James Calbraith is a Poland-born writer, foodie and traveller, currently residing in South London. His debut historical fantasy novel, "The Shadow of Black Wings", has reached ABNA semi-finals. It was published in July 2012 and hit the Historical Fantasy and Alternate History bestsellers list on Amazon US and UK.

Praise for *The Shadow of Black Wings*

"Fast paced and full of energy."
— Adrian Tchaikovsky,
author of the *Shadows of the Apt*

"This manuscript is full of highly crafted detail that will make readers shiver at times with fear and delight...a familiar yet highly original fantasy that is a worthwhile road."
— Publishers Weekly

"The real-world cultures are incredibly well-researched and truthful, and yet well-balanced with the fantasy elements. An intriguing and impressive series."
— Ben Galley,
author of the *Emaneska Series*

By James Calbraith

THE YEAR OF THE DRAGON
Book One: The Shadow of Black Wings
Book Two: The Warrior's Soul
Book Three: The Islands in the Mist
Book Four: The Rising Tide
Book Five: The Chrysanthemum Seal

The Year of the Dragon Books 1-4 Delux Edition

Transmission
Dragonbone Chest

Visit James Calbraith's official website at
jamescalbraith.com
for the latest news, book details, and other information
Or sign up for the newsletter at:
tinyletter.com/jcalbraith

The Chrysanthemum Seal

Book Five of
The Year of the Dragon

James Calbraith

FLYING
SQUID

Published May 2014 by Flying Squid
ISBN-13: 978-83-936713-7-3

Cover Illustration: Daniel Kordek
Map Illustrations: Jared Blando, Flying Squid, Metruis
Cover Design: Flying Squid

TABLE OF CONTENTS

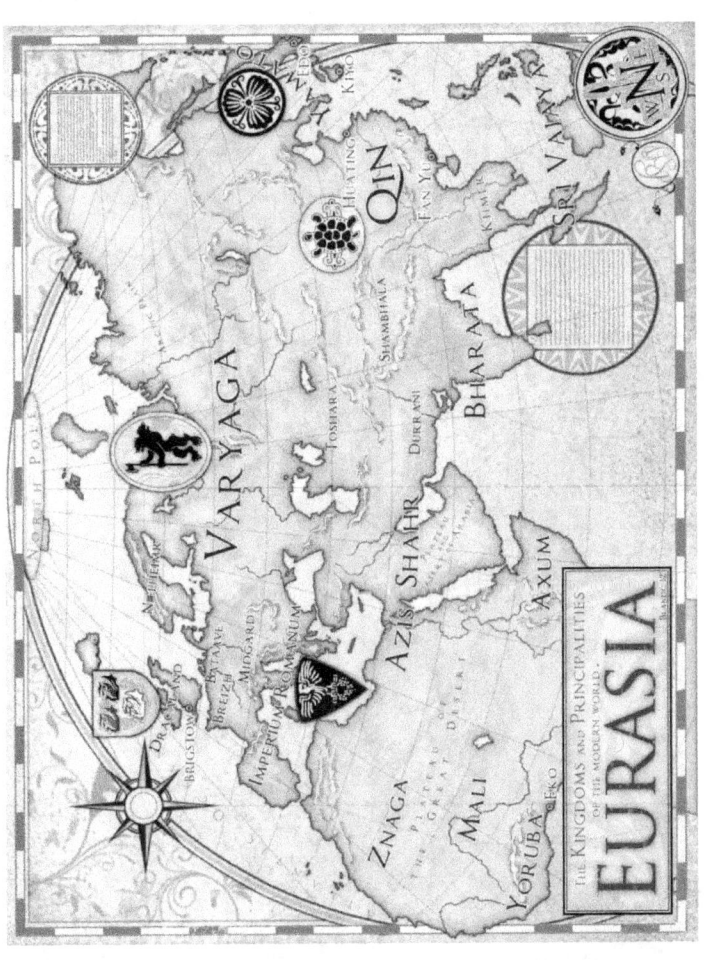

EURASIA

THE KINGDOMS AND PRINCIPALITIES
OF THE MODERN WORLD

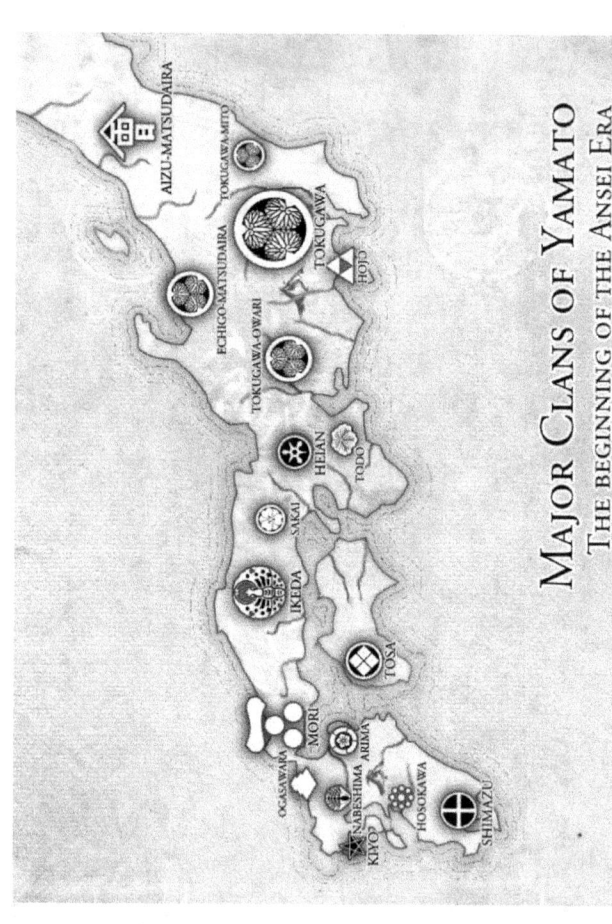

Major Clans of Yamato
The Beginning of the Ansei Era

AIZU-MATSUDAIRA

TOKUGAWA-MITO

ECHIGO-MATSUDAIRA

TOKUGAWA-OWARI

TOKUGAWA

HOJO

HEIAN

TODO

SAKAI

IKEDA

TOSA

MORI

OGASAWARA

NABESHIMA

ARIMA

KIYO

HOSOKAWA

SHIMAZU

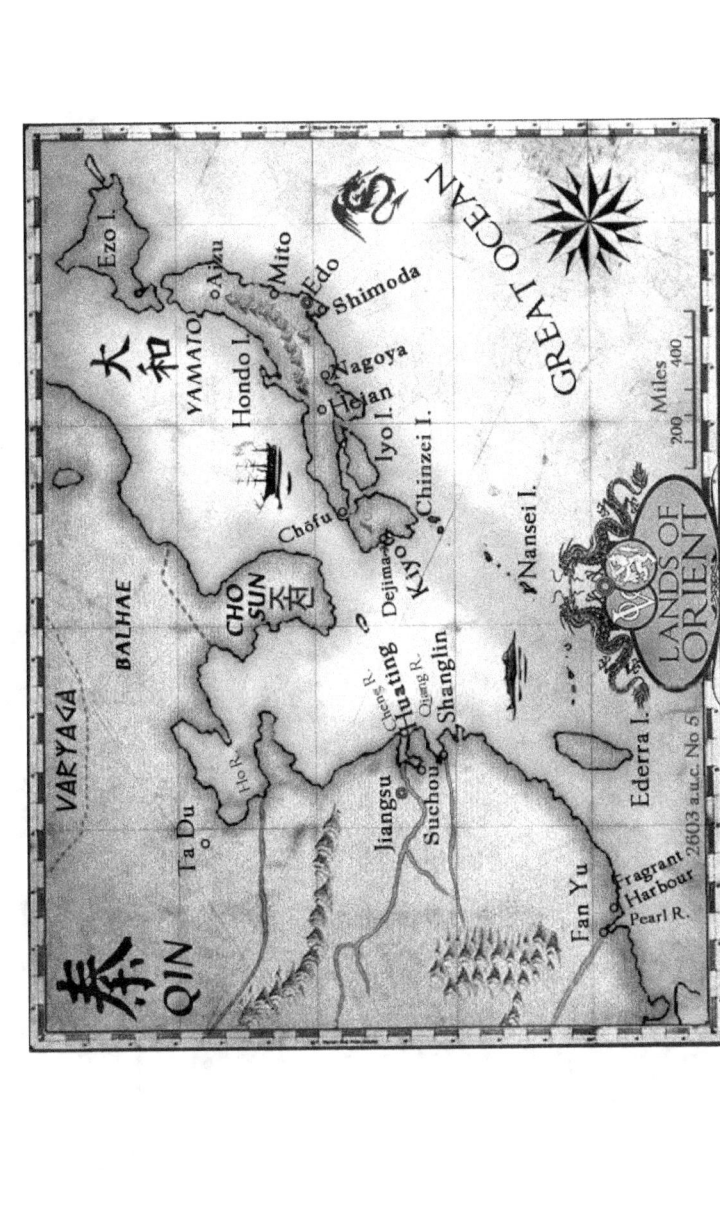

GREAT OCEAN

Ezo I.

YAMATO

大和

Hondo I.

Aizu
Mito
Edo
Shimoda

Nagoya

Heian

Iyo I.

Chōfu

Chinzei I.

Dejima
Kiyo

Nansei I.

VARYAGA

BALHAE

CHO
SUN
朝鮮

Ta Du

Ho R.

Chens R.
Huating
Qiang R.
Shanglin

Jiangsu
Suchou

Fan Yu

Ederra I.

Fragrant
Harbour

Pearl R.

秦
QIN

Miles
200 400

LANDS OF
ORIENT

2603 a.u.c. No 5

And if we were never

To meet again

Neither my mind nor my body

Would regret anything

Chunagon Asatada

PROLOGUE

The shuttlecock whizzed past the Overwizard's ear and with a flutter flew into the rose bush behind him. Curzius sighed and picked it gingerly from among the thorns.

"I had no idea you were such a keen player, *kakka*," he said.

His opponent smiled. "We have a game like this one," he said, "something for the women and children to play. This *'feather-ball'* of yours is a man's game."

He waved the racket a couple of times, tilting his head to hear the satisfying whistling sound.

"Even the *raketto* feels like a sword," he added.

Curzius wiped the sweat from his brow, adjusted his spectacles and served. The shuttlecock bounced off the stretched parchment in his opponent's racket and flew back to him, over the thin silk string. With effort, the Overwizard lunged forward and managed a return. Soon Curzius had to bow down again to pick up the missile from the dirt.

"I shall have all my vassals learn how to play this game," the other man said. "This is good training."

"I'm glad you enjoy it, *kakka*. But, I'm afraid I must take a break. The day is too hot for me."

Nabeshima Naomasa, the *daimyo* of Saga, though short in stature, was built of sinews and muscles. They had been playing for a good half an hour now, and he didn't even break a sweat. The portly Curzius, on the other hand, was almost at the end of his strength.

"*Ah*, of course!" the *daimyo* said, nodding. "How thoughtless of me; I'd forgotten how far you have travelled, Curzius-*dono*."

The *daimyo* clapped twice, and from out of the rose bushes emerged a servant with two flat pillows and a tray of cold saké.

Curzius smiled weakly. He threw the racket away and sat down on the dusty ground of the courtyard.

"It took you two weeks to get here from Edo, yes?" Naomasa asked, raising the saké cup in two fingers. In an instant he was transformed from a tough sportsman into a delicate gourmand.

It will never cease to amaze me, thought Curzius, quaffing the ice-cold liquid in one gulp. He reached out and the servant poured another cup.

"Yes, but I wasn't in such a hurry at first. I was in Nagoya, meeting with some friends and relatives of my… late concubine when I received the first letter from Dejima."

The *daimyo's* face turned grave.

"I am sorry. I know how it is to lose someone to the disease."

14

He put his hands together and recited a brief prayer for the dead.

Curzius nodded sadly, waiting for him to finish. He had known Misato less than a year, and most of it he'd spent travelling alone… Still, he had grown very fond of her, and her sudden death from smallpox had caused him as much distress as the recent events in Kiyō.

"From Nagoya I travelled almost without stopping, day and night," he continued. "Today is the first day of rest I have taken since then – I could not pass through Saga without spending some time with Your Excellency."

"You honour me," the *daimyo* said, bowing lightly, "but, why not go straight to Kiyō?"

"Once I'm back behind the sealed wall of Dejima, it won't be as easy to gather information."

Naomasa raised a cup to his mouth to hide a smile. "I see."

"My men don't know everything, and can put even less in the letters."

"You don't trust your own couriers?"

"Do *you*, *kakka*?"

"Hah!" Naomasa laughed into his cup, spluttering the drink.

Curzius sipped the second cup slowly, waiting. He didn't have to wait long. Naomasa put the cup down, slid the tray aside and waved the servant away.

"What do you want to know?" he asked sternly.

Curzius quickly ran through the list of questions in his head. Which matter was the most pressing?

"What exactly happened to Takashima-*sama*?"

The *daimyo* nodded, as if expecting the question to come first.

"Dead. Or rather, destroyed."

"*Destroyed?*"

"Tell me, *Oppertovenaar-dono*, how much do you know of the events in Kiyō?"

"I... know of the man dressed in crimson," Curzius said carefully. This was the part where the letters were at their most vague and confusing. *Demons. Blood magic. Is this really happening? It's like the Wizardry Wars all over again.*

Naomasa nodded. "Shūhan-*sama* was turning into... some sort of dark being. He was burned down by his own daughter before it was too late. Most tragic."

"And what of her?"

"Oh, that's a whole different story to tell. She fought the demon and, somehow, defeated him. But that's all over now. Last I heard she was heading for Kagoshima. That seems to be the right place for her."

"The school of magic?"

"That's right. Nariakira-*dono* may seem a difficult ally, but you can't deny his devotion to the *Rangaku* arts. Those cups are a gift from him, by the way."

Curzius noticed that the saké in the cup remained pleasantly cool despite the heat. He traced the rim with his finger and found a faint ice rune scratched into the clay.

They learn so fast.

"Defeated the demon, you say?" he mused.

"With a lot of help, of course. Shimazu-*dono*'s Arch-wizard was with her, if I remember right, and a few others."

"And the... boy?"

"The foreigner? He was there too. But he's gone now, I hear. Found a way home by himself, perhaps. I hear there was a *dorako* involved."

Curzius let out a discreet sigh of relief. *That's one burden less to worry about.*

"The Spy's daughters," said Naomasa, "I assume you took care of them?"

The Overwizard nodded. "As long as they stay in Nagoya, the Itō family is safe. That's as far as our arm can reach."

"That's impressive. Right under the *Taikun*'s nose, too." Naomasa raised his cup. "Things are looking up, it seems."

Curzius did not return the toast.

"We got rid of one foreigner... and got a whole lot more in the bargain."

"The black dragons, yes. And the Varyaga Khaganate. You are worried that your monopoly of Sea Maze crossing is broken?"

Are you *not worried about any of this? You're the protector of Kiyō!* Was what he wanted to say, but instead he said: "That's one of the two reasons I was in such a hurry, really. My masters in Noviomagus will demand answers."

"I have sent my engineer Tanaka-*sama* to Kiyō to investigate what kind of vessel the Khaganate used, but he has not yet returned. What do you think of them, Curzius-*dono*? Even though they are the nearest of all Westerners, I admit I know almost nothing about them."

"They are shrewd," said Curzius, shrugging, "and they are a wizard nation, too. I will have a report sent to you once I get to Dejima."

"I will be obliged."

Curzius wiped his brow again and reached for the saké flask to pour himself some more of the cool drink. He noticed the breach of etiquette at the last moment and offered to fill Naomasa's cup first, but the *daimyo* shook his head with a smile.

"I'll just say this," Curzius said, "their arrival may yet be a blessing in disguise."

"How so?" asked Naomasa.

"We may be able to use them as a counter against the Black Wings – if they ever decide to return."

"*Aah,* have they really departed? That's somewhat disappointing. And after making such a show of it."

"That's what I heard. They were still in Edo when I left the city, but then they just flew away, back across the ocean. It was almost as if they got what they had come for."

"Some kind of… secret deal with the barbarians? That would've been a grave departure from the *Taikun's* policy. Perhaps even enough to stir some of his *fudai* retainers to action…"

Rebellion? Among the inner clans? Is that even possible?

Naomasa put a finger to his lips in thought. "You said *two reasons…*"

"Oh, the other one concerns only Dejima. It's nothing for you to worry about, *kakka.*"

"Anything that concerns my friend, concerns me, *Oppertovenaar-dono.*"

Curzius coughed. *Why did I even mention that in the first place?*

"If you must know, it's about the Ship. It hasn't arrived yet, and we haven't heard from it."

"Oh, I'm sorry to hear that. I hope it's nothing serious."

"This much of a delay is nothing out of the ordinary yet. You know we are forced to use only the old vessels, and they are not the most reliable. We will need to prepare ourselves for winter if the Ship will not come at all."

He was trying to sound nonchalant, but in truth, the Ship was the matter that worried him the most. It was bad enough to not receive the supplies and cash that came with the Ship every year; but this was not a normal year, and this ship was not the usual one. It wouldn't just disappear in a storm, as happened a couple of times with the old galleons. *Something* must have happened. Something bad.

19

"Would you like my Scryers to try to find out what's going on? If you'd only give me a few more details…"

Oh, you'd like that, wouldn't you?

Suddenly Curzius felt very tired of this conversation. He did his best to smile and bowed his head.

"Thank you, *kakka*, but I'm afraid until the Ship comes through the Sea Maze, there's very little we can do."

"Then I will order my monks to pray for its safe return."

"You are too generous, *kakka*."

"Nonsense. We must stick together. This will be a difficult year for all of us," said Naomasa, pouring Curzius yet another cup. "This year of the Dragon."

"And it's barely half-way through," agreed Curzius, wiping his brow with a silk handkerchief. His face, reflecting in the saké was beetroot-red. "I dread to think what the summer will bring."

Naomasa smiled broadly.

"Would you like to have another game of *'feather-ball'*?"

CHAPTER I

The ringing of swords and chaotic cries coming from behind the thick, bronze door filled the dark, narrow corridor briefly, soon replaced by gurgles of agony and then silence.

Lord Shimazu Nariakira nodded at the tall, burly samurai, who pushed the door open. The torch in his hand shone at a bloody scene: four men, lying in pools of their own blood on the stone floor. One of them wore a Satsuma uniform, the other three – that of the Hosokawa of Kumamoto. Five other Satsuma soldiers, bleeding from many wounds but still alive, stood back, bowing, and formed a corridor down which Lord Nariakira approached the dead men.

"Those were the last of the rebels, *kakka*," said the samurai with a hint of pride in his voice, wiping the blood off his face.

Nariakira nodded. "They fought well. Make sure they are buried with honour."

He was in a sour mood. He disliked unnecessary bloodshed. The rebels had to be dealt with, of course, but it didn't make the loss of useful lives any easier.

Somehow, a few of Hosokawa's retainers had got wind – a mere suspicion – of how the handover of power had come about, and rebelled against the *daimyo's* son, and, by extension, Lord Nariakira, his new protector. The fighting was brief, and confined mostly to the winding corridors of the Kumamoto Castle.

"How did they know?" he asked nobody in particular.

"We believe perhaps… Hisamitsu-*sama*…"

My dear little brother?

He stepped over the bodies.

"I know this man," said Nariakira, leaning over the last of the dead men, who fell defending a small wooden door: the last door at the end of the last corridor at the top level of the donjon.

"That's Captain Kiyomasa, their leader, *kakka*" the tall samurai explained. "Half our losses are down to him alone."

The *daimyo* punched the wall in anger.

Damn you, Kiyomasa. You lived through dragon fire for this…?

"Give his family four hundred *ryō*. Tell them he died in the line of duty."

"But *kakka*…!" the samurai burst out before remembering to whom he was speaking. He bowed sharply. "Of course."

"And, Commander…" Nariakira wished he could remember the man's name. Bushy-browed and square-jawed, he had the kind of face one does not easily forget. But recently the *daimyo* had too much on his mind.

"Find as many of Kiyomasa's former soldiers as you can."

"Certainly, *kakka*. What do you want me to do with them?"

"Make sure they remain loyal to us. They are some of the best men in Yamato. In a month, I want you to turn them into my personal guard."

The samurai's square face beamed and he bowed deeply. The office of a *daimyo*'s bodyguard commander was more than enough reward for his prompt dealing with the short-lived rebellion.

Nariakira turned his attention to the wooden door.

"What was it that they were defending so fiercely…?"

The door was unlocked and swivelled open under his touch. Behind it was a tiny room, more of an alcove. The *daimyo* waved his hand, and one of the soldiers got nearer with the torch.

It was a small armoury. Not the main arsenal of the Kumamoto Castle – they had taken it over a long time ago; this one seemed more like a treasury of weapons. Ancient halberds and pikes, elaborate spears, and precious swords, hanging on walls, scattered all around the room, and lying on the floor; a prized coat of armour, made of gleaming white lacquer scales stood prominently in the middle. Nariakira had seen an identical one in Hosokawa's personal quarters below.

The original.

The fierce mask gazed at the man with its empty eyes. But something else drew the *daimyo's* attention: a sword stand

23

of dark red lacquer at the foot of the armour. The longer *katana* was missing, and only *wakizashi*, the short sword, remained, in a plain black sheath. It was marked with the Hosokawa crest – and the horned circle; mark of the Roman priests.

"Where's the other sword?" asked Nariakira, his voice suddenly hoarse.

The Commander answered in a whisper.

"We didn't know these were in here."

The *daimyo* made a step forward and slowly reached for the short sword. The hilt buzzed in his hand. He unsheathed it carefully, by an inch, smoothly and noiselessly. The blade was jet black, as if glowing darkness, and it let out a high-pitched, quiet hum. The sword called for blood. But not his…

"Get me Yokoi-*dono*," he ordered.

A quick, loud rapping on Satō's door stirred her from a shallow dream.

"*Later, Dad,*" she murmured, annoyed.

"Come quick, Takashima!" a rasping, male voice said.

She opened her eyes at once and sat down. It was pitch black in the room.

"What is it?" she asked. "It's the middle of the night."

"You wanted me to let you know when the Ship arrives. So hurry up!"

24

"*Eeh!*"

She jumped up in an instant and stumbled about on the floor in search of clothes and light. She threw on the vermillion *gi* jacket and the black *hakama*, tied it hastily and parted the door with a crash.

"Well, what are we waiting for, Yukihige-*sensei?*"

The man grinned at her and led the way, out of the dormitory, past the school gates and out onto the sleepy, dark, ash-covered streets of Kagoshima.

"Actually, there's no need to hurry," said Yukihige, slowing down. "It just emerged off Sakurajima."

Satō only knew this man by his nickname – Yukihige, Snow Beard – referring to some seldom-told laboratory accident from his youth. Now he had a real beard, black with threads of grey, framing a mature, sharp face. He was the head teacher of Ice Wizardry at *Shigakko*, Nariakira's *Rangaku* Academy in Kagoshima. And, of course, he had known her father, though he was reluctant to share too many stories of their youth.

Their sandals shuffling on the ash-covered pavement, they emerged onto the harbour, where several other wizards had already gathered, awaiting the Ship's arrival. The largest pier in the harbour had been prepared for its welcome, blocked off by a make-shift bamboo barrier and a row of armed guards. Only a few men were allowed beyond; in the hazy-grey light of rising dawn, Satō recognized the *Daisen, Torii* Heishichi, lanky and unassuming as always, setting up some complex apparatus on a tripod.

25

THE CHRYSANTHEMUM SEAL

The wild rumours had started circulating around the Academy not long after her arrival in Kagoshima. That the Bataavians would openly sail into a harbour other than Kiyō was of itself a major break of the *Taikun's* rules; almost a declaration of rebellion on Satsuma's part, but that wasn't all: the Ship was supposed to be something else this time, something unexpected. Something *big*.

"There it is!" shouted one of the men. They were all men, of course.

She reached out on tip-toes.

That the Ship would at least be a mistfire one, she had no doubt; why else would the Bataavians and Shimazu-*dono* go to so much trouble and secrecy? Perhaps it would even be an ironclad. As the rumours grew, so did the ship in her mind: at first, it was an armoured gunboat, then – a frigate; the last batch of gossip made it out into an enormous *dorako* carrier.

"My uncle works on a merchant ship to Nansei," one of the students kept saying, "he told me he saw a huge black ship pass him by, filled with dragons! It *must* have been the Bataavians!"

The clouds finally parted and the first rays of the rising sun lit up the Bataavian vessel. It was closer than Satō had expected; less than a quarter of a *ri* from the shore.

"But… it looks just like the ones in Kiyō," she said, slumping in disappointment.

The vessel approaching the pier, led by a small pilot barge, was the usual Bataavian merchantman of the sort Satō had grown up watching moor every year at Dejima.

"No, look!" cried the sailor's nephew into her ear, "between the main-mast and the fore-mast."

"Between the what and the what?" she asked, annoyed.

"The middle one and the one at the front," the young man said, pointing.

Satō squinted and saw a narrow metal funnel, about half the height of the middle mast, jutting out of a box-like structure. As the ship turned to its side, she noticed the large paddle-wheels, silent, rolling slowly back and forth on the waves...

"It *is* a mistfire..." she whispered.

The ship was listing slightly, battered and bruised, boards torn from the planking, the masts crooked; the main mast in particular looked as if it had just been mended, and in some haste, too. Patches of timber planking on the sides were missing, revealing sheets of iron cladding, ripped and charred in places.

"She looks like she's been through a war," Snow Beard said, frowning.

"Maybe the *Taikun's* ships found it..." pondered Satō.

"No way, they have nothing that could match this ship," said the sailor's nephew. "Look, she's got more guns than our entire fortress!"

The ship struck its sails, and the sailors heaved the anchors overboard. Satō had watched this kind of vessel at Dejima enough times to know it would take hours before it fully moored and anyone on board could get off onto the pier.

"I'm going back to sleep," she said to no-one in particular. "Nothing else will happen until noon."

"What's that on the forecastle?" asked the sailor's nephew. Something in his voice made Satō stop and turn her head. On the front deck of the ship, a huge coil of gold lay, glinting and shimmering like a giant snake skin.

As the ship heaved at the anchor, the coil stirred, and a coal-black eye opened.

"It's… it's…" Satō gasped.

It's a dragon!

The city was in disarray.

The Kagoshima wizards may have been prepared for the Ship's arrival, but the ordinary townspeople had been kept in the dark. And when the first panicked citizens ran down the streets, shouting about an "invasion", and "monsters", dread erupted and spread everywhere like the ash cloud of Sakurajima.

The commoners and nobles alike crowded the paths leading for the hills, looking for shelter in the thick woods. Some of them remembered the dreadful news from Qin; others heard vague tales from the North, gossips of the monsters invading the coast near Edo. But for most, the arrival of foreign ships in Satsuma meant only one thing: the Civil War. The memory of Vasconians and Bataavians roaming Yamato freely among the chaos and bloodshed was all too alive.

Lord Nariakira's heralds tried to play the Ship's arrival as proof of Satsuma's importance. "Our *daimyo* made allies with The Bataavians!" they cried in the cross-roads and markets to whoever listened, adding only to the confusion.

Satō would have loved to stay and find more out about the golden dragon, a Qin *long* that in some inexplicable way found itself on a Bataavian ship bound for Yamato. She wanted to study the Bataavian machinery of the Ship, too. She would have given much to discuss the finer points of mistfire technology with the crew. To feel, for even a moment, a part of the greater community of wizards spread all over the world, instead of being always kept in the dark on one, small, remote island.

But it was not to be. The final time she had seen the Ship and its crew was as she looked back from a hilltop north of Kagoshima's gates, where the Hitoyoshi highway looped around Lord Nariakira's summer gardens. It was little more than a speck of brown and grey, recognizable only by the three masts rising above the roofs of the city like mighty cedars.

The order to march off had arrived in the afternoon of the Ship's day of arrival. It bore the *daimyo*'s seal; there was to be no protest, no grumbling. The departure was imminent: they only had one day to prepare.

"A lode of Ice was discovered high on Mount Ichifusa," Yukihige had explained, unhappily. He was also ordered to accompany the expedition.

"Mount Ichifusa... where's that?"

Satō had hoped yet it would just be a brief excursion. But her hopes were promptly shattered.

"On the eastern end of Hitoyoshi Valley."

Hitoyoshi…?

"*Eeh*, but that's days away!"

"I know," Yukihige said with a scowl. "Best be off quickly, then. Wear something warm," he added with a weak smile.

I bet they'll be long gone by the time we get back, Satō thought, resigned to her fate.

The gold-enamelled panels slid open and Dylan saw before him a large, formal chamber, with the floor of packed yellow straw and walls of painted wood. The only object out of place in this austere room was a man-sized Qin vase of blue and white china.

This is the land of riches the Bataavians were so secretive about? he wondered, not for the first time.

They had been kept on the Bataavian ship for a week, waiting for an audience with the man Dylan understood to be the local warlord, and a friend of the Bataavian Captain. From the window of his cabin he could see the calm, round bay and the tall, conical volcano, spewing columns of smoke and dirt.

It's certainly picturesque, he thought, *like the Bay of Neapolis in summer.*

30

But even the natural beauty of the city was marred by a constant layer of black volcanic ash that found its way into the food, water, and bedding.

There is nothing here that would be of interest to anyone.

From the deck he had been observing this strange city of low-rise wooden buildings. There was some golden glint on the roofs and walls of the larger buildings, but even if it was pure gold leaf it wouldn't amount to more than a chest of the stuff. There were no ships in the harbour other than fishing junks and a few wooden barges carrying rice and timber. One detail was jarring – a battery of modern-looking iron cannons on the harbour wall – but Dylan assumed they were simply a gift from the Bataavians, an expensive, but useless, decoration.

Short, squat men in plaid skirts, with their heads shaven, walking everywhere on foot, purposefully and with grim expressions on their faces, and women, wearing elaborate robes and haircuts, following them with forced smiles which turned into grimaces of tiredness as soon as their men turned away. Soldiers going to and fro, brandishing spears and sabre-like swords, wearing bits of ancient armour which looked as if they wouldn't stop an arrow, much less an air-gun pellet. Once in a while some of them came by, either to watch the vessel itself, or to check on Li's great golden dragon, now sleeping in lazy coils on the forecastle.

On the fourth day Dylan saw a thin man in an orange jacket and black skirt, who stood on the pier and studied the *Soembing* with great care, while the sailors were busy mending the damage done by Afroleus to the quarterdeck. He heard a

31

nasty crack as the wooden crane carrying a platform of crates snapped; the load rolled straight towards the men and, in an instant, the lanky Yamato reached out his hands and shouted something Dylan could not hear in the din. Flame spurted from his fingers and the crates burst into harmless splinters. The Yamato man cleaned bits of burnt wood from his robe, adjusted his spectacles, and returned to studying the mistfire capstan.

Dylan's knuckles tensed up on the railing.

That was a… Chwalu'r dân! *Western magic!*

The man from the harbour was in the audience chamber. Dylan recognized his gangly form instantly. What he hadn't noticed before were the burn scars covering the bespectacled face. The kind of injury Dylan had seen many times before.

He also had the sunken, absent eyes of an addict.

Cursed Weed, thought Dylan. *Or worse.*

He scanned the rest of the room. There were no chairs or benches, everyone was kneeling or sitting cross-legged on the straw floor, like musicians in the Qin court. Right in front of Dylan, on a small raised dais of packed straw, sat the local warlord, "*daimyo*". His clothes were plain, a dark grey vest and skirt over a black tunic, marked only with a crossed circle sign on the shoulders. He was holding a wooden paddle in his right hand, a mark of office, Dylan guessed, though it looked more like a fly swatter.

He's dressed almost like a commoner.

He couldn't tell whether the austerity of the place was real or merely symbolic. The robes were plain, but made of fine, precious silk. The sheaths of the swords were simple, yet masterly crafted.

The other men sitting around the warlord looked similar, wearing the same hair-styles and robes as their master. The only difference was in their poses: solemn, subdued, with none of the self-importance and certainty of power beaming from the man in the middle.

There was also a young woman sitting to the right of the warlord; her eyes were pale with advanced cataracts. She must have been completely blind, yet she seemed to be looking straight at Dylan from the moment he had stepped into the chamber.

And who might she be? His truth-sayer?

He had seen such people employed at the courts of the Orient before. Trained in the arts of subtlety, they allegedly sensed the emotions of those they interrogated. Sometimes they would deliberately blunt one of their "conventional" senses, claiming it increased their attunement to the "hidden truth". The girl, if that was indeed her role, had a natural advantage...

Her blank eyes slid away from Dylan, as she turned her unseeing gaze to the other men accompanying him: Captain Gerhardus Fabius of the *Soembing*, Li Hung-Chang, the Qinese interpreter from Huating, and the Warwick's son, Wulfhere. Dylan got separated from Gwen before entering the room, but with True Sight could still see her strong energy just behind the thin paper walls, in the antechamber.

The truth-sayer paid little attention to Li, and focused on the blond boy. A slight frown marred her face.

Is she wondering what he's doing here? You and me both, girl…

At a nod from the usher, they all knelt down, bowing deeply as instructed beforehand. There was silence, as the warlord studied them without hurry. Dylan knew better than to speak first.

"He's fluent in Bataavian and classical Qin," Captain Fabius had explained to him, "but he will prefer to use an interpreter with you."

The warlord said something in his staccato tongue.

"You have caused some great trouble to my good friend, Captain," the Bataavian interpreter said, with some difficulty.

Dylan raised his head to answer. At that moment, the sun peered through a ceiling window and glinted off a piece of gold and blue on the *daimyo's* hand.

"The ring…" he said, his throat suddenly dry. The interpreter dutifully translated it before Dylan could stop him.

"This?" The warlord raised his hand to the light. "What keen eyes you have. A certain foreign boy gave it to me as a gift for helping him."

Blood rushed to Dylan's head, his entire carefully prepared speech forgotten. Suddenly, all was clear. He knew that ring all too well. He remembered giving it to Bran on his eleventh birthday, the boy's finger too small for the twisted band of gold…

"You have my son," he said slowly.

"Your son, is it?" The warlord said, his lips pressed into a thin line. "I'm afraid he's no longer with us."

"He... what...?"

Fabius gave him a stern look. Everyone in the room tensed. Dylan assessed his situation. He wasn't afraid. Neither the soldiers, nor the Bataavian trinkets of the Yamato worried him. He noticed tiny flames dancing around the fingers of the lanky man.

He's the only one here who's a threat.

"You're trying to figure out how to defeat everyone in this room," the warlord said, looking him straight in the eye. "That's some courage."

"It's no courage when I know I'll win."

The warlord touched his bottom lip with his paddle.

"Fine words. Tell me, is your... woman as strong as you?"

Dylan froze. *Gwen?*

At that moment, a muffled sound of fighting came from behind the door, and all Yamato guards jumped to their feet immediately, their hands on the long hilts. A man burst head-first through the paper wall, dropping his sword as he flew, and landed on the floor with a thud. Gwen followed, with two more soldiers trying vainly to hold her down.

"What on Owain's Sword is going on?" she asked sharply.

Anger and surprise flashed on the warlord's face. Dylan glanced to his left to see Wulfhere standing up, his eyes opened wild, and Gwen's attackers scrambling to their feet. Throughout the ordeal Li remained seated, smirking.

The warlord lowered his paddle.

The lanky Yamato wizard lunged forward, uttering a spell word: "*Los!*"

Lightning traps erupted from the floor, hitting Dylan in the chest. His own defences triggered in time and the attack merely knocked the breath out of him. Frost chains snaked around his hands and legs. The spearmen surrounded him, steel blades pressed against his *tarian*.

"*Ffrwydro darian,*" he spoke calmly. The *tarian* exploded, smashing the men against the walls, their useless weapons shattered to splinters. Gwen aimed her Soul Lance at their throats, but they were too stunned to oppose her.

Dylan's hands burst aflame.

The enemy wizard whirled his arms in a circle. His eyes were now bright and clear. A cone of flame flew towards Dylan, enveloping his shield with spiral coils.

What the – ?

His *tarian* tightened on him, the air inside grew hot as if in a furnace.

"*Diffodd!*" he cried. The flames turned yellow and vanished in a blink. That at least still worked… He dropped the *tarian* to gain more energy, and formed his fingers into an ice rune.

He's a fire wizard, he thought quickly. *That will teach him.*

36

He readied himself to launch the devastating attack, pouring enough power into it to flash-freeze everyone in the room. He had little time – his True Sight was telling him there were more wizards in the building, gathering around the audience room for a concerted assault.

"*Halt!*"

Everyone turned to the warlord.

Red-faced, he barked another order, shaking the paddle. The wizard stood still, his hands clasped together, bowing. The guards prostrated on the floor, face down. Dylan remained standing, poised, tense. The crackling of the ice on his hands was the only noise in the room.

"Sit down," the warlord said in Bataavian. "*Please,*" he added in Seaxe, half-mockingly.

One of the old men patted out a singing hem of his robe. The wizard kicked a lightning trap aside, before returning to his seat. His face adopted its vague expression.

Reluctantly, Dylan and Gwen obeyed. The guards left the room in a hassle, picking up their weapons.

"That was a brave show, but futile," the warlord continued. "I told you, your son isn't here."

"Then where – "

"I don't know," the warlord cut him off. "It's true that I've met him, as you guessed, but I have no idea where's he gone now. I can't chase after somebody who flies a *dorako*."

Dylan frowned.

Does he mean… Emrys? That frog managed to get as far as here?

"How do I know you're telling the truth? Your wizard," he said, pointing at the lanky man, "has dragonflame marks all over his face. You threatened my… officer. And you're wearing Bran's ring on your finger. Why would he have given it to anyone, especially you?"

The warlord lowered his head and stared at Dylan; his gaze would send shivers down the spine of most men. "You'd do wisely not to question my words in my own home."

He leaned back.

"I can see it in your eyes. You think I'm some primitive chieftain on a poor, far-away island. Your son was far more perceptive. That's why I agreed to help him. And my help does *not* come lightly, wizard. Now, the question is, will I agree to help *you*?"

"I don't need your help. You don't know where he is."

The warlord twirled his paddle in his short fingers.

"If your son is still in Yamato, I'm the only man who can help you find him. Outside this city you're nothing but a gibberish-talking barbarian. Ask him," the warlord pointed to the Bataavian Captain. "Fabius-*sama*," he spoke, changing the language seamlessly to Bataavian, "I see you haven't explained properly the situation in Yamato."

"N…no, *kakka*." The Captain bowed and turned to Dylan with a pained expression on his face.

"Foreigners are banned in Yamato on pain of death. Outside *Dejeema*, we are only tolerated here, in Kagoshima."

"And the *Taikun* allows that because…?" the warlord prodded.

"Shimazu-*dono* is one of the most powerful men in Yamato. Some say he's second only to the *Taikun*, its ruler."

"*Some* say?" the *daimyo* chuckled. "I need to make sure it's not just 'some'."

"And why would such a powerful man help somebody like me?" asked Dylan.

"Why indeed… What could the Dracalish officer have to offer in exchange for my assistance? It would have to be… substantial."

"I have nothing," said Dylan, straightening up. "I even lost my dragon coming here."

The *daimyo* chuckled again. "I'm sure we can think of *something*. We'll talk again in a few days. For now, this audience is finished."

The usher urged Dylan, Gwen, and the Captain to stand up. Li and Warwick rose also, but the warlord pointed at them with his paddle.

"No, you two stay. I still don't know why *you're* here," he said in Qin.

Li bowed and gestured the Warwick boy to remain in place, as the guards prodded Dylan out of the room.

THE CHRYSANTHEMUM SEAL

They returned to the harbour the same way they had arrived – separately, in closed palanquins carried by servants. When they were back in their cabin, Dylan looked around with True Sight; as far as he could tell, they were alone.

"I blew it," he said, rubbing the bridge of his nose. "I underestimated him, and then I lost my temper. I know how to handle these things… but when it's Bran, or – or you, I just…"

He slumped heavily on the leather armchair. Their cabin must have once belonged to someone hefty – the seat was sunken and wouldn't hold much longer.

Gwen leaned towards him and stroked his head.

"I've never seen you start a fight with the natives before."

Dylan scratched his scar. "I don't know what came over me."

"Maybe it's because it's the first time you actually *care*," she said.

He raised his eyes.

"What do you mean? I always care deeply about what I do. I couldn't do my job otherwise."

"That's just the thing," she said. "It's not your job this time. It's your family."

He held her hand. "And I always tried to keep them separate."

"We both know it cannot go on forever, right?"

"Are we still talking about the audience?"

She stopped smiling and pulled her hand back.

"You hesitated," she said. "In a fight. That too was unusual."

"The spell he used… I haven't seen one like it before. Is it possible they're developing their own magic here?"

She shrugged. "Must be something old they've learned from the Vasconians. Even you don't know all those ancient charms."

"Must be." He nodded. His eyes fell on the Qin jewel glinting playfully on her neck. His mood brightened.

"Come," he said, standing up and pulling her towards him, "let's give our minds some rest."

THE CHRYSANTHEMUM SEAL

CHAPTER II

Wulf and Li followed one of the Yamato servants down the narrow, winding corridors of the palace. They walked far longer than it had taken them before to reach the audience room. At some point, they passed through a garden filled with bushes blossoming pink and blue, which he didn't remember seeing.

This isn't the way to the harbour, Wulf thought.

At last, they reached another sliding door; the servant opened it, bowed, and disappeared into the shadows.

"We're not staying at the ship tonight," said Li, nodding at him to come inside. "I'm a guest of the palace. And so are you."

The room was furnished sparsely, with a single thick mattress, and a low wooden writing table.

Is this a servant's room, or a prison cell?

Li sat down at the table and began taking out the writing utensils from a small drawer, unperturbed in the slightest by their situation.

"Are we going to stay in this shithole?"

"What do you think of our host?" asked Li, ignoring his question.

Wulf got used to this kind of behaviour, but it still angered him. He shrugged.

"I have no idea what you were talking about. I don't speak this gibberish."

The local warlord and Li had been speaking Qin, ignoring Wulf's presence; to his ears, they both sounded identical.

"Good!" Li exclaimed to his surprise. "Words obscure the truth. What did you see?"

"*See?* Nothing," he said, looking for a place to sit down. *We don't even deserve chairs?* "You sat and talked."

"Ah, Master Warwick", Li smiled, smoothing the tip of the brush, "if you want to make history, you must do better than that."

Wulfhere was gave him an annoyed look. Truth was, he could barely recall anything except the pale, striking face of the girl sitting in front of the warlord.

"Well, the old guy seemed... strong-willed. And he kept laughing, even though nobody else did."

"Good, good. Anything else?"

Wulf focused. Now that Li mentioned, there was something odd about the man...

"It was as if he was thinking of several things at the same time. His eyes kept darting about, and he kept twitching his fingers. Like this," Wulfhere said, and tried to imitate what he'd seen.

"Ah! That is remarkable. He's doing mental arithmetic – it's a trick learned by Qin accountants. But to do that and talk at the same time…" Li shook his head. "It will be good to have him as an ally."

"Is that what you were talking about? An alliance?"

Li lay one piece of paper aside.

"We were discussing the Chosen Sayings of Master Kong, and Master Sun's Rules for Soldiers."

Wulf scoffed.

"Chosen Sayings? Are you kidding me?"

"*All things have their roots and branches*," Li quipped, dipping his brush into the black ink. "All undertakings have their ends and their beginnings. Thus says Master Kong."

"That's it? You debated philosophy?"

"That's the best way for two learned men to get to know each other. See a person's ways, observe his motive, notice his result, as Master Kong advises. Now, if you please, I must write down my thoughts. Your room is behind that wall." Li pointed the brush at a sliding panel decorated with flying swallows.

Wulfhere opened the door with a whack. He reeled back.

"She… she's here!"

The girl from the audience chamber was sitting in the middle of the room, on the narrow mattress. She was

45

wearing a flowing robe of golden silk. The light of the oil lamp she was holding danced on her snow white neck. Her raven-black hair was loose and falling around her shoulders.

"Yes, it seems she's a gift from our host," Li explained. "He noticed you liked her," he added, coldly.

"A gift...? I don't want – "

"Now, now, you can't turn away a gift from a *daimyo*. That would be a gravest insult."

Wulf took another step back, and whispered, pointing at the girl.

"But, what... what am I supposed to do with her?"

Li raised an eyebrow. "You're a man, aren't you? *What you know, you know, what you don't know, you don't know*, says Master Kong. Don't worry; I'm sure she's trained enough that the language barrier will not be a problem."

Wulf looked at the girl again and gulped.

"I've changed my mind," he heard Li saying. "I think I'll go for a walk in the castle gardens."

He sat down beside the girl. In the silence of the dim room he could hear only his heart beating. She was waiting, motionless, like a doll, still facing the door.

"I'm sorry, I..." he broke into the quiet. She stirred and turned towards him. "I don't even know your name..."

She reached out and put her finger to his lips. Her touch made him shiver. An unwanted memory ran through his head, almost spoiling the mood.

46

"You're a Warwick," his father had said to him, before sending him to the Academy. "King Richard's blood runs through your veins. Don't forget that when some low-born girl takes your fancy."

Somewhere in Dracaland, a daughter of some other aristocratic clan was already promised to him, a bride-to-be, chosen by his father a long time ago, waiting for his return. Everything was already sorted for him back home.

Knowing this, he had ignored the girls at the Academy; the only one who had caught his eye was the red-head from the Geomancy... But now, he couldn't even remember her name.

She was always around those Prydain boys, wasn't she?

It all seemed so distant now, trivial. He'd been through war since, he almost died – and had seen soldiers his age die. The Academy was now just a strange dream. So were his father's warnings.

The girl took his hand in hers and led him between her breasts, peeking from under the loose robe.

"Yoko," she whispered.

"Is that... is that your name?" he whispered back. "I'm Wulfhere – Wulf..."

"U... *Urufo*," she struggled with the words.

"That's good enough."

She ran a hand over his face, as if trying to remember its shape. Then she reached for the thin strip of material holding her robe together and untied it. The golden silk slid to the floor like a cascade of autumn leaves.

She blew out her oil lamp.

Shimazu Nariakira finished reading through the report and put the paper down.

"Just as expected, the crop from the Hayato fields is trebled."

"Yes, *kakka*."

The young man sitting before him nodded sharply and nervously ran his fingers through the bushy, unkempt beard.

"Very well. Get the fourth engine out. The one with the experimental drive shaft. Put it on the sweet potato field."

"Right away, *kakka*."

"You're doing a great job, Shosuke-*sama*."

"I live to serve, *kakka*."

Nariakira grunted irritably, the matter of traction engines had already bored his impatient mind. The young man prostrated then shuffled backwards out of the room on his knees.

"Call the girl in!" the *daimyo* shouted after him.

Yokō entered noiselessly, her golden robe shimmering around her like the scales of a temple carp.

She's wearing that thing as if she was born into it, thought Nariakira

"How was he?" he asked.

48

The girl sat down, or rather, folded like a twilight flower.

"Clumsy and eager, like all virgins," she said quietly.

"Will he do what I want?"

She raised her blind eyes. Her face was pale, bloodless, tired.

"Right now, he'll do everything I ask of him."

Nariakira let out a half-chuckle.

"The question is, can he do it?"

"He studied in the same school as Bran-*sama*."

"They knew each other, then? Are you sure?"

"I saw it all in his head. The... animosity is clear."

Nariakira laughed. "Oh, that is precious! It's as if the Gods were toying with my plans. Rivals, eh? Splendid, just splendid."

He turned serious at once.

"We're not letting this one go."

"No, *kakka*. I'll make sure of that."

Nariakira reached for the simple cup of white clay. Water; he never drank alcohol when dealing with matters of the province.

He considered the girl before him and remembered her arrival, just a few weeks ago. All she had to her was a single piece of silver... and her gift. The guards at the castle gate had mocked her at first, and pushed her away; that was until she told their Captain all their little secrets. Nobody had since dared to mock her.

Takamori chose him well, thought Nariakira. One of Kiyomasa's men. Loyal, and a bright one, too.

The guards' heads hung from the battlements, and the girl was introduced to the *daimyo* the next day. Seeing her now, it was hard to believe she wasn't born at the *Mikado's* court.

He caressed her hair in a fatherly gesture, and she flinched slightly.

"Yokō, you... you don't mind doing all of this, do you?"

"My liege!" She sounded almost offended. "I am thy most humble servant."

She's made remarkable progress.

He stepped back.

"It's strange," he said, more to himself than to the girl, "I don't mind sending any of my men to their death, or worse, if need be. And they do it, eagerly. But it's different with you."

Is it because she reminds me of Atsuko so much? he wondered, swirling water in the cup.

"If only you were of noble birth..."

I might have adopted you, too.

She touched the floor with her forehead. "A month ago I was a kitchen girl at a shrine, *kakka*. I can never repay what you did for me."

"Let me know if I ask too much," he said at last.

She rose slowly and retreated towards the door. She stopped when she reached the exit and turned an unseeing gaze towards the northern wall.

"He's coming."

Nariakira raised his head.

"Oh? How long?"

"A few days, maybe a week."

"He's already too late, anyway," Nariakira waved his hand. The girl bowed one last time and disappeared in a golden shimmer.

A line of Yamato porters and Bataavian sailors moved in a slow and orderly fashion up and down the gangways of the Soembing. Dylan and Gwen moved to the side, out of everyone's way, and watched as the engineers dismantled the engine and the paddle wheels under the Captain's watchful eye.

Most of the modern equipment on board the ship, including all weapons, had been stripped and taken on land in big metal crates. The decks were full of serious-looking Yamato men, inspecting, checking, and measuring the ship, and ordering about a mass of porters.

"What will happen to all those things?" Gwen asked.

"My orders were to deliver her here intact, that's all," Captain Fabius replied, shrugging. He was drained, grey-faced. Dylan almost felt sorry for him. "Those barbarians can turn her into matchsticks for all I care. Hey!" he shouted at one of the Yamato porters, struggling with some heavy device of coils and glass tubes. "Careful with that, it will fry your face off!"

He cursed and ran off to assist with the removal.

"Do you trust this man?" Gwen asked Dylan. "This Nariakira."

"I don't," he replied, "but I have little choice. He controls everything here: Fabius said so, and I believe him. I will need his help if I want to find Bran."

"So you will keep your part of the bargain? We don't want to start another war, Dylan."

"I don't think he really can do anything with a single, rider-less dragon" He waved his hand. "I'll worry about it when we get to this Keeyoh and figure out how things are in Qin. Maybe I won't be able to contact Edern after all. For all we know, he may not even be alive anymore."

"I'm sure he's fine. He is much stronger than you."

He pulled her closer. "You were always fond of him, weren't you?"

She laughed. "Are you now jealous of Edern?"

He laughed back. "How can I be jealous of someone like him?"

"Some men would be."

"I'm not *some* men. And I've known him for a long time."

"Yes, I've often wondered about that," she said, her eyes smiling.

"Now who's jealous?" He kissed her. "You're in a good mood today."

"Oh, Dylan," she said leaning back into his embrace, "I know this is a bad moment, but I'm just happy we're here together. I was ready to fight our way through; I was preparing myself for bloodshed. But apart from those guards... everyone here is so unobtrusive and agreeable..."

"It's all pretend. It always is. It will – "

"Who cares! It makes a change. Did you like the food they made for us yesterday? I loved it," she said.

He winced. "It's all tasteless to me."

"You're impossible," she said and pulled him away from the ship. "Actually, it's almost lunch-time. Let's see if we can convince them to cook us something that will change your mind." She looked at the porters. "This looks like it's going to take a while..."

Wulfhere watched Commodore ab Ifor and Reeve Gwenllian ferch Harri descend down the gangway, close to each other, almost hand in hand.

Didn't the Commodore have a wife back in Gwynedd?

He decided he didn't care about it any more than he had about his bride-to-be. He reached his left hand back and felt Yokō's gentle, slim fingers touch his. Li was standing next to them, his hands behind his back.

The Commodore approached and looked him over.

"Where's your uniform, Lieutenant?"

"It's... stained, Sir" Wulf replied. "I got this from Lord Nariakira, while the uniform's being washed."

The Commodore's finger poked him in the shoulder, where the circle-in-cross was stitched in white thread. "Do you know what that means?"

"It means it's a gift from Lord Nariakira."

"It means you're his *vassal*, you fool. You shouldn't be wearing this. Not while you are a subject of Her Majesty."

"Y-yes, Sir."

"Have you packed your things back to the ship?"

Wulfhere took half a step back.

"I'll be coming with Master Li, later."

The Commodore looked sharply, first at the Qin interpreter, then at the blind girl behind Wulf.

"Nonsense, you're coming with us – and that's an order."

Wulf took a deep breath and squeezed Yokō's hand.

"Commodore *Dí Lán*," he heard Li speak, "I believe you have forfeited your rank when you decided to come here. This boy only takes orders from Ardian Seton."

The Commodore's eyes hardened. "Seton knows you're here?"

Wulfhere gulped and opened his mouth, but decided saying nothing was a better idea.

"Was that your idea, Li?" the Commodore turned to the interpreter, who bowed his head slightly, his lips curled.

"Lord Nariakira has invited both of us to a hunting trip tomorrow," Li said, "It would be unwise to refuse."

"Just the two of you?"

"He knows the ship must sail today."

The Commodore paused to think. His eyes glinted with sudden understanding.

"So *that's* what he is planning," he murmured. "You're a damn fool, Warwick. You have no idea what games they're playing."

"I'll be fine, Sir."

"You should come with us now."

"I'll be fine," Wulfhere repeated. "I'll be in Kiyō before long."

"Not if she has something to say about that," the Commodore said quietly, looking past him, straight at Yokō. He nodded at the interpreter.

"I'll be watching you, Li. Tell Nariakira that if you come alone to Kiyō, the bargain is off."

"He would be most displeased," said the interpreter, bowing slightly again. "And you'd have gone all this way for nothing."

The Commodore's eyes narrowed. "Let me worry about that. And you – " he added, staring Wulf down, "don't forget where your loyalties lie, boy."

He turned on his heels and marched off towards the Bataavian ship, Reeve Gwenllian following, limping slightly.

"What did he mean?" Wulf asked. "What games? We're only staying for the hunt, aren't we?"

The interpreter's mouth raised in a wry smile.

"He's a good one too, your Commodore," he said, absentmindedly. "But Lord Nariakira will outplay him, just watch."

From half-way up the slope, Satō could see all of Hitoyoshi Valley, like an enormous, multi-faceted emerald; bright green embedded in the dark, verdant forests around it. She saw the white lightning that was the foamy Kuma River, sparkling in the summer sun, and the town itself, the vermillion of the Aoi Aso Shrine a distant, but bright dot peeking through the haze of steam beaming from the hot spring pools and narrow chimneys of the shōchu distilleries.

This is where we stayed, she remembered. *The day before we fought the bandits. And met Master Dōraku.*

It was only a month ago – but seemed like a different age; a different life. That last time she really laughed and enjoyed herself. Before she killed her first man, before everything that followed…

How long did it take us to get through that forest…?

The scientific expedition had left Kagoshima a mere week earlier and now they were just a few hours from reaching the summit of Mount Ichifusa. The pace was a lightning one now, despite the heat.

Apart from her, two other students, some armed guards and a few porters, carrying all the necessary equipment up the mountain made up the remainder of the expedition, led by the Snow Beard. The mountain they were climbing was one of the few places in all of Satsuma where snow fell in winter. That meant that, somewhere in the crevices, fissures, and narrow caves of its summit, the Frost Elementals could survive even until the height of the hot Chinzei summer.

Satō knew how precious these were, but she still could not understand the purpose of the expedition. Why not wait until winter, when the Elementals were so much easier to extract and capture? Were the needs of the Kagoshima wizards so dire and urgent? Surely all available magic-users should have been at the harbour, studying the ship and its contents?

And the dragon — am I not the best dragon expert they have? Why send me out?

"Stop brooding, Takashima," Yukihige prodded her. "We need to get to the top before dusk."

They broke camp around an old, dilapidated shrine on the summit of the mountain. Some pilgrims were still coming here – Satō noticed an offering of stale rice cakes and withered wild flowers at the altar; but they hadn't passed anyone along the road, and both the altar and the offerings were covered in dust and cobwebs.

"Our lode starts from this outcrop," Yukihige guided his students to a jumble of cracked and weathered boulders the size of a tea house and the shape of a crooked hood. A narrow prospecting shaft, protected by timber scaffolding, had already been dug into it, and something silver at the bottom gleamed. "It reaches at least a hundred feet into the rock, maybe more. It should provide a good haul."

"But," he added, raising a licked finger, "it's a nice, warm day, even so high up, so we'll need to be careful. We don't want our precious elementals to evaporate as soon as we get them up on the surface, now, do we? You two, start building the ice dome."

"Yes, *sensei*." The two young men stood on the opposite sides of the shaft and started weaving long, thin strands of ice.

"Let me know if you need any help," said Yukihige. "I know it's your first time."

"Yes, *sensei*."

The teacher dispatched the porters to various jobs around the camp, and sat down on a large, flat stone, looking down into the valley.

"What about me?" asked Satō, who alone had not been given any task.

"Save your strength, Takashima," he replied. "You'll be the first one going into the mine." He leaned back against the rock and stretched his arms.

"That golden dragon sure was something, eh?"

The night was cold and filled with snoring.

Everyone was already sound asleep, even the guards; there was no need for them to stay awake here, at the top of the mountain. An unwatched campfire was sizzling down in the dew, its expiring glow dancing blue on the walls of the unfinished ice dome. Far below the mountain, a few dots of light twinkled through the haze: the great bonfires on the grounds of the Aoi Aso Shrine.

Satō was wide awake. Not for the first time; rare were the nights when she could simply fall asleep before midnight. Sometimes she asked the Daisen for one of his herbal essences, but she didn't like how her mind was always blurred the next day. Most of the time she just struggled on.

Tonight her mind wandered from one thought to another, none of them happy. She had a lot to worry about in the darkness. The machinations of the *Taikun* and the Eight-headed Serpent. The fate of Yamato. The well-being of her friends in far-away Nagoya. But most worrying of all was her own future.

She counted the coins on her waist; her fortune had dwindled to a few pieces of gold. What would happen when there was no gold left? Not even she could live and study for free at the Academy forever.

Adoption or marriage? The only two options left. She had counted on Shimazu-*dono*'s help in either, but the *daimyo* had been ignoring her pleas so far.

Maybe it's for the better. I don't want to owe anything to anyone.

And then, unwittingly, she remembered Bran, and the last time she had seen him, or rather, his *dorako*, the green cross-shape in the clouds. She didn't like that memory, but somehow, in the end, it always haunted her.

She liked to think that she understood why he had to do it, that she got over it – over him. But understanding did not mean forgiveness.

"You could have at least said goodbye," she whispered into the night. "What am I supposed to do with myself now?"

The dome was ready, and the shaft had been cleaned and prepared for her to climb down.

"Be careful, Takashima," said Yukihige. "This may be routine for us, but it's still slippery and dangerous."

"Yes, yes."

She rolled up her sleeves and put on a miner's headband with a burning candle tied to it.

How primitive, she thought. *Bran could summon a flamespark with a snap of his fingers. We still have so much to learn.*

She grabbed the rope ladder and began her descent. The walls of the shaft were covered with a thin layer of frozen water, turning plain limestone into precious, polished onyx. In the cold of the mine, she turned into a living mistfire machine, producing puffs of white steam with every breath.

She reached the bottom, some twenty feet below ground; from here the shaft went deeper into the mountain at a slight angle. She took the candle off her head and stuck it in some wax on the wall. The layer of frost ended after a few feet; there was nothing else here but dry rock.

"Something's not right," she shouted up. "I can't see any vein here!"

High above her head, the ice dome formed a reflector, casting strange rays of light and shadow on the mine floor. Yukihige's head showed in the narrow opening.

He said something, but she didn't hear him clearly.

"What did you say?"

"I said I'm really sorry about this!" he repeated. "But those are Shimazu-*dono*'s orders."

"What orders?"

The teacher's head disappeared for a moment.

"What's – "

She looked up just in time to notice the rope ladder tumbling towards her, followed by rain of shattered bamboo.

A shadow of Yukihige's hands danced on the floor, weaving threads of ice into a dense lattice. At first she couldn't grasp what she was seeing, but then, with sudden, terrible clarity, she knew.

"No!"

Threads of frost, like tiny waterfalls, trickled down the shaft's wall. The dome above her head was closing up.

"A most unfortunate accident," said Yukihige. "A young life cut in its prime... I will leave you a window to look at the stars," he added. "I know how you like the stars. I'm sorry," he said one last time.

He finished his task by casting a transparent sheet of ice over the opening. It looked like glass, but she knew it was as firm and unbreakable as diamond.

"Why?" she cried, but there was no answer.

CHAPTER III

Lord Nariakira shut the window and dusted his clothes of soot.

The night sky over Kagoshima was dark, moonless. Clouds, rare at this time of year, hid all but the brightest stars. The air was thick, heavy and steamy, muffling the distant lights and noises of the entertainment district.

The mountain was acting up again, and the thin dust was getting everywhere. The *daimyo* switched on the wind machine, and revelled for a while in its rhythmical clacking. The air and fire elementals inside purred, and their inexplicable interactions caused the hot wind to blow through a long brass funnel. By the time this wind blew out into the room, it was cooled by a thin layer of True Frost.

Ice was a rare and expensive element in this part of Yamato, and without it, the wind machine would only be a glorified fireplace; only a few aristocratic houses had the machines installed, each painstakingly crafted in the workshops and laboratories of Satsuma's wizard school. A few more could afford it, Nariakira knew, but were afraid to flaunt their wealth too much in case it attracted too many tax collectors and lost relatives in search of inheritance.

THE CHRYSANTHEMUM SEAL

A candle on the desk flickered and went out. The *daimyo* turned the wind machine off. The air was cool enough without it. Nariakira winced.

How does he do that? I have so many traps…

They were at the top floor of the castle keep; the doors and windows were locked shut; just outside the room stood Saigō Takamori, the square-jawed Captain of his bodyguards, watchful.

"You're late," Nariakira said, lighting a new candle, his hands shaking slightly.

"I keep hearing that," the cold voice replied. "I make my own time."

Nariakira touched the grip of his short sword; it buzzed reassuringly. He turned slowly around to face the intruder.

Most men, he knew, would welcome the visitor with nothing but dread. But Nariakira was almost glad to see him. There was something strangely calming in the sight of the invariably garish cloak, ever the same dark shade of purple, and the familiar twin *katana*s at the Swordsman's waist.

"I don't just mean today," said the *daimyo*. "Where have you been? I needed you here."

"Here and there. Mostly Chōfu," replied Dōraku. "Where is Takashima?"

"On a scientific expedition to the northern borders. Chōfu, you say? What's young Mori-*dono* up to these days?"

Dōraku produced a pipe and lit it, deliberately slowly, before answering.

"He's established his own school of *Rangaku*."

"*Mori?*" Nariakira cried out in genuine shock. "*This* Mori? He hates everything Western."

"Strange, isn't it?" Dōraku puffed on the pipe. "Perhaps the recent events changed his mind."

"Have you talked with him?"

"No, I don't have his trust anymore. He grew up in the shadow of Ganry   jima. He hates my kind more than he hates the Westerners."

Nariakira sat down, laid his hands on his knees and straightened his back. Dōraku hesitated for a moment and then sat down too. The casual part of the conversation was over.

"Speaking of Ganryūjima…" started Nariakira.

The *daimyo* had learnt about the events at the island fortress from the Daisen and the Takashima girl. By now, he had managed to calm his fury over the disappearance of the dragon rider – though not enough to forgive Dōraku his negligence.

The Swordsman scowled. "I know what you're thinking, but I assure you, the boy is still somewhere in Yamato."

"But not here. And neither is his dragon. I trusted your judgement and I lost everything."

Do you have any idea what I would do to my own vassal if he'd failed me like this?

Dōraku shrugged.

"This is temporary. Everything's going according to my plan."

Nariakira slammed his fist on the floor.

"It's not *my* plan! I don't have time for this – I've made my own arrangements."

"You have a knack for attracting foreign castaways," said Dōraku, unperturbed. "But I've seen that new boy. He's nothing like Bran-*sama*."

"Good!" Nariakira waved his hands in exasperation. "I don't need another disobedient Westerner. This one will do just right."

"You'll still need a *dorako*."

Nariakira's eyes glinted. "I know."

Dōraku puffed on the pipe to conceal his surprise. "Looks like you really don't need me anymore."

"Oh," Nariakira tried his best to sound casual. "I'm sure I can always find use for your services."

The Swordsman's eyes turned cold and dark. Nariakira fought the urge to reach for the sword. The candle on the desk flickered in the icy wind coming from nowhere.

"I don't *serve* anyone," said Dōraku slowly. "I help you because we share common goals."

Nariakira smirked. "Noble words, but empty. I need more commitment than that."

Dōraku raised an eyebrow. "*More* than that?"

"I'm thinking of the future. I might do things you will not approve. I can join forces with people you dislike. I know my men sometimes disagree with my methods – but it doesn't bother me as long as they remain loyal to me."

The Swordsman leaned forward, stone-faced.

"What have you done, Shimazu?"

Nariakira felt his fury rising. He knew it was a test; if they were to remain allies, he would have to swallow the insult. But if he was to assert his authority…

He's like a feral dog… that needs whipping.

Though rich and powerful, Nariakira was merely a mortal after all. Not even a *Taikun* could stand against the Fanged. Perhaps…not even the *Mikado*.

But if I let this slide now, in my own castle, how will I be able to tame him once I rule Yamato?

He put a hand on his wakizashi and felt it vibrate gently. Dōraku's eyes focused on its black sheath and his own hand moved slowly towards the grips of his swords.

You can feel it, can't you? It calls for your blood, demon.

"I call it Wolf Bite," Nariakira said, revelling in the Swordsman's unease.

"How… fitting," the Swordsman replied. They both knew of Dōraku's distinct lack of fondness for the wolves.

"I found it in Hosokawa's armoury," the *daimyo* added, "After you helped me depose the old man – remember?"

Don't even think of doing the same to me.

67

A sudden thought struck Nariakira.

Who told Captain Kiyomasa about the coup…? I thought it was my dear little brother, but what if…

"Why did you *really* send Takashima-*sama* away?" the Swordsman asked, not letting the sword out of his sight. "It's because of the Ship, isn't it? When is she coming back?"

She is not, Nariakira thought, and licked his lips.

It was as if the Swordsman had heard his thoughts; he froze suddenly, and then stood up. Nariakira stared straight at him, unblinking, straining his eyes and tightening the grip on the hilt.

"You've gone too far, Shimazu," the Swordsman said quietly.

"Everything I do is for the good of Yamato."

"Yamato… or yours?"

"There is no difference, Swordsman. Can't you understand that?" he said through gritted teeth. "The time of darkness is upon us. Only I can lead the country safely through it."

Dōraku's eyes glinted gold.

"I'm wasting my time here," he spat.

The world around Nariakira swirled. He stumbled forward in a daze, drawing the black sword and slashing the air blindly.

When he came to, he was alone. The candle on his desk was burned half-way down.

"Takamori!" Nariakira roared.

The Captain burst through the door, sword in hand. His expression turned from fury to relief in an instant when he saw the *daimyo* unharmed.

"Have you seen anyone coming in or out of the castle?" Nariakira asked.

"No, *kakka.*"

"Gather your men. Call a manhunt."

Making no noise, Dōraku opened the door to the Daisen's room. He didn't expect anyone inside: all the wizards of the Shigakko Academy were working through the night on the artefacts retrieved from the Bataavian ship. But the room was not empty; a girl in golden silk robe was sitting beside the Daisen's desk, so quiet and discreet he barely noticed her. It took him a moment to recognize the white-daubed face.

"You look well, Yokō-*sama.*"

"Thank you."

"Are you here to stop me?"

She giggled. "Me? I'm just a weak, blind girl."

"Then why are you here?"

"Shimazu-*dono* is a good man." she said. "He would have made a good *Taikun.*"

"The first Tokugawa was a good *Taikun*, too. And look where we are now."

She tilted her head to the side. "I'm a mere shrine servant who got lucky. I don't know much about history."

He reached for the documents strewn on the desk. There had to be a clue to Takashima's whereabouts somewhere among them…

The girl lay gentle fingers on a piece of paper and slid it towards him.

"I will have to report this to Shimazu-*dono*, of course," she said.

His keen ears caught the sound of cries and alarm gongs, and feet stomping across the courtyard of the Academy. He had little time. He grabbed the paper from under her hand and looked at her inquiringly.

"The wizardess was the first who was kind to me," she said, her voice even quieter, almost a whisper. "Please save her."

Dōraku moved towards the door, but stopped at the threshold, listening to the noise outside.

"You will tell them where to find me, won't you?"

"Of course," she smiled and bowed her head slightly.

"Good girl."

"What's wrong, boy?" asked Li, noticing Wulfhere brooding in his room. "Your silk-clad beauty abandoned you?"

"She's busy tonight," said Wulf. "It's boring here without her. When do we fly to *Keeyo*?"

"Soon."

Wulf sighed. Li eyed him from under a raised brow.

"Are you sure you want to fly with me? Kiyō will be even more boring than Kagoshima. You won't even be allowed to go outside the Bataavian district."

Wulfhere shrugged, resigned. "I can't really stay here, can I?"

"Can't you? I know you've even started learning the language."

"The Commodore said — "

"Let me deal with your Commodore. Here in Yamato he's not as important as he thinks he is."

Wulfhere's eyes lit up. "Well, I could stay a few weeks if Lord Nariakira agrees. Yes, I'm sure I'd manage that." He smiled to himself.

Li smirked. "I thought you would. I'll let Lord Nariakira know."

He suddenly stiffened and his nostrils flared as if he'd smelled something nasty.

"What is — " Wulf started, but the interpreter silenced him with a raised hand.

"Hush… can you not feel it? All my hair is standing on end!"

Slowly, Li stepped towards his bedding where his sword lay. Wulfhere had seen this weapon only once out of its sheath — an old Qin blade, broadened and split at the end, fit for ceremony rather than battle.

"Get your sword," the interpreter whispered, "and hide in your room."

"Hide? What's going on?"

"A Black Lotus is here."

"*Black Lotus?* In this castle?" he whispered back.

Li unsheathed his sword and waved at Wulf, impatiently.

"Hide, hide! I can sense it's near."

Wulf slid the door to his room; it had never seemed as thin, as fragile as now. Just to be sure, he extinguished the oil lamp, and waited in silence and darkness.

I'm not hiding, he told himself. *I'm waiting in ambush.*

He heard the main door slide open. The room turned cold. There was silence, and then a voice spoke, cold, emotionless. It spoke in Qin, with some difficulty.

Wulf's heart pounded furiously; his hand, tightened on the hilt of his sword, got cold and clammy.

There was an even longer pause before Li replied, shakily. The two exchanged a couple more sentences in this manner, and then Li spoke a sentence in which Wulf recognized the Qin word for "the boy". He clenched his teeth.

I did it once. I can do it again.

He heard steps again, across the straw floor, moving towards his room, and he raised his right hand. The door started to slide open slowly.

I can do it!

Wulf summoned the Soul Lance and lunged forward with what he planned to be a roar, but turned out a feeble cry.

The man leapt aside. Wulf swept the Lance around wildly, and felt it hit something soft and fleshy. The next thing he knew somebody turned him around and twisted his arm painfully; his Lance shimmered away.

"Stop!" cried Li.

Wulf struggled and gasped, but it was futile to try to wrestle from the tight grip. He felt cold fingers on his windpipe; the arm they belonged to bore the deep and wide cut of a Soul Lance blade; a dark gash running down the entire forearm. But there was no blood, and as Wulf watched mesmerised, the edges of the wound started drawing together. Before long, the gash was gone without a trace.

The man holding him said something in Qin again, then in Bataavian; Wulfhere looked helplessly at Li.

"I don't – "

"Don't move, boy," the interpreter said sharply. "He says he can crush your neck with that hand, and I believe him."

"Is he a Black Lotus?" Wulfhere tried to twist his head to face the enemy, but the grip on his neck forced him away. He choked and coughed.

Before Li could answer, Lord Nariakira and his guards burst into the room. The *daimyo* pointed a blade at the man holding Wulf; the short sword was at once black and translucent, shimmering and humming, like the scales of a Highland Grey. Wulf didn't need True Sight to tell it was a magic weapon.

Wulfhere followed little of what happened next. There was a lot of arguing in both Qin and Yamato tongues, shouting, threats, and waving swords in the air. The Lotus's hold on his throat and arm once slackened, once tightened, as the argument progressed, but was always firm enough to ensure Wulf could not even think of getting himself free.

At long last, the argument quietened down. Lord Nariakira stepped back and lowered his peculiar blade, resigned and coldly furious.

The Black Lotus shoved Wulfhere forward.

"Do what he tells you, boy," said Li. "We're going to the dragon."

Something twinkled next to the hair-thin crescent of the new Moon hanging low in the southern sky.

A shooting star?

The golden sparkle disappeared, only to return a few seconds later, a bit to the left. Again, it vanished, and again it returned, and Satō realized that whatever it was, was coming in and out of clouds. With difficulty, she stood up leaning against the hard, cold, wet wall.

The shining dot grew to the size of the evening star, then a sesame seed, and it kept growing; it was moving fast, in what she could tell by now was a bobbing movement. Her heart fluttered.

Could it be… a dragon…?

Satō couldn't see the wings yet, but she was now certain the gleaming dot – now almost as big as a grain of rice – was heading in her direction.

Bran! He's coming to save me… she thought, watching the fast-approaching beast.

She had lost count of the days at the bottom of the frozen mine; she was tired and hungry. The piercing cold sapped all her strength. She had used everything she had, every spell she could think of, to get out. She climbed on ice bolts stuck in the rock – but they were too brittle. She tried various fire spells to shatter the shield, but those never worked for her well, and the dome didn't even begin to melt. It didn't surprise her – Snow Beard was among the most powerful ice wizards she had ever met.

She'd gathered splinters of bamboo and set them on fire to stay warm. Now this fire was also gone, and with it, her remaining power.

The humiliation she felt was worse than the cold; a shame that burned her inside out and kept her awake at night. They wouldn't even leave her the sword. For all she was worth, for all she had done to prove it, the good and the bad - she was still unworthy to die with the dignity of a samurai.

She drew one last blade of frost, long and sharp. But it splintered on her stomach into painful shards. She hid her face in her hands.

Endless hours passed. The night turned into the day and again into the night. By the time the dragon appeared, she could barely move.

The shimmering of the ice sheet was playing tricks on her eyes – the dragon was not jade green but golden. Her heart sank. The long wasn't coming for her. Lord Nariakira had sent it and its rider to fly across Satsuma in the dark of night on some urgent errand.

The Taikun *will never stand for this, she thought, feebly.*

The dragon vanished from her sight. She lay down, resigned, barely registering the cool of the cavern floor on her cheek.

She closed her eyes.

Goodbye, Bran.

She woke up with the warm sun on her face and the howl of wind in her ears.

She tried to sit up, but was too weak; she got dizzy and lay back to the ground. Her body was light.

"Careful, Takashima-*sama*," spoke a voice she hadn't heard in a long, long time.

I'm dreaming.

A flask was put to her lips; cold shōchū spilled into her mouth, and she started coughing. Slowly, she opened her eyes and sat up, shivering. Her head was spinning and her cuts started to burn.

76

Master Dōraku put the flask away, looked her over and touched her forehead. His hand was cold, like the walls of the ice mine.

"Good. You're not sick."

Satō glanced to her left. She was sitting just a few feet from the ice dome, the shattered remains of which melted quickly in the sun. That meant only one thing... Several hacked bodies lay beside the rocky outcrop, Yukihige among them, his grey beard splattered with drops of red, his neck sliced through, his mouth open, silenced forever in mid-spell.

Still dizzy, she looked to her right, and saw the dragon.

The beast was a lot longer than Emrys, but slimmer, more a flying snake than a lizard. Its scales shimmered purest gold, like tiles on a temple roof. Satō couldn't help herself and gasped.

So it's true. Qin dragons evoke awe, she remembered. *Not fear.*

A man stood beside the *long* and stared at her with an angry, resentful glare. He had a strangely angular face underneath a blue hat, and he wore the kind of clothes she had only seen worn by the officials in the Qin district of Kiyō.

Master Dōraku smoothed his moustache with his fingers. His eyes were black as coals, and his face seemed even paler than usual. If such a thing was at all possible, Satō would think he was... tired.

Why is he here with that Qin man?

"You look terrible," she said weakly. "What happened?"

He laughed. "*I* look terrible? Oh, that's a good one." He reached into his bags and gave her a rice ball. "You must eat."

She sank her teeth in the rice and took hasty bites; it was the best thing she'd ever tasted. She felt her strength slowly coming back. She finished her rice ball and before she could ask, Master Dōraku put another in her hands and then another.

"How long…" she asked, licking rice off her fingers.

"I don't know. Three, four days, maybe? I got here as soon as I could."

"Are you… in trouble because you came here?"

He grinned, his dark teeth showing.

"You could say that. I don't believe I'm welcome in Kagoshima anymore."

She stood up shakily, supporting herself on the Fanged's shoulder.

"My sword – my things – …"

"It's all here," he pointed to the saddlebags hanging over the dragon's side. "Luckily that man was still here – watching you die I guess."

Master Yukihige… How quickly you gained my trust, and how quickly you betrayed it!

She staggered towards the dragon and the Qin man. He didn't move when she bowed slightly and said her greetings,

78

unsure about his role. She looked to the magnificent golden creature. The beast stared right back at her with curious, wondrous eyes.

Unable to withstand that gaze, she turned back to Dōraku.

"I came to Satsuma to help fight the *Taikun*," she said. "To avenge my father. I... don't understand."

"You've become too much of a burden for Shimazu-*dono*." Then after a pause he added. "You knew too much... you knew about me. You knew about Bran."

Bran...

"But why now...?"

He shrugged. "Even I can't pierce Nariakira's thoughts. We must be going now," he added.

"Go? Where?" she asked, angrily. "I can't go back to Kagoshima; I can't go back to Kiyō... I'm wanted everywhere else."

"You are going to Chōfu. There's an opening for a teacher of Ice Wizardry."

She looked and him and blinked.

A teacher? Like Snow Beard?

"But I can't... I'm just a student..."

"I'm sure you'll be more than perfect for the job. Didn't you use to teach in your father's school, in Kiyō?"

He's right. I was a teacher!

It seemed almost like some previous life now.

"Chōfu is so far away…" she said, her will slowly breaking.

"The dragon would get you there in no time."

I'd get to ride the dragon…?

She reached out to touch the scales of the *long*. They were warm and soft under her touch, and yet firm, like cloth made of the purest silk. She felt the body underneath vibrate gently with each of the beast's breaths. A spark of static electricity struck her fingers. She jerked back.

"Chōfu it is, then," she said, and laughed.

The morning sun was reflected in the steel-blue sea below the hill. Funai harbour was waking to life.

Master Dōraku helped Satō dismount. The Qin man, who had kept morbidly silent all through the ride, remained on the dragon, staring at the sea in the distance.

"A ship goes out for Chōfu at noon," the Fanged said. "Do not linger too long. This is Ogasawara land, the place is brimming with the *Taikun*'s spies."

"You're not coming with me?"

He shook his head.

"I have to be somewhere else, as usual. But," he reached into his sleeve, "I have something for you."

He handed her a ball of crystal the colour of fresh blood and the size of an orange. She touched it carefully; it was warm and perfectly smooth.

"It belonged to Ganryū – well, ever since he stole it from somewhere else, that is. He was using it to control Emrys. Bran-*sama* wanted you to have it."

"Bran… wanted me…"

She took the orb and held it in both hands. It grew hot and bright, almost too hot to hold, like a piece of cinder.

"I was hoping to ask the Daisen to research it, but that is no longer possible. You may have more luck."

"But what is it?"

"This is a Tide Jewel."

"*Eeeh*…a Tide Jewel? You mean like in the legend…?"

The *kagura* dancers of Kirishima Shrine flashed before her eyes, but she struggled to remember the details. She hadn't exactly been paying great attention to the performance that night.

"In every legend, no matter how embellished it is, there is a grain of truth," said Dōraku. "There used to be more than two of these. Always came in pairs, too – a white one and a blue one."

"This one is red," Satō pointed out, raising the stone to the light.

"It was corrupted by Ganryū's blood. It was originally white."

"How can you be so sure?"

He smiled. "If you could see its magic glow, you'd understand. I've seen the blue one of the pair before – just a shard – and the energy signature is unmistakable."

"The blue shard... you mean Bran's ring."

"Shimazu-*dono*'s ring now, I'm afraid. The boy got back the copy."

"Does Bran know?"

"He does now."

She rolled the orb in her hand and put it into her own sleeve.

"You know where he is, don't you?"

He grinned and got on the dragon's back.

"The war will come to Chōfu first," he said. "It stands between Edo and the South. Make sure you are well prepared. Goodbye, Takashima-*sama*."

He patted the Qin on the shoulder and the golden beast shot into the air like a striking viper.

Satō stood in front of the sand-yellow gates of Chōfu Castle holding a bundle of her few belongings, wearing a freshly cleaned and mended set of the *Rangaku* vermillion-and-black clothes and a nervous smile. The townspeople passed her by in a hurry, giving her curious looks; the guards watched her with bored interest. Once more, she made sure her breasts were wrapped flat, her jacket clean, her male haircut in order. A lonely female on a ship was asking for trouble, and in Chōfu she couldn't count on the protection she had enjoyed in Kiyō or Satsuma.

For the first time in her life she had nobody to help her, to guide her or to put in a good word for her. She was all alone.

But it felt good to be dressed as a samurai again. Almost as if the woman's body had been the disguise all along. She shifted her Matsubara sword and stepped forward.

"What do you want, boy?" asked one of the guards, bored at last to irritation.

She bowed. "I... I request an audience with the *daimyo*."

The guard chuckled. "Mori-*dono* is a busy man. What clan are you from? I don't recognize the crest."

"Takashima, of Kiyō."

"Never heard about you."

Satō tensed. He was more of an usher than a guard. No mere soldier: he was a retainer, a vassal with a high position at the castle. His entire behaviour – the words, the posture – was an insult, and she had a good mind to teach him some manners. But he was right: she was a nobody. She had to earn her respect the hard way.

"I'm here to ask about the *Rangaku* job at the Meirinkan School."

The samurai looked to his companion with a raised eyebrow, and then spat at Satō's feet.

"The barbarian school is up there," he pointed with his thumb to where a street branched off the castle approach and wound up a dusty slope.

83

Satō bowed. As she walked off, the man mumbled, just loud enough for her to hear:

"Another dirty half-barbarian. Send someone to clean the spot where he stood."

"…and finally, here is the *onmyōji* class. They are researching how we could bind the old Yamato magic with *Rangaku*."

Shōin opened the door to a small room where two older men in silk robes were leaning over a pile of yellowed papers. He smiled apologetically, they nodded at him, and he closed the door.

This finished the brief tour of the school. Shōin stood with his head slightly bowed, the smile of apology still on his lips.

"This is very small," said Satō. There couldn't have been less than thirty pupils in the entire school; in Kagoshima, this would have been just a single class.

"There aren't many in Chōfu who are interested in anything Western, *sensei*," the boy explained softly. Apart from bags under his eyes and a pale, worn face, he didn't seem any different from the eager pupil she remembered from Kiyō. He was now wearing nobleman's clothes, marked with the Mori crest – three circles under a line – and they fitted him badly, hanging loose on thin, narrow shoulders.

"You are now a Mori clansman, are you not?"

"Yes, *sensei*. A minor branch adopted me last month. I could not teach the samurai sons otherwise."

How come he's the headmaster here…?

84

They headed back to the small garden at the back of the school. The veranda looked out on the castle town below, neat, straight lines of sand-yellow walls and grey slate roofs of the residences of the noble-men, all built in a very traditional style she had rarely seen further south.

That's right; I'm not on Chinzei anymore.

"On the ship, I overheard that even the *daimyo* hates the West. The people on the streets here despise us."

"I'm afraid so."

"Then why have a school at all?"

A sparrow landed on the wooden veranda's edge. Shōin sat down on the floor and gestured to her to do the same. Outside, he seemed even more frail.

He bit his lip.

"Mori-*dono* believes it's the only way to stop the Westerners from coming to Yamato."

"Stop them…? But that would mean – "

This was not what she wanted at all.

"They call it *jōi,*" Shōin continued, "'expelling the barbarians'. This is what the *daimyo* wants. Mori-*dono* thinks not even the *Taikun* is forceful enough – and now with all those rumours from Edo…"

What rumours?

"I haven't come all this way from Kiyō to help enforce the *Taikun*'s laws," she said.

"I know, I'm sorry," the boy replied with a wince. "I don't think I agree with it myself. After all, in Kiyō... But he is my liege and I have to obey. And for now, there aren't any barbarians to *expel*, so I can simply focus on my studies. I'm really glad you're here, Satō-*sensei*," he turned to her, his eyes glinting. The sparrow fluttered away. "There's nobody here who would know even half as much about *Rangaku* as you do."

She felt herself blush. "I will do my best, but in Satsuma _ "

"But this isn't Satsuma. Or Kiyō. There are some decent *onmyōji* here, but with the Western magic I'm all alone. I'm stumped in my research. I really hope you can help me."

"Well, as soon as I get the job..."

He winced again. "There is a small problem."

Another sparrow landed on the gravel below Satō's feet; it started a fight with a stubborn worm.

"A problem? Why?"

"I've mentioned you to Mori-*dono* yesterday. It was all going fine, until, well..."

"Until what?"

Shōin crumpled the hem of his kimono in a gesture which reminded Satō of Nagomi.

"Until I mentioned you're a woman." He bowed his head. "He almost threw me outside. I'm afraid he's rather conservative in these matters. He doesn't believe in women teaching men."

"Bastard," she hissed.

The boy gasped. "*Sensei*! He's my overlord!"

Satō glanced at him coldly. "I don't care. He's exactly the kind of man I always despised. It looks like this isn't a place for me after all."

She started up, but Shōin grabbed her by the hand. She looked down at him in shock. He released her immediately.

"I'm sorry." He stared at the cedar wood floorboards again. "There is still one option…"

"What option?"

"I pleaded with the *daimyo*… He understands the need of the school. He knows I can't cope with it myself. He agreed on one… one condition."

"Well, what is it?"

"That you marry."

She laughed out loud.

"Well *that's* not going to happen. I'm not marrying some fat old samurai just to get a job. Thanks, but I'll manage just fine. Take care, Shōin."

She cast one last look at the town below.

What was Dōraku-sama thinking? This place is terrible.

"He doesn't have to be…" Shōin's voice trailed into bashful silence.

"What did you say?"

"It wouldn't have to be a fat and old samurai."

"It doesn't matter." She waved her hand and prepared to leave. "I'm not marrying anyone."

"You could marry me, *sensei*."

She stopped with one foot on the veranda and one in the door. She turned slowly around. "Shōin... you're just a boy..."

"I'm of marrying age," he replied quickly. "You're a noble woman, so you may see it as an insult of course...but since I am Mori now...and this job is..."

Avoiding his worried eyes, she looked at the sparrow in the gravel, that finally tore the stubborn worm in half and jumped away with the rear part of it in its beak.

"That means Mori-*dono* would have to approve of this marriage."

"He already has."

She looked at him sharply. *Already - !*

She noticed Mori's guards standing in front of the school gate. She felt dizzy; blood rushed from her head to her feet, and back again.

Why were things in her life always happening so fast?

Not even two months had passed since she'd had to leave Kiyō forever... a month ago she had burned her father... a few days before coming to Chōfu she had been betrayed and buried alive, forgotten and alone... and now she was being proposed to by her own student!

"Isn't becoming a Mori a far better option than staying an exiled Takashima?" the boy asked in a whisper.

This would solve all my problems with one strike of an official's brush. Position, protection, power... This was almost too ideal.

And what would I tell Bran...?

She remembered the green dragon disappearing into the clouds. She shook her head.

He's never coming back. Forget it already. It's time to move on.

"It would just be for show, you understand," she said at last, biting her lower lip.

He beamed at her and then prostrated, showering the veranda floor with thanks and apologies.

The stubborn worm's upper half slithered away into the shadow.

THE CHRYSANTHEMUM SEAL

CHAPTER IV

"This looks like it," said Azumi.

The steep road winding up the mountain between small shrines built of withered grey cedar wood in a sequence of stone stairs and slopes slippery with mud ended at a blind *torii* gate, leading nowhere; a few feet beyond it rose a sheer wall of volcanic rock, like a frozen waterfall of lava; pillars of black obsidian blotched with light grey and yellow-green veins. Above, the mountain rose tall and bald; no trees grew around its summit, not even the hardy spruce.

Near the top, bathed in mists and rising clouds, a slate-gabled temple-like building perched over the slope. Its jutting balcony was supported on a lattice of thick pillars. There was no obvious road leading to it, almost as if the only way to reach it was by flying.

"It sure does," agreed Ozun.

She tied tighter around her waist the rope holding the basket with his head, spat into her hands, and started to climb up the pillars of lava. The rock was smooth and polished with very little hold. At times she had to leap from one hole to another. Her toes slipped, leaving her hovering over the precipice by just her fingers, the muscles in her

91

limbs tearing apart from the strain. The cold, wet wind tore at her clothes, piercing her with a thousand ice needles and bringing down mist from the top to moisten the grips even further.

"You're almost there, love," Ozun encouraged her.

"I know."

Her fingers bled and her feet swelled up with blisters. She felt she could not climb any longer. And just then, her hand seeking another hold point found nothing but air. The rock ended. She'd reached the top.

There was a path here, a narrow and precarious shelf, but good enough to rest awhile before walking further. It climbed up for another hundred feet before reaching a gateway arch built of great black boulders.

Two guards, each dressed in armour of black lacquer adorned with polished emeralds, spotted her as she reached the last bend, and jumped up in surprise. One of them pointed a spear at her; the other drew a short-bladed sword, of the sort used by the assassins of the Iga province.

"Go back where you came from," ordered the swordsman. "There is nothing for you here."

Azumi put the basket with Ozun's head on the ground, and slowly pulled the chain-sickle from her belt. She swept it a few times from side to side with a swish, to show she knew her business. The swordsman narrowed his eyes and stepped forward.

"You wield the weapons of the *shinobi*," he said, "but do you know how to use them?"

"Do you want to know how many men like you I've killed to get here?"

She spat and covered her face with the ashen-grey mask of her uniform.

"*Koga*." The swordsman recognised it. "You were all destroyed."

"And yet here I am."

She whirled the sickle in a complex pattern and stepped closer.

"Hey," the spearman shouted, "that's enough talk. Either get out of here or die."

"Aren't you at least interested why I'm here?" asked Azumi.

"There's only one reason," replied the swordsman, "and for that, you'll have to pass through us."

"So be it."

As she spoke the last word, Azumi let the sickle fly. It bounced off the swordsman's short blade with a soft chime. She followed the momentum and struck again from the same direction, faster and stronger this time. The chain whirled around the sword, and the swordsman jerked it forward to tear the weapon from Azumi's hands, but she held fast.

She swivelled her hips to dodge the spear point thrust towards her, and leapt up, bouncing lightly from the shaft, over the spearman's head, behind the swordsman, pulling the chain with her around the swordsman's neck. The swordsman rolled back and around, releasing himself from the chain, and, reaching into his belt, threw a volley of poisoned darts towards her. Azumi dodged one, parried another, and caught the third in flight, then threw it back; the swordsman barely managed to reflect it aside.

The two men got serious now. The initial bout over, they circled her slowly, looking for an opening in the whirlwind wall she formed around her out of the chain and blade. They struck at the same instant from opposing directions, the spear slashing at her legs, the sword aiming at her neck. She jumped up and twisted her body in the air, for a brief, gravity-defying moment suspended horizontally between the two blades. Looking straight in the eyes of the swordsman behind her, she cast the sickle forward and felt the chain slacken when the blade hit its target. She made a half-roll and landed on her hands and legs, letting go of her weapon; the spearman staggered and fell forward, clutching the sickle embedded in his neck.

Azumi stood up quickly, drawing twin forked sai daggers to counter the remaining enemy's sword. It was now a duel of short blades, of parrying, glancing and feinting; the swordsman had an advantage of skill and experience, but was visibly shaken by the sudden death of his partner. She pressed on with all her strength, forcing him back.

She did not have much energy left for a lengthy battle. She was an assassin, not a samurai. Rather than by stamina, she was driven by desperation – and that would not last long. This had to finish fast.

The swordsman sensed her exhaustion, and the force of his blows increased; but he was growing tired too, and his slashes and thrusts began to miss their target, sliding off her daggers in a flurry of grinds and sparkles. The shards flying off his blade pierced her hands, and rivulets of blood trickled down her tired wrists.

"His left leg," whispered Ozun.

She noticed it too; the swordsman was shifting his weight on to the right foot whenever he could. At some point in the melee he must have sprained his ankle. Azumi had just enough strength for one last trick.

She feigned a trip and a fall to her right. The swordsman followed with a desperate thrust, but his left leg gave way and the blade missed her shoulder by an inch. She caught the sword in the fork of her left dagger and drew the point of the right one straight into the enemy's now open thigh. He knocked her and she fell on her back, this time for real; the dagger dropped from her hand and the swordsman stood above her, raising the short sword to deal the final blow.

"Enough!"

A tall, full-figured woman in an emerald-green hooded robe moved noiselessly towards them.

"Can't you see she defeated you already? You're going to bleed to death from that wound."

The swordsman lowered his weapon and dropped to his knees, his head hung in shame.

"Chiyo-*sama*," he said, breathing heavily.

"Get that looked after," she ordered. "It's enough that Mishima's dead. I don't want to have to look for two new guards."

The swordsman cast Azumi a vengeful look and hurried inside the stone gateway. Azumi's heart skipped a beat. The woman's thick silk robe was almost identical to the one her old Master had worn. The colour was different, yes, but it was adorned with the same black eight-headed serpent crest that flew on his banners.

"That's her," said Ozun.

"I know."

Azumi knelt on one knee and bowed her head. The woman approached her, closed her eyes, and brushed Azumi's head with long, cold fingers.

"You were with Mars when he died," she said, opening her eyes.

"Mars?"

"Mars of the Crimson Robe. What was the name he used among mortals?"

"Ganryū, my lady. I was there when Ganryūjima fell."

"Do you know how he was killed?"

Azumi reached for the bundle at her waist and unravelled it, revealing the blackened remains of the sword she had found in Ganryū's garden. She presented it in outstretched hands. The woman's eyes widened and she drew back her hand as if burned.

"*Kuso*. You did well, girl. Come with me."

The woman in the emerald robe walked seemingly casually down the timbered corridor, but Azumi knew she had to observe and follow her every step.

It was the kind of house Azumi would have built if she had unlimited time and resources. A complex maze of hallways and stairways, joining at mad angles, with double walls hiding concealed rooms, false exits and escape routes at every corner; every inch of it booby-trapped. In short, a house fit for a master assassin.

The last corridor was a tunnel carved into the meat of the mountain, leading to a balcony looking out over the valley, suspended above the forest and the quiet, sleepy village below. A piercing gale howled in the treetops. Azumi tightened her clothes to ward off the elements, but the woman seemed unfazed by the cold wind raising her robe in emerald billows, revealing glimpses of a dark grey *shinobi* uniform underneath, even tighter and more form-fitting than Azumi's. She cast off her hood, revealing luscious black hair, tied in a long, thick ponytail.

"I'm glad you're here. I was a Koga too, you know," she said, leaning against the railing. She took out a long pipe and lit it with a snap of her spider-like fingers. "A long time ago. Even I didn't know anyone had survived the raid."

Azumi put the basket with Ozun's head carefully in the corner.

"It was Ganryū-*sama* himself who saved me," she said. "That's why I swore him loyalty, lady…"

"Call me Chiyo. Or Venus of the Emerald Robe, if you want to be formal." She puffed smoke in Azumi's face.

Chiyo? Without the honorific? Azumi could never be so informal with a noble lady like her. Was she really the same kind of person as Ganryū-*sama?*

"Was it Mars who told you where to find me?"

"No. I followed hints and clues for the last month... Hajime-*sama* set me in the right direction... but of course you don't know him, lady..."

"Oh, I know *him*," the woman laughed, covering her mouth with the back of her hand. "A sword for hire, right? Did a few jobs for me, too. And others. Did he mention the others?"

"I didn't even know there were any others until the last few weeks."

"Why, what happened in the last few weeks?"

"I saw another Fanged for the first time. The one called Dōraku."

The woman's eyes hardened.

"So you've met the Renegade. Have you seen him kill Mars? With this sword?"

"It wasn't him. There was a boy – "

At the end of her tale, Azumi was shuddering from cold, her lips were numb, and her teeth were chattering.

Why can't we go inside? Doesn't she feel anything?

The woman, who asked to be called Chiyo, exuded none of the dread and power Ganryū had done. In fact, she was completely *normal*. She even sounded like a commoner.

She was still leaning against the railing, having filled her pipe up twice already, tapping ash into the precipice below, deep in thought. The sweet smell of the Cursed Weed lingered in the air.

"You're thinking you've got the wrong person," she said at last, chuckling.

"I'm sorry?"

"Mars liked to be theatrical. Grandiose. *Terrifying*, wasn't he?"

"Y- yes," said Azumi, remembering the fear the Crimson Robe had struck in her heart.

Chiyo laughed out loud again. "Mortals! You're so easy to play with."

There was a sudden gust of wind and Azumi found herself looking straight into Chiyo's black, cold eyes, inches away from her face. The woman's teeth were long and twisted, and her skin pale like paper. Her breath was sweet and nauseating. Azumi gagged.

"Why did you come here?" Chiyo asked. "You are free now. You could've gone wherever you wanted."

Azumi stepped back. "Ozun says you can help him."

"Ozun?" Chiyo frowned. "Who's Ozun?"

Azumi reached for the straw basket and raised the lid. A couple of flies buzzed out and disappeared into the wind.

"The love of my life," said Azumi, gazing fondly at the *yamabushi*'s severed head. "Aren't you, dear?"

"And you mine," said Ozun.

Azumi turned to the woman in the emerald robe.

"Will you help him? I'll do anything for you in exchange."

Chiyo reeled backwards in disgust.

"*Cheee...!*" She covered her nose. "Girl, it is you who needs help!"

The watchman whistled out two in the afternoon, but the sky outside the window of Bran's cabin was the shade of twilight.

The steel-grey sky and the steel-blue sea rolled back and forth in a titanic struggle for the horizon. Rain the size and hardness of gravel lashed the window with fury, deafening all conversation and thought. Once in a while a white shape – a face or a limb – showed in the billowing darkness outside, trying to pierce the thick glass. From the surface, and from the outside, the Sea Maze was nothing like the straight-edged wall of cloud Bran remembered flying over with Emrys. It had been growing steadily, as the ships of the Gorllewin flotilla pushed on slowly, day by day, in the general direction of Yamato. First the winds picked up slightly, almost beyond notice. The currents grew strong and twisted, bubbling up in whirlpools, throwing whole shoals of confused fish out onto the surface. The waves changed direction and danced about the ships, crashing, and roaring.

When the stars started changing positions in the night sky, and the sun and the moon rose in the wrong place on the horizon, Vice Komtur Aulick had ordered the anchors down. There was no point pushing through anymore – they couldn't even tell if they were moving forwards or backwards. They waited.

Bran returned to his desk to add a few finishing touches to his "homework" – describing the four major festivals of the Old Faith: Yalda, Nowruz, Tiregan, and Mehrgan. He couldn't remember which was the more important one: Tiregan or Yalda? The subtleties of the Gorllewin religion kept escaping him.

He adjusted the chafing collar and reached for the tin cup hanging on the peg. He was hot and sweaty in his new uniform; a tunic of rough grey wool of the kind worn by everyone else on the ship apart from the officers. He was pouring himself some water from a pitcher, when a freak wave heaved the ship and he spilled most of it over himself.

"Great."

Leif barged into the room without knocking. Bran sighed inwardly. It was Leif's room, and Bran was just a prisoner turned dubious guest. Still, a little courtesy would have been welcome. The giant blond Norse, oblivious to Bran's annoyance, leaned over his head to read the paper.

"Good, good," he exclaimed. "You are making progress. Vice Komtur will be glad. It's Tiregan, by the way."

"Ah. I was wondering," said Bran, and wrote down the missing sentence.

And I though alchemy was boring.

"Although some would argue otherwise," added Leif, scratching his bushy, golden beard. "Yalda is more popular among common people... Tiregan is more important to priests."

Leif was a Grey Hood through and through, so orthodox he didn't even need to wear the ceremonial hooded robe any more: the light of his faith was uniform enough. Or so he said. The only outward symbol he bore was the crossed and horned circle tattooed on his forehead; like all members of the Sun Warrior's caste.

Sometimes Bran thought he'd rather stay in the prison cell where Vice Komtur Aulick had first thrown him, uncertain whether to believe the story he had hastily prepared after capture: that he had been living as a castaway among the fishermen and was not even aware they were not Qin. It was a gamble, but it had paid off for now. The Gorllewin had no means to check whether he was telling the truth. They had heard, however, of the *Ladon*'s disaster, and that part of the story checked out. This had bought Bran some time during which Vice Komtur Aulick deliberated whether or not to throw both him and his boisterous dragon overboard.

The only person, other than the Vice Komtur, who could visit him in his cell at the lowest deck, stuck between crates of onions and barrels of dragon fodder, was Leif, the ship's chaplain. Bran asked him to teach him more about the Old Faith and it didn't take much convincing. Leif jumped on the opportunity with great enthusiasm.

Bran was taken out of the cell dressed in the uncomfortable uniform of a Gorllewin ensign, put in Leif's small cabin, and given a bundle of books on the basic tenets of Mithraism. Bran did his best to feign interest. What he really wanted and what he was trying to get from the chaplain, were details of the history and geography of the western continent.

"So, what's a Norseman doing among the Old Faithers?" was Bran's first question. From what he knew, neither the Snaellanders on their remote icy islands, nor the inhabitants of the cold fjords of Niflheimr had much love for Rome and her priests. "And how come you speak Seaxe?"

"I'm not a Norseman. I'm a Vinlander," replied Leif, shaking his golden mane. "Don't you know the difference?"

Bran had no idea. Leif sat down on his bunk and reached for an old map of the world.

"It's an old story. Older than that of New Rome, older than the Gorllewin itself. It begins in the days of legend, of Arthur the Faer and Beowulf the Geat. You remember those?"

"Of course. Arthur is the greatest Prydain that ever lived."

Leif nodded.

"I guess he was. But he was also the greatest scourge of my people. You see, when Beowulf's Geats betrayed us, my ancestors fled their savage mountain home. Most of them went East, where they built the Varyaga Khaganate among the barbarians – but some rode their white dragons West, over the frozen ocean…"

He traced the line on the map. Bran expected it to light up, as when Dylan drew things in the air, but Leif was no wizard and his finger left only a smudge of grease on the parchment.

"They flew for days, searching for a new home," the chaplain continued, "they say many perished in the winds of the North. At last they reached Snaelland – an island of mist and lava, where nothing grows apart from moss and lichen. Many said that that was enough, but seven warriors and their shieldmaidens jumped on their dragons again."

"Why?" asked Bran, sensing a deliberate pause in the narrative. When Leif told a story, he seemed to channel an old skald telling a saga to an enraptured audience in the mead hall.

Leif shrugged. "Who knows, after all these years? The sagas are silent. Maybe they were still afraid of Arthur's wyrm armies. Maybe they sensed there was a better land further west. What matters is that they found it." He pointed at the map. "A new continent, plentiful and ready for the taking. The natives fled before their dragons, and the warriors founded their settlements. Vinland... Markland... Helluland... such were the three chief provinces, but the entire country they called Hvitramannaland, the White Men's Land, for the seven warriors wore white capes when they rode their white dragons."

He pointed to a large swathe of land in the north-eastern corner of the western continent, not saying another word. Bran sensed another cue.

"And what about the Gorllewin...?"

"Ah, that's a whole other chapter of this old book," Leif replied, raising his head. A spark of ancient Norse fierceness flashed in his eyes. "Six centuries had passed in Vinland and the land grew rich and prosperous, but lazy and feeble in its isolation; and when Madoc ab Owain and his Gwynedd sailors arrived on our southern coast, we could not push them back to the sea. They captured our harbours and built their fortresses where our mead halls once stood... and they called it Tyr Gorllewin, the Land of the West. But their worst crime, in our eyes, was that they tried to force their faith upon us."

"Faith? You mean the Old Faith?"

"That was long before the Prydain and others turned heretics. The Sun Priests of Rome held sway over half the known world... except the North. We have always been faithful to the Spirits and Gods of their forefathers. They worshipped the Sun, we prayed to the Wolf and the Raven. They culled their dragons; we treated them as our own blood. There could never be peace between us. We fought, and we died, and so did they. For generations the border between Tyr Gorllewin and Hvitramannaland burned with dragon fire... until Dee came."

"Dee?" Bran looked at the wall over Leif's bunk, where, among the bronze reliefs showing stages of the Mithraic cycle, hung a portrait of a solemn-looking bearded man. The man wore a grey hood and grey cloak with a large frilly collar and upon his forehead was carved the same horned circle that Leif and other Grey Hoods bore.

"Yes, that one." Leif's eyes lit up with pious fervour. "He went among the Vinlanders, not with a Soul Lance, but with a wise and powerful word. He taught us that our real enemies were the demons in the hearts of men, not the men themselves. He taught us how we could keep our dragons and our magic and still be faithful in the eyes of Mithras. And then, just as he had prophesied when he first stood on Gorllewin shore, he died."

"Died?"

"Killed by the agents of the Dracalish Queen. But she was too late. He had forged us into one nation, and upon his grave we built New Rome, a new city cleansed from the filth and depravation of the old world."

"He sounds like… an intriguing man," said Bran, in a voice which he hoped indicated polite disinterest.

"He taught us and wrote down his words in the Seaxe tongue, which is now sacred to us more than Latin is in Rome," continued Leif, "although I speak Norse at home, and the soldiers from the South will speak Prydain when they get together, as you've noticed."

Bran nodded. He wanted to hear more about the history of Leif's country, but it seemed that particular saga was over, and he wasn't yet ready for a lesson in theology. Many of those would follow in the days to come.

Leif stood alone by the bulwark, looking forlorn to the east, ignoring the wind and rain lashing his face. The sky in the east was slightly clearer and brighter than in the west where a dark wall of clouds rose high in the sky, illuminated from the inside by rolling lightning bolts.

"Missing home?" asked Bran, raising his voice to shout over the noise of the waves.

"Don't we all?" replied Leif.

"I sense more," Bran prodded. It was rare to see the good-natured chaplain so solemn.

Leif sighed. The wind tore up his reply.

"What?"

"I said I'm worried about my country!"

"Gorllewin? Why, have you heard some bad news?"

Bran looked instinctively to the sea to see if there was any new ship on the horizon, but of course, there couldn't have been one. They were in the middle of an open ocean, inside a fierce storm which reduced visibility around them to less than a mile. There was no way anybody could find them here – not even, this time, by accident.

"No And that's partly the problem. Because of that," he pointed to the wall of clouds, "we've had no messages from home for weeks."

"Surely everything's fine?" Bran said. "You said yourself; it's far from the wars of the old world. What could go wrong?"

He was trying to cheer Leif up, but, much more so, he was intrigued to learn anything new about the chaplain's land.

"I can't help thinking our dragons could be better used to keep the peace back home," Leif replied with a sad smile.

"There are tensions between the provinces, conflicts, even violent confrontations…"

The irony of the situation became clear to Bran. If his suspicions were right, the Black Wings would be used in quelling a Yamato civil war, while conflict grew in their home land unabated. This made the question that was constantly on his mind even more burning.

"What do the Gorllewin really want from Yamato?" he asked. "What were you looking for in Qin?"

A way to win your own war?

Leif smirked.

"What do all nations want from others? To discover… to trade…"

"To conquer," Bran added helpfully.

"We are a warrior people, true," Leif nodded, "but I don't think we are ready to strike at the country as powerful as Yamato just yet. Not while our own straits are still so dire."

"And yet, this is no merchant ship," Bran said, waving his hand, "and your dragons are not here to help you haul the gifts from the ambassador."

"From what I hear, the Yamato are notoriously difficult to talk to. It helps to have an… edge to the negotiations."

"But what is the aim of the negotiations? You wouldn't go through all this trouble just to get first dibs on…" Bran bit his tongue; he had to be careful – if his questions were too detailed, it would betray his intimate knowledge of Yamato, "…whatever it is these people have to sell."

Leif stroked his golden beard.

"You're right, I suppose, but I'm just the chaplain. The real deals are being settled right now on the other side of that demonic storm."

The ship heaved from side to side. Bran grabbed the rails tight to stop himself from sliding away.

"How long are we supposed to stay here like this?" he asked.

Several days had passed already since they'd reached this featureless expanse of the sea and stopped, using just enough engine power to prevent the storm from pushing them back out into the open ocean.

The flotilla had been sailing at full steam for the previous three weeks, and from what Bran could tell – checking the positions of stars with what he remembered from his journey – they almost circumnavigated the whole of Yamato, from south-west to north-east. Bran wished he still had Von Siebold's map with him, but he'd got rid of it before the soldiers decided to search him. Even without it he could roughly guess that they were nearing Edo.

"Until the Sea Maze opens," replied Leif, "and only the Vice Komtur knows when that will happen."

"And how does he know?"

"He knows," Leif said with a mysterious smile, "and you shouldn't be asking so many questions."

Bran had long suspected the Grey Hoods had some way of communicating with the Yamato mainland; of sending messages across the Sea Maze. Leif either didn't

109

know what it was or refused to divulge such sensitive intelligence, but Vice Komtur Aulick's moves were clearly coordinated with some source of information on the other side.

Another freak wave wobbled the ship and Bran came dangerously close to losing his teeth on the railing. After that, came a lull in the storm and wide cracks emerged in the clouds, letting in the sun not seen for several days.

"I'll go check on Emrys," he said.

Leif looked at him suspiciously. According to his deal with the Vice Komtur, he should be accompanying Bran everywhere on the *Star of the Sea*, but it was plain he couldn't be bothered.

"Just don't do any tricks."

The Gorllewin had agreed to keep Emrys with their own dragons. The jade-green dragon was so small compared to the other three Black Wings that it managed to fit into what amounted to storage space next to the big stalls.

When Bran made his way to the stable deck, the three dragon riders were already there, also making use of the respite to make sure their mounts were in good health. One of them nodded at the boy; it was Frigga, a flax-haired shield-maiden, the third rider, who had not taken part in Bran's capture on Tamna Island. The other two gave him cold looks. They weren't friendly – Bran suspected they had as little warm feelings for the Wizards as he had for the Sun Priests – but, he had to admit, at least they treated him fairly.

So far, he had no reason to complain about his treatment on the ship.

Grey Hoods. Old Faithers. Sun Priests. Growing up, he had learned to associate those terms with fear and revulsion. The Wizardry Wars may have been ancient history, but Rome was still a sinister presence on everyone's minds, just beneath the horizon of their thoughts. Dylan would certainly have expected Bran to think of the *Star of the Sea*'s crew as enemies. And it should have been even easier to hate the Gorllewin now that he knew that they were making deals with the likes of Ganryū and Black Lotus, that they were preparing something sinister in great secret from the rest of the world. But, after the month he'd spent among them, things weren't so easy anymore. Enemy or not, he had more in common with them than he ever had with the Yamato. He may have been a prisoner, but at least he wasn't a barbarian. Frigga, Leif, Thorfinn, even Aulick… those were real people, real lives, not vague threats and slogans from Miss Farnham's history lectures.

He nodded back at Frigga and passed the others quickly by with his eyes at his feet.

He entered Emrys's "stall". Even this was far too big for the little dragon, which seemed almost lost in the vast space of the cargo hold. There were still crates, barrels, and iron drums piled under the walls, leaving just enough of the floor for the jade green dragon to stand with its wings folded.

The Black Wings were noticeably absent from Leif's sagas, Bran noted. The dragons of the Gorllewin that he had seen before were either the stocky, resilient Whites of the

Norsemen, or the all-too-familiar Reds of the Prydain. Nothing out of the ordinary, certainly nothing that would explain the origin and existence of beasts as enormous and powerful as these. It seemed a wonder that they could even fly, let alone be useful in combat. The Imperial Golds, the largest breed Bran had ever heard about, had a wingspan of a hundred and twenty feet, but these had been bred for size and prestige, and were used only for ceremonial fly-throughs of the Dracalish royal family. The wings of the black dragons, Bran assessed, spanned easily a hundred and fifty feet, if not more. And yet the mounts were as sleek, fast, and agile as the Blues or Silvers of the Royal Marines.

To Bran's surprise, Emrys was asleep, unperturbed by the raging storm outside. The rider sent a mild stirring pulse, and felt the grogginess of the beast's waking thoughts affect him as well. He rubbed his eyes and yawned.

"I can't believe you slept through all that," he said, stroking the dragon's scaly neck. Emrys raised its head, hissed lazily, and snorted a puff of gaseous steam. The entire room was filled with the smell of methane, but Bran had gotten so used to it he barely noticed it. It did mean, however, that he was left alone with his thoughts in the stall most of the time.

"We're almost across the Sea Maze," he said. "In a few days we'll be back in Yamato."

The dragon shook its head, annoyed.

"I know, I know," said Bran, "but it'll be different this time. We'll make a run for it as soon as we're safe on the other side. With my knowledge of Yamato and your wings, we'll lose them in no time."

112

And then what…?

For a brief moment before his capture he had considered returning to warn Satō and Nagomi of the impending danger. But it'd been over a month since he had last seen the girls. Who knew what happened to them in the meantime, or where they ended up…?

And would they even still care about what he had to say?

When he was leaving Ganryūjima, Dōraku was certain a war was inevitable. Perhaps it was already too late. Perhaps Yamato was already engulfed in a bloody conflict.

"Satō was supposed to go to Satsuma," he mused loudly. "She would be safe there. And she probably took Nagomi with her… but Satsuma is so far away. Getting there will be almost as hard as getting to Qin."

Emrys snorted in protest. Bran patted it on the snout.

"You're right. We'll worry about that later."

First we need to get out of here in one piece.

THE CHRYSANTHEMUM SEAL

CHAPTER V

The baby in Nagomi's embrace started crying as she squeezed its arm gently in her left hand and made a shallow incision with a two-pronged needle. The drop of poison seeped into the wound and the baby's cry grew louder and more frantic.

"Shh…" she tried to calm it down. She felt the tiny wound with her finger. Nothing happened. She frowned and pressed harder. The finger traced a blue glowing line and the wound healed at once. She handed the baby back to the worried parents.

"Is that it?" asked the mother, wrapping her child back in its simple rags. The father, meanwhile, carefully unrolled a single silver coin from his belt.

They were poor commoners – not peasants, but townsfolk who'd fallen on hard times – and she knew that that single coin represented most of their fortune. She would never have dreamt of accepting it in the old days, but now she knew better.

"They won't believe it works if it's not costly," her father had explained when she first started administering the vaccine. "At first I was giving it away for free to the poor –

you can't control the disease if the poor are sick – but then they became suspicious and stopped coming. Some people started spreading nasty rumours… they thought, we're poisoning them. So I started charging."

The coin would go to the local priests, who would then redistribute it among the needy. Such was the agreement, though Nagomi had her suspicions; since the Itō family began the inoculations, the local shrine had gained a new shiny roof and the priests' robes had grown more opulent. The poor, on the other hand, seemed even poorer.

She received the coin and put it on a small pile on the low table.

"Your child is now safe."

The mother and father looked reluctantly at the baby, now quiet and smiling. She felt their distrust. She may have been a priestess, but curing smallpox seemed a wonder only Gods themselves were capable of. Eventually, they bowed deeply and left the little room where she accepted patients.

There were four similar rooms in the house; in each one member of the Itō family administered the vaccine. The lines of people coming for the cure seemed endless – they came not only from Nagoya, but all around the domain; Nagomi's father finally managed to convince the *daimyo* to allow free passage for anyone who wished to get themselves and their family vaccinated: nobleman and peasant alike. It was a grave breach of the law but fighting the epidemic required drastic measures.

The door opened one more time. Nagomi reached with calloused fingers for another needle from the bamboo box.

"That's it," she heard a deep voice, "there's nobody else."

Nagomi started putting the medications away into the vials and boxes, but Torishi grasped her hand.

"I'll clean that up. You should rest, take a bath."

"Thank you."

"It's the least I can do. You're all miracle-workers to me."

The bear-man bent down to collect the utensils. He lived in a small hut he had built for himself in the garden, and was helping around the hospital, but did not work with the patients – they were too afraid of his long hair and beard, and foreign-looking clothes.

Nagomi entered the steam-filled bathroom. She untied the red ribbon and shook her head, letting her hair tumble down her shoulders. They were black – dyed with indigo her father used to produce some of his medicine. Her fiery locks would not go down as well in Nagoya as in Kiyō.

She took off the shiny white coat she was wearing as a physician's assistant and folded it carefully into the basket, along with the vermillion *hakama* and obi belt, parts of the uniform she wore during her morning work at the local shrine.

It's like there's two of me, she thought, watching her reflection in the steaming water. She touched the scar between her breasts; a memory of another time, another life. She stirred the water, and the reflection danced and split on the ripples. She sat on the edge of the cedar-lined bath, struggling to gather enough strength to wash before plunging in. Lately she was growing more and more tired at the end of each day, something that could not be explained by her daily duties. It worried her.

She ran her fingers through water. *It's going to get cold,* she thought. *The servant worked so hard to heat it up.*

Old Yoshō had died a few weeks earlier, and the Itō household had gained a new servant in his place; a young girl from a nearby village.

She never seems tired. Neither does Ine, and she's studying all night after the hospital closes. What is wrong with me?

Sacchan would have an answer. She giggled. *Not necessarily the right one, but she'd have one.*

She wiped her hand and reached into the basket. Hidden in the folds of the white coat was a letter she had received from Kagoshima a few days ago. It had gone through many layers of the complex censorship of the Owari province, but most of its contents remained intact. The wizardess had written about setting up at the Academy, her first lessons and experiments, her teachers and fellow students, local politics and rumours.

She's doing what she always wanted, Nagomi thought. *And this* – she glanced around the bathroom – *this is what I have always wanted. Living with my family and helping people.*

It should have been a happy thought, but it wasn't.

It is *what I've always wanted, isn't it?*

"Nagomi, dear," her mother knocked at the bathroom door, "dinner will be ready soon."

"Just a minute, mom."

She filled the small cedar pail with bath water and grabbed the bran soap. She froze. The surface of the water turned black, glistening like tar, pulsating with energy. Some vague shapes spawned in the ripples...

No. Not again!

She poured the water back into the bath and the shapes vanished. She was in no mood for another vision.

I'm not washing today, she decided, and put her clothes back on.

"There you are," said Torishi. "We were worried about you."

The tiny Inari shrine was a little more than a wooden box on stilts at the end of a narrow path branching out from behind the Offertory building. She was kneeling between the two statues of foxes with her head bowed low, but she wasn't praying.

Inari was her favourite *kami* – the foxes' fur reminding her of her own red hair. She often came here to think and meditate.

"There's another family with a child, waiting for the vaccine."

She stared at him blankly. "I'm sorry, I can't do it today. Let Ine see them."

"Your sister is busy as well." He studied her eyes. "Are you alright?"

"No, I'm not. I'm tired."

He crouched down beside her and stroked her hair in a way her father no longer had the time to do.

"It's fine, little priestess. You can rest today."

She shook her head. "It's not just today."

He scratched his long beard, twisting its ends in his fingers.

"You are sick? What did your father say?"

"He said there's nothing wrong with me, physically, and that I should stop brooding and take an example from Ine," she said bitterly.

She turned gruffly towards Torishi. He looked just the same as he had when she first saw him; rough and gentle. He gave her an encouraging smile. It calmed her down.

"I know he only wants me to be safe, and that he's glad we're all out of Kiyō after all that trouble with Kazuko-*hime*, the Crimson Robe, and the Takashima family, but... Dad still treats me like a child, as if nothing out of the ordinary happened over the last two months."

"It happened to you, not to him," Torishi said. "He would not understand."

"But you do, don't you? You know what's wrong about all – this...?"

She waved her hand around, hoping he would help her put in straight words all the complex thoughts running through her head. He bared his teeth in a way that others took for an angry snarl, but she knew was a smile. "I know what it is. You miss adventure! Mountains! Forest!"

She let out a quiet laugh. "I'm not like you, Torishi-*sama*. I didn't grow up in the wilderness."

She knew he wasn't being serious – it was just an attempt at lightening the mood. But, in a way, he was right. Her current life was nowhere near as exciting and fun as those few weeks she had spent with Bran and Satō.

She thought about the High Priestess and the cause she had believed in – the cause which urged her to help a castaway barbarian and a banished wizardess. Nagomi had always been a part of her plans. The High Priestess had given her a *mission*… She never quite understood what the mission was, but it certainly went beyond simply helping Bran and defeating the Crimson Robe. The Prophecy was not yet fulfilled.

The mightiest will fall.

And yet here she was, cosy and safe with her family, while Lady Kazuko had died a traitor's death in shame and infamy.

And all for what?

In far-away Chinzei there may have been rebellious factions and voices of discontent, but from the perspective of Nagoya, those were just murmurs far below the surface. Nobody in the city was even aware of any disruption. To her parents, the disturbance of recent weeks was all over, and they were grateful for it. Nothing had changed in Yamato and, it seemed, nothing was going to change.

"Maybe you should pray for a vision to guide you," Torishi suggested.

She glanced at the shrine before her. The sunlight turned the brass key in the fox's mouth into a little ball of flame.

"I am sick of visions."

That's it, she realized. *That's what's making me so tired!*

"What do you mean?" asked Torishi.

She rubbed her eyes and exhaled, gathering her thoughts.

"Ever since... ever since Ganryūjima, really," she started, slowly, "I've been having these – flashes. Not full visions, like one sees in the Waters of Scrying... rather, various bits and pieces, random premonitions, blurred images I can't quite piece together."

She moved her hand in a vague motion, trying to express her confusion.

"They are growing more frequent, more intense. It's sapping my strength just trying to control them."

Torishi ran his fingers through his beard.

"Didn't you always see these omens?" he asked.

"Not like this." She shook her head. "Rarely outside a shrine. Kazuko-*hime* said I had a talent for Scrying, and tried to teach me how to harness it, but my training was never finished – and now..." She bit her lips, "now it's too late."

"Can't the priests here help you?" Torishi looked to the main courtyard where a couple of acolytes were sweeping the sand.

She scoffed. "They are worse than those in Kirishima."

"Another shrine, then?"

"All the shrines and temples in Nagoya are the same. It's this city – it's too new, built from scratch by the first *Taikun*... it brings out the worst in people." She shook her head.

Torishi scratched the back of his neck.

"What about that place... we were passing it when we first came here?"

Nagomi strained her memory. More than a month had passed since she and the bear-man had disembarked from a ship which had carried them across the Inland Sea and around the Kii Peninsula. It was a long journey – the longest in her life, by far; an adventure in its own right, weeks at sea, raging storms at night, scorching sun in the afternoon... Cities, harbours, people – all of this passed around her, changing like the colourful images in those paper tube toys the Bataavians gave away to kids in Kiyō...

What was it that she was trying to remember? Oh, that's right.

The shrine.

The huge, crowded complex of ancient buildings straddling the Tokaido highway just south of Nagoya, all fresh, bright green thatch and golden cedar wood. Mom and dad had shown it to her briefly on the way from the harbour.

"Atsuta," she said, "that was the name. We will go to Atsuta."

This may have been the largest shrine compound Nagomi had ever been to; greater than Suwa, far more impressive than Kirishima… From beyond the mud walls and forest gates the size of the complex could hardly be appreciated. It was a city within a city; the main approach stretched for almost half a mile from the first vermillion *torii* to the vast courtyard in front of the main building, and it branched off into a myriad of wooded paths leading to smaller shrines and temples. The crowds reminded Nagomi of the streets of Kiyō during a festival, yet she knew this was just a normal summer's day.

Torishi followed her closely, stooped, and with his shoulders raised like a frightened dog. Unfortunately for him, this made him even more of a curiosity. Men snarled at him, women shrieked and a small troop of children ran after him, taunting.

Nagomi felt bad for him. Had she not been dyeing her hair, she probably would have met with the same derision, or worse. Nagoya may have been a big city, but its townspeople were the same as everywhere in Yamato. She missed Kiyō's open-mindedness.

"You should wait in here," Nagomi said, pointing Torishi to a small tea shop. Hidden away in the azalea bushes, it was almost empty. "I'll be fine on my own."

"Why are there so *many* people here?" he asked, as they made their way through a narrow crescent-shaped bridge

124

separating the inner and outer precincts. "Is this place so important?"

She giggled. "Yes, it's quite important."

Once she had recalled the name of the shrine, she began remembering all the other details. Atsuta was famous; perhaps the most famous in the land, after the Great Shrine of Ise. Deep within its sacred hall lay the Emperor's Sacred Sword, Kusanagi, one of the Three Imperial Jewels; a source of great power and proof that the Gods protected Yamato... There was no point explaining all this to Torishi – he didn't care much neither for Yamato theology nor the Emperor and his treasures. She led him to the tea shop – the few remaining patrons excused themselves promptly – ordered some food and a drink and hurried back to the main alley, into the throngs pouring straight from the Tokaido highway.

The wrinkle-faced priest took off his tall cap to wipe the sweat from his balding, shiny head.

"A vision, you say... It's not something that we usually do here."

He poured Nagomi another cup of *cha*. They were sitting in one of several tea houses in the shrine garden, in the shade of a giant camphor tree, which the priest had assured her was at least twelve hundred years old. It was the only place in the entire shrine – in all of Nagoya, perhaps – that was cool on that merciless summer afternoon.

"The *daimyo* does not want us to waste our talents on Scrying. He needs healers more."

"Waste your talents?" She picked up the cup. "What do you mean?"

He looked at her strangely. "Don't you know? Scryers can't be good healers, and vice-versa. The Spirits won't let this happen. It's common knowledge among priests. I'm surprised the High Priestess didn't explain this in your training."

Why... wouldn't she mention something so crucial?

"I still find it hard to believe Kazuko-*hime* is dead," he shook his head. "News from the South does not reach us here as fast as you might think."

"Did you know her?" she asked, hiding her confusion.

She was surprised that the name of the High Priestess was recognizable even so far north. Nagomi had omitted the details of her death, and the priest seemed oblivious to the charges.

"Oh, certainly." A smile flickered on his lips. "I met her a few times... First time was in Heian, a long time ago... She was buying pottery on the approach to Kiyomizu. We were both very young, and she had such beautiful eyes... " He forced a chuckle and wiped his eyes with the edge of an embroidered sleeve. "She will be missed."

"Isn't there anything you can do to help me?" Nagomi pleaded, sensing a chance.

He slurped his cha in thought.

"There's a place at the back of the Kagura stage... it's a bit run-down, I'm afraid. An ancient well of sacred water. It may still retain some of its former power... But as I said, it hasn't been used in a long time."

"Can I see it?"

"It's normally off-limits to the public… but then, you're not really 'public'. Yes, I'll take you there after the evening worship, if you are willing to wait."

The sacred grove at the back of the Kagura stage was a far cry from the hustle and bustle of the inner precinct. Not even the smell of the giant incense cauldron standing in the courtyard reached through the camphor trees. The few tiny shrines standing here were dedicated to a minor associate *kami*, not as important as those worshipped in the main building. The shrines were simple wooden huts with no ornaments other than the decorative writing on the lantern posts. As the wrinkled priest had described it, the area was pretty run-down; the pilgrims rarely came here, and it seemed that the acolytes only cleaned and repaired the tiny huts before major festivals.

Nagomi apologized to the spider *kami* before sweeping away the thick cobwebs guarding the well's narrow, rectangular opening. She could barely see the surface of the water.

"Will this do?" the priest asked, looking worried.

"I will try," she said. She threw a copper coin into the offering box and jingled the small bell to waken the Spirits. She stretched out her arms and began the shrine maiden's dance, hoping for the best.

Nothing happened. She grew tired, hot and sweaty, but the trance was not coming, and the water remained as still as ever. But she *did* feel something… Some power had awoken in the grove, but it was not coming from the healing well. She looked around, searching for the source.

"What's in that building?" she asked, pointing at a half-ruined shack overgrown with vine.

"This is Doyō Den, the Midsummer Hall," the priest answered. "This is where the Sacred Sword was once kept after it was retrieved from the thieves, a long time ago."

Nagomi stepped nearer the Midsummer Hall; her body quivered in the familiar way, first the tips of her fingers and toes, then her shoulders and legs. The fire within her body was waking up.

"There is great power here," she said through suddenly parched lips.

She heard a distant, female whisper, multiplied as if spoken by a thousand mouths.

The Storm God's sword… the Storm God's sword…

It's the prophecy, she remembered in an instant. *The Storm God's sword is sheathed.*

She turned to the priest to tell him about the voice but her words didn't come out, and the priest stepped back in fright.

The sacred grove spun around her and everything disappeared.

A bamboo flute trilled in the distance.

She was looking out onto a city street in Nagoya. Her family stood outside with their bags packed, her mother sad, her father graven-faced, Ine rolling her eyes with annoyance. Nagomi shouted at them, but they didn't notice her. She ran down to the door and struggled to open it, but it was locked shut from outside.

The corridor was long, disappearing in the darkness on either side, with many identical doors along it, all closed. She waited, uncertain, until she heard the sound of the flute again, and the same female voice as before, whispering in the distance.

What was whole is now in shards,

Man and beast are torn apart.

She wandered towards the sound, down the dark, stuffy passage, touching the wall, trying the doors along the way. They were all locked, except one, which was trimmed with golden leaf. When she touched it, the flute stopped. She slid it open by a crack.

The stench hit her nostrils. Inside, surrounded by lit candles in the shape of a five-pointed star, sat a young girl in a long, flowing, crimson robe of silk. She turned around to face Nagomi.

The priestess gagged and reeled back. The girl's face was half-rotten, falling apart, and yet, somehow, familiar.

I've seen her before.

The decaying lips opened to speak.

"You should not be here," the corpse said with surprise. "Go away!"

Nagomi shut the door and fled, stumbling, panting. The flute played again, and she heard torn fragments of the voice, carried by the draught.

Turning, turning... three... stone... see...

She raced until she ran out of breath. She stopped and dropped to her knees, heaving. When she looked up, the corridor around her changed. It was now a well-lit, and small vestibule, much like that inside her old house in Kiyō. Before her was a staircase to the upper floor. She climbed it carefully; the mouldy timber creaked dangerously under her every step. She reached the top and stood before a door of what, in her old house, used to be her room. The door, too, was decomposing, covered with rot and mildew.

She heard a faint temple bell behind it. Holding her breath, she slid it open. It almost fell apart in her hands.

Lit up by brass candlesticks and oil lamps, the room was decorated like the hall of a *Butsu* temple. A small golden *Butsu-sama* sat in the alcove, over a simple altar. Somewhere outside, the temple bell was ringing out a late hour. A monk brushed past her, carrying an orb of white crystal in his hands. He put the orb on the altar, and whispered a quick prayer – or maybe a spell? – before closing the black lacquer door. He turned around and raised a hand pointing at the darkness behind Nagomi. His face contorted in terror; his hand turned into a black dragon's claw, black.

She felt a creeping presence behind her; cold and powerful. She knew that presence well. She didn't want to see the rest. She slid the door shut, and the presence vanished.

She took a deep breath. The vision was far longer and more vivid than she had hoped for. She was growing tired of it.

When will this end?

The voice spoke again, crisp and clear. It was downstairs this time, and this time Nagomi understood the entire sentence:

> *What was pure is now unclean.*
>
> *Find the boy who can't be seen.*

She ran down, faltering, and searched for the voice; the corridor was now dark again, as if the day had already passed. The hazy grey light of dusk seeped through the dirty paper windows. A half-opened door stood at the end and she rushed towards it. As she ran, the wooden corridor morphed into a stone cave carved out of dirt-grey limestone. Something shone blue at the end.

It was a large orb of blue crystal, the size of a skull, standing on a roughly-hewed stone column. Gathered around it, kneeling and praying, were little, dark-skinned men, wearing tunics of tree bark and bear teeth necklaces.

Nagomi stepped nearer to the blue orb. She recognized the shade of the stone, and the way it muddled the light; it was the same material from which Bran's ring was made. She brought her trembling hand nearer to the surface – it radiated heat, like the scales of Bran's jade dragon. Cautiously, she tapped the stone with her finger and it cracked into three large shards. The little men cried out in anguish, and the light went out. Her feet were touching timber floor again, her hand reached out to pat a grimy wooden wall. She was back in the house.

The disembodied voice whispered again. Nagomi tilted her head and listened. She was certain she would now find the source of the whispers; it was just around the next corner, just beyond the next door, in another corridor...

She staggered on, stumbling and stopping for breath every few steps. She felt as if she'd been running around this strange house for days since the vision began. A sudden light came from outside; the fiery blaze of a bloody sunset. The flute was wailing a sad melody.

There were no more unlocked rooms, and she already made a full circle around the house. She remembered one more place she hadn't looked: the garden. She retraced her steps, and this time, found her way to the backyard. She slid the panels aside, squinting from the sun. The garden was filled with smoke and the smell of sulphur.

A giant green dragon filled the entire garden, long-necked, serpentine. It was greater than Emrys, larger than the house; a giant monster from some nightmare. It roared in rage, spewing fire and lightning from its terrible jaws.

Nagomi cowered behind a pillar. She summoned all her courage to peek out and noticed the sun reflecting off something near the dragon's front leg... a sword. Not the sleek *katana* of the samurai, but an ancient bronze broadsword, stained and notched. It was embedded in the dragon's claw like a thorn in a cat's paw, pinning it to the ground.

She heard the tinkling of a tiny bell. A white fox with a bushy tail jumped out of the flowers and hopped across the garden, stopping briefly by the bronze sword, before leaping away.

As she struggled to overcome the paralyzing fear she heard another sound behind her. A rumble came from inside the house. She felt the air in the garden suddenly grow cold, and the same dark, dreadful presence she had sensed in the room above, creeping towards her. Hoar covered the grass.

The veranda door creaked and cracked under a powerful blast. She screamed. Another bang and the door burst into splinters. A slobbering monster slithered forth from the corridor, an eight-headed, eight-legged serpent. Each of its black scales was marked with the hollyhock crest; each of the eight pairs of eyes burned gold, each of the eight jaws had teeth black and twisted, and each of the eight feet was clawed with sharp nails. Ripping the wood from the floor, it charged at her.

The green dragon in the garden raged at the monster with a roar so powerful it tore tiles from the roof, adding to Nagomi's terror. Covering her ears, and blind with panic, she

133

forced her legs to move, but tripped and fell into wet dirt. Mud trapped her legs. She struggled to crawl, but she couldn't budge an inch. The hissing demon caught her and plunged its many teeth and claws into her soft flesh.

She kept screaming and crying long after she woke up.

"We were so afraid," Nagomi's mother wailed, holding her daughter in her arms and stroking her head frantically.

"You slept for two days," said her dad. He was standing at the foot of Nagomi's bed with his arms crossed. "Tossing and turning, and crying."

Two days...? No wonder I was so tired.

"Even the priests of Atsuta didn't know what to do with you!" her father added. "They – "

"It doesn't matter," her mother interrupted him, "what matters is that she's awake. We can finally start packing for the journey."

Nagomi released herself from her mother's embrace.

"The journey? What journey?" she asked, still in a daze.

Itō Keisuke showed her a piece of paper sealed with a hollyhock crest.

"The High Council invites us to Edo, to present my research before the *Taikun*," he said proudly.

Hollyhock...

She gasped and dropped the letter. "You can't go," she said.

Her dad laughed nervously. "You're not asleep anymore, child. Don't spout nonsense."

"No – you must refuse – "

Her father exchanged worried looks with her mother.

"Refuse the *Taikun*'s invitation? Why would I do that?"

"You will die – "

"I will die if I refuse! You are still tired and addled. Taki, dear, let her sleep some more."

Nagomi's mother nudged the girl gently down onto the bedding.

"It's all right. Rest now. We will talk later."

"What about the other letters?" Keisuke asked his wife.

"Later," she replied firmly.

"What other letters?" Nagomi rose again.

Keisuke looked at Nagomi's mother. She nodded. He reached for a bundle on the clothes chest.

"You received two things while you were asleep," he said, "one is from Kiyō, the other… Chōfu? Do we know anyone in Chōfu?"

She grabbed the bundle from his hand impatiently. The missive from Kiyō was a small, but heavy parcel, unsigned, and with no word describing its contents. She opened it carefully and spilled it onto the bed with a jingle.

"*Ah*, how beautiful!" Her mother clapped her hands.

THE CHRYSANTHEMUM SEAL

It was a golden necklace studded with a few small emeralds and one large jade stone embedded within. It took Nagomi a moment to recognize it, and when she did, she could do nothing to stop the tears streaming from her eyes.

"What is it?" Keisuke asked, grumpily. Anything that reminded him of Kiyō was throwing him in a sour mood.

"It's Kazuko-*hime*'s necklace," she replied, swallowing tears.

Jade, the bringer of Life.

"What about the other letter?"

This one had no crest other than the stamps of Owari domain's censors. Normally, it meant that the letter was from Satō, but... Chōfu?

She tore the seal open. As she read it, her eyes grew wide open.

"You'll never guess – " she said, "Sacchan is inviting me to Chōfu for..."

A wedding?

CHAPTER VI

Atsuko stood in the main gate of the eerily silent compound of gardens, tea huts, and guest houses, trying to understand the situation, while servants moved around her with the luggage brought from the ship. A maidservant walked up to her with downcast eyes.

"What's going on here?" the princess asked, uneasily. "Where is Shosuke-*sama*? Where is Kuroda? Why did noone welcome me at the pier?"

The girl dropped to her knees and bowed deeply, stifling tears.

"They're all gone, lady! Banished from Edo… on orders of the High Council… only us servants remain."

Banished?

"We thought you knew…"

"I was stuck in some small village for days because of that damn storm. I had no news. When did it happen?"

"The orders came a week before your arrival. The last of the retainers left just three days ago."

"Which one?"

"Kuroda-*dono*, lady."

"He can't have gone too far. Right," Atsuko intercepted one of the samurai of her entourage, "you, take some men and find Kuroda-*sama* on the western road. Bring him here – but be discreet about it."

"Yes, my lady." The samurai bowed sharply and hustled off to fulfil the order.

"And you, girl," she turned to the maidservant, "how far is the castle from here?"

"The castle... you mean His Excellency's...?"

"The *Taikun*'s, yes."

"About a ri if you go through the merchant district."

"A merchant district... isn't there a shorter way?"

"There was a shortcut through the Zōjō Temple, but I think it's still off limits after the Black Wings."

"The Black Wings? What are you talking about, girl?"

"Oh, my lady," the maidservant clutched her face between her hands, "there is so much you don't know about!"

Atsuko dismissed the lectern porters once they'd passed the canal separating the residence ground from the merchant district, and insisted on walking the rest of the way to the castle on foot.

She had to see the streets of Edo with her own eyes, trod on it with her own sandals. The greatest city on Earth, as the *Taikun*'s propaganda would have it, and despite what Atsuko had studied in Satsuma, it was easy to believe. Everything here was greater than anything she had known before; the streets were wider, the houses bigger, the lights brighter, the crowds denser, the people louder and more rude than in Kagoshima. The smells of a thousand street carts selling any food imaginable, the dazzling colours of a thousand shop curtains, clan flags, lanterns, wall decorations, the noise of a million throats talking at once, all hit her like a gust of an autumn typhoon.

"Is there a festival today?" she asked the maidservant who walked by her side

"No, lady," she replied, "it's always like this. It even feels a bit quieter than usual."

Atsuko was stung with embarrassment. She was the daughter of a mighty *daimyo*, and grew up in what she had once thought was a great city, the capital of a rich and populous province... and yet Edo made her feel now as if she was a mere rustic churl.

The crowd before her parted from left to right this time, letting through a troop of fierce-looking soldiers bearing Aizu and Hojo banners fluttering on their backs. They were heading for the harbour in a great hurry.

"Is this usual too?" asked Atsuko, frowning.

"No, I don't believe so..." the girl answered. "I don't think I've ever seen soldiers openly in the streets before."

Atsuko tried to ponder the consequences of what she was seeing. Dragons landing in the Zōjō Temple... a new Chief Councillor... armed soldiers on the streets of Edo...

All were in some way connected, of that she was certain. But she couldn't think clearly. The number of people on the street alone was enough to suffocate her; the din, the chaotic disarray all around her didn't help... She shook her head, felt dizzy, and stumbled. The maid supported her arm.

"Are you well, my lady? Perhaps we should take the palanquin after all…"

"No, I'm fine. How far is it?"

"Half a ri still. But the worst part is behind us."

As she spoke, the high street ended on a tall arc of a bridge over a canal, beyond which lay a silent, sleepy neighbourhood of sprawling rich villas hidden behind striped ochre walls.

"What is this place?" asked Atsuko, taking in the warm, calm air. She could still hear the commotion continuing on the other side of the canal, but it was as if from behind a curtain; the cries of the crowds beyond subdued by the nostalgic shrill of cicadas – kikikikiki…

That's right, it's summer already… she remembered. I almost managed to forget about it on the ship.

"These are residences of the fudai clans. They stretch from here all the way to the castle, in order of importance."

"But the Shimazu residence…!"

She clutched her fists. The Satsuma residence may have been far greater in scale than any of the villas here, but it was on the outskirts of Edo, far from the castle walls, beyond the hills, beyond the canals. Until now Atsuko thought this was the norm – that all the clans chose to live away from the

140

downtown hubbub and noise… but now she realized the truth. Satsuma just wasn't that important here in Edo.

But that would change soon – she was going to make sure of it.

Atsuko's entourage crossed the outer moat along with other visitors going about their daily duties, passed through the enormous courtyard – an open space that alone would easily fit a small Satsuma town – and stopped before the inner gate leading into the *Taikun*'s castle. Cut through the mighty, angled wall built of straight-hewn stone blocks, and coated in gold leaf, it was supposed to both impress and terrify, but Atsuko was by now too dazed by the rest of the city to care either way. Upon the heavy timbers lay a long blockhouse with a large window covered by thin slats of black wood. She felt upon her the watchful eyes of the guards hidden behind the slats.

"We're going in," she decided suddenly.

"Are you sure, lady?" the servant girl worried. "We are unannounced… and alone."

"I want to see my future home."

The girl tilted her head down to hide a smile. She was one of the few in the household who yet knew about the real reason behind Atsuko's arrival in Edo. The princess moved forward. A guard at the gate stepped forth to stop her.

"I am Shimazu Atsu, Lady of Satsuma, daughter of Shimazu Nariakira," she said forcibly, before he could ask her anything. "I come to speak with His Excellency on behalf of my father."

The guard reeled back, opening his mouth a few times like a fish.

"Please wait here, lady," he said at last, and disappeared to summon his superior.

She managed to take a peek through the gate while he was gone. Standing in the courtyard, not far from the walls, stood a man she recognized from the drawings she had to learn by heart before leaving for Edo: Councillor Munenari, one of the few real allies her father could trust within *Taikun*'s inner circle.

"Date-*dono*!" she cried, but he was too far away and too engrossed in conversation with another aristocrat to notice.

The guard returned with the Captain of the gate's garrison; a meaty-faced officer bearing the 'ai' character of the Aizu on his clothes, similar to all the other senior guards she had spotted around the castle.

Looks like the Aizu-Matsudairas have taken over the city, she reflected. The *Taikun* chooses to surround himself only with close kin.

She stepped towards him and again spoke first.

"How long are you going to keep me waiting?"

"The Shimazu are no longer welcome in the Inner Palace, Lady," the Captain said calmly, unfazed by her brazenness. "You should know. In fact, I'm not sure you're even supposed to be in Edo."

"I've only just arrived," she explained. "I had little time to catch up with the news."

"Nonetheless, I'm afraid I will have to ask you to – "

A clash of swords interrupted the exchange. Atsuko turned towards the sound – two small groups of samurai were fighting around an overturned palanquin, inside of which, a small, bald courtier was huddled, terrified.

"Mito assassins!" cried the Captain, drawing the sword. "Lady – wait here!" he ordered Atsuko, before charging into the fray followed by the rest of his men, leaving only the hapless guard with whom she had first spoken.

The princess spotted her chance. She pushed the lone guard aside with a force and resolve which must have stunned him and ran through the gate, losing her clogs on the threshold.

She found herself in yet another world, as separate from the villas outside as they were from the commercial district on the other side of the canal. Beyond the stone wall lay another city, tiny but densely built; a whole labyrinth of houses, towers, and corridors, roofed chambers, and open verandas, and lush gardens of blue ponds, and verdant groves.

"Date-*dono*!" she shouted again, and this time the old Councillor had no choice but to notice her running barefoot across the gravel courtyard.

He stared at her incredulously for a second, before noticing the tiny onnamon crests of the Shimazu clan on her shoulders. He glanced towards the gate, then back.

"Come with me, quick, quick" he urged, and beckoned her towards the nearest open door.

"You're Nariakira's daughter, aren't you?"

She bowed as deeply as she could, catching her breath as she did so. The day was proving to be much more exciting than she'd expected when disembarking from her ship in the morning.

"Shimazu Atsuko, at your service, Councillor."

He winced. "I'm not a Councillor anymore. What are you doing here? The Shimazu are banished!"

"So I heard," she replied.

"You have to cancel the plan. Even I could be arrested for taking to you."

"I was hoping to see young Iesada-*dono* and explain – "

The nobleman raised an eyebrow. "Young *tono*, did you say?"

"Yes, why? Is he not in today?"

The Councillor drew in his breath. "So, you haven't heard the news?" he asked.

"Everyone keeps asking me the same question. No, I haven't heard anything."

He scratched his nose.

"Ah, that makes more sense. I think we had better go and see the new Chief Councillor," he said.

"I think we better should," she agreed.

"Out of the question," said the Chief Councillor, not even raising his eyes from the paper he was studying, glossing with a small brush he kept dipping in red ink as he read. A straight, tall pile of similar documents rose on the left side of his low desk, and another, even greater, leaned precipitously over its right edge. "Iesada-*dono* will be the new *Taikun*. He cannot be seen socializing with the daughter of a lord who is all but accused of rebellion."

"New *Taikun*...?"

"Tokugawa Ieyoshi-*dono* died a few days ago. I'm preparing the official proclamation of the mourning period right now – and I don't with to be disturbed anymoe."

Atsuko's heart sank, but her mind raced. Councillor Date was right. If she couldn't even see young Iesada the entire plan devised by her father was doomed to failure.

Her true, secret mission was to guile him with her womanly charms and convince him to marry her. A desperate, last ditch attempt to avoid an all-out war, it might have just about worked –rumour had it that Lord Iesada had expressed his interest in Atsuko ever since he'd seen a woodcut portrait of her while visiting the Shimazu residence – if only she could have met him, alone, on her own terms...

Lord Ieyoshi dead... what does it mean for me...? There's no time to write back to Satsuma – it would take weeks to get the messages there and back, even by hikyaku couriers...

145

This was exactly the sort of thing for which her father had trained her. The situation in Edo could change overnight, and the distance between the capital and Satsuma made quick reactions impossible. She had to think for herself; Lord Nariakira had given her enough au*tono*my in all matters.

"I did not come here for idle chatter, but to negotiate on behalf of Shimazu clan," she said, trying to hide the nervousness in her voice. "The alliance between our clans that my father and Councillor Date have worked so hard on…"

"Ah, but Munenori-*dono* is not a Councillor anymore. He hasn't been for a long time, in fact," said the man behind the desk. She didn't even know his name yet, but she already deeply disliked him. "And what was good for an heir, is no longer suitable for a ruling *Taikun*. I know why old Nariakira really sent you, but you can forget it. Iesada-*dono* will choose a bride from one of the inner clans. Aizu-Matsudaira, probably."

"My father will hear about this!"

"Oh, I'm sure he will. But he won't be able to do anything about it. I'm planning that the wedding will be a quick affair."

"Then there is nothing else for me to say."

"No, I suppose not."

Atsuko stood up and gave a sharp bow. The Chief Councillor at last looked up from his papers to say goodbye, and froze, his mouth agape, with the brush in his hand suspended over the table dripping the red ink like blood. He

146

was staring at her waist – a reaction with which she was not unfamiliar, but which she expected more from young samurai sons rather than an old Edo aristocrat.

Do I have to seduce him as well? she thought quickly, with revulsion. Is that the key to this man?

"Councillor-*dono*?" she said, sweetening her voice. "See anything you like?"

"I'm sorry," the man replied, blinking, "I was just admiring the craftsmanship on your obi buckle, lady."

Obi buckle? The sudden change of topic threw her off. She looked down and remembered she was wearing the golden buckle she had received from the foreign boy. She had not given the choice much thought when she was dressing that morning, but now, somehow, it felt significant.

"You are... interested in antiques?" she asked.

It was an odd thing for a man to notice, but then she had been warned of Edo aristocrats and their strange ways.

"This pattern..." He licked his lips. "I haven't seen one like it in a long time. Where did you get it?"

"It was a gift."

Where is this going?

The Chief Councillor pointed at her with the end of the brush. The red ink splashed on the paper, forming a line of splatters in her direction. It made her shudder.

"Perhaps I was too hasty. After all, a war is in no one's interest, especially with the Mito situation... Why won't you come back here tomorrow? I'll see what can be done."

She bowed deeply.

"That is all I ask."

What was all that about? she wondered, as a courtier escorted her out of the inner palace, where the servant girl waited anxiously. The commotion, whatever it was, had by now calmed down. The guards at the gate had been replaced, she noticed. The new ones let her pass without a word.

She touched the cold metal surface of the obi, remembering the night at the Kirishima Shrine – now a distant memory she rarely returned to. What did it have to do with the Chief Councillor's sudden turn? Did it take his attention away from the office business long enough to reconsider the situation? Or was it a very clumsy attempt at courtship? Not that it mattered much, for now. One way or another, she had gained what she wanted: one precious meeting with lord Iesada. She still had allies in Edo, friends at the Council; she could still work the situation to Satsuma's advantage. She would bring Kuroda and the others back to the residence. She would work on this as hard as was expected of her, and harder. The wedding was not off yet.

She ran through the list of names in her head.

"I need to speak to… Toyo-*dono* of Tosa," she told Lord Date, who was waiting outside to hear of the results of the meeting. "Does he still reside in the palace?"

"No, lady," he replied, "not since his retirement. But I can take you to his residence. It's not far, in the fourth citadel."

A shrill shriek of a black kite tore the sky, bouncing a dozen times off the steep, wooded walls of the canyon, creased and wrinkled like the hide of some giant, old animal, before echoing one last time down the single road of the quiet mountain village.

The tall, strapping man who emerged from behind the dark blue noren curtain of the bath house struck an imposing presence. He was naked except for a great sword, the biggest Koyata had ever seen, slung on a harness across his back. Steaming water trickled down rippling biceps and the face of a fierce tiger tattooed across his chest which made it seem as if the beast was crying.

He leaned down over a small stream running across the garden and splashed his face and torso with water. Koyata, observing all this from his breakfast table on a veranda, winced, imagining the hiss of freezing cold water striking the hot skin. The man spluttered and shook his head like a wet dog, and went to pick up his clothes from the straw basket.

Now is the time we should attack, thought Koyata, gritting his teeth. If it was up to him, he would charge the bath house with all the men. But he was only a deputy chief of the city guards in Heian – his benefactor, *daimyo* of Saga's power reached only so far – and had to obey the orders of one Lord Sasaki, an old fashioned aristocrat who believed that attacking a nobleman in his bath was "dishonourable".

It had been the oddest capture order Koyata had ever seen. The man with the tiger tattoo, and the small group of swordsmen accompanying him, were wanted both by the *Taikun* and the Lord of Satsuma. What crime did they commit that so angered two most powerful men in Yamato,

Koyata didn't know. In the conflicting missives they were branded variously as rebels, assassins, and thieves. They were accused of burning down a shrine, of stealing from the *daimyo*'s treasury, of fostering murderous intent towards Edo officials... quite a dossier. One thing was certain – these men were brutal and dangerous.

A tip-off from a trusted source had led them to this small hot spring village on the northern outskirts of Heian, and Koyata had been observing the outlaws' movements for the last few days. He had learned they were heading for the shores of Lake Biwa, and then to Edo, taking the longer, less travelled way across the mountains – and today was the final day before their departure.

Koyata finished his breakfast and settled the bill for the guesthouse – all the while not letting the Tiger Tattoo from his sight – and moved outside to meet his men, positioned around the only road. To the south, it led back to the wide-open Heian plain, but in the north it narrowed to a single-file path as it cut through the Momoi Pass – and that was where the chief of the guards had planned his ambush.

The Tiger Tattoo's group counted merely half a dozen men; judging by their accent, they had come from somewhere around Kumamoto. They bore unmarked clothes of the rōnin, but had the manner of people used to court living. None of that mattered to Koyata as much as what he could tell at a glance: that they were all strong and fierce warriors, no doubt members of the bodyguard of some rich southern family. This was not going to be an easy fight, even if the guards had come in with the full force of fifty-odd men.

150

If anyone wanted to raise trouble in Heian, today's the day, thought Koyata.

About half an hour after he left the guest house, the man with the tiger tattoo and his group followed. They moved cautiously, but nonchalantly, like men aware of being pursued, but not willing to show it.

As they passed him, Koyata rubbed the smooth ivory grip of his teppo and checked if the charge was full. Ordering the thunder gun from Master Tanaka had cost him most of his life savings, but after witnessing its effectiveness in the battle on the volcano, he decided he simply had to have one to stay ahead of the increasingly sophisticated criminals roaming the streets of Heian.

"Stay in formation," he told his men, "this may get ugly."

They moved on, disguised as a train of servants and porters following their master – Koyata – on a leisurely trip to the hot springs. He had hand-picked them himself from among the city guards, not by how tough they were, but by how clever and loyal they seemed. Among them was Tokojiro, the one-eyed interpreter, who proved surprisingly deft with the sword once some of his confidence had been restored.

"And listen only to my orders," he warned them as they neared the spot where the trap had been set up.

"What about Sasaki-*dono*?" asked Tokojiro.

"What about him?" Koyata replied with a grin, and the others chuckled. They knew there was no love lost between the Chief and his Deputy.

"Let's just hope he doesn't do anything too… rash." He wanted to say stupid, but that would not be proper, not even among his loyal subordinates. "Slow down, we're almost there."

The road descended down a steep slope, entering a small hollow carved by a shallow stream running across it. Looking from above, Koyata had good view of the six fugitives as they stopped before the ford.

"He's good," Koyata murmured to himself. "He knows it's a good place for an ambush."

He gestured to his men to crouch down out of sight and prepare their weapons. But there was no need for stealth. A large group of guardsmen – Koyata counted at least thirty, meaning between them and his own men, there were very few left to guard any escape routes – approached openly from the north, led by lord Sasaki. They stopped on the other side of the stream, and the Chief stepped forward, his hand on the sword.

"Kawakami Gensai!" he cried. "You are under arrest. Lay down your weapons and surrender peacefully."

Koyata shook his head. What is he doing? Where are the archers? Reserves? Is he just planning to swamp them with numbers? They were trained samurai, after all – each worth ten of our men in hand-to-hand combat…

"Under arrest? By whose authority?" replied the Tiger Tattoo.

"I have warrants on your heads signed by both Shimazu Nariakira-*dono* and the *Taikun*."

The man laughed. "At last, the two houses are well and truly allied! And all because of me. How utterly delightful."

"You are an outlaw, Kawakami. A *rōnin*. Your lords denounced you. Surrender now and you will be granted the right to die like a man – and your families will be spared."

Koyata winced. It was a good offer, but he would have hated to be in the position of the six men in the valley, to be given this choice. Whatever they did, he was certain, they did with conviction – they didn't look like the common rōnin cut-throats and robbers he was familiar with. He almost felt sorry for the Tiger Tattoo. But he needn't have.

"Our families are dead to us," the Tiger Tattoo said, "and we are to them. And soon, so will *you*!"

He charged, drawing the short wakizashi – the big sword remaining in the harness on his back. In one great leap he jumped over the stream, landed in front of Lord Sasaki, and cut him right across the chest. The Chief fell backwards with a cry, his arms apart. The other five samurai followed in grim silence, their *katana*s as cold as their resolve.

"*Kuso*," swore Koyata. "Tokojiro! Stay here in case any of them tries to get back to Heian. Ishida, Hirata, take half of the men and follow me. We'll cut them off at the head of the valley."

He ran parallel to the road through the thin cedar forest, tripping and falling several times on roots and brambles. By the time he reached his intended destination, he was tired, irritated, and in pain. His knees ached, unused to such effort. He leaned against a cedar tree trunk, catching his breath, and looked back to the road.

To their merit, the Heian guardsmen stood their ground bravely, even if their chief had fallen. The fugitive samurai all fought with the fierceness of men with nothing to lose, and with skill of highly trained martial artists but, to Koyata's surprise, they were slowly being overwhelmed by the sheer number of the enemy. The reason became clear to Koyata as he watched the fight unfold and he studied the movements of the swordsmen: most of them already struggled with injuries from some previous encounters, and fought, at best, at only half their strengths.

The Tiger Tattoo, in the midst of this mayhem, remained calm and composed, his wakizashi carving the path through the guards like a farmer's sickle through a field of barley. A short glimpse at the way his arms and legs moved as if in a delicate, precise dance, was enough for Koyata: this was, by a long way, the finest swordsman he had ever seen.

Why won't he draw the big sword? he wondered, uneasy. He could finish this in no time.

Slowly but inevitably, the swordsmen cut through the ambush, leaving a bloody trail of slain guards in their wake. Koyata positioned himself in the fork formed by twin trunks of an old maple tree, and aimed the thunder gun at the approaching group.

Even in flight, the six men retained order and tight formation: two in front, then the Tiger Tattoo, then the remaining three, two of them limping and bloodied. Koyata waited until he was certain of the shot and squeezed the trigger.

Through trial and error, he had learned a lot about how the weapon worked over the previous weeks. He knew that

154

if timed well, and with the targets close, he could hit two with one forked lightning. He learned how to adjust the power of the charge so that it would merely stun rather than kill outright. He taught himself the best way to aim to compensate for the recoil and lack of precision of the copper electrodes that produced the shot. The only thing he didn't know was how, exactly, the weapon worked. Not that it mattered. *It's magic*, was all he needed to know.

The sudden thunderbolt rolled through the valley. A murder of crows fluttered from the treetops. Just as Koyata intended, the lightning forked, hitting both men in front at the same moment. One fell down instantly, but the other, astonishingly, remained standing, staggering backwards, clutching his chest, where a hole in his kimono smouldered.

"Gensai-*sama*! Run!" the man yelled. "I will stop them!"

"Miyabe, don't – " The Tiger Tattoo cried, but was too far to stop his companion.

"The Blade must reach Edo – it's our only chance!" the first one replied, and charged straight at Koyata's position.

The Deputy watched the dial of recharge move excruciatingly slowly, as the samurai ran towards him. He kept squeezing the trigger frantically.

Move, move, move!

In the corner of his eye he saw his own men running to intercept the swordsman, but he knew they would be too slow.

At last, the dial reached its final stop and the gun thundered again. Just as it did, Koyata realized his mistake.

The lightning was still set to fork – and the samurai was now only a few feet away. The discharge struck them both; the feedback blew the gun in Koyata's hands apart, and a split second later the acute pain in his chest knocked out the air from his lungs. He fell on the grass and the maple trees whirled around him.

Deputy Koyata stumbled out of the lectern and took the crutch from the porter. Limping, he climbed up the stone stairs of Lord Matsudaira's residence.

His chest ached when he breathed, and his right hand was still out of use – the doctor warned him it might never be fully functional. But the summons from the man of Matsudaira's stature – brother of the *daimyo* of Aizu, and the closest kin the *Taikun* family had in Yamato – could not be refused, even in his state.

The villa, overhanging the slope of a low mountain in the eastern suburb of Heian, was a simple building, exhibiting the kind of deliberate scarcity and modesty that only the very rich and powerful could afford. A small vestibule led straight to the main room, whose walls slid open revealing a meticulously maintained small garden and a stunning view over the entire city bathing in green summer haze below.

Lord Matsudaira turned towards him and frowned.

"I wasn't told you're still in such a condition," he said, "I would have waited."

"It's nothing, *tono*," Koyata replied, bowing with some effort. "May I sit down?"

156

"Of course!"

A servant brought an extra pillow, and another gave him a cup of ice-cold cha, which Koyata drank in one swallow.

"You're probably wondering why I'm here," said Lord Matsudaira.

"Respectfully, I'm wondering why I'm here," replied Koyata. The nobleman chuckled.

"We'll get to that. But first things first. Much like you, I was summoned here, to take over a new office. Since yesterday, I am the new Head of Security in Heian."

"Head of Security? What about Sasaki-*dono*?" Koyata asked hopefully. The Chief of Guards somehow survived the battle; the Tiger Tattoo's cut turned out to be shallow and never much of a threat, despite Lord Sasaki's dramatic performance.

"Oh, he will remain in his position. He's a good administrator, regardless of what you may think of his prowess in the field."

"Ah." Koyata slumped.

"You see, the situation in the city grows more difficult with every passing day. Not only in Heian – in all of Yamato. The seeds of rebellion are spreading. Lawlessness is on the increase. And now that the *Taikun* is dead and old loyalties are put to the test, the government fears things might get even worse. We even begin to fear for the *Mikado*'s safety."

"That would be unthinkable."

"The unthinkable is already happening, Koyata-*sama*. A hatamoto retainer was recently slain in Mito, in broad daylight!"

"I was not aware of this, *tono*." Koyata raised an eyebrow in genuine surprise, less at the assassination, more at the mention of Mito. Wasn't Mito one of Tokugawa family's personal domains?

Have things turned that bad already?

"No, we managed to keep it under wraps for the time-being. But that brings us to you, Koyata-*sama*. I hear your name mentioned a lot lately," said Matsudaira with a thin smile, "not only in Kurama, but in many other actions; you and your men keep distinguishing themselves with no regard to your own safety. Rest assured, it did not pass unnoticed."

"I only do my duty, *tono*."

The man with the Tiger Tattoo had fled safety from the ambush at Kurama, but for Koyata, despite his injuries, the battle was a resounding success: his men managed to capture three of the fugitives, including the man called Miyabe, who turned out to be the brains of the entire operation, of which the Tiger Tattoo was mere muscle.

"If only more Yamato did their duty with such diligence!" Lord Matsudaira sighed opening a fan. "Your words are modest, but your actions speak for themselves. Putting you under Sasaki-*dono* was a mistake. How would you like to lead your own force, independent of the city guard?"

"I would like that very much, *tono*. But… "

"Yes?"

"Where would I get the men? I have some under my command right now – I even brought some from Kiyō – but they are too few to be effective in any major action. I would feel bad about taking any more of Sasaki-*dono*'s troops from him."

Matsudaira nodded. "Ever the practical mind. Don't worry, I've thought of everything. As it happens, I was recommended a group of rōnin in search of employment passing through Heian. Their loyalty to the *Taikun*, I was assured, is impermeable."

Rōnin...? Loyal...? That's a first...

"Assured by whom?" asked Koyata, incredulously.

"Men whose authority will not be questioned by either you or me," replied Matsudaira vaguely. "The leader of the rōnin is here today, and I wanted you to meet him. Hajime-*sama*!"

A side door slid open and in came a man at the sight of whom Koyata jumped up, forgetting his injuries. His hand wandered to the grip of the short sword at his belt.

"You!"

"You two know each other?" Lord Matsudaira asked.

"Yes – " replied the other man with a smile. In the corner of his mouth hung a half-lit cigarette, "I do believe we've... met."

Koyata prided himself on never forgetting a face, but even without his skill, it was impossible to forget this one. The broken nose, the crooked eye, the scars... there was no doubt – this was the commander of the grey clad rōnin who

159

had attacked the Magistrate prison in Kiyō. Only the uniform was different this time – not plain grey, but white with blue teeth-like chevrons along the edges.

"You – scoundrel!"

"Come now, I was merely following orders. That's what I'm best at, you'll find out."

"Koyata-*sama*, Hajime-*sama*!"

Lord Matsudaira struck the floor with his fan. He glowered from one man to another.

"Whatever your history, you're working for me now. I need you both – you for your wit, and you – " he pointed at Haijme, "for your swords. Understand?"

"Of course," the broken-nosed man replied. The mocking smile did not vanish from his lips.

"Koyata-*sama*?"

"I – yes, Matsudaira-*dono*," Koyata surrendered with a bow, "I will not fail you."

CHAPTER VII

The great crowd pouring down the main street of the town of densely packed inns, guesthouses and shops that had grown around the Miya-juku checkpoint was relentless; it waited for no one, it parted for no one... except a giant, broad-shouldered man in exotic clothes, with a long, thick mane of hair and the beard of a mountain hermit, walking briskly through the middle of the road – and a small, young priestess following a few steps behind him.

The pair reached the long lawn before the checkpoint gate. Low guardhouses ran along both sides, where bored spearmen on the verandas peeked from under the shade of white cloth adorned with the black hollyhock emblem of the Owari-Tokugawas – the ruling clan of Nagoya, a close branch of the *Taikun*'s family. The entire courtyard was filled with a long, winding queue of people trying to make their way along the Tokaido highway from Edo to Heian, and all points in between. Here the tensions reached the zenith, and nobody would make way, not even for Torishi and Nagomi.

The queue moved steadily until at last Nagomi found herself before the low black table and a grumpy samurai sitting cross-legged behind it.

"Itō?"

She gulped; she had never before had to queue at the Tokaido checkpoint – when she and Torishi had arrived in Nagoya, it was by boat. But now her family could ill afford to send her back the expensive way; moving the entire household to Edo at short notice was costly enough.

She handed him her *tegata* – an official travel permit her father had obtained from the magistrate. He looked over his list.

"You're at the wrong gate. I have you on the Edo list."

"It must be some mistake. I have a *tegata* to Chōfu." Nagomi pointed to the permit.

The official studied the paper with great scrutiny. "No, no, no. Definitely Edo. And who are you?" He turned to Torishi. "An appointed male guardian? *Ano na…* it doesn't say what clan you belong to."

"I'm a servant of the Itō family, *tono*," Torishi answered with a trained, studied bow.

"What accent is that?" The keen-eared official tilted his head. "Not Nagoya, that's for sure."

"He comes from Kiyō," explained Nagomi. "I'm sure you have that information somewhere in your documents."

The official's face turned red. He was a man perfect for his position: a stiff bureaucrat, who didn't like his authority questioned by anyone. Nagomi tried her best smile, but it worked little.

She now wished she could disguise herself as a man, like Satō. Since their control had started, half a dozen male

162

travellers had passed her by with nary a glance from the guardsmen at their travel documents.

The official browsed through a pile of papers on his desk with increased irritation.

"There's nothing here. We'll have to contact your family," he said, even more grumpily than before.

"But they are already on the ship to Edo!"

"Well then, you'll have to wait until they're back. Now, go away…"

Nagomi put her hands on the table.

"I have to leave – "

Another samurai came up to the official with another, much shorter list of names. He whispered into the official's ear, and they both gave Nagomi a look which made her shiver. They whispered some more; Nagomi heard only bits of their conversation: "…Suwa…Kiyō…treason…"

The other samurai walked away, and the official snapped his fingers. Two spearmen appeared immediately at Nagomi's side.

"What's going on?" asked Torishi.

The official ignored him. "You will go to the women's inspection room," he ordered Nagomi. "It's just a routine procedure."

Nagomi hesitated, but the spearman bumped her on the shoulder to hurry up.

Dark, cold, bamboo cage, of ropes and chains.

Grim light reflecting off the executioner's sword.

Dirt in the wide-opened eyes.

She squeezed Torishi's hand.

"Run away," she whispered, "now."

"Huh?" the bear-man looked at her perplexed, but then nodded sharply and turned to flee. A spearman blocked his path.

"You too – " the man started. One swipe was enough to crash both him and the official's table upon which he fell against the wall. Shoving another guard aside, Torishi hurried back outside towards the traveller-filled courtyard. He parted the crowd before him like a ship in the sea, and not one of the guards dared to stop him.

Hurriedly, the guards led Nagomi to a small, windowless room at the back of the gate office. A woman in a green kimono, looking almost as grumpy as the official before, waited until the men left them alone.

"Undress," she ordered sharply without looking up from a document she was writing.

Nagomi took off her clothes slowly and put them in a neat pile on a rectangle of packed straw by the door. It was the kind of humiliating inspection she knew most women travelling alone were subject to, and which she had hoped, being a priestess, she would have avoided.

"How old are you?"

"Sixteen."

The woman studied Nagomi's body for a while, then stood up, and walked closer. She poked the sickle scar between Nagomi's breasts, then ran her yellowed nail along the white line on Nagomi's left forearm.

"Your body is scarred like that of a seasoned warrior," she said.

"I was... prone to accidents in childhood."

"Accidents with swords?"

Nagomi didn't know how to answer her. The woman leaned closer to smell her hair, and then with a swift move of a hand, she pinched a handful.

"Ow!"

"Why do you dye your hair?" the woman asked, narrowing her eyes.

"I... I don't want people to mock me in the street," Nagomi answered. She started to shiver, even though it was a hot summer's day outside.

"The description on your *tegata* says your hair is red."

"I'm sorry, I forgot..."

The woman waved her hand. "It doesn't matter. You're wanted for far more serious crimes than not fitting your description. I just needed to make sure you are you."

Nagomi raised her head.

"Wanted...?"

"Don't play innocent with me, girl." The woman smirked. "You should have stayed in Nagoya. Now put your clothes back on before those spearmen return. Unless you want them to see you like that."

Nagomi rubbed her shoulders. They were still sore from the firm grip of the prison guards. She thanked the Gods for choosing her to serve them. The men had handled her roughly, but were still wary of bringing a priestess to any real harm. They even allowed her to keep the jade necklace, refusing to touch it as if it was cursed.

The door of the bamboo cage squeaked open and a hand slid in a bowl of gruel. Nagomi grabbed the hand.

"How much more of this?" she whispered.

The hand struggled briefly, but then surrendered, and a face appeared in the opening – a pock-marked and wrinkled face of a man with a small moustache and scarce hair greying at the ends.

"They are taking you to Edo tomorrow, priestess-*sama*," he said. "I'm sorry."

Edo. So that's how this ends.

She remembered the stories of the *Taikun*'s own executioners in Edo repeated like dreadful fairy tales by the people of Nagoya. So close to the capital, the shadow of the *Taikun*'s castle hung long over the thoughts of the townsfolk.

"Wait, please. Don't I know you?"

The man's eyes darted to the sides. "Yes, your honoured father saved my family from the pox."

"I'm glad to hear that," Nagomi said with a gentle smile.

His lips trembled. "Priestess-*sama*, we are all here... guards, servants... your father's work – I wish we could help, but there's nothing – "

"Shh," she silenced him. "I understand."

"I'm sorry," the man repeated, and disappeared.

She slurped the gruel in grim silence. She had long lost count of the hours in the cage. A night had passed since her imprisonment, and another day was coming to an end.

What should I do?

There was nothing she could do. Only a miracle could save her now – but she felt she had long ago used up her share of miracles... and if the Spirits could affect politics, Lady Kazuko would still be alive. She could only hope her crimes were not severe enough to warrant the worst punishments. But that was a feeble hope.

Who am I kidding, she thought, playing with the necklace, *the* Taikun *does not show mercy to traitors*.

The door of the cage opened again. The same man showed in the gap, holding something in his hands.

"We thought..." he whispered, "...you might want to send a message to your family."

"Oh, thank you!"

He disappeared, leaving Nagomi with her own racing thoughts. She knew how much he risked. *Is that my miracle?* One chance, just one letter. Warn her father about the danger of arrest? Say her farewells? Ask them to pass the message over to Satō…?

In the end, she chose none of those things. By the time the old man returned, she had the letter ready.

"Find the man named Torishi," she said, "you'll know him – he's taller than any Yamato, and has long hair and a big beard… Give it to him before tomorrow."

The wagon squeaked to a halt; Nagomi bumped into the wall.

She stood up on tiptoes and looked through the narrow air vent. The leafy forest around stood still, stuffy, breeze-less.

"Can you see anything?" asked one of the other two prisoners in the wagon.

They were both in chains, unlike Nagomi, who had freedom of movement within the confines of the iron box. Not that it mattered. The wagon was locked shut, and escorted by a troop of armed men.

"The woods are quiet," she said, frowning.

"Oh, woods are quiet. I'm sure that's important."

"Give her a break," the other prisoner said, "she's just a kid."

"I don't need advice from a Satsuma dog," snarled the first one.

"Trust a Chōfu bumpkin to be rude to a lady."

"Quiet, both of you!" Nagomi snapped. The two men fell silent in bewilderment. There was something in the air; something that had stopped all noise. She listened.

"One of the guards is coming … he looks nervous."

The guard rapped on the iron wall with the butt of his spear. "Sit down! Don't try anything!"

"Don't try what?" replied the Satsuma prisoner. "What's going on out there?"

"Just – just don't move!"

"Bandits?" the man from Chōfu guessed.

"Not so close to Nagoya," the other one said with a grin. "Maybe Shimazu men are coming to my rescue, after all."

"Shimazu? *Pah*! It's the Mori retainers coming to rescue me."

Nagomi said nothing. The guard disappeared from her sight, then another appeared for just a moment, then vanished. Somebody was shouting orders at the front of the convoy; men were running about in confusion.

A sudden roar stopped all this commotion.

"Come back here, you cowards!" she heard the commander call. "It's just a damn bear!"

169

A second later the guards ran past the wagon, slipping in the mud, dropping their spears and losing their black tin helmets. Then the commander himself appeared in her field of view, backing up slowly, his sword raised in a trembling hand.

"Nagoya scum," he mumbled, "never mind, I'll deal with it myself."

He yelled and charged forward; the next thing Nagomi heard was a swipe and a sickening crack of bones. She strained her neck to see further, but managed to see only the bristling, hairy back of the beast as it blurred past the side of the wagon, leaving behind the fading growl and stench of wet fur.

Both prisoners jumped to their feet, and pressed their faces to the bars.

"What the – "

A moment later, a series of mighty blows on the back door sent the two men into a panicked frenzy; they retreated as far into the back of the wagon as their chains allowed. One more blow and the door burst into splinters. The muzzle of a giant black bear showed in the opening.

"Torishi-*sama*!" Nagomi cried, throwing herself on the animal's neck.

Nagomi knelt down, put her hand on the dead samurai's eyes, and whispered a quick prayer. Torishi stood by, scratching the back of his neck.

"He charged at me…"

"I understand," she said softly.

The commander wore a kimono embroidered with the symbols of hollyhock and the character "Ai".

He was a servant of Edo — an enemy, as she now understood. Killing a bandit or a rōnin in a fight was one thing, but now a government official was dead. There was no turning back.

Now I really am a traitor, she realized, strangely calm.

"We should move on," Torishi said, looking at the road. "The other guards may come back at any moment."

"Just a minute."

She searched his body and found a pair of square-shaped wooden keys. She returned to the wagon and threw the keys at the two prisoners.

"Wait," said one of them as she turned to leave. "Where will you go? We should stick together for now."

"Little priestess," Torishi pressed, "we have to run into the mountains."

"No, we *must* be at the — wait..." She looked at the two prisoners who now stood on the muddy ground getting rid of their remaining chains, "isn't one of you from Chōfu?"

The nearer of the prisoners had already unshackled himself and was now rubbing his wrists, wincing.

"That's me," he said. The other man was still struggling with the key.

"Can you take us there?"

He nodded. "I know people who can help us. We just need to get to the sea."

"Then let's go," said Torishi, "and fast."

"What about you?" Nagomi asked the other man. His rusted chain finally let go. "Are you coming with us?"

"To Chōfu?" He spat. "I'd rather go straight to Edo."

He jumped out of the wagon, glanced around, and, with a quick "thank you" thrown at Nagomi, disappeared into the woods.

Nagomi picked up Torishi's bow and quiver from the ground. She walked up to the edge of a bluff and looked at the nameless harbour town below. A few fishing boats bobbed on the waves, and a large flat-bottomed ferry rowed between them across the narrow bay. It didn't seem like the kind of place that had ships fit to take them all the way to Chōfu.

She turned back towards the tiny lumberjack shack that their new friend had found; a place where they could hide. Meanwhile, he went down to the town to seek safe passage. "It's best if I do it alone," he had said, "you two are not exactly... inconspicuous."

She had to agree. Her hair was now a mess of dirty red and washed-up indigo, and Torishi's bulky frame would have made it all too easy for the Edo agents to track them down.

She strung the bow with some effort, nocked an arrow, and aimed at a nearby birch tree. The released missile grazed its bark and vanished into the forest. She nocked another one. She wasn't sure if being able to shoot the bow would ever be useful, but she found the practice soothing. It demanded focus and emptying one's mind, almost like a prayer.

Torishi stepped out of the hut and studied her stance.

"Put your elbows closer. This isn't a Yamato bow," he said. The Kumaso bow was much shorter and more curved than the ones she had seen the samurai use at the shrine contests. This was a hunting tool, rather than a weapon.

She let the arrow fly and it missed the birch by a good inch. It didn't really matter.

"Do you think he'll come back?" asked Torishi, returning with the two arrows from the forest. He handed them to Nagomi who put them back into the deerskin quiver.

"I don't want to worry about it now," she replied, brushing the hair across her forehead. "If he doesn't, we'll think of something."

Torishi looked down, shielding his eyes from the afternoon sun. "Is that our boat?" he asked.

Nagomi stepped as close to the edge of the bluff as she could. The flat-bottomed ferry had just moored up at the pier. She expected the usual commotion of travellers lining up to enter the boat, but something else was happening. The pier was empty, cut-off from the rest of the harbour by a thin line of guards. Men poured forth from the ferry in small, neat groups, each carrying a rectangular banner bearing the same "Ai" design Nagomi had seen on the clothes of the dead official. Thirty, maybe forty warriors trotted towards the small square in front of the pier. Only when their muster was over, were the queuing passengers allowed to enter the boat.

"What do you think is happening?" asked Torishi.

"Is it because of… us?" Nagomi asked.

"No. They're garrisoning the entire coast," came an answer. The man from Chōfu emerged out of the forest, grey-faced and tired. "All the ports from here to Edo now have a military presence. These are Aizu troops," he pointed down to the town, "but other provinces are sending soldiers as well."

He called himself Takasugi, but that was all he was willing to divulge.

"The war," said Nagomi, "the one everyone's been talking about."

"It's all Satsuma's fault," Takasugi said, shaking his fist. "They act too rashly. Taking over Kumamoto, openly dealing with the Bataavians… They will draw Edo's wrath. We'll all be doomed because of their impatience."

"Can we still get on the boat?" Torishi asked.

"Not this one, but we *will* get out of here. I have a fishing boat coming for us after dark. That should at least take us to the other side of the bay. Trust me, I need to get to Chōfu just as much as you do."

The only light on the beach was coming from a small campfire around which the fishing nets were draped on bamboo racks. As she got closer, Nagomi made out the shape of the shallow boat in the darkness, drawn out halfway onto the sand, lapped by the glimmering waves, and the shadows of two fishermen sitting quietly and unmoving in their bamboo hats.

Not far to the north, the harbour light flickered from the end of the pier. But the town itself was asleep; even the noises of revelry coming from the inn where the Aizu soldiers were stationed had by now quietened. Nothing disturbed the silence of the night except the crackling of the campfire, the rush of the waves, and the occasional hooting of an owl coming from the forest.

"Where did you find those fishermen?" Nagomi whispered as they approached the boat.

"In the town, at the tavern," replied Takasugi.

"Can we trust them?"

"They're just some commoners looking for a quick profit," he whispered back. "I don't think we have to worry about them."

Nagomi gave Torishi a warning look. The bear-man returned her stare, but said nothing. The three of them passed by the drying nets – the type used to trawl for the small *shirasu* fish, Nagomi noted – and emerged into the light of the campfire. The fishermen stirred at their entrance. The older one stood up to welcome them, while the younger went to prepare the boat for departure.

"As agreed, payment after passage," said Takasugi. The fisherman nodded.

"Come now, that is hardly a fair deal," said Nagomi, smiling, "what if we run away without paying?"

"I'm sure there's no need – " the fisherman started, but Nagomi interrupted him.

"Torishi-*sama*, can I have some money?"

Torishi reached into the bundle containing a few of Nagomi's and his own belongings, and handed her a few copper coins. Nagomi took the fisherman's hand and pressed the cash into his palm.

A dagger glinting in the night.
A splash of blood on the wood.

"I don't like when things aren't settled properly," she explained, putting on her most innocent expression. "It's just the way I am."

The fisherman grunted, shrugged, hid the coins in his sleeve, and went on to help with the boat. Takasugi stared at her.

"What was that all about?"

"They're assassins," she whispered through her smile. "Strike them when we're out at sea."

In the darkness, they quickly lost sight of the land. The older fisherman was sitting in the bow of the boat looking at them curiously, sharpening a stick with a short knife. The young one rowed the vessel forward with broad oar strokes.

The mood was tense. Apart from their knives, the fishermen were unarmed, as far as Nagomi could tell, but then so was she and her companions, and if her suspicions were right, the men were trained fighters. She wasn't sure if the Chōfu man was any good in a fight; lean and dishevelled, he didn't seem like much of a brawler. She glanced at Torishi – the bear-man was sitting on the edge of the boat, bobbing nervously from side to side; he was obviously wary of having to fight in a small, wobbly boat in the middle of the black ocean.

She looked over the prow. In the bleak distance she saw the gleaming light of another harbour. The same light flickered behind them. The boat was half-way across the bay.

"Now!" she cried.

Torishi lunged forward, grabbing the older fisherman with him and dragging him beyond the side of the boat with a loud splash. The boat wobbled back and forth as Takasugi grappled with the oarsman. He had surprise on his side, but his enemy was stronger and larger. They struggled for a few seconds, and then the fisherman toppled Takasugi down, pinning him to the floor of the boat. He raised a short knife to strike. Nagomi looked around, spotted Torishi's quiver, pulled an arrow and stabbed the enemy in the back with all her strength. The iron-tipped shaft tore through the muscles with sickening ease.

The man howled in pain, his blade brushing Takasugi's arm. Takasugi kicked him desperately with all four limbs, and threw him overboard. The boat wobbled again and Nagomi fell on her knees.

"Get the oar!" she ordered, grabbing the sides of the boat to keep balance. Takasugi reached for the wooden pole. She leaned over the side, trying to spot Torishi. A gurgling cry came from the front of the boat. She reached out, and a hairy arm grabbed her hand. With Takasugi they helped Torishi climb back on board, wet and grim, spluttering blood and heaving.

"Thank the Great Otter," he said between coughs, "I was sure I'd drown."

He noticed the pole in Takasugi's hand.

"I hope you know how to steer this thing."

The boat hit the sand with speed, and they all fell out, splashing into the shallow waters on the other side of the bay. It took them a while to scramble back up, gather their scattered belongings, and find a place for shelter among the rocks.

Fire was out of the question – even if they could somehow prepare it from the wet tinderbox and driftwood, – they did not want to draw attention to themselves. It was going to be a long and cold night.

"How… how did you know?" asked Takasugi, panting. He had done most of the frantic and clumsy rowing that brought them ashore.

"The nets were for *shirasu* trawling... but this is not the season."

He squinted. "The season...? Are you a fisherwoman?"

"I grew up near the greatest harbour in Yamato. Every child in Kiyō knows the fishing seasons by heart."

"And that money thing...?"

"I had to make sure – I wanted to touch their hands. The fisherman's hands have a certain pattern of calluses, cuts, and furrows... The old man had the hands of a swordsman."

"Again, how – ?"

She smiled sadly.

"I worked with all sorts of patients in my father's clinic. Fishermen, peasants, samurai..."

He stared from her to Torishi, his mouth agape, scratching the back of his head in wonder.

"Who *are you* people? Back then, on the road – "

"I think it's time you told us about yourself." Torishi leaned forward, wiping seawater from his brow. "We've saved your life twice now."

"Yes, yes, of course," Takasugi laughed nervously. He rose slightly to a bow, almost slipping on the wet rocks.

"I am Takasugi Hiro, student of Meirinkan, the Chōfu School of *Rangaku*."

"You're a wizard?" Nagomi asked, genuinely surprised. "Why didn't you use magic to fight?"

"I'm not a very good spell-caster," he answered, scratching his head, "I'm more interested in the technology side of things. I lack the ability... – if you know what I mean. Though you probably don't know the difference."

Nagomi chuckled. "Don't worry about that. Did you say Meirinkan?" She reached into her sleeve where, sewn into lining, was the letter from Satō, and unravelled the soaked paper. "Is that where the headmaster is a boy called Yoshida Shōin?"

"You – you know of him?"

"*Know* of him? We are invited to his wedding!"

The dawn was near, and the air grew warm, foretelling the scorching heat of the morning to come. They spread their clothes high on the rocks, hoping to dry them in the salty breeze. Nagomi huddled into the nook of a rock, wrapping her arms around her knees. The rush of the battle had now passed, and she started trembling at the very memory.

She looked at her right palm... How did Torishi's arrow end up in her hand? She had never struck anyone in combat before... and she didn't plan to ever again.

If this is what war is like, let the warriors have it, she thought, bitterly. Even in self-defence, even justified, bringing physical harm to somebody made her feel sick with herself. Her instinct was to heal the wound she had caused. But it was too late... the assassins were now somewhere at the bottom of the ocean, beyond her or anyone else's help... She wiped her eyes and turned to the man.

"Why were those men after you?" she asked, drawing her blanket tighter around herself. "Why were you in prison?"

Takasugi sneezed. Naked and trembling in the moonlight, he looked frail and weak.

"I was sent to Edo by my domain to recruit students and teachers to the school."

"There are *Rangaku* scholars in Edo?"

"You'd be surprised. Chief Councillor Abe was a remarkably lenient man. He may have been fierce with the outlying clans, but under his rule, in Edo, the Western arts flourished."

"That's good, I guess?" She said without conviction. Whatever the Edo politics were now, it was too late to help either the Takashima family, or her own.

My family, a thought flashed through her mind. *What's going to happen to them?*

But she was too tired, her thoughts too muddled, to worry about it now.

He shook his head. "After the *Taikun*'s death," he continued, and Nagomi barely registered the news at first, "the new Chief Councillor began to purge all those whom he saw as threat to the government."

She raised her eyes.

"Wait, did you say the *Taikun* is dead – ?"

The mightiest will fall.

Somewhere in among the snippets of the visions she remembered scenes which seemed completely enigmatic until now: *An old man in hollyhock-embroidered robe, dying in spasms. Dark-eyed man with bloodied face, holding him in a tight embrace...*

The foe lurks within.

"Yes, it was a sudden illness... or so they said. A brief succession dispute ensued, led by a Mito branch of the *Taikun*'s family... The *Rangaku* were the first to fall under scrutiny, and we in Chōfu doubly so. We are always suspected of plotting and conspiring against them after all."

Conspiring against the Taikun. This was the accusation that led Lady Kazuko to her death.

"And do you?" she asked.

There are no coincidences, the High Priestess had always said.

He grinned. "They did send assassins after me, didn't they?"

"You don't seem like very safe company," Torishi said.

"*Safe company?*" Takasugi chuckled, eyeing the bear-man's rippling muscles and grim face. "I wonder which one of us has more to fear."

"You can go your own way," Torishi grunted, "as soon as you want."

"No," replied Takasugi. He nodded at Nagomi. "Twice you've saved me now. You must let me repay the debt. This is Todō land, I believe," he said, looking towards the mountains rising in the dark to the west. "I have many

182

friends here. They will help us cross over to Naniwa. No more snags from now on, I promise you that."

CHAPTER VIII

It was an unlikely place for a naval base, Bran thought. The beach was a perfect crescent of golden sand, bounded by tall dunes. A summer paradise. If there was a harbour here, it must have been hidden by the teeth-like hills covered with the kind of lush, almost tropical forest Bran was by now so familiar with.

He looked back towards the eastern horizon. The forbidding black wall of clouds and winds had already closed, and was now just a thin dark line – he could only see it because he knew it was there. As Leif had predicted, one day the Sea Maze had simply vanished all around them; the winds quietened down, the waves calmed, and the compass pointed north again, long enough for the entire flotilla to pass through to the other side.

The Gorllewin sailors had not known what to expect, for them it was just another phenomenon of the unknown Yamato magic. But Bran had flown through the barrier, and had known the reverence with which the Yamato people spoke about it. Only the *Taikun* had the power to control the Divine Winds. And that could only have meant one thing: that the Grey Hoods had finally struck some kind of deal with Edo. The potential repercussions were staggering… but for the moment, Bran had something else on his mind.

The *Star* dropped anchor at the head of the crescent-shaped bay and, for a few hours, nothing else happened. The bay was eerily empty; no boat appeared on the horizon, no curious peasant emerged from among the trees. The only living thing he spotted were several black kites circling over the ship trying to figure out what to think about this new arrival.

He felt something at the back of his head, a tingling buzz of the Farlink. It quickly grew irritatingly strong. Somebody nearby was flying a dragon, and they were getting closer. Bran looked up, but he still couldn't see anything over the hills.

Over the weeks spent on board of the *Star*, Bran had been honing his newly found talent. He still wasn't sure how it worked exactly, but he could now distinguish with ease, from within the confines of his cabin, whether the rider flying out on patrol was Thorfinn, or either of the other two men. He began to wonder how far he could reach with this skill, or how detailed the information he could get. At times he could swear he could not only sense that the Farlink was active, but also *what* it was transmitting – orders, emotions, of both the mount and its rider.

This would make spying a breeze, he thought.

But those moments were fleeting and they left him with a pounding headache that was almost unbearable.

The dragon he had sensed finally appeared from beyond the hill; another Black Wing, maybe even larger than the ones on the ship. Bran watched it fly heavily, when he felt a hand on his shoulder.

"Come," said Leif, unhappily. "I'm afraid I must lock you up. Vice Komtur's orders."

Bran cast one last look at the black dragon swerving to avoid an invisible current of the Ninth Wind. He remembered how difficult it was to steer his own mount in the lands of the Orient and he almost felt sorry for the unknown rider.

"Can you at least lock me up in the cargo hold, rather than in the cell?" he asked Leif, trying to sound casual. "I don't want to leave my dragon all alone."

The chaplain scratched his blond head.

"I don't see why not. Locked is locked."

Bran leaned down and touched Emrys's neck with his cheek. He closed his eyes and focused. He didn't know what the result of him melding with Emrys looked like, and wasn't sure he wanted to. Perhaps he turned into some kind of two-headed, two-bodied monster... or maybe his human form simply vanished...?

With everyone above busy welcoming the arriving rider, Bran thought he had his last chance to try. He calmed his mind, focused and called on the Dragonform. His entire body jolted. For a moment he found himself in complete emptiness; he smelled the red dust around him. Emrys was not keen on letting him in without a struggle. Bran panicked; he was out of his own body, but not yet inside the dragon's, stuck in the limbo between minds. But he remembered how he had fought back and forth with Shigemasa, and firmly forced his way in.

He opened his eyes. The stall was cramped and stuffy, and he hated it, but it was better than being locked up in a cage, forced to sleep, or in that box of steel, at the mercy of the glowing red ball. At least here his mind was clear and he could stretch his wings a little.

He wanted to fly so badly. Lately, humans did nothing but kept him locked in strange, dark places.

There were other dragons here. He sensed them through the wall. Big, strong dragons, like the ones he used to play with before – before the white light came, before he flew over endless water… Before he lost his rider. He didn't want to lose his rider ever again.

Three of the dragons he knew already; the fourth one was new. He was older than the others. He beamed with arrogance and pride. There were none like him, anywhere in the world.

The Firstborn.

He'd hatched from the first egg their brood-mother laid. A distant memory: an oval-shaped cave, flat, with a viewing gallery above it, like an arena. Other eggs hatching, in their dozens. The body of a bull thrown into the ring from the gallery. Dragons, fighting for the meat, with claw and teeth, too young yet to breathe fire. There's not enough meat for everyone. Those who get killed, get eaten by others. At last, only four remain. The Firstborn among them, the prince of the brood. Chosen for greatness. Chosen for the secret mission.

Another memory: a long flight over a never-ending expanse of the sea. Lesser dragons would balk at such effort; they would revolt, throw their riders down, show their fury. But not him, never him. The Firstborn trusts in the rider's judgement. He must have been someone important if he was chosen to ride *him*. So they fly into the unknown, into the maze of winds, clouds, and angry Spirits.

A little pale man comes to greet them in a forest on a mountain. He's bowing a lot, smiling nervously. But his shadow is great and terrible, greater even than a dragon's. The Firstborn had never seen a human like him.

The little man with the big shadow is riding the Firstborn. The dragon doesn't like it. His skin feels cold where the little man sits. The scales are defiled, stained; they must be scrubbed clean. But other humans don't notice anything. Why can't they see it?

Oh, good. The little man is leaving. He and the Firstborn's rider bow and shake hands. They sign a long piece of paper. They are both happy about it. The Firstborn is happy, too. Happy that the little man with the big shadow is gone.

The other dragons are coming. The young ones – the second batch of hatchlings; they are weaker, of course. The Firstborn knows, because he… had seen them in the other world, the world of the red dust, where the rider sometimes takes him. It's different than the world of blue sky and yellow sun. There are no trees there, no sea, no birds, no wild animals to feed on. But there are mountains – tall, grey, cold mountains – and hills, and the immense plain of red dust. And towers, with red lights on top, many, many towers. How the rider knows his way around it, the Firstborn doesn't know, but he's glad that they never get lost among the beaming turrets…

Bran broke away from the dragon's mind, and, breathless, fell to the floor. He coughed, exhausted and sick from the mental and physical strain. His limbs and back ached, as if his entire body had been stretched on some torture device… But it was worth it. He was now sure that he knew the secret of the Black Wings.

The red dust plain… the Otherworld.

Somehow, they had found their way to the same place Bran had been visiting with General Shigemasa… He never got quite around navigating that place himself, but he knew the distances and barriers from the physical world meant little in the Otherworld. *Of course* it could have been used for communication. It now seemed so obvious. All it took was two people with the ability to travel through it and find each other's position…

Too bad I don't know anyone I could reach that way, he thought. Although… hadn't Torishi mentioned that the Kumaso could travel through the Otherworld as well? But there was no chance he could just randomly stumble upon the bear-man taking a hike through the red dust plain, was there?

"I could never get past all the walls and wards," Shigemasa had told him. That meant he'd tried… and that he thought it was possible. Perhaps Bran didn't need another person to actually *be* present in the Otherworld… perhaps… perhaps…

The stall lock rumbled, and the door slammed opened. Bran scrambled to his feet and, squinting, saw the man coming in from the light, followed by four soldiers. He was short and somewhat portly in his grey hooded cloak, bespectacled, with greying, receding hair, shaved around the horned circle tattoo. He walked briskly across the floor towards Bran, and looked him over through the thin, wiry spectacles. He murmured something Bran didn't understand.

"Is that him?" he asked, louder.

"Yes, Komtur," said Vice Komtur Aulick from the corridor.

Emrys snorted angrily. The Komtur glanced at the dragon, raised an eyebrow and then returned to studying Bran.

"Fishermen village, eh?"

He gestured at one of the soldiers, who opened a jute sack he was holding and emptied it on the floor. It contained the indigo kimono and sandals Bran had been wearing when the Grey Hoods had caught him.

"That doesn't look like fishermen clothes to me," he said, picking up the silk kimono.

He turned to the Vice Komtur.

"Clean the boy up. I'm taking him with me to Shimoda. Maybe the Councillor will want to explain what's going on here."

"What about the dragon, sir?"

The Komtur looked over his shoulder and narrowed his eyes.

"That's your mount, boy? Your only hope to get home, eh?"

Bran nodded slowly. He didn't like where this was going.

"That's funny, I'd swear I've seen it somewhere before... No matter. Keep it here," the Komtur said to Aulick. "Set up the Bomb Lance. If the boy tries anything – kill it."

"I know where I saw that dragon of yours," the Komtur said, slamming his hand on the desk. "Goa, when we were all waiting for that storm to pass."

The ancient desk was hewn out of thick oak and decorated with peeling strips of gold leaf. It was the sort of furniture Bran had not seen since the teaching halls of the Academy. Like the heavy chairs and the tall cabinet in this strange room, it was marked with the Eagle of Rome, but the pieces did not belong to one set; rather, it seemed like they had been assembled in a hurry. Bran imagined the furniture taken from private collections of the wealthy samurai to accommodate the barbarian invaders, and chuckled at the dishonour this must have brought them.

Everything else in the room was typical Yamato: the straw floor, the painted panels on the walls, the shallow alcove with a calligraphy scroll and a vase – which, Bran noticed, was filled with fresh flowers.

There are Yamato in this building, he thought, *even if they are just servants.* He didn't suspect the Komtur or his men to bother changing the flower composition every day.

The room where Bran was being interrogated was part of an administrative building inside a *Butsu* temple complex overlooking a small fishing town on the northern edge of the crescent-shaped bay. Both the temple and the town were eerily empty, cleared of all the locals before the Black Wings had settled.

"You were there?" Bran asked. "So you must've been in Fan Yu, too."

"Briefly," the Komtur nodded. "*Ladon* was a magnificent ship. More's the pity."

He knocked the frame of his spectacles repeatedly on the edge of the oak table, piercing Bran with his slightly short-sighted eyes.

"How did you come by these clothes?"

"I… it was a gift."

That was not a lie, after all.

"Who from?"

"From the people who helped me."

"Look, boy, I know you think you're being clever, but I'm a Komtur of the Western Navy, and you're just a kid.

You're not your father. You can't outsmart me. So let's drop this charade, shall we?"

Bran said nothing. The Komtur put the spectacles back on, steepled his fingers and leaned forward.

"All right, let's start differently. How did you know how to find us?" he asked.

"I'm sorry?" Bran blinked.

"Stop playing games with me!" He slammed his hands on the table. "How did you know that the *Star of the Sea* was anchored off Tamna Island?"

"I didn't," Bran answered, swallowing. "It was an accident."

His thoughts raced. He didn't know how the Gorllewin treated spies – or people they suspected of being spies – but he knew it would be a lot harder to defend himself against false accusations than the truth.

The Komtur scoffed.

"The most secret operation in the history of our nation. Months of preparations, weeks of avoiding detection. Most complex glamours ever devised. We make sure nobody – *nobody,* not the Dracaland, not the Varyaga, not even *our own people* – knows we're here. And you, a single boy on a small dragon, stumble upon us *by accident?* Oh, that's good, that's good indeed." He turned serious abruptly and leaned forward. "Don't think anyone here is on your side, boy. If you don't tell me your story, I'll be more than glad to give you back to our Yamato friends – and something tells me you know full well what they might do to you."

"I'm not a spy!" Bran almost cried. The memory of the "little man" he had seen through the Firstborn's memories still haunted him. A man who could terrify a dragon must have been either one of the Fanged, or their monstrous servants.

"I never said you were," said the Komtur, with a wry smile, "but you'll admit, the idea does sound appealing in the circumstances…"

I can't tell him the truth. He's making deals with the Eight-headed Serpent. But… I can make my lies more convincing.

"I admit – I was in Yamato before," he said. The Komtur leaned back with his hands behind his head.

"If I tell you the truth," Bran continued, "will you *promise* not to hand me over to the Yamato?"

"No," the Komtur said. "You can't bargain with me – you have nothing, but I might *consider* it – depending on what you tell me."

"Have you heard of a place called Satsuma?" asked Bran.

The Komtur raised his hands in exasperation. "*Heard* of it? The Councillor wouldn't shut up about it. Yes, I've *heard* of it. What of it?"

So he is planning to use you against Nariakira…

"After the disaster on *Ladon* I was washed ashore on a beach in Satsuma," said Bran. "I was captured and kept prisoner for a few weeks."

"Whom have you met there?"

Bran pretended to think. "I don't know. Several people came to meet me in prison, but I wasn't introduced to any of them."

"How did you communicate? Don't tell me you've learned to speak that gibberish of theirs in a month."

"Oh, no!" Bran forced a laugh. "They had an interpreter – a Bataavian."

The Komtur tapped his spectacles on the table again. "How did you escape?"

"I… uh…" Bran clenched and unclenched his hands under the table. His mind was coming up blank. The Komtur's lips curled into a smirk.

I have to think of something… If I'm caught lying again, Emrys…

"Emrys…" he whispered.

"I'm sorry?"

"Emrys, my dragon. It found me. It must have been lost somewhere in Yamato, and trying to locate me all those weeks. As soon as it got near enough I used dragon magic to break free. Then we simply flew away in what I thought was the direction of Qin – that's where you found me."

The Komtur scratched his nose. "And the clothes…?"

"I stole from the guards. They took my uniform in prison."

"And you didn't think to tell us this sooner, because…?"

Bran said nothing.

196

"Well," the Komtur said, standing up. "that all sounds very plausible, I admit. Should be easy to verify, too. In a few days I have the delegation from Edo coming here to finally sign the treaties. I'm sure they would have heard about a Western dragon wreaking havoc in the palaces of Satsuma."

"A delegation from Edo… here?" Bran asked, through clenched throat.

A few days…that Councillor may know who I am. I must run away before he gets here.

"Yes. In fact, I'm surprised they're not here yet – they seem as eager to get that treaty signed as we are. But don't worry, boy," the Komtur stood up and walked to the door, "if your story checks out, you'll be safe with us. I hear the chaplain of the *Star* has grown rather fond of you. I would hate to disappoint him."

He opened the door and beckoned one of the guards to take Bran away.

"Lock him up somewhere," he said, "and get me the Seneschal at once."

THE CHRYSANTHEMUM SEAL

CHAPTER IX

There were no prison cells in the temple, so Bran was locked up in a clay-walled hermit's hut in a bamboo grove above the temple's cemetery. Through a tiny window near the roof he could see a bit of the crescent-shaped beach and the turquoise waters of the bay.

He mulled over his options. They were limited. He had his magic to rely on – Emrys, though on a ship on the other side of the bay, was still near enough to provide him with some dragon power. But he couldn't simply fight his way through the camp. At the least sign of trouble, the men on the *Star* would execute Emrys – the Komtur had made it clear enough. And even if he did manage to sneak out somehow without alarming the guards, he couldn't just fly or swim to the ship on his own... He needed help from outside.

Apart from the three guards Bran could see with True Sight outside the hut – two at the front, one at the back, where the bamboo grove grew thicker – the only other people he was allowed contact with were two Yamato servants who twice a day brought him food and cleaned out the waste pot: an older, sour-faced woman in the evening, and a young girl with a squashed face, small, spry eyes and a snub nose, in the morning. They wore no shoes, and the simplest clothes he had ever seen on a Yamato – single pieces of crude linen, thrown over one shoulder and tied with hemp rope. They were both deeply tanned, their hair uncombed, and the older woman's skin was covered in warts and seeping lesions.

"Please help me," he tried the second morning. The girl jumped away, startled.

"*Oraya...*" she muttered.

"Can't you understand me? I'm speaking Yamato!"

"*Araya*," she muttered again and retreated hastily out of the door.

He hoped the older woman would not be as jumpy.

"Please," he spoke in the morning, trying to sound softer and more gentle, "save me from those barbarians."

She didn't look surprised; the girl must have warned her.

"But ye'r barbarian ye'self," she replied in a crude manner.

"I'm not. I'm Yamato like you, trapped in this body by their foul magic."

She sniffed. "If ye'r Yamato, ye'd know not to talk to us."

"What do you mean?"

"'Cus we are *Eta*."

Bran gritted his teeth. *Eta*. He had heard the word before. The Untouchables, the outcasts, living even below the unhappy peasants. Of course they would be the only ones allowed to stay in the village. They were fit to deal with dung, dead corpses – and foreigners. Were Gorllewin even aware of the insult?

"Even so," he tried again, "surely you must hate the barbarians as much as I do?"

She shrugged. "I don't hate them. They don't treat us like animals. Slaves, yes – but human slaves."

He tried another approach.

"See this?" he asked, showing her his ring. It may have been a copy, but it was still a well-made piece of jewellery. "It's pure gold. If you help me, it's yours."

She stared at the ring without any expression on her face.

"If I were found with that amount of gold, I would be boiled alive as a thief."

"I would vouch for you. I have powerful friends. I would get you and your daughter out of here, out of this squalor – you have my word."

She laughed bitterly and shook her head. "Now I know ye'r no Yamato. A promise made to *Eta* is worth less than the contents of this pot."

She left, still shaking her head and laughing.

Bran's time was running out. Any day now the Council's delegation was expected to arrive. The girl steadfastly refused any contact. "*Oraya*," was all Bran managed to get out of her. "*Araya*."

Didn't your mother even bother to teach you to speak?

As she handed him his usual breakfast of a bowl of rice and shredded fish, he grabbed her hand and pulled her closer.

"Listen to me!"

She wriggled out of his grasp, surprisingly nimble; her skin was moist, slippery, almost snake-like, almost as if...

A sudden thought struck him. *Could it be...?*

He braced himself for the unexpected, but still what his True Sight revealed shocked him. The girl's body was covered with thick, oily fur, brown at the back, white at the front and the 'face'. The head was that of some cat-like animal, whiskered, blinking with tiny black eyes, darting back and forth in panic.

"I knew it – you're a *yōkai*!"

"*Araya!*" the creature whelped and burst out the door, sobbing.

Bran overheard the two guards outside, guffawing lewdly.

"The boy's so desperate he tried it on with a native!" said one.

"And an ugly one, at that!" laughed the other.

The whistles and cries of alarm were Bran's cue. He peered through the small window and saw the bright glow of a nearby fire. His True Sight revealed the guard at the back run off to see to the trouble. The two in front remained on an uneasy watch.

He waited for several excruciating seconds. The plan was far-fetched, but hope was all he had left.

Somebody scratched at the wall on the side of the bamboo grove, twice. A signal Bran had been waiting for. He summoned the Soul Lance and cut through the wattle and daub wall with ease. Getting out of the hut had never been the problem.

The dry summer bamboo burned quickly; steam trapped in the trunks hissed and exploded with deafening, gunshot-like noise; the entire grove sounded like a battlefield. There was no way anyone could spot him running away in all this chaos.

The heat was becoming unbearable, but the bamboo trees burned quickly, and the grove was small; it would soon burn out. Bran raised his hand and with a quick shot of dragon flame set fire to the hut's roof. The blaze shot up like a firework.

It will take them a while to find out if I made it out alive.

"Where's your daughter?" he asked the older woman, who was guiding him through the blazing forest.

"Beach," she said. Her voice was filled with a revulsion which hurt him almost physically.

He had no choice – he had to blackmail the old woman with revealing the truth to the Gorllewin and their Yamato hosts. The girl was a *Kawauso*, an Otter-demon, she'd told him. Another remnant of the Yōkai War, hiding among the Untouchables in place of the woman's late daughter.

"I will find you and repay you for your help," he said, but the woman gave him a pained look which told him she didn't believe a word of what he said.

The grove ended abruptly before a three-foot high stone wall. Bran recognized the administrative building in which the Komtur had him interrogated: the field headquarters of the Black Wings. The lights inside were out, and judging by what True Sight revealed, the building was mostly empty.

This is my only chance to find out what this is all about, thought Bran.

He told the old woman to wait. He leapt over the wall, crossed the tiny, single-tree garden and entered the building, thankful for the fact that the Yamato doors rarely had locks and that the Gorllewin had trusted enough in the strength of their arms not to fix that oversight.

The headquarters was small enough for Bran to find his way around without much hassle; only four rooms along a single corridor. There was a guard at the main entrance, but not at the back, where the compound was walled off. Bran scoffed at the lack of diligence at first, but then realized the reason: the original mission had arrived here on dragonback; it must have been formed of no more than a dozen Grey Hoods. The Komtur simply did not have enough manpower to guard every entrance. Only now were the reinforcements from the *Star* being discharged around the compound, and most of them must have been sent off to tackle the forest fire.

Barefoot, Bran paced the corridor as silent as a cat and reached the interrogation room door. He closed it behind him and lit up a faint flamespark.

He didn't hope for much. He expected the really important documents the Komtur kept in his private room, under lock and key. But there had to be *some* clues in the pile of densely written papers he found in the cabinet and desk drawers. He stuffed it all under his uniform and, as quietly as he came in, he walked out, leaping the wall and landing next to the old woman, who was crouched under a bush like a frightened rabbit.

They emerged onto the beach, at the far corner of the bay.

"There," the woman said, pointing at the sea.

"Where's the boat?"

"No boat."

Bran came up closer to the waterline until he saw the young girl standing waist-deep in the waves; naked, forlorn.

"What – "

The old woman forced him forward. "Quick."

He waded towards the girl. When he reached her, he turned back to the old woman for a second, wanting to say something. She stared back at him blankly, her features sagging and faltering. He had never before seen such resignation on a human's face. He had to turn away.

"I will repay you, I promise!" he said. The woman waved her hand, dismissively.

"*Oraya?*"

Before he could react, the girl wrapped her slippery arms around him tightly, pressed her lips to his and pulled him under the surface. He thrashed about in panic. He almost struck at the girl with magic, but then he realized he could still *breathe*. The air pushed into his lungs from the *Kawauso*'s mouth smelled of seaweed and mud, but was perfectly fine.

He opened his eyes, but could see nothing in the dark, murky water. The pressure tightened on his body. He could only hope the girl was taking him in the right direction, propelling them with strong strokes of her muscular legs and coils of her slim body, with the speed and ease of a fish. He had thought Yamato could not surprise him with anything anymore, but this was the strangest experience yet.

They emerged right by the side of the *Star of the Sea*. He spluttered and cleared salty water from his eyes. The fire on the shore had not yet died out. The ship, and the auxiliary vessels around it were all lit up as if on a parade, with colourful lanterns and signal lights hoisted above the deck.

In the moonless darkness the Gorllewin watchmen still hadn't spotted him.

They think that they are too powerful. That the Yamato are just spears and swords.

He felt anger bubble inside him at this recklessness. A single saboteur, like the one on *Ladon*, could easily wreak havoc in the flotilla. They were lucky, Bran thought, that all he really wanted was to get his dragon back and run away.

"I'll be fine from here," he said. The girl vanished noiselessly into the depths.

He swam up to the anchor chain of the *Star* and started climbing it, aiding himself with a little enhanced acrobatics. He leapt the last few feet to land on the deck, hoping he sounded as light as the otter-girl had in the water... The fore watchman was near; too near. Bran hid between the crates. He still hoped to sneak down to the stable decks, but it was unlikely; at some point, he would have to fight his way through.

The watchman lit a cigar and puffed out a cloud of white smoke, looking at the dying flames on the shore. Bran slipped behind him, but a moment later found himself almost face-to-face with another guard, leaning against the barrel of a cannon. Bran dropped to the floor in the shadows, and waited, but the guard didn't move. He, too, was enraptured with the infernal spectacle across the bay.

How lazy and complacent are these guards?

He felt Emrys directly below. He linked with the beast to see the situation through the eyes of the dragon. There were two men in the stall; one was watching the door, the other – he recognized Thorfinn, the rider – stood by a large, harpoon-like device aimed straight at the dragon's heart.

Any minute now they will receive their orders, thought Bran and forced himself to stay calm. Crawling, crouching and sneaking, he made his way to the iron stairwell leading to the lower decks.

"Who's there?" the guard finally noticed something was amiss. Bran scrambled down the stair as quietly as he could. It was pitch black down below, and he dared not shine a light. The guard's torch swept the floor. Bran hid in a small side corridor. The door at its end was locked.

Somebody was coming from down the main hallway. Bran was trapped; he clenched his right hand, ready to summon the Lance. The shadow of a man crept towards him.

The mane of golden hair was unmistakable.

"Leif!" Bran whispered.

The chaplain turned, surprised. "Bra – "

Bran sprang, covered Leif's mouth with his hand and pulled him back into the small corridor.

"Be silent."

"Leif, is that you?" the guard cried from above. Bran snapped his fingers; they burst into flame before the chaplain's face.

"If you try anything, I'll burn your eyes out," he whispered. Leif nodded; Bran released his mouth.

"Yes, Madoc, don't worry. I just stumbled on these damn stairs."

The guard chuckled and walked away.

"I need your help, Leif," Bran said. "They're going to kill my dragon."

"I know. I just spoke to the Vice Komtur. I'm sorry, Bran, but I can't go against the Komtur's orders. It would be treason."

Bran summoned his Lance. Clenching his teeth and frowning in its faint, blue light, he could only hope he looked as desperate as he felt.

"If Emrys dies, I will have nothing to lose. How many men will get killed before you subdue me, do you think? In these cramped corridors, where you can't count on your black dragons…?"

Leif opened his mouth then closed it. Then opened it again.

"What do you want me to do?"

Leif opened the stall door. The soldier leapt up and aimed his rifle at him before sighing with relief.

"By the Bull, Leif, don't you ever knock?"

"I'm sorry. You're wanted upstairs."

"Me?" The soldier looked at Leif suspiciously. "What for?"

"How do I know?" Leif shrugged and smiled nervously.

Don't be so nervous, thought Bran, observing the exchange from the shadows. He had one distinct advantage over the men inside: watching the scene through the eyes of his dragon, he knew exactly where each of the guards stood, and could plan out his attack in detail.

The soldier shook his head. "I don't know. There's supposed to be two of us here at all times."

"Oh, I can wait," volunteered Leif. "I can't sleep tonight anyway."

The two soldiers looked at each other; Thorfinn shrugged.

"Who wants me?" asked the other one.

"Madoc, I think. He's by the cannon."

"Right. This better not be some kind of a prank. I'm not in the mood."

He passed Bran by a breath, muttering curses to himself. As soon as he disappeared up the stairwell, Bran charged inside, straight toward the harpoon gun.

But Thorfinn was faster than Bran had expected; in a swift move he swivelled the cannon and squizzed the trigger, releasing the giant lance.

"*Rhew!*"

Bran's fiery missile met the harpoon mid-flight. The explosion threw both men apart, showering Bran's *tarian* shield with debris and hot oil.

Leif howled and ran outside, screaming for help.

The Gorllewin rider scrambled up first. Ignoring his scorched wounds, he drew a gunpowder pistol. The bullets bounced off the boy's *bwcler*. Thorfinn dropped the gun, grabbed the eagle-shaped hilt of his sword and charged forward. The blade burst with bright red dragonflame. A round shield of thin, folded metal unrolled instantly from a bracer on his left arm.

Bran swept his Lance in panic. The weapons clashed with a loud crackle, Thorfinn's sword surprisingly resistant to the blade of light.

I don't have time.

He panicked. He wasn't planning on a *sword fight*. Thorfinn was the better fencer of the two of them. He struck again, a deft, swift cut, which nearly took Bran by surprise. He parried it with the *bwcler* and missed his chance to strike. Another blow made the *bwcler* flicker; the flame burned hot against Bran's face. He pushed the Gorllewin away and whirled the Lance, aiming low, at the enemy's legs.

At that moment, a thick plume of bluish dragon flame enveloped Thorfinn's head and upper body: Emrys had decided to join the fight. The Gorllewin screamed, shielded himself from the fire and fell forward.

Straight on Bran's Lance.

The blade of pure light sliced him neatly in two with no resistance, just below his unprotected waist. Blood and guts splattered around.

For a moment yet, Thorfinn lived; he reached his hand towards Bran, twitching on the sword hilt in spasms, his mouth twisted, wheezing. The other half of his body lay strangely separate, jerking in deathly throes.

Bran stood transfixed. *No time*, he repeated to himself in shock. *No time.*

211

He forced himself to look away. He wiped the blood off his face, cut through the chains holding Emrys, and leapt onto its neck. The dragon roared and spat a ball of fire into the corridor, and then turned around to face the ramp leading out of the stables onto the quarterdeck.

Tearing its way through the thin metal bulk, Emrys climbed outside into the night. Bran heard gunshots but bullets could not pierce the dragon scales, reinforced now by the rider's shields.

Don't they have any dragon-slaying weapons?

He got his answer immediately. With a whining of chains and the hissing of mistfire, the great turret in the middle of the quarterdeck rotated until the twin barrels of its missile launcher were aiming straight at Emrys.

"Up!" cried Bran, and pulled Emrys into the air just as the first rocket whizzed underneath them. The proximity fuse exploded, throwing the dragon and the rider aside. For a moment, Bran found himself hanging upside down, holding on to the dragon's horns. Another rocket burst right above Bran's head, deafening him; the *tarian* buzzed blue, showered with shrapnel.

But they were getting away. The shore was close. Emrys was giving all it had, flying for its life at breakneck speed. Soon they were above the fishing village, the temple, and the sizzling bamboo grove.

Bran looked back. The great shadow cast by the Black Wings was unmistakable. The first of the dragons was already in the air, rising swiftly from the deck of the *Star*.

The ship was far behind, and Bran was sure this time he'd be able to get away. He relaxed his grip on the dragon's horns...

In the corner of his eye he noticed another dark shape dimming the stars to his left.

Annwn's Hounds...!

He had forgotten about the dragons on land. The Firstborn and its brethren had already caught his scent. Another rose to his right, heading for the mountains rising on the moonlit horizon to cut off his escape route.

At his current speed he could lose two, maybe three pursuers... but not all seven. His heart sank. Was everything lost after all? He needed some trick.

As skilled a rider as he was, he was a burden to his mount. Alone, Emrys got through the Sea Maze and flew across the wide ocean to Yamato, without a rider trying to steer it according to his own whims and needs.

Bran unbuckled the thin leather belt of the Gorllewin uniform and tied his hands over the dragon's neck to make sure he wouldn't fall off during the swift manoeuvres. He was not yet in the blind, mindless rage necessary to summon the Dragonform, but if his guess was correct, he no longer had to be.

A deep breath and a brief invocation later, he world around him slowed down and magnified. The wind, the lights, the smells, all became brighter and more powerful. Looking below, he saw a tiny squirrel jumping from tree to tree with an owl in grim pursuit. Above him, the stars beamed like tiny Suns. He sensed the Ninth Wind like currents of water washing over his body. There was no need for him to steer, he let the dragon pick its own path through the streams of air, making sure only that it headed in the right direction – deeper inland, into the mountains.

In his-their-mind, Bran-Emrys drew a complex, twisting flight path, shooting madly through river canyons and forested gullies, until all below – the trees, the rocks, the forest shrines, the mountain streams – was just a dark grey blur.

Still they came; the Black Wings in relentless pursuit. They weren't letting him go easily this time. The Firstborn was leading the chase. Bran could sense its primeval, snarling joy, like that of the chief wolf at the head of the pack. And the others were not far behind. The buzz of the Farlink commands coming from all seven riders was almost unbearable. The forest around Bran-Emrys erupted with the fire balls the dragons started spewing in excitement. Splinters and scorched particles of earth rained from the sky.

And then, suddenly, it all stopped. Bran returned to his own body and looked back to find that the Black Wings had halted as if they'd come up against some invisible barrier. A couple of stray fireballs flew past Emrys, sizzling the treetops, but no more.

They almost had us. Why did they stop?

He looked down and saw a silver-grey ribbon of a wide river valley cutting right across the mountains from east to west. *A border river*, he realized. *They can't fly farther than this. Not until the treaties are signed.*

He felt his left leg burn with sharp, intense pain. One of the fireballs must have grazed it. Emrys' scales, too, were blackened in several places.

I have to get down before I fall off...

He flew around a few wooded hilltops and found one remote enough to hope he would not be found by a search party before dawn, and landed between two towering cedar trees.

"We made it," he said, stroking the dragon's scales. "We made it."

But he was in no mood to celebrate. The dying gasps of Thorfinn the dragon rider rang in his ears as he fell into a tired sleep.

Komtur Perai coughed and squinted, forcing a few tears out of his eyes. The scorched bamboo grove was still smouldering billows of grey, sharp, biting smoke.

He picked up a shard of the hut's wall, baked by the heat into a piece of pottery, and weighed it in his hand.

"That's cut off neatly," he muttered to himself.

Just like poor Thorfinn.

He turned to face his Seneschal, running up the hill from the temple below.

"The Councillor's boat is coming," the Seneschal announced. "The patrol's seen it right off the Narcissus Cape."

The Komtur threw the shard back onto the pile of rubble and wiped his hand on his uniform. "Hurry up with that," he ordered the soldiers, cleaning up the debris, "and pay attention to tracks, if you can find any. I need to know who helped him escape."

"You think he had help?" asked the Seneschal.

"He must have. How else did he get to the ship?"

"But who would betray us?"

"Not my men, that's for sure. I've known every one of them since they were ensigns. I can't vouch for those who came with the ships, though. That chaplain, Eiriksson, for example… I'll raise this with Aulick tonight."

"What about the Yamato?"

The Komtur looked at the eerily quiet fishing village sprawled beneath the temple. It had been emptied of all the inhabitants prior to their arrival, except a few chosen by their Yamato hosts to serve the needs of the dragon riders. He never trusted any of them.

"I'm sure they have spies among the servants, but they don't speak our language. And the boy wouldn't know theirs."

"That's what he said. We know he's been here before."

"And we know a month ago he was on a Dracalish ship bound for Huating. It would take a genius to grasp this language in such a short time. Has the girl been found yet?"

The Seneschal shook his head. "Gone without a trace. We have her mother, but she's just blethering some gibberish about demons."

216

The Komtur wrinkled his nose. "I don't think I trust Otokichi with this interrogation. These are his own people, after all. The better we have our own interpreters the better."

"Brother Gwilym is trying his best, Komtur."

"I know, Seneschal. But sometimes, our best may not be enough."

He raised his eyes to the horizon to where a thin plume of black smoke still rose from the deck of the *Star*.

So much damage caused by one boy. He'll pay for it…

A large, ornate rowing barge, painted bright red and festooned with flags and lampions, appeared slowly from beyond the tip of the peninsula, and stopped. The Komtur imagined the chaos aboard; the scrambling officials, the confused orders. This was the first that the Yamato delegation had seen a Gorllewin ship, and it didn't help that the *Star of the Sea* was one of the largest and most modern in the fleet. Compared to her, the barge was a mere speck.

"What do we tell them?" asked the Seneschal.

"Nothing."

"But – they will ask…"

"About what, a fire in the bamboo grove? These things must happen all the time." The Komtur took off his spectacles, cleaned them of soot and put them back on. "What do you want me to tell them? That we lost a prisoner? That we allowed a *boy* to run free all around our base? That a foreigner whom, let me remind you, *we* brought to Yamato, is now somewhere *out there*, in the non-treaty territory, probably on his way to *Taikun*'s enemies in Satsuma? That he

217

stole our treaty drafts? Do you know what that would do to our prestige? We need that settlement, Seneschal. Our country needs it."

"What if they find him?"

The Komtur glanced one last time at the damaged *Star* and shook his head with resignation.

"Well, Seneschal – let's just pray that they won't."

CHAPTER X

There was no respite in the night.

The ground shook from the elemental bombardment, as blasts of dragon flame and lightning tore the darkness apart. The siege of Suchou, the rebel capital, had entered its final stages.

Edern stood on the battlements of a small fortalice they had captured a week earlier, and watched the violent fireworks erupt over and beyond the mighty walls of the city, as the wizards and dragons tried with all their might to pierce through the magic shield surrounding it – a miniature version of the bubble barrier protecting Qin. Somewhere in the west, a squadron of Blues fought against a patrol of *longs*, a flicker of colourful sparks marked their complex manoeuvres. In the north, a rebel hill fort was slowly dying in the shower of rockets fired from a gunboat which had managed to make its way far up the Wusong River.

Edern stretched his arms and rubbed his cat-like eyes. The bright colourful flashes of the magic eruptions, which he could see without the need for True Sight, were hurting his head. The Tylwyth Teg could survive long without sleep or food, but this was his fifth waking night in a row, and the strain was beginning to take its toll. There was always the danger of a night sally from Suchou, and Edern believed he had to be there for his men just in case.

The responsibility of commanding the entire great Western army was a heavy burden, and one that Edern had never prepared for, despite his long service in the Royal Marines. He had been trained more than sufficiently to be able to replace the Ardian if he fell in battle. But the rank of a *Commodore* was never in his sights.

It's not that he lacked ambition. But a Tylwyth reaching such a high position was unthinkable in the predominantly human Dracalish army. Simply put, it didn't happen. He wasn't even a real soldier, a conscript – but a mercenary bound with a temporary contract with Her Imperial Majesty's army. He fully expected to be relieved of his rank as soon as this damn war was over. And the day could not come sooner.

He may have been Arthur's Kin, but he was no Arthur the Faer and his dragon was not Y Ddraig Goch. He tried his best to manage, but with each day he was growing more exhausted and restless.

Edern tried his best to emulate Dylan's strategies with what little resources he had to spare, and had done so with considerable success. That he could plan and conduct operations all day and night was certainly to his advantage, as was the natural swiftness of reflexes and intuition which, when applied to strategy, allowed him to react to the events faster than any human commander. A chain of surprising victories led his army to the walls of Suchou in what must've been record time. It wasn't the end of the war yet – Jiankang,

Qin's Southern Capital, still remained in the firm grip of the rebels, and their vast regional armies were still spread far and wide all over the hinterland, but the inevitable fall of Suchou was bound to be at least the beginning of the end.

This should have been a reason to celebrate for the victorious commander. But Edern's thoughts were far from celebratory. He was tired, irritated, and above all, bored of this slog of a war that he and his men had to take part in for reasons he could not fathom. His contract with the army obliged him not to question his orders openly, but that didn't mean he never pondered them in his head.

His soldiers were itching to move on to another campaign. They were marines: mobile, brutal, fast; used to jumping from one frontline to another wherever a short, sharp, surgical strike was needed. But this was a different kind of war. At some point, after another lost battle, the rebels had lost their technological advantage: either they ran out of resources, or their suppliers ran out of patience. What they lacked in machines and strategy, they made up for in numbers. Thousands after thousands of their fighters poured at the fully mechanized defensive lines in a massive suicidal rush.

This was a moment when, according to the rules of the kind of war Edern was familiar with, the dragoons should have been replaced, or at least supported, by the regular infantry; it was the grunt's role to stay in one place and bear the brunt of an onslaught, and then push the frontline slowly onwards. But Dracaland had no more soldiers to spare. Rumour had it, the Taurica situation, that Roman wart in the Varyagan underside, had finally burst open. Scythian Sea was much closer to home than far-away Qin, and much more important. The grunts were needed over there.

And so here they were, stuck in an endless chain of sieges and set-piece battles, month after month, just because the General Staff couldn't find anyone better to send as their replacement. They'd become victims of their own success, the name given to them by the Qin – the Ever Victorious Army – was now a curse.

That their commanding officer, the man who had brought them here in the first place, had gone missing – presumed dead – didn't help the morale either. For a few weeks, Edern had expected to hear something from, or about, Dylan, but eventually, he had lost faith and interest. Perhaps the Ardian – and Edern would always think of him as an Ardian – had perished on the clandestine mission, or perhaps it was still on-going in full secrecy. Either way, Edern had enough on his plate to gradually forget about the matter altogether. It was only in nights like this one, when there was enough time for his mind to wander, that he wondered where the Ardian had gone and what secret had required him to abandon his troops so abruptly.

Why didn't you take me with you? he thought. *Why only Gwen?*

A complex web of lightning tore the veil of the Suchou Barrier apart. This was not the breach everyone waited for. Edern's keen eyes pierced the darkness, and he saw clearly a troop of enemy cavalry sallying forth from the opening on the backs of the leaping Bishiu beasts. He surveyed the field quickly. A flank of the besieging army lay wide open before the attack.

He stretched sore muscles. His reserve force, resting in the camp, was the closest to the breakout. He blew the alarm whistle, and then ran towards the dragon enclosure where Nodwydd, his mount, waited impatiently to join the action.

Samuel stood in the middle of the steel corridor rooted to the spot in fear. Freezing-cold mist was rising around him, seeping from underneath the iron door with a hiss.

Something banged on the door from inside, repeatedly, a rhythmic, metallic thud. Once, twice, three times. The door bulged, cracking and heaving; the rivets flew out of their sockets. The fourth bang smashed it open, showering the corridor with metal splinters.

He woke up. The bell-tower was ringing out the fourth hour. A rhythmic, metallic thud...

I must have dozed off in the heat, he realized. *What did I dream about?*

The remnants of the nightmare quickly vanished from his memory, leaving just a lingering feeling of dread. It took him a moment to remember where he was, and why he was there: a small, walled garden of fragrant roses and rainbow-coloured tulips.

Dejeema.

It was an almost perfect imitation of a piece of the Bataavians' homeland. How they had managed to create it here, in a different climate, on a tiny artificial island in a hostile country, on the other side of the globe, was the source of Samuel's unceasing wonder.

He plucked an unripen rose from a bush and placed it thoughtfully on top of a large rune-stone set in the middle of the herb plot.

"Ah, there you are, *Doktor*."

The Admiral appeared behind Samuel, wearing his most elegant uniform and full regalia, his beard trimmed and his golden buttons gleaming; immaculate.

"I see you've come straight from the meeting with the Magistrate," said Samuel.

Otterson nodded. "*Alle* sorted. We are leaving in a few days."

"Leaving? Where for?"

"*Yedo*. The *kapital*."

"That's – good, isn't it?"

"*Ja*. The *Magistrat* was most eager to finally get rid of us, and the only way was to make us somebody else's problem."

"How come? The Bataavians I spoke to were certain we would get nowhere with the Yamato."

Otterson smoothed his long, black beard.

"Things are changing, *Doktor*. The revolution seems to have started without us… And that other power I told you about? They are already in *Yedo*. Nobody's saying it, but I can read *mellan raderna*… between the lines well enough."

"Ah, the other power. You still haven't told me who they are. Is it still a secret?"

The Admiral glanced around before answering.

"No, I think not. You'd learn as soon as we reached Yedo anyway. We call them Vinlander – but you know them as the Gorllewin."

Gorllewin?

Samuel blinked and then slowly nodded. The mystery proved not as surprising as he had thought it to be. There weren't that many nations sending merchant ships out into the waters of Orient, and the Admiral had already ruled out most of them, so the Gorllewin were always one of the prime candidates. Besides, the question of who was never as important as the *how* and *why*. Otterson had a state-of-the-art under-sea ship that let him sail past the Sea Maze... what did the Gorllewin have? And what made them aim for Yamato as the first target?

"Whose *grav* is this?" the Admiral asked, nodding at the runestone.

"Oh, it's not a grave," replied Samuel. "It's a memorial stone set up by one Bataavian physician in memory of his predecessor."

"Ah, another *Doktor!* I see."

"I knew the man who founded it. I met him last year in Transvaal. I never knew he was in Yamato as well."

The dragon figurine I got from him... I gave it to the Ardian's son, he remembered. He tried not to think too often of the ship's disaster and the death of so many of good people, so many of his friends. Death at sea was a sailor's lot – a navy-man's even more so. But he did feel sorry for the boy – his life had been cut far too short...

225

The Admiral leaned in to read the runes. "Von Siebold…" His eyes widened. "That's the spion who led us to Yamato!"

"Ah. So not *just* a physician, then."

"That's quite a… coincidence," said the Admiral, frowning.

"Not that big, when you think about it," replied Samuel. "Bataave does not have that many colonies left. A well-travelled man – a spy and a scientist – was bound to find his way through most of them, eventually."

The Admiral stood over the runestone for a while in silence, thinking intently.

"You *Drakalanders* and Bataavians have much in common, *nej?*"

"How so?"

"You are just tiny nations on the edge of the *sjoe* – and yet you are now everywhere. Even here. So strange."

He shook his head, his beard swaying from side to side.

"The Khaganate is here, too."

"Ah, but that is different. With us, it was inevitable."

He crouched down by the tulips and ran his fingers through the p*Eta*ls, his bulky frame made to seem even greater by the contrast with the dainty flowers.

"There is a legend in my country," he said. "When Reurig, the first Khagan, was fleeing from Arthur the Faer's armies, he found a *kulle* – a hill on an island in the middle of a lake. On its top he had a vision: to the *Vaest* stretched a

226

great wall of stone, manned by warriors clad in steel. To the *Oest*, an empty forest, ready for the taking. He built a great city on the island – *Holmgard*, our *kapital*. And we have been looking Eastwards ever since."

He stood up and turned his back to the slowly setting sun.

"But the forest was not empty. It took us a thousand years to wrestle it from the man-beasts, the varulvs, the *bjorn* shamans, the tiger-skins… along the way, we've conquered the steppe from the Horse Lords, and the desert from the Tosharans, and we've built the greatest Empire the world has ever seen – and finally we reached the *Stora Havet* – the Great Ocean. We thought that was enough."

"And then you've learned about Yamato."

The Admiral nodded.

"There are small islands far to the north of here near the icy wastes… the Varyaga built outposts there to trade seal fur and *valspaek* – whale fat with the local tribes. They told us of another island, big and rich, from which *kopmen* – traders came wielding steel swords and paid with gold and silver for the furs, not with glass and pig iron, like us. And it lay to the east of our shores, where we once thought there was nothing more… we simply *had* to find it."

"I thought this spy… this Von Siebold told you all you needed to know?"

"*Nej.*" Otterson shook his head. "He filled out the gaps in our knowledge, but we knew where to look long before he came to us. The *kopmen* the tribesmen spoke of… ten years ago, we – I raided their outposts and captured some men, though most preferred to die rather than surrender. We interrogated them with the help of the island tribesmen. Only then were we certain that the kopmen were coming from Yamato through the Sea Maze, and not some Qin or Chosun dependency."

"So you've met the Yamato before."

"*Ja.* I even know a little of the language. Made the negotiations run a bit faster."

The Admiral was unexpectedly frank today, and yet Samuel sensed there was still something important Otterson wasn't telling him. That thing at the lowest deck, he remembered with a shudder. *What is it for? What else did the Varyaga learn from the Yamato merchants?*

"I should go," he said, rolling a tulip stem in his fingers. "The Bataavian doctor asked me to help him with a patient. Although I think he's just happy to have somebody to talk to."

Nagomi absentmindedly picked at the rice with a chopstick. She still felt as if the earth beneath her feet rolled slightly back and forth, but that was just an illusion – they were on dry land, at an inn in some small castle town somewhere past Okayama.

Half-way through a yawn she realized what she was doing and covered her mouth, looking around nervously. Luckily, the bear-man seemed equally distracted, playing with the small wooden slat upon which a piece of silken paper was glued – their permit of passage, a forgery produced by the Chōfu conspirators who had helped them get across the mountains of Todō province.

After a week's journey together, they had split from Takasugi in Naniwa. He boarded another, smaller ship, to get any pursuit off their backs. Nagomi promised to pray for his safe arrival in Chōfu, but she soon forgot about her pledge.

"How many more of these stations before us?" Torishi asked, rolling the *tegata* in his fingers. The forgery was good, but every time they had to present it to the officials along the way, the tension was unbearable.

"I'm sorry?" Nagomi raised her eyes from the breakfast. "Oh, I'm not sure. The boats are not checked as often as the roads. We should be fine from now."

"You seem distracted. Visions, again?"

She paused for a second.

"I had the dream today."

"The one with the dragon?"

She nodded.

"You must pull that sword out."

"I know, but... I'm too terrified to move. You know how it is with dreams."

"You must try, little priestess," he said, clenching his fist in encouragement. "Something is waiting at the end of that vision. The third verse. It must be the key."

They had been pouring over the words she'd heard in her vision, trying to decipher their meaning. Who was the boy who couldn't be seen? What man and beast were torn apart? Neither of them could guess.

"I understand. I will try next time."

"Think of the sword before you go to sleep. It helps."

She nodded and pushed the rice bowl away and stood up. The floor beneath her swayed. She wasn't sure if it was a tremor or her still weary legs.

"What did you say?" she asked.

Torishi raised his head.

"I didn't say anything."

"Strange. I'd swear I heard somebody calling me."

There she was again, on the veranda of the Itō house in Nagoya, with the rampaging dragon roaring in the garden. The floor beneath her feet rumbled with the approaching steps of the slobbering monster.

She bit on her lips until blood trickled down her chin. The pain tore her out of her petrified stupor. She stumbled down from the veranda and ran up to the sword stuck in the dragon's paw. The beast spat a cloud of steam and vile gas all around her, but it let her pass and she pulled with all her might, drawing out the sword; black blood splattered her snow white kimono. The dragon roared with the force of the hurricane – and disappeared.

Nagomi was left alone with the ancient sword in her trembling hands. The eight-headed monster burst into the garden. Nagomi retreated. The monster crawled towards her with all of its sixteen eyes staring at the blade with hatred.

Somebody stepped beside Nagomi and took the sword out of her hands. A tall boy, roughly her age... She had a feeling she had seen him somewhere before, but she couldn't see his face clearly enough to recognize him.

He charged at the monster and, with one strike, cut off all of its eight heads. The black, oily carcass fell down, dead. The boy turned back to Nagomi, wiping the sword on the silk of his robe – a robe marked with the golden seal in the shape of a chrysanthemum flower.

The bamboo flute trilled once again. The whispering female voice returned, at last.

What was dead will be reborn,

What was lost shall not be mourned.

The boy nodded at her. He opened his mouth to speak, but the monster behind him rose again, growing eight new heads and fell on the boy, throwing him to the ground and tearing him apart as Nagomi watched, unable to run, unable to fight.

When she woke up, she tasted blood.

The peasant's wife looked over the yard one last time, then went back inside the house and shut the door. Bran waited a while longer, hidden in the tall grass until the faint candle light inside went off and the family went to sleep.

He crawled through the grass to the granary shed. Underneath the floor of the thatched hut, between the four tall oaken pillars, stood several clay jars, each half the height of a man, their lids weighed down with heavy stones. This was exactly what Bran was looking for. He removed the first stone, trying to make as little sound as possible. He winced at the burst of pain in his leg.

The first jar seemed to be filled with sour, fermenting rice, but Bran already knew that was where the best food was hidden. He reached deep into the stinking brown mass and pulled out juicy morsels of marinated fish. He put them into a small jute sack he had stolen from the previous farm, and then reached into another jar. This one was full of soured forest veg*Eta*bles; an unappetizing pile of deep green and brown shoots and leaves, plants, the names of which Bran didn't know, but already knew were filling. He packed them into the sack too.

He already had enough to last him for the day, but decided to try the third jar. As he raised the heavy boulder, it slipped from his hands and crashed into the lid. In the silence of the night the sound reverberated like a gunshot.

The door of the hut slammed open, and the farmer ran out, naked, brandishing a sickle. Bran grabbed his sack and, without looking back, ran off through the tall grass as fast as his injured leg allowed him, trampling the barley field and splashing across a small rice paddy, towards the forest.

He reached the line of trees and fell panting to the warm, moist ground. The farmer had abandoned the pursuit, too scared to venture by himself into the forest at night.

Limping and hissing, Bran found his way to the glade where he had left Emrys. The dragon looked at him, yawned, and returned to the carcass of a deer it had almost finished eating. Like the great reptiles it descended from, Emrys could go for several days without food, but eventually, Bran had to allow it to venture deep into the mountains to prey on the wild animals there. The Yamato deer were too small to share.

Bran himself had neither the skill nor the strength for hunting. He had once caught a snake, but he couldn't cook it properly, and the meat, burned to crisp with dragon flame, was disgusting. Hungry, tired, and increasingly feverish, he had to resort to stealing food from the mountain farmers.

He reached into the sack; the fish and the vegEtables were squashed together into a brown-green pulp, but he was too hungry to care, and devoured the contents of the jute bag, gagging on the strong taste of vinegar.

He touched his leg. The wound was taking a long time to heal. In fact, it didn't seem to be healing at all. The skin on his thigh was still a mess of seeping red blisters.

If I don't treat it soon, I might lose that leg, he thought with cold clarity.

He limped over to a small spring and washed the wound in the freezing cold water. He splashed some on his itching cheeks. He had not shaved since the Grey Hoods put him into his cell. It was the least of his worries, but it did irritate him more than he'd expected.

Two days earlier Bran had decided that he could no longer simply keep to the coast; he was certain it was taking him too far the wrong way, so he turned inland, towards the setting moon. Soon wild mountain ranges rose across his path, and it was there, trying to find yet another shortcut, that he finally lost his way for good. Whenever Bran tried to cut short through what he thought was a bay or gulf, he would end up far out into the sea with no land in sight, and had to retrace his route before Emrys ran out of strength. That they had to fly at night didn't help with the orientation. Bran dared not risk being spotted by a passing fishing boat or a harbour watchman. At night, his only guidance was the moon and the stars, and the lingering glow of the waves dashing against the shore.

"Come on," Bran said with some effort, "it's time. Let's try to get *somewhere* tonight."

Slowly, gritting his teeth in pain, he mounted Emrys. A thousand knives pierced his leg. Wobbling, they flew off into the warm summer night. He didn't want to accept it, but it was becoming apparent that they were hopelessly lost.

From the top of the bald hill Bran watched the sea stretching before him in a scattering of tiny islets and small, narrow capes, jutting out like the fingers of a giant. Fishing boats launched into the dawn, and the farmers marched off into the fields; an obedient army of workers, each his own quartermaster.

What sea it was, and what lay beyond it, Bran had no idea. What he thought he remembered from studying the Yamato map had long vanished, leaving only the faint outline of the complex archipelago. Was Satsuma more to the west, or to the south? Where was Kiyō? Or Ganryūjima? The scale of this land evaded him; several times already he had thought he'd seen the peaks of Kirishima, only to discover it was yet another nameless and featureless range, with the same indistinguishable forested gullies and villages in the narrow valleys.

"For all I know, we could be going in circles," he said.

Emrys belched a ball of flaming methane. Its digestive system was just finishing dealing with another mountain deer. Bran, on the other hand, was still hungry – and thirsty. The summer heat was beginning to take its toll on him.

A small castle rose at the edge of one of the finger-like capes, layers of snow-white walls and curved slate roofs, like a wedding cake. Bran imagined himself storming the castle with Emrys and terrorizing the town below, demanding to bring before him the local healers and all the best food the domain had to offer: fresh fish, white rice, cold noodles, summer fruit... his mouth watered at the thought.

He wondered how long he would manage to leap from one castle to another before *Taikun*'s wizards came after him, and how long he could fight them before they finally subdued and killed him.

Every time he took to flying it was getting more difficult. Even in a saddle, a rider's strong legs were his most important asset. Bareback, they were essential. Soon he would be unable to ride at all without some way to alleviate the pain. He shook his head. There was no point going anywhere further like this. He had to try something else.

He knelt down in the tall grass, with his feet straight, as Shigemasa had taught him. The aching in his leg felt a little weaker that way. He put one hand in his lap, and the other on the dragon's warm neck, breathed in deeply, closed his eyes and, trying his best to ignore the waves of hunger, exhaustion and pain, focused on his own mind.

It seemed to take ages, but eventually, the howling of the wind around him and the cries of the men below ceased. He smelled blood and opened his eyes. It was the plain of the red dirt, and he was looking at it from above, from the top of the red light tower; at last, the only lord and master of his own private domain in this strange land.

He called on Emrys, and the dragon came flying, dazed at finding itself all of a sudden in another world. Bran mounted it deftly.

"Where now?" he asked aloud.

The plain seemed as empty as ever; only the misty peaks of the mountains marking the border of the world of the dead loomed far on the horizon. And yet, Bran knew there were others here, and there was a way to navigate to them…

How did the Grey Hoods manage this?

He tried to first detect the Black Wings, the way he had before. He felt them in the distance, faintly but clearly; seven dots, seven pulsating beacons. If he so wished, he could trace them… but he didn't have time. He had to find his friends.

He figured he had more chance of finding Nagomi's presence in the Otherworld, so he tried to visualize her, to remember as much about her as he could: the fiery hair, the white and red clothes, the dark, almond-shaped eyes, the quiet, shy voice...

He remembered her naked in the stream near Kumamoto, where the girls bathed; he remembered her warm, clumsy lips on his, in the dark corridor of the Kagoshima inn; he remembered carrying her dying, on the cold floor of the cave at Kirishima. All those moments burst into his mind, more vivid and forceful than any memory. These were no longer mere recollections, he realized – these were visions. And they were *coming to him* from one direction.

He opened his eyes. The outside world returned, attacking him with noises and smells; but the clear sense of direction remained.

THE CHRYSANTHEMUM SEAL

CHAPTER XI

The view from the walls of the Meirinkan stretched all the way down to the sea; a narrow, crowded strait framed by the hump of the Mekari Mountain on the other side. This was the busiest shipping lane in Yamato – one could almost imagine getting across it just by leaping from one boat to another.

But none of these boats carried the passengers Satō was waiting for.

"Still no news?"

She turned away from the sea. Shōin stood in the shadow of the wall, smiling and nervously crushing the edge of his *hakama*. Since she'd agreed to marry him, he'd become even more timid and anxious in her presence. It made her angry.

"She will come," she replied, "she promised."

"I know. It's just... Mori-*dono* is growing impatient. It's been so long – "

"I'm not having a wedding without Nagomi," she interrupted him fiercely. "I've known her since we were babies. She's – "

Her voice broke. *She's my only family. If something's happened to her...*

"How are the new recruits?" she asked, changing the subject.

"Promising," he said. His smile was genuine this time. "Once the word came out we have a new teacher from Kiyō, they started arriving from all over the province. Everyone knows that's where the best *Rangaku* scholars come from."

"I'm hardly a scholar."

"Well – before you came, I was the best they had," he said, and laughed briefly. He didn't laugh often – his laughter was high-pitched and wheezing, and he was ashamed of its sound.

"Ah, that reminds me," she said, leaping off the wall. "There is something I wanted your *onmyōji* to investigate. Now that we have more students perhaps they can spare some time?"

"Of course – what is it?"

"Meet me at the laboratory – I'll bring it over."

She carried the red orb carefully in the fold of her sleeve. It was warm to touch, though not as hot as when she had first received it from Dōraku. The temperature and the brightness of the flickering light inside were the only things she could observe on her own. There was little else she could do to pierce the jewel's mysteries. Her father had a knack for analysing artefacts, but it was exactly the kind of meticulous and painstaking research she had never found the patience for. In more peaceful times, she would send it to another scholar like Master Tanaka, or Master Zōzan… but that was out of the question now. She could not risk the orb falling into the wrong hands, again.

If it even was some kind of ancient anti-dragon weapon, right now it remained nothing but a curiosity. Even

Ganryū must have been keeping it in some dark corner of his treasury, not expecting to ever find a use for it, until Bran came to Yamato… and with the boy gone, so was the only *dorako* she could test it on.

She reached the doors of the main hall and halted. She took a deep breath, grit her teeth and went inside.

To reach the laboratory wing, at the far side of the building, she first had to pass through all of the classrooms and lecture halls. And that meant walking past all of Meirinkan's students, who now knew who she was. The rumour of the Headmaster's engagement spread fast throughout the school, followed by the mind-boggling revelation that Takashima-*sensei* was a *woman*.

Boys she could ignore. Many of them, younger and less experienced, still had a shred of respect for the wizardess. It was the older men…

The jeers started from the moment she entered the hall.

"Hey, it's the *sensei*'s woman!"

"Are you sure it's a woman? Doesn't look like one to me."

"It's easy to check – just look under that *hakama*."

"I'd rather fondle a boar!"

She bit her lips and tightened her fists. *It doesn't matter*, she kept telling herself. *You're better than this.*

"What's that at her belt? Is that a thunder gun?" asked somebody in the next room. Her heart skipped a beat. Was there actually somebody interested in *Rangaku* technology here? She turned to speak to whoever said it, but all around her were the same mocking, lecherous faces.

"I wouldn't mind her polishing *my* gun," was the jeering response.

She cursed inwardly. It was all just a set-up for another joke. She shoved aside a small boy who stumbled in her way by accident and pressed on.

"You'd have to ask the *sensei* for permission first," the anonymous clown continued.

"That upstart kid? I'd only need to speak to Mori-*dono* and he'd have to bring her to my bed tonight," guffawed the first voice.

"Right, that's *enough!*"

She stopped and turned slowly. She raised a hand. Ice crackled around her fingers and started forming into a sharp spear. The men stepped back, the mocking smiles melting from their faces.

"Takashima-*sensei*, no!"

Shōin grabbed her by the hand and pulled her towards him. She stumbled, and the ice spear flew over the heads of the students, shattering into a thousand splinters on the ceiling.

"The – the laboratory is ready," he stuttered, swallowing hard. "Please, come with me."

"Why did you stop me?"

Satō still trembled with fury. She had forgotten all about the red orb; all she could think of were the smirks of the men in the lecture hall, and the pleasure with which she'd have wiped them off their faces.

Shōin sighed heavily.

"They are Mori-*dono*'s direct vassals. Anger them, and this school is no more. Hurt them, and *you* could be arrested."

"So they can just do whatever they want?"

"After the we- wedding this should all stop," he stuttered again, swallowing hard. "You too will be a Mori, just like them."

She prodded him.

"You're one, and it doesn't help you much."

"Believe me, it does," he said with a pained smile.

"Why are they even here?"

"I think it's the *daimyo*'s orders. He wants some of the high ranking samurai to learn magic too. That makes them even more resentful... and they're taking it out on us."

"I don't care *what* makes them like that. Tell Mori-*dono* that either this stops, or I'm leaving. No more *teacher from Kiyō* for his precious academy."

Shōin cleared his throat.

"You must understand, my position here – " He stopped, noticing her murderous look. "I... I will do what I can, of course. But, wasn't there something you wanted to show me?"

It took her a moment to remember. "Ah, yes." She reached for the orb. "I thought the *onmyōji* could take a look at it."

She handed him the red jewel. The light within grew bright in Shōin's hands – and so did his face.

"Leave it to me," he said. "*That* I can certainly help you with."

The boat rounded the sharp tip of a craggy cape. Nagomi's eyes welled up. The land before her was Chinzei, the island she still regarded as her true home; somewhere beyond the hills lay Kiyō, and the Suwa Shrine, and the sunny streets of Sōfukuji district that she knew so well. She wondered if she would ever go back to the city.

I'm a wanted person everywhere now, she reminded herself. *There's no home for me to come back to. I can only hope the news won't reach Chōfu before the wedding…*

As the ship entered the mouth of the narrow strait separating Chinzei from the main island, the wind died down, but the waves rose in fierce billows. Despite the single sail faltering into futile flapping, a strong current drew the vessel away from Chinzei and closer towards the Chōfu castle town, guarding the western side of the passage. Nagomi shivered; the last time she had seen these waters was when she boarded the ferry towards Nagoya, a few days after Ganryū was killed.

She thought she would be able to spot Ganryūjima easily, but from a distance the island melted with other tiny islets and reefs crowding the southern entrance to the straits.

The ship turned left – "to starboard," Nagomi remembered, though she wasn't sure when and where she had learned that word – and the crewmen headed to the front of the boat to prepare for docking at Chōfu.

Nagomi turned to take one last glance at Chinzei. Near the end of the arrow-shaped peninsula rose a single hump-backed hill; near its bottom, by the beach, she noticed a tinge of vermillion: a gate of a small shrine.

Part of the vision from Atsuta come back to her: the inside of an ancient temple, and a monk putting the white orb on the altar, turning in terror to face an unknown enemy. Only the enemy was not unknown this time. She saw him clearly: it was the Crimson Robe.

"Come, little priestess, we need to get our things." Torishi's voice broke the spell, but not before Nagomi remembered where she had seen the inside of the ancient

244

temple before – in another vision, her first ever glimpse of the Prophecy at Suwa Shrine.

She stopped one of the sailors who walked past with a length of coarse rope in his red hands. "Excuse me," she asked, pointing to the temple, "what do you call that place?"

"Mekari, priestess-*sama*," he answered.

"Mekari…" she repeated. The name meant nothing to her, and yet, she felt as if she'd heard it before…

I'll ask Sacchan's husband, she told herself and chuckled at the thought.

Satō's husband.

Of all the things that had happened to them, this one seemed the most ridiculous.

Nagomi climbed the narrow wooden staircase to the second floor of the guesthouse and knocked on the door.

"Come in," said a familiar voice. Nagomi took a deep breath and stepped into the room.

Satō was sitting by a teak cupboard, wearing a flowing red kimono. In one hand she was holding a sponge with white powder, in the other – a bronze mirror. She put away both things and stood up to welcome her friend.

Nagomi hesitated for a second, then ran up to the wizardess and embraced her. The wizardess stood rigid, not returning the hug at first. Finally, she raised her hand and patted Nagomi on the back. They stood motionless for a while.

"You look… beautiful," Nagomi said finally, looking the other girl over. Satō's hair was bunched up, not quite yet fully coiffured, but not the cropped boyish haircut, either. Half of her face was already daubed with peach-coloured chalk, her lips ruby red, one eye blackened with charcoal.

The effect was slightly disturbing, even without accounting for Satō's distinct lack of skill in applying the makeup.

"I hate it," Satō replied, pushing the cosmetic utensils off the cupboard with an angry swipe. "I hate having to wear this, and I hate having to have this wedding."

"Then why did you agree to it? And – why aren't you in Satsuma?"

Satō grimaced and reached for a wet sponge. "Let me get this off, and we'll come down to drink some cha. I'll tell you everything." She looked at Nagomi curiously. "Have you come all this way alone?"

"Torishi-*sama* stayed at the inn. Do you want me to send someone for him?"

Satō shook her head. "No, let it be only the two of us for a moment. Just like the old days."

"…and worst of all, I was running out of money. That's why he sent me here, to get this job." Satō finished her tale and gulped a hearty sip of saké. Nagomi poured her another cup. "Look at this place," Satō added, "it's all I can afford these days."

"It's not that bad," Nagomi said, but she had to admit that it wasn't up to the level she had normally expected of Satō.

To think the Takashima family had a walled mansion in the finest district of Kiyō.

"I don't even have a wedding kimono," Satō continued to spill her woes, her face flushed with saké, "I had to borrow it from Shōin's mother."

Yoshida Shōin.

Satō had spent a long time describing her life in Satsuma, and Lord Nariakira's treachery, but out of their entire conversation this was what stood out in Nagomi's mind. Shōin. The timid, well-behaved son of a cloth merchant. Of all the men, all the boys Nagomi had expected Satō to end up married to – if anyone at all – he was the last.

And yet, now that it was about to happen, somehow, it felt just right. The boy, from what Nagomi remembered, was an eager and talented student of *Rangaku*. And he had good ear of the *daimyo* himself. *Still, Shōin? That kid?*

"Do you remember when you laughed at your students for not being able to hold their swords straight?" Nagomi said and giggled.

Satō scratched her chin in thought. "Did I? It must have been a long time ago…" She laughed. "That must be why Shōin decided to come up with his own style of magic!"

Nagomi joined Satō, though she wasn't sure what they were laughing about.

"I was hoping," she said when they turned serious again, "you could have come with us to Nagoya and work at the hospital… But now, I don't know what will happen to us."

Satō shook her head and sipped more saké.

"Nagoya? Its *daimyo* is the *Taikun*'s cousin! I would be arrested at the first checkpoint. I'm surprised they let *you* in. Or out."

"Actually, we did have some – " Nagomi started, but Satō interrupted her with a sweeping gesture.

"Besides, I'm a wizard, not a doctor. Shōin's school has potential. With me and him at the head it could soon come to rival the one of that traitor Shimazu, and then…"

"Shhh!" Nagomi covered Satō's mouth with her hand. "People are listening!"

Satō removed the hand. "They don't care. Nobody here cares for Satsuma." The wizardess lowered her voice. "They don't like anyone who's in close cahoots with the Westerners. They barely tolerate us wizards."

"And what about you? What do you think about the Westerners now?"

Satō's lips set in a straight line. They both knew what Nagomi really meant by that question.

"He did what he had to do," she said eventually, with a forced shrug. "I would have done the same thing in his place."

"Would you?"

Satō crossed her arms.

"It doesn't matter. He's gone now, isn't he? We have a life to live here, in Yamato. He's got his own, in Dracaland, or wherever he's gone to. For him, for us… it was just a short adventure. Real life is what happens *between* such adventures."

"Your wedding sounds like quite an adventure," said Nagomi, smiling.

"It's all a sham. I have divorce papers in my room, signed by Shōin. But," she sighed, "for now, I don't have much choice."

"Will you have to wear these clothes?" Nagomi pointed at the rich, flowing kimono.

"Only when I'm outside the school gates. I don't plan on doing it often. After the wedding I can move back to the school, to Shōin's rooms. Now," Satō said, reaching for the flask; she noticed it was empty and called for another. "Tell me more about your journey."

A lone crow cawed, trying its best to sound louder than the cicadas crawling up the old pine tree, and the waves of the Dan-no-ura Strait nibbling at the beach beneath the Akama Shrine, where the wedding ceremony of Satō Takashima and Shōin Yoshida was taking place.

The procession marched down the vermillion-pillared cloister in the slow rhythm of the priest's chime. Nagomi and Torishi followed in the third row, just behind the parents of the groom. There weren't many guests at the wedding; some students of the Meirinkan, a few friends of the Yoshida family, and a burly samurai sent by lord Mori to see if everything was proceeding as it should be. He had spent most of the day so far giving Nagomi a suspicious glance.

The final guest to arrive at the ceremony was Master Dōraku. The Swordsman had come at the last moment, in great hurry, and Nagomi didn't even have the time to talk to him yet beyond a nod of greeting. He waited outside, just beyond the red *torii* gate.

The young couple – Shōin, in a splendid, simple black kimono embroidered with the Mori family crest, and Satō, almost lost in layers of flowing crimson, tripping constantly over the hem of her crane-embroidered gown, her head hidden inside the broad white hood – turned left, leaving the cloister, up a few steps, and onto the great ceremonial platform of the Akama Shrine. The jagged, wooded slope of the Hinoyama Mountain rising beyond the shrine formed a dark, ominous backdrop to the ritual. The celebrant, in tall black cap, and the two shrine maidens, waited until all the guests sat down at their positions, before beginning the first stage of the ritual.

THE CHRYSANTHEMUM SEAL

At the celebrant's behest, everyone stood up and bowed. The priest took a great paper wand from beside the altar and shook it in four directions, blessing all four corners of the platform – and the world. He then returned to the altar and spoke a long, mumbling prayer, announcing the marriage to the gathered Gods, after which came the part that Nagomi alone of the gathered was looking forward to: the shrine maidens' dance.

Nagomi remembered herself performing similar duties in Suwa; she knew the ceremony by heart. The dance was always her favourite – a chance for a hitherto anonymous maiden to show off in front of a captive crowd – and her heart went out to the two girls trying their best to keep the guests from dozing off, shaking their holy sakaki branches and jingling the bells at their hands and feet in perfectly – almost perfectly, Nagomi couldn't help noticing – timed intervals.

The dance over, the priest approached the young couple with three cups of saké. First Shōin, then Satō, sipped from each cup three times – once for Heaven, once for Earth, and once for all of Mankind.

It was now time for Shōin to speak the vows and ask the Gods to bless their union; from that moment, he and Satō would become lawfully wedded and Nagomi could no longer hold the tears welling in her eyes.

If only her father were here to see it...

Shōin unrolled a piece of snow-white paper, cleared his throat and, with a voice that was quiet and trembling at first, but soon grew proud and booming, read out the prepared formula.

Today is an auspicious day
And so we come before you, the Gods,
To perform this wedding ceremony
We vow to live together in peace and harmony
To share our joy and sorrow
To prepare a life of fortune and happiness for our descendants
This, we humbly vow
And beseech thee, protect our union
And bless all that results from it.

When he finished, the shrine maidens stepped forth, each holding a holy branch. Shōin and Satō took each in a hand and moved towards the altar, to finish their vows.

A sudden noise came from the direction of the sea, whooshing and whistling like a rising storm, an autumn typhoon in the middle of the summer. Nagomi, the acolytes, and all the visitors in the shrine courtyard cried in great alarm. A priest barged onto the platform, his face white with fear, waving frantically towards the Dan-no-ura Strait.

"A mo – " he stuttered, "a monster is coming!"

Some of the guests started running away, others – mostly the wizards from Satō's school – stood on tiptoes, trying to see what was going on over the roof of the shrine gate. Nagomi rushed towards Satō.

The wizardess stood still, frozen, morbid in her pale makeup, looking at a point in the sky; she alone saw what the others couldn't yet spot, and Nagomi followed her gaze.

A jade-green missile, blurry in its speed, came lightning-fast and bounced off the peaked gable of the shrine gate, showering the panicking crowd with shattered tiles, then shattered through the roof of the Offertory Hall, and flew

251

straight on, madly, blindly; just as it seemed that it would crash into the face of the Hinoyama Mountain, it leapt up again and disappeared into the thick forest beyond its jagged crest. Nagomi was the first to break the silence.

"Wasn't that…"

"Bran," Satō said quietly, and then added: "*Shit.*"

She tore the wedding hat off her head, lifted the hem of her wedding gown and, cursing the uncomfortable sandals, ran down the platform stairs.

"You knew, didn't you?" Satō asked Master Dōraku, struggling with the stubbornly clingy wedding kimono. "You knew Bran was coming. I did wonder why you suddenly appeared."

"I could not miss your wedding, Takashima-*sama*," the Swordsman answered with a smirk and mocking bow.

"*Bollocks.* I didn't even send you an invitation."

With a heave and a pull she finally managed to free herself of the many folds of the kimono and under-kimono and started putting on her *Rangaku* clothes in a hurry.

"Is that true?" asked Nagomi, staring at the Swordsman intently. "You knew he was still in Yamato and you didn't tell us?"

Dōraku scratched the back of his head. "Well… I suspected, but wasn't certain…"

Satō threw the wedding *obi* sash at him. "You always know. *Why* is he here? Why didn't he fly away?"

"I really don't know. You'll have to ask him about it. Perhaps, he missed you?"

Satō gave him a murderous stare, and then looked out the window onto the school courtyard, where the Mori samurai among the students formed a separate group and prepared themselves to march out.

"What's going on there?" she asked.

"Takasugi-*sama*!" Shōin called out. He had already managed to change from his wedding clothes into combat gear.

"*Takasugi...?*" whispered Nagomi.

Takasugi Hiro was a broad-lipped man in his early twenties, recently returned from Edo. He was perhaps the closest to Shōin of all students, a relationship Satō didn't really understand. Takasugi was a proper samurai, of good family, trained in the art of war – he and the frail and scholarly Shōin made an odd couple.

He now barged into the room, his face flushed with exertion, and stopped abruptly at the sight of Nagomi.

"Priestess-*sama*! You made it safe!" he exclaimed with a bright smile. He bowed and Nagomi bowed in response.

"I am glad you are well, Takasugi-*sama*."

"It could only be thanks to your prayers," he said happily.

Satō stared at the two of them. "You – when – how – ?"

"We met... on the way here," Nagomi answered, embarrassed.

"What's this commotion all about?" Shōin asked from the window.

"Mori-*dono* ordered that the monster on the mountain be captured, and announced that the first group to find it will receive a great reward."

Everyone had seen the creature fly over Chōfu, but few managed to take a good look at it. Rumours and tall tales spread like wildfire, fuelled by the strange, disturbing news coming from the north; of foreign invasion and beasts landing at the gates of Edo.

"*Group?*" Satō fumed. "They are no *group*!"

She tied her jacket tight, thrust the sword into her sash and stormed outside, ignoring Shōin's attempts to stop her. She stood in front of the leader of the samurai group with her hands on her hips.

"What do you think you're doing?" she barked at the surprised nobleman. "You're students of the Meirinkan! We're supposed to search the mountain together!"

The samurai laughed at her. "Oh no, the *sensei* is scolding me!" His men joined in the mocking laughter.

"Step aside, girl." He turned serious. "It's time for adults to act. For *men*."

"She's right, Kunishi-*sama*," Takasugi said, standing in the door of the hall. "If you wish to study here, you must – "

The samurai sneered and tore off the white sash marking his allegiance to the school. "I've had quite enough of this!" he snarled and pushed Satō aside – she almost fell.

"Filthy barbarian magic," he said, "is not fit for a samurai, no matter what Mori-*dono* says. We'll prove to him we can capture the monster with just our sharp swords and pure hearts! *Jōi*!" he cried, shaking his sword in the air triumphantly.

His men did the same, and they marched out the main gate, in tight formation, toward the Hinoyama Mountain.

CHAPTER XII

The mountain was small compared to the peaks of Chinzei, and the forest was sparse, broad, leafy, criss-crossed by narrow paths trodden by lumberjacks and hunters. Still, it was large enough to get lost in if one wasn't careful, and Satō, reluctantly, had to give leadership of the chase to Shōin and his wizards; the local boys. Even so, they didn't seem to be getting anywhere.

"You'd think it would be easy to find a dragon in this place," she mumbled, panting. She wafted herself with a paper fan. Deep in the woods, the air was thick and sticky with moisture.

They stopped to catch a breath on some crossroads, but they couldn't afford to rest long. Somewhere in the forest the samurai search party was on its way, and they could not be allowed to reach their quarry first.

This reminds me of something... but what?

Shōin finally gathered the courage to put the question he'd been wanting to ask since they had left the Akama Shrine. Things had been happening so fast since the incident at the wedding that they hadn't really had time to discuss what was really going on.

"It seems to me, *sensei*... Satō... that you know about this – monster."

She looked at Shōin in surprise before realizing he had no way of knowing what was going on; she had never told him about anything that had happened since the Takashima School disbanded.

"Not the monster. The rider," she answered.

It was an odd feeling. She had come to regard her adventure with Bran as just another part of her life – important, crucial even, but something that could have happened to anyone... but no, the confused look on Shōin's face told her otherwise.

"The rider? You mean – we're looking for a man, as well as the monster?" Shōin said, wide-eyed.

"A foreigner."

"A *foreigner?*"

Nagomi came closer.

"You're talking about Bran," she said.

Satō nodded. She studied the priestess's face; despite the long climb up the mountain, her cheeks were rosy and her breath was calm.

Where did she get that stamina from?

"I can – I think I can *feel* him," said Nagomi carefully. "I thought I heard him call me before... on the ship, and yesterday – but I wasn't sure if I wasn't imagining things."

"And now you are sure?" Satō asked.

256

"No. But it won't hurt to try."

"We'll follow you, then."

Mogi, she remembered at last. *That's where we chased Bran before. I was the one tracking him through the forest then...* She couldn't help feeling bitter that it was Nagomi who sensed Bran's presence; priestess or not.

Shōin looked as if he wanted to ask a hundred questions, but couldn't decide which one he should pose first.

"Trust me on this, Shōin," she told him, "I'll explain everything later. We have to get to that *dorako* before the samurai. We must keep the rider safe."

"But – if he's a foreigner, he must be brought before the *daimyo*!" protested Shōin.

She shook her head with disapproval. "Haven't you learned *anything* in Kiyō?"

She heard the dragon's roar before she saw it. Her stomach filled with cold and her breath quickened. She pressed forward with sheer willpower, her body suddenly very heavy. The others slowed down as well; some froze in the spot.

Dragon fear.

They emerged out of the forest onto a scorched glade, right in front of the snarling dragon. The beast roared and spat out a whirling cone of flames and smoke. It stood on spread legs, with its tail to the steep rocky cliff, snarling and fuming at them. A tight ring of fire surrounded it on three sides.

Satō looked to her companions. Dōraku returned her gaze, scratching his thin beard. Torishi stood in front of Nagomi. But Shōin and his wizards were transfixed, staring at the beast. She pitied and envied them at the same time. She, at least, had seen Emrys in the flesh, even so, it was still a stunning sight.

The sensation of dread slowly left her body.

"I can't see Bran," Nagomi said, her voice trembling.

Satō remembered why they were there and tore her eyes from the magnificent creature to search for the rider.

"Over there," she pointed, "under the front legs."

"Is he – is he alive?"

"You tell me! I don't think the *dorako* would still be here if he wasn't. He must be wounded."

"We have to get him out of there," the priestess said and lurched forward. Satō grabbed her by the hand and held it strongly.

"Wait! It's dangerous."

"But – Bran!"

For Nagomi, that was argument enough. But Satō hesitated.

Why am I doing this? Why should I risk anything for him? He wouldn't care. He ran away as soon as we got him the stupid dragon back.

"Sacchan," the priestess pleaded, "we must help him!"

Satō swore through her teeth and stepped forward. She drew her sword and pointed its tip at the beast.

"*Ijsschild!*" she cried. A thick shield of ice rose between her and the dragon. She made a slow step forward.

"It's me, Satō," she said in what she hoped was a soothing voice. "You may not remember me, but you should remember Nagomi?" she pointed to the priestess. "We're Bran's friends," she said, making another step. "We're here to help…"

The dragon spat fire at the ice shield; it shattered into shards. She leapt back at the last moment, clutching a singed arm.

Now what?

"Whatever you do, do it fast," said Dōraku. "Those samurai are right behind us."

"Why won't you go?" she snapped. The tension of the situation was getting to her.

She tightened her fist, ready to go into the flame again, when she heard Shōin call.

"Hot!"

He struggled with his sleeve and dropped something bright and red to the ground.

My orb.

"I took it from the laboratory… I thought it might be useful," said Shōin.

"Good job, boy," Dōraku said with a grin.

Satō reached to pick it up from the grass. It was quickly cooling off in her grasp. There were a few long strips of paper glued to it, marked with Qin characters. She gave Shōin a questioning look.

"Something our *onmyōji* had left…" he said. "Research *ofuda*."

She tore the papers off. The orb vibrated in her hand. She felt her hand pulled towards the raging dragon.

It's now or never, she thought.

Unsure what to do, she stared at the orb and poured her energy into the stone, the way she would have done with a sword in the Takashima School style. She'd done it countless times before with the jewel, with no discernible effect.

But this time it felt different. The world around her slowed down. Everything turned white-grey. The people around her became wisps of smoke and light, shapeless clouds of white flame. Only the dragon before her remained solid, fierce and even greater than before.

She had never felt so much power surging through her. The jewel became a part of her – no, it was she who had become a part of it. It was all-encompassing. A series of images flashed before her eyes, lightning quick: a miner's pick, carving the twin crystals out of a rock; a gathering of small, dark people in the cave around a gleaming white orb; a flock of wild, rider-less Yamato dragons dancing in the sky…

Ancient history.

The orb in her hand turned warm and strangely soft. She looked at it – it was no longer a crystal, but a heart, beating regularly, spurting blood down her arm. She squeezed it, and its beat slowed.

Emrys roared, recognizing the threat; she knew that, somehow. She knew what the beast felt, and what it felt was fear, anger and terrible pain. It opened its jaw to spew once again, but the fire died in its throat. She squeezed harder. The dragon swayed from side to side, like a drunkard.

Can I really make it fall...? She sent one more blast of power into the heart. The *dorako* staggered forward, snorted and hit the dirt with a great thud, rising a cloud of dust. She swayed too. She dropped the Tide Jewel to the ground and supported herself on the sword, exhausted.

The world returned to normal. Nagomi could wait no longer. Hiding her face in her arms, she jumped through the wall of fire with Torishi in tow. Satō wiped the sweat form her face with her sleeve and followed them both, shielding herself from the flames with a layer of ice.

Nagomi knelt down beside Bran. Satō looked over her shoulder.

Lying unconscious, in the sand, she thought briefly, we've got to stop meeting like this.

His face was white, wet curls of black hair stuck to his forehead. Dark blood and pus were seeping through the tatters of the uniform trousers on his left leg. The entire thigh was covered in torn blisters and ripe burn scars.

"What happened to him?" asked Nagomi, pressing on the wound gingerly. Her fingers glowed with the blue light of healing. "Was it his *dorako*'s fire?"

Satō looked the dragon over. "No, look – " Satō touched the scales on Emrys' neck. They were singed and cracked in two places where, she guessed, a rider would sit. "It's hurt as well."

Another dragon...? she thought. *Is that what you've come to tell us about?*

"Can you heal him?" she asked the priestess.

Nagomi cast her a panicked look.

"The wound is too old," she said, shaking her head. "He needs a proper healer."

Satō frowned.

What do you mean, proper *healer...?*

"We have to hurry, then. I'll take him by the arms, and – "

She felt a tap on the shoulder and turned to Torishi.

"Trouble," the bear-man said, pointing with a thumb behind him.

Mori r*Eta*iners had finally caught up with them. They stood along the edge of the scorched glade, their spears and swords aimed at those gathered around the *dorako*.

"Dōraku-*sa* – " she started, and stopped. The Swordsman was nowhere to be seen. She realized she had not seen him since she'd used the Tide Jewel. She turned to Torishi, instead.

"Torishi-*sama*, help me carry Bran away."

"Yoshida-*sensei*!" Kunishi, the commander of the Mori r*Eta*iners shouted. "Get away from that barbarian. All of you. He's under arrest!"

The dragon grunted in its stupor. The samurai leapt back and shook his sword furiously.

"I can carry him myself. But where do you want to take him?" asked the bear-man, throwing the boy over his shoulder. The boy moaned and opened his eyes, but was too weak to speak. His gaze slid from Satō to Nagomi.

"Out of here, first," the wizardess ordered, "then back to Meirinkan, if we can."

"What about them?" he nodded at the r*Eta*iners.

The samurai now barred all the exits from the scorched glade, in two rows, spear points aimed straight at Satō and Torishi. Worse than that – more warriors poured from among the trees; archers and arquebusiers, ready to shoot.

"Put. Him. Down." The commander stepped forward.

Satō reached to her waist, but stopped short of drawing the sword.

Damn it, Dōraku-sama, where are you? Now is when we could really use your help…

Shōin patted her on the shoulder. She turned towards him: his face was gravely serious.

"*Sen*… Satō – can I really trust you on this?"

"Yes, Shōin."

"And this foreigner… is he really that important?"

This made her pause again.

Is he important at all?

Her eyes fell on Nagomi. The priestess was pale, biting her fingernails, her eyes wide open and darting about, she looked like a trapped rabbit. Satō did not remember ever seeing her friend so worried before.

"He may be the most important person in Yamato," she said with conviction.

Shōin nodded and then turned to his wizards. He raised a hand.

A barrage of ice and fire missiles struck the samurai. The earth wobbled beneath their feet. Wind carried the released arrows and bullets harmlessly through the air, shattering treetops and rocks around the glade.

"Now, go!" cried Shōin and pushed Satō forward. "We'll hold them."

"What about you?"

The boy smiled weakly. Satō noticed only now how tired he seemed.

"Don't worry. I swore before the Gods that we would always be together. I'll meet you at the Meirinkan."

Satō and Torishi barged their way through the chaos, pushing the few still-standing, confused samurai out of their way. Running headlong down the slope, leaving the noise of the battle behind, she almost bumped into Master Dōraku. He dragged her to the small, flat glen; a bowl of sand dug by a narrow mountain stream. In the middle of it, drawn in red in the sand was a complex six-pointed pattern. He beckoned them to hurry.

"Lay him here, in the middle," he ordered.

"Is that a – " Satō began.

"A transportation hex, yes. I did go through Ganryū's library, remember? Now step back, this can only take two of us."

"But you don't know – "

"Meirinkan, right? I'll be waiting there – if you can make it."

He looked up – the samurai were pushing through the undergrowth towards them. He knelt down and pressed the tips of his fingers to two opposite points of the pattern. The spell whirled and blasted Satō with wind and light. When she could see again, both the Swordsman and the dragon rider were gone.

The compound that formed the Meirinkan School had once been part of the outer bailey of the Chōfu Castle. As such, it was a well-fortified place, with a tough oaken gate and a dry moat encompassing the six foot wall. It may not have been enough to withstand a full-on siege, but served just fine to stop Kunishi's samurai from charging in.

The students patrolled the perimeter in twos, ready to stop any intrusion; no attack was forthcoming. The troops of the domain gathered around the school in force, but the

265

commanders were unsure what to make of the situation. No orders had come from the *daimyo*'s castle, no condemnation of the rebellious wizards, no demand to hand over the foreigner. The soldiers marched back and forth along the walls, waving spears and shouting abuse, and could do nothing to the men inside. As long as Lord Mori remained silent, it was stalemate.

Satō and Shōin sat on a bench in front of the school dormitory. Behind them, inside the building, the students of the Western Medicine faculty were doing their best to save Bran's rotting leg. Satō wished desperately to take her mind off what would happen if they failed.

"So, have you found your attunement yet, Shōin?" she asked. "I saw you cast all sorts of spells back there in the forest."

The boy looked at her in surprise, and then shook his head. He spoke slowly. "Not yet. I can't figure it out. No kind of magic comes any harder to me than any other... or any easier, for that matter."

His face was not even pale anymore – it was a rainbow of colours, all of them sickly: his cheeks were sunken, almost green, his eyes rounded in deep purple.

"You should rest," she said.

"I'll be fine," he replied, and bent over in a sudden coughing fit. She leaned to support him.

"It's always like this after I use too much power..." he added when he finished coughing. "I just need to be careful, that's all. I don't often have to fight half of Chōfu's garrison," he smiled.

"I was surprised," she said, "by the loyalty of your students. The Satsuma wizards would never go against Shimazu's men like that."

"You saw how the Chōfu nobles can treat those beneath them. Most of these boys come from common families, like mine. To tell you the truth, they were itching to bloody the noses of a few samurai for a long time."

"I can imagine." She forced a smile.

An agonizing howl came from the building. Satō winced, recognizing Bran's voice.

"What now? We are all going to be condemned as rebels," she said. "The school is finished."

Shōin shook his head.

"If that was the *daimyo*'s wish, he would have ordered the attack already."

"Then what's he playing at?"

"I don't know – but I'm going to find out." He stood up abruptly, but then he swayed as blood rushed from his head. Satō allowed him to lean on her shoulder.

That's right, she thought, *we are a married couple now. I keep forgetting it's no longer improper for him to touch me.*

"I'm…I'm sorry. As soon as the foreigner wakes, I am going to go to the castle," Shōin decided, "to parley with the *daimyo*. He trusts me more than his samurai advisors."

"They will arrest you the moment you step out of that gate."

"I am still a Mori r*Eta*iner, equal in rank with all those samurai outside."

"You've learned to play the role of a nobleman quickly," said Satō. She was finding it increasingly difficult to reconcile the memories of a boy scribbling clumsy notes on the floor of a Takashima Mansion with this… man, almost a leader of other men.

I thought we had grown over the recent months… but he's grown far more.

"I had a great teacher in Mori-*dono*," Shōin said. "Chōfu is rife with politics, always has been. We're a frontier domain – stuck half-way between those loyal to the *Taikun* on Hondo, and the rebellious *daimyo* on Chinzei. I thought, as a son of a cloth merchant, I could have avoided all this… all I wanted was to learn some *Rangaku*… You know, the original reason why my father sent me to Kiyō was simply so I could make some contacts among the Bataavian traders, to see if we could sell them our silk."

"I'm sorry you got involved in all our trouble."

"Not at all." He shook his head. "Had I stayed in Kiyō, I wouldn't have all this," he waved at the courtyard. Then he looked her in the eyes. "And I wouldn't have – "

Cries and commotion coming from the direction of the wall interrupted him. The main gate swung open, and the wizards guarding it dropped to their knees.

Satō stood up.

"What are they doing?"

A young man entered the gate with purposeful steps, sweeping the courtyard with a lordly look. Satō did not recognize his face, but his stature was enough: the only other man she knew who bore himself like that was Shimazu Nariakira. This must have been Mori Takachika, the *daimyo* of Chōfu.

He nodded at somebody beyond the gate and it shut, leaving him alone inside.

"*Kakka...!*" Shōin gasped, and prostrated as the *daimyo* approached them. Satō knelt down.

"Where is he?" Lord Mori asked curtly.

"In the infirmary," replied Shōin from the dirt. Another howling cry confirmed his words.

"Take me to him."

All dropped to their knees when Lord Mori entered the infirmary room. Satō and Shōin followed him closely. She eyed the room quickly. Three medicine students were kneeling at the head of Bran's bed with morose faces. Nagomi was down by his leg, still touching it with faintly blue-lit fingers. The wound was a thin maze of healed scars among the black and purple mass of dying flesh.

"What's wrong with him?" the *daimyo* asked.

"His...his leg is burned," said one of the students, stuttering, "and not with normal fire, either. The damage looks magical in origin."

Lord Mori frowned.

"Can he be moved to the castle prison?"

"The rot is too deep, *kakka*," the student replied. "We have to cut here and now, or he dies."

The other two nodded in agreement.

"No!" protested Nagomi, rising from her knees. "It can be saved, *kakka*. We only need more power. Another priest that can – "

"Silence, girl!" the *daimyo* thundered. Everyone turned pale. The priestess beat the floor with her forehead.

"Yoshida-*sama*," Lord Mori turned to Shōin, "I have been very lenient to your school so far. But I did not expect it to become a nest of fugitives and traitors."

"I understand, *kakka*..." the boy replied, downcast, pale. "But the situation with this *Gaikokujin* ..."

"I don't mean the barbarian," snapped the *daimyo*, "I mean *her!*"

He raised an accusing fan-holding hand at Nagomi.

"*Me...?*" the priestess gasped, "why...?"

Lord Mori stood over her. "Don't talk back to me, mongrel."

She pressed her forehead to the floor.

"*Kakka...*"

"I know you killed an Aizu r*Eta*iner. You're wanted from Kiyō to Tsugaru. And that half-ape companion of yours – I saw him in the courtyard."

"Nagomi...?" Satō stared at her friend.

270

"I… I was going to tell you," Nagomi whispered. "I am sorry…"

"I told you to stay quiet!" Lord Mori slapped her over the head with his fan. "Yoshida-*sama*, give me one good reason why I shouldn't have you all thrown into a dungeon, and that barbarian cast to the dogs?"

Satō felt somebody push her gently aside from the door.

"Will this help?" Master Dōraku said, holding up a bundle of papers.

"*You*." The *daimyo* spared the Fanged only the coldest of glances. "I thought I told you never to set foot in Chōfu again."

"The fate of Yamato hangs in the balance," Dōraku replied grimly. "I'm afraid I had to stop pretending to listen to orders from mortals."

"You insolent…" The *daimyo* raised his fan to a slap, but his eyes caught the papers. "Give me those."

He grabbed them from the Fanged's hands and perused them briefly. Looking over his shoulder, Satō noticed hastily written Seaxe runes. She thought she could understand some words, but she didn't dare speak out of turn.

"I can't read these," the *daimyo* said.

"None of us can," said Dōraku. "Only the boy. These were found on him, and are likely the reason why he's here. He wanted to bring these to our attention, *kakka*."

Lord Mori's lips were a thin line. He studied one of the pages: a fairly dEtailed map of southern provinces drawn on it in elegant ink, and he frowned.

"The boy speaks Yamato," Fanged pressed.

"And why should I care about any of this?"

"That wound on his leg," Dōraku said, pointing, "that's *dorako* fire."

Lord Mori put a hand to his chest in mock surprise. "It can't be! A *dorako*, you say? Where on Earth could the boy – ?"

"*Another* dragon's fire," Dōraku interrupted.

The *daimyo*'s eyes narrowed. He pondered for a moment.

"Where is his beast now?" he asked.

As if in answer, an ear-piercing shriek came from outside, followed by a roar and a fiery hiss. Satō caught Lord Mori's eyes and he nodded, suddenly pale.

She ran out, Shōin behind her. She sheltered her eyes from the dust raised by the wind. The dragon hovered over the courtyard, roaring and spitting balls of flame. A few wizards tried to fight back with missiles of ice and lightning, but the elements bounced off the jade-green scales with a shower of shards and fizzle.

"Satō, do it," she heard Shōin whisper.

She drew the red orb from her sleeve, burning now with renewed energy. In an instant the dragon dived at her. She focused her energy into the jewel, just as she had done in the forest. At once it turned into a beating heart. The surge of power was even greater than before. The dragon was right above her. She squeezed the heart tight. The beast hung in the air, flapping its wings desperately.

Down!

One more squeeze and the beast dropped to the ground. It smashed into the sand of the courtyard a feet away from Satō and lay there, not moving a muscle.

Did I – did I kill it?

Carefully she moved closer and gently touched the scales. They were warm, and she felt something ripple beneath, blood vessels or maybe relaxing tendons… The beast was alive, but barely.

"Impressive," she heard *daimyo*'s voice right behind her. She bowed down without turning back.

"So this is a *dorako*…" Lord Mori laid a hand on the dragon's head beside hers. He seemed unaffected by dragon fear. "How long can you keep it that way?" he asked.

"I… I don't know, *kakka*."

"Can anybody else do it?"

Nobody else tried.

"No, *kakka*."

"Very well. I order you to focus on this task for now," the *daimyo* said. "And *only* this. As for the rest of you…"

He turned to Shōin and others, who waited in the door of the infirmary.

"You are all under house arrest for now. Forbidden to leave the school until I think of further punishment."

He thrust the papers into Shōin's hands. "Bring the barbarian to me as soon as he wakes," he ordered. "Leg or no leg."

He drilled the tip of the fan into the Fanged's chest. "And I want *you* out of here."

He gave them all one last tired, mocking look, rolled his eyes and marched off towards the gate in a huff.

As soon as the *daimyo* disappeared, Satō turned back towards the infirmary.

"But – the *dorako* – " Shōin tried to stop her. "The *daimyo* – "

She gave him a scornful look and brushed him aside.

"*Sensei*, please! What if – "

She didn't hear the rest. Inside the infirmary, the three students were preparing their instruments. One of them already had the hacksaw in his hand and was busy choosing the best place to cut. The others were preparing tourniquets and bottles of distilled alcohol.

"All out," she said.

She knelt down beside Bran's bed. He was awake, his green eyes clouded with fever.

"Do you understand what's going on?" she asked.

Bran reached out and grabbed her hand, weakly.

He opened his parched lips. She leaned down to hear him whisper:

"The Black Wings… are coming…"

She frowned.

"Don't worry about it now. Bran, listen to me, this is important. We may have to cut your leg off."

"How… much… "

She examined his thigh. "Almost all of it. There will barely be a stump left. Will you be able to ride again…?"

He turned his head to the wall. That was all the answer she needed.

This was tough. She didn't know why he had returned, or how he knew where to find them, but she was sure that, whatever his plans were, they would all come to naught if he couldn't fly Emrys anymore.

"What about blood magic?" she overheard one of the students speaking behind the paper wall.

"What about it?" another asked.

"Well, you know what they say. If it can bring back the dead… maybe it could work here."

They started arguing vigorously.

"There are no adepts of blood magic here, Aoki," said one of them, "unless you wish to tell us something."

The voice of the one they called Aoki trembled.

"No. No. How can you say that?"

Satō stood up and opened the doors. "Keep an eye on him," she ordered the students, "but don't do anything yet. I'll be right back."

Master Dōraku gave Satō a heavy look from under a furrowed brow. He ran his hand down his face and stared at the wall for a long time before answering.

"If there was no hope, you'd say so already," said the wizardess, breaking the brooding silence.

The Swordsman sighed. "It's not that easy, girl. Blood magic – "

"I know all about blood magic," she said. "I also know what it does to people – or have you forgotten why I had to bury my own father?"

"No, I remember. I remember everything. That's why I think your family has dabbled in it enough."

"I'm willing to take the risk."

His eyes turned golden as he leaned towards her, black fangs bared.

"Are you?" he spoke. A cold stench of decay burst forth.

She stepped back and covered her mouth in disgust.

"Are you really? Would you give your life for the boy? Your very soul? And maybe *his*?"

She failed to find a quick answer to that. After all, it was just a leg... Bran could live without it. Besides... he only had himself to blame. Why did he have to endanger himself like that? What was in those papers that was so important?

"I see you hesitate." The Swordsman scoffed, his pupils black again. "The power of blood is not for the weak-willed."

"No, wait!"

The power of blood.

The words burned bright in her mind, like a beacon, beckoning her forth.

Greater than Rangaku. *Greater than that of the shrine healers. Invulnerability. Immortality. Could I really harness it? Even at the risk of...*

"My soul..." she whispered.

"No." Master Dōraku stood up.

She grabbed his cold, dry hand in hers.

"Please... Grant me the power, one last time. Think of Nagomi – it would break her heart if anything happened to Bran."

She was surprised how easy it was for her to say those words. In some part of her mind she rarely visited she had long known the priestess had fallen in love with the foreigner. Maybe even since that day when they had found him at the beach in Kiyō...

The Swordsman released his hand. He rose and came up to the door, looking out at the courtyard in deep, brooding silence.

"None must know," he said at last.

"None will," she assured him in a heartbeat.

He turned back to her.

"Do you still have Tanaka's glove?"

"I do."

"Bring it to the infirmary in an hour. And your dagger."

"Thank you."

"Don't thank me. I know you will come to rue this decision one day," he said. "And so will I."

"Then why did you agree?"

"Sometimes…" He pinched his thin beard. "Sometimes the only way to move on is to let go of the cliff's edge."

CHAPTER XIII

Satō picked up the glove and the dagger from her room and crossed the courtyard – passing at a safe distance from the unconscious *dorako* – towards the infirmary. She could only hope it would not wake up while she was dealing with Bran. Sitting on the same bench she had earlier shared with Shōin, was Nagomi and her inseparable Kumaso companion.

The priestess stood up and barred her way.

"Don't do it, Sacchan."

"Don't do what?" she said, trying to sound casual.

Nagomi grabbed her by the shoulders.

"Whatever it is you're planning. I don't know exactly, but I know it ends badly."

"How do you know?" Satō asked.

"I know – I've seen it…"

"Tell me."

Nagomi leaned closer and whispered.

"You and Bran, standing on the threshold of the Gates of the Otherworld. Bran was on this side but you... you were on the other, in the shadows."

Satō brushed her hands off.

"That could have meant anything. It doesn't have to apply to today."

"But you are planning something," said Nagomi, staring at Satō with eyes wide open, worried. "Something you dare not tell – "

None must know.

"You love him, don't you?" Satō asked.

Nagomi blinked, her cheeks turned crimson. Her mouth opened and closed a few times, as if she was catching her breath.

"I don't know what you're talking about," she whispered quickly, looking at her feet.

"What I'm about to do, I'm doing for you as much as him," said Satō. "I know that if you could, you'd do anything to help him. But you can't. So it's up to me."

"Sacchan..." Nagomi said, quietly. "I've known you all my life. I barely met him a few months ago. So please... don't make me have to choose."

"You don't have to choose anything." Satō forced a laugh. "We will both be just fine, and we'll all be laughing about it in a few days. Trust me."

She glanced nervously to the infirmary.

"I have to go. I'm already late."

280

There were soldiers posted now before the infirmary, two Mori samurai from the r*Eta*iners group. She looked around the courtyard and noticed more of Kunishi's men guarding key positions around the school. The short-lived siege was over, and Meirinkan was under complete control of Lord Mori and his samurai.

One of the guards stepped forward. He had a flat, pudgy, dull face.

"Only physicians and healers are allowed in," he said. "Are you one?"

"I – yes, I am a physician," she replied, "I'm here to help with the surgery…"

He nodded and moved aside, but the other guard stared at her attentively, frowning, thinking – with visible effort. She reached for the door.

"Wait!" The other guard reached for her. "You're a woman, aren't you?"

"What if I am?"

"He said not to let the woman one in," the guard told another, "remember?"

"Oh, yeah!" The first one slapped his forehead. "He's right. You can't come in."

I don't have time for this, she thought.

Satō stepped back. Her hand reached for the sword. The samurai did the same.

That they understand.

She tensed up, ready to strike. The infirmary door slid open quietly behind them. Master Dōraku appeared outside and, in a blur of movement, struck the two guards on the necks with his hands. Before they started sliding to the ground, he grabbed them and propped them up against the wall. They looked as if they were dozing off in the afternoon sun.

"Not a drop of blood more than necessary," he admonished Satō. His eyes darted left and right around the courtyard. "I don't think anybody saw anything, but we won't have much time. Come quickly."

The walls and the floor of the infirmary were covered in complex patterns drawn in red ink: spirals, concentric circles, stars, polygons, straight and zig-zagging lines, all interconnected in hellish, mind-numbing arrangements. Satō was straining her memory to the limits, trying to remember as many of the drawings as she could.

Master Dōraku was kneeling beside Bran's mattress, finishing a long line made of interlocking crescents and angled strokes running straight through the blanket across the boy's body.

"How can you remember all this?" Satō whispered in awe. "I know you've lived long, but still…"

The Swordsman put a final dot on the pattern and stood up, heavily.

"It's not a matter of memory. The Blood Runes are like letters of the kana alphabet, only instead of words, they form spells. This — " he said, pointing to the wall, "is more than just a simple incantation: it is an essay in blood magic."

"How many Runes are there?" asked Satō. Now that she knew what to look for, she was beginning to spot smaller, repeating patterns in the greater design. She even recognized some of the runes from the inscriptions on Ganryūjima.

I could learn this. It looks no more difficult than Qin writing.

Master Dōraku shrugged. "Who knows? A thousand, ten thousand… I know several hundred off the top of my head. For more, I would need to consult the ancient scrolls, but I don't need more for this spell."

"And this is enough to bring Bran back to health?"

"Don't speak so lightly of what you don't understand," the Swordsman scoffed. "Come here, we must begin."

He led her to a corner between the floor and two walls, from where the complex pattern started.

"Put on the glove. Don't use the needle — it's too small for the job; I just want you to keep an eye out for that dial."

Too small…?

"Give me your dagger."

She handed him the weapon. Master Dōraku took her hand in his and studied it before slashing straight through the forearm at an angle.

Satō hissed, but didn't twitch.

"Fill the pattern with your blood. Don't put too much at one time — you will have to last for the entire process."

283

The entire thing!

"*Eeeh*! But it would take all my blood…!"

"Not at all, if you let me drain it. It takes a certain… skill. But hurry, it's drying up."

She dabbed a finger in her wound and then ran it along the line of red ink. The pattern glowed – just like the runes at Ganryū's gate – and swallowed the blood hungrily.

"Thousands of years ago," the Swordsman spoke, as Satō continued with the ritual, "when the first men discovered blood magic, they carved simple patterns into the stones. Spirals, angles, dots and lines. They did it at random, trying many things out, improving and developing the patterns for generation after generation."

"How do you know all this?" she asked. The incision dried out and she came up to the Swordsman for a new cut. This one was slightly more painful than the first.

"I studied Vasconian lore for decades, trying to find a way to cure my condition. It was they who brought blood magic to Yamato. Long before the Bataavians, with their *Rangaku*."

Satō looked at the wall. It seemed she had barely just started… there was so much to go. But, strangely, it didn't worry her as much as it should have. She felt oddly light-headed.

"You're using too much," the Swordsman warned her. "What does the dial say?"

"It's barely up."

Bran moaned and stirred. Satō stopped to check on him.

"Don't worry," said Master Dōraku, "I gave him a sleeping extract. He will not wake. Continue."

He stepped further away from Bran's bed; his face hid in the shadow.

"Those small patterns," he picked up the lecture from where he had finished, "were initially harmless. The shamans and later priests felt the danger, but nobody believed them – they were natural rivals of the blood mages, after all."

Satō's hand slid across the slippery wall. She giggled.

"All of this happened before history, before the written word, and we only know it from the sagas and legends. All writing came later, born out of increasingly complex blood runes… What we do know is that they started going mad. Some simply went insane, and harmed only themselves. Others became power hungry, and grew stronger and stronger, enslaving others with their magic. The wizard-kings of Ejiputo, Babiron and other kingdoms the names of which are forgotten in the mists of time, controlled tens of thousands, and the more slaves they had, the more blood was at their disposal. They became unstoppable, immortal beings of immeasurable power."

Why is he telling me this? Satō wondered. I'm getting a headache from all this talk.

"What happened to them?"

"The dragons ate them."

She burst into uncontrollable laughter. Master Dōraku waited patiently. When she finished laughing, her wounds were all mended, and he had to cut her again. It was even more painful this time, but she didn't mind. In fact, it was perversely pleasant.

"Seriously, what happened?"

"I am serious. The elemental wizards fled to the East and hid in the marshes of Bharata and Qin. They used crocodiles and giant turtles they found there as the basis to create creatures strong enough to fight the blood-crazed kings."

She blinked.

"The dragons… dragons were made by humans?"

The Dragon Book didn't mention that.

The Swordsman nodded. "That's what some of the legends say. There were wars — we do not know for how long, how many people died, what treasures and secrets of ancient lore were lost to us forever… but when the elemental wizards and their dragons emerged victorious, blood magic was banished for centuries, pursued only in secret by sinister, devious men — who wished for more power than…"

Satō didn't hear the end of the sentence. The world around her turned and she fell to her knees, dizzy.

Master Dōraku lifted her to her feet and looked at the dial on the glove. "Almost half-way there… and you're half-way through. This is going to be close."

"I'm fine, really…" she said, slurring her words. Her tongue felt like cotton wool.

"Too late to go back now, anyway. We must finish this, or we are both damned."

His hands trembling, he cut her again. She didn't feel pain at all; the wound radiated warmth and bliss. She felt the same warmth emanating from her left shoulder, but could not remember why. The inside of her mouth tasted of iron.

"From here on, I won't be able to help you. I will need to leave the room. Do you understand why?"

She nodded, though she could barely make out his words, coming as if from a great distance, muffled through the white mist rising from the floor.

"Izzit… is it because of your addiction?"

"You must make the final cut yourself," he said, ignoring her question. He pressed the dagger in her slippery hand. "Here. Along the inside of your shoulder. No deeper than a grain of rice. Takashima Satō!" He shook her awake.

"I hear you," she said. "A grain of rice. I'll be all right."

"Remember why you are doing this. Remember Nagomi. Remember Bran."

She pushed him away. "Enough. Let me finish."

She could barely see the red ink symbols. The walls and the floor glowed bright white, and the trace of her blood was a line of deep, thick, light-consuming black. There was nothing else in the world but that line, and those walls. She no longer remembered anything, or anyone; all she knew was that she had to finish drawing the pattern.

THE CHRYSANTHEMUM SEAL

She crawled on her hands and feet across something soft, a bundle of colourful lights, and, at last, she reached the final dot.

The walls around her disappeared, leaving only the black pattern suspended in nothingness, whirling, turning and pulsating, a source of unending power, pulling the entire universe towards it. With a jolt, Satō felt her soul wrenched from her body.

She was standing feet-deep in soft, red, dry dirt, in a place of darkness, looking out through a great stone portal onto the slope of a bald, rocky, boulder-strewn mountain.

Cold wind picked up loose gravel from the surface and scattered it over the grey boulders, and into the slow-flowing river below. Everything on the other side was the same shade of morbid, sickly grey, even the sky; and yet, Satō knew that the mountain was in the land of the living – unlike the red dirt place where she was stood.

She dared not turn around. She heard whispers behind her, and laughter, mocking and sinister, growing in the darkness. They were getting closer and louder with every second.

I could just step through that door, she thought, but she didn't move. She couldn't. Her will was already bound to the darkness.

The voices behind her grew to a loud din, like a nest of angry hornets, and she felt their gaze upon her body. It was cold, slippery; she shivered with disgust. Still more came, wrapping spiny limbs around her hands and legs. Their heads bobbed in the air in the corner of her eye, pale white, wispy, laughing skulls. She ignored them and stared ahead, at the grey rocks, at the grey sky.

They started dragging her back; she struggled, planting her feet firmly in the red dirt, but she was sliding, slipping. They called her with sweet voices: "Come with us... you'll be happy here... there's no pain here, no suffering..." Then others, snarling angrily: "Come with us, or you'll regret it... we will torture you... tear your soul apart..."

She was losing her strength, her will faltered. Tears ran down her face, as she dared not even to blink, not wanting to lose the sight of the land of the living. But she was being dragged away from the portal, little by little, inch by inch. More ghostly hands grabbed her, more voices hissed obscenities into her ears. She fell down to her knees, then on her face, scratching the red dirt with her hands, trying to grab onto something – anything – that could slow her down. But there was nothing here but the sand the colour of blood.

A thunderclap struck, and a web of lightning buzzed all around her, then another. In an instant, all the wraiths were gone. She was free.

She stood up, and started turning slowly, when a voice she would have recognized always and everywhere, stopped her.

"No, don't turn around. You must never turn around in this place."

"Father!"

She felt him come closer – almost close enough to touch. Her chin trembled.

"Don't weep, daughter."

"I thought …I'll never hear you again."

"Well, this time probably is the last one," Shūhan said.

"How did you …?"

"This place has strict rules. A balance that needs preserving. My death… broke some of those rules. I had to break a few more to bring back this balance. That is all I can say."

"I understand – I think."

"I hope it was worth it, Satō."

"I… don't know."

"What will you do next? What will you do when it's somebody's life that needs saving, not just a limb?"

"I will be stronger next time."

Even without seeing him, she knew he shook his head.

"This wasn't just about the boy, was it?"

"You condemn me… and yet you studied blood magic yourself. As did Tanaka-*sama*. You two gave me the glove in the first place! Did you really expect me to ignore it all?"

"I was hoping you'd be wiser than us."

"I am. I'm not doing it alone."

He clicked his lips. She knew that sound well, a sound of harsh disapproval.

"You trust one of their kind? Do you not remember what they did to me?"

I do, Father, she thought, *but I also remember what others did to me.*

"The Fanged are no worse than humans. They just have more time."

"More time to develop their cruelty."

"And skill with magic."

"That's not how I wanted to raise you."

"Didn't you always want me to be the strongest wizard in Kiyō, Father?"

"No!" protested Shūhan. "I only wanted you to be safe."

"Then why did you not name me your heir, Father? What were you waiting for?"

She almost turned around to shout at him, but he stopped her again.

"I'm sorry, Satō," he said, his voice fading into the distance. "My time here is coming to an end."

"Don't be like that again! We never had time to talk – "

"Satō, you must step through that door now. If you tarry, *they* will come back."

"Father! I – "

But he was gone; she felt nothing but the cold emptiness behind her – and the wraiths, gathering slowly again in the distance.

" – I just wanted to say goodbye."

The ceiling was unfamiliar.

She squeezed her left hand – it didn't hurt, but was neatly bandaged.

"Where am I?" she asked.

"This is our room," she heard Shōin answer. "The one we are supposed to share now that we're married."

Of course – she remembered. *I got married this morning!*

She turned to him.

"Why do you look so worried?" she asked.

"You died," Shōin replied.

"I – what?"

"Your heart stopped beating," he explained. "The Fanged told us to wait. So we waited."

"How long was I out?"

"Over an hour," said Shōin. "It's almost dark outside."

"How is Bran?"

"The foreigner? His leg is like new… and he's conscious – but still too weak to move."

A soft roar rumbled through the air.

"The *dorako*!" Satō sat up, groggily, and searched for the Tide Jewel.

"It's fine," said Shōin softly. "Ever since the Westerner woke up, the *dorako* has been sitting in the courtyard, making noises."

"Thank the Gods… that thing was really draining all my strength."

She felt dizzy and had to lean against Shōin's thin shoulder.

"Did he say anything?" she asked.

A barely discernible shadow swept across Shōin's face.

"Shōin? Did Bran say anything?"

"He… he called your name."

She struggled to stand up. "I must go see him."

"You're also tired," Shōin said, holding her by the hand. "It was a long day. Surely it can wait till tomorrow…"

She released herself. "It might be too late tomorrow. The *daimyo* will want him at the castle."

She staggered outside, propping herself up against the passing walls and pillars.

Dōraku and Nagomi waited for her in front of the house.

Satō opened her arms to accept Nagomi's embrace. The priestess pressed her face to her shoulder, not speaking for a long time.

"There, there," Satō said, patting her on the head, "see, I'm not dead after all."

"I was so worried!"

"It's all over now. Really, I'm fine. And Bran is fine too. In the end, there was nothing to worry about."

She pushed her gently away and turned towards Dōraku. "I have to see him."

"They've doubled the guards," he said. "I can get you through one last time, but you'll have to make it brief."

"Why must we sneak around like that? Those guards are no match for either of us."

"Where will you go if you lose favour with Mori-*dono*?"

She had no answer.

They walked briskly towards the infirmary. She felt the *dorako*'s angry stare as she passed it, but the beast remained silent, watchful. Several students examined the beast at a distance. They noticed her and bowed. She bowed in response.

The Mori samurai stood rigid at the door. Dōraku hesitated.

"I can only take one of you past them…"

"I'll… I'll wait here," said Nagomi. "I already saw him."

Dōraku nodded. He pressed his fingers together and whispered a quick incantation, then gestured at Satō to follow him quietly. She walked between the entranced samurai, as if invisible, entered the infirmary and closed the door behind her, leaving the Swordsman on guard.

Bran was asleep, lying on his back. She sat down by the side of his bed and sighed.

"Why did you fly away, Bran?" she said quietly, careful not to wake him up. "And what have you returned for?"

She reached out to touch his hair. "Was it just to warn us about something? That dragon that got you, or…?"

His breath was ragged, breaking. She looked around. In the light of a single candle she saw that the walls were clean, bearing no mark of the blood ritual. Yet somehow, she could still sense the soft pulsing of the invisible runes.

"There's so much I have to tell you…" she continued, her pent-up emotions spilling out as if a dam in her heart had suddenly broken open. "So much has happened. But what was I supposed to do? I didn't have a dragon to jump on and flee Yamato. I had to stay and live here… Should I have waited your return, like a good Dejima Wife?"

His silence made her irrationally angry.

"I was destitute, orphaned, banished, I had no clan and no money, and all of it thanks to you!" she cried.

"I'm sorry," he whispered. He opened his eyes – there was anguish in them that cut right through her.

Satō put a hand to her mouth. "I…I didn't mean to…!"

He sat up slowly, and leaned against the wall.

"You're right," he said. He spoke so quietly she could barely hear him, weighing each word, pausing. "Everywhere I go, I bring nothing but trouble."

"That's not true." She wiped a tear from her eye.

Why am I crying?

"My Father…he warned me against stagnation. You brought us *change*. Things started moving, when once they were stuck in a rut."

295

He forced a smile.

"Things seem to have been moving around even more while I *wasn't* here."

"How much... how much do you know already?" she asked with bated breath.

"Dōraku told me what happened to you in Satsuma... and what you did for me today," Bran said. "You shouldn't have done it. It's just a leg."

He doesn't know about Shōin, she realized, half relieved, half anxious.

"I thought you couldn't fly without it," she said.

"So what? I would still be alive."

"Well, it worked, didn't it? Show me."

He unravelled the *yukata*, baring his left leg. It was whole, the skin had healed perfectly, pale and bald where the scars had mended. All over his thigh and knee ran a long, winding, black pattern of the Blood Runes, carved deep into the skin, like a tattoo. She gasped at the sight.

"I know," Bran said, chuckling. "It's an odd souvenir."

"I'm sorry. I didn't know."

He shrugged. "A small price to pay. What matters is that you are unharmed."

He reached for her hand and squeezed it gently. "I am forever in your debt."

"I am... I am really glad it worked." she said. Her voice now as quiet as his.

He leaned closer. "If there is anything I can do to thank you…"

She felt his hot breath on her face. Her heart raced. Their eyes met – and, a moment later, their lips. Their tongues danced, their breath quickened. Bran ran his fingers through Satō's short hair, down her face. One of his hands caressed her back, the other moved down from her face to her neck, and then lower, to where her kimono parted…

She pushed him away.

"What's wrong…?"

"I can't – " she searched for words, but her mind was a jumbled mess of thoughts and feelings, racing and breaking. "I'm – I'm not…"

She bit her lips. *How do I tell him?*

The door slammed opened. She stood up, adjusting her kimono swiftly.

"We have to go," Dōraku said.

"Wait – " Bran wouldn't let go of her hand. "Go where? Why can't you stay here? What's going on behind that door?"

The Fanged scowled, impatient. "The guards will wake at any moment."

"I'm sorry, Bran," she slipped her hand out of his grasp. "I know it must be confusing." She walked to the door and turned around for a moment. "There are things…I will try to visit you…. I may be – "

She ran out of the room mid-sentence.

THE CHRYSANTHEMUM SEAL

The door slid shut, and Bran was left alone and baffled in the twilit room. He sighed, closed his eyes and linked with Emrys.

He studied the surroundings through the dragon's senses. It was a broad, sandy courtyard, surrounded by low, long buildings on all sides, and a tall stone wall beyond – some kind of military compound, Bran guessed. He counted a dozen samurai, in pairs, guarding entrances to the main buildings. He did not recognize the markings on their clothes, or on the flags on the walls: three circles under a straight line.

There were other men, too. Some walking about the place purposefully, avoiding the dragon in the middle of the compound, others opposite, trying to get close to Emrys with lanterns and devices of copper and glass which reminded Bran of the measuring apparatus he had seen the Satsuma wizard use on the mistfire boat.

A school of wizardry, he thought. *A tiny one.* Through the dragon's attuned senses he could see the magic energies of the place, and of the men around him.

Of course – where else would Satō end up… but why isn't she in Satsuma?

He bade Emrys fly up, the wind from his wings scattering the scientific devices, and their owners, aside. The samurai guards cowered behind pillars; the wizards shouted in excitement. He ignored them all.

Where am I?

There wasn't much that he could see in the quickly falling night. A castle keep on a hill, and a small city sprawling beneath, down to the sea… a narrow strait, a dark shadow of a hill on the other side… a small, ship-shaped island to the south…

I know this place.

The dragon refused to fly nearer to the island. It, too, recognized the location – but even more so, it felt the faint remnant of the sinister presence.

Ganryūjima. I'm back where I started.

He grew tired. He bade the dragon return, once again scaring away the wizards from the courtyard. He noticed Satō, standing firm in front of Emrys, unflinching. A fleeting emotion ran through the dragon's beastly mind. *Anger.*

Why?

Bran searched through the dragon's memories. It wasn't easy, but he caught a glimpse of a red orb in Sato's hand.

The Tide Jewel.

"It's all right, Emrys," he sent a soothing thought. "I gave it to her. She's a… a friend. Just a friend."

Another wizard emerged from the shadow, standing right behind Satō, a young boy – younger than Bran, short and timid-looking. He put a hand gently on the girl's shoulder and said something. She turned to him and they disappeared together inside a small house.

Just a friend.

THE CHRYSANTHEMUM SEAL

CHAPTER XIV

Two black palanquins waited in front of the infirmary, surrounded by a throng of Chōfu samurai. Lord Mori was taking no chances. The path leading from the building to the gate was cut off by a row of armed men.

Satō watched as the guards escorted Bran outside. He squinted and shaded his eyes from the sun. He looked sad and comical in a too-big *yukata* he'd borrowed from one of the medical students.

She marched straight at the line of the samurai. One of them tried to stop her.

"You can't come – "

She pressed her hand to his chest. His breastplate crackled with frost.

"Let me through or the next thing to freeze will be your heart."

The samurai looked back at his commander. Kunishi rolled his eyes and waved at him to let the wizardess pass.

"Satō!" Bran beamed at her. "Are you coming with us to see the *daimyō*?"

301

She got close to him, so that nobody else could hear them.

"You don't have to do this, Bran," she whispered.

"Do what?" he stared at her. "This is just an audience, isn't it? I spoke to *daimyo*s before."

"This isn't Satsuma. Mori-*dono* is not as keen on foreigners as Nariakira."

"You worry too much. What can they do to me now that I have Emrys back?" he smiled. "I'll be fine."

He reached out a hand to her face, but she swerved to avoid his touch.

"Just… be careful," she said and quickly turned back to hide her embarrassment.

Another domain capital, another *daimyo*'s palace… Bran felt like a monkey in a travelling menagerie, carried from town to town to perform. At least he was spared the humiliation of being shown on the main streets of the city. He journeyed, once again, incognito, in an enclosed, stuffy palanquin.

In the middle of Yamato summer, the inside of the vehicle was even worse to bear, hot like the inside of a furnace, and filled with the smell of sweat condensing on the thick black cotton curtains. By the time the cavalcade arrived at its destination, his cotton *yukata* was soaked through.

"I can't see the *daimyo* like this," he said, after emerging from the palanquin. "I need a bath."

"There's no time," said the boy leaving the other palanquin. He was the boy whom Bran had seen the other night with Satō.

Shōin-something.

"Besides, to us, you foreigners smell no matter how much you bathe."

He smiled, but Bran knew it wasn't exactly a joke. He wiped his forehead with a sleeve, but it was a futile gesture. The garden around them, overgrown with densely canopied maple and ash trees, was almost as hot and humid as the inside of the palanquin.

A haughty-looking samurai came out to greet them. His bow was the slightest of nods, his face frozen in a badly concealed scoff.

"It is great honour to host the *daimyo* in my house," the samurai said to nobody in particular. The meaning was clear: "my position in the domain is high, and don't you forget it". Bran guessed this was aimed at the boy beside him, rather than himself.

As they walked through the garden, he recalled Satō's words before his departure. He was keen to dismiss them as needless worry. This whole Lord Mori could not have been all that bad: like Nariakira, he funded a school of *Rangaku*, he tolerated Satō and others' presence in his capital – even Dōraku's. At the very least, that meant he was not an ally to the *Taikun* or the Eight-headed Serpent. How dangerous could a man like him be?

And yet Nariakira wanted to kill Satō, he remembered, and his blood ran cold.

303

THE CHRYSANTHEMUM SEAL

After they entered the vestibule, the nobleman turned around and stared, unashamedly, at Bran. He seemed taken aback by the fact that the dragon rider remembered to take off his sandals before stepping onto the straw floor; he looked like somebody who'd had the punch-line of a joke taken away.

He led them down the corridor. The door at the end opened, and for a moment, Bran thought they were facing yet another rEtainer, before he realized the truth. The young man sitting on a dais in the middle of the room, barely in his twenties, *was* Lord Mori himself.

The councillors surrounding him were all old, hoary-headed, wrinkle-faced men – Bran guessed they'd been inherited from the previous lord's entourage. The tension in the room was tangible, even before Bran and Shōin crossed the threshold and prostrated themselves before the *daimyo*.

"Rise," said Lord Mori in a tired, gruff voice.

He studied Bran in silence for what seemed like an eternity.

"Can you really speak our language?" he asked.

"Yes, *kakka*."

"Is that one of your *Rangaku* powers?"

"No, *kakka*. That talent was bestowed upon me by the Spirits of the Suwa Shrine, in Kiyō, when I first arrived in Yamato."

"Ah, I see," the *daimyo* replied, and turned to one of his councillors. "You were right, Murata. Our Yamato magic is still good for *something*."

304

The plum-faced councillor bowed with a faint, forced smile.

"Ah, but what a poor host I am! You must both be thirsty after all this talk."

He clapped twice, and the servants brought in bottles of saké, pots of cha, and plates of small salty biscuits.

"So you've been to Yamato before?" Lord Mori asked, reaching for a cracker.

"Two months ago I was shipwrecked in Kiyō. I left a month later."

"And now you've returned. Do you not know what the laws of this land say about foreigners?"

"I am aware, *kakka*, but I had no choice. I had to warn my friends of the danger they're facing."

The *daimyo* pointed to Shōin. "Is Yoshida-*sama* one of your friends?"

"No. I mean, I haven't known him before. I came to see Takashima-*sama*."

"Ah, of course. She's from Kiyō, too. That makes sense. Each to his own, I suppose..." He scratched his chin. "This warning. I assume it's something that concerns more than just the fate of your... *friend*."

What was that? Bran perked up. *How would he know?*

"Yes, *kakka*," he said. "I believe it concerns the future of Yamato – especially domains like yours and..." he bit his tongue.

"You wanted to say Satsuma," the *daimyo* stated coldly. "Despite our differences we are both equally despised by Edo. It is Edo you came to warn us about, isn't it?"

Bran nodded. "It's…" He stopped and looked at the councillors. How many of them were spies of the *Taikun* or agents of the Serpent?

One way or another, they are involved in everything, he remembered Dōraku's words.

The *daimyo* caught his wandering look and smiled. "Elders," he said, "will you please leave us alone for a moment."

"*Kakka!*" the eldest-looking councillor's jowls shook with indignation. "Your safety – !"

"Yoshida-*sama* can guarantee our safety. Isn't that right?"

"Of – of course," Shōin stuttered.

He's not certain at all, thought Bran. He couldn't blame the boy. *After all, this could all just be a very long ruse on my part to get near the* daimyo.

He hit the floor with his forehead. "Upon my honour as a dragon rider, I vow no harm will come to you in my presence, *kakka*," he said.

The *daimyo* smiled again. "Surely that is sufficient for you, Murata."

"A barbarian's word is worth less than manure," the councillor scoffed.

I've heard that before.

"Now you're insulting my guest, Murata."

The councillor bowed. "I'm sorry, *kakka*. But it is my duty to express my opinions clearly."

"And it is my right to ignore them. Now leave, everyone."

He waved the wooden paddle and said no more until the room emptied.

"It's not much, and most of it is written in some kind of code," said Bran, sipping hot *cha* from a frail terracotta cup; he'd had no idea how much he'd missed the bitter-salty taste. "But it's enough to gain a basic understanding of the proposed treaty."

On the *daimyo*'s invitation, he and Shōin sat next to the dais and all three were now poring over the papers which Bran had stolen from the Gorllewin Komtur's desk.

I was hoping to discuss this with Satō and others first, Bran thought. I still don't know how much I can trust this man...

"These two pages are interesting," he said, presenting the pieces of paper on which were roughly drawn several tables. Each table had two columns: one bearing brief, coded words, the other – simply rows of crosses and ticks.

"Some of those marks are from a different brush," noted Lord Mori. "That's a Yamato hand."

"Well spotted, *kakka*. The Grey Hoods must have been working on it with the Council," said Bran. "I noticed the crosses and ticks in each table always add up to seven: as many as there are dragons in the squadron."

307

"Seven?" asked the *daimyo*. "Is that significant?"

"Seven is an important number for all Sun Priests," said Bran. "I learned a little of their religion while I was their prisoner. There are seven ranks in their holy order of warriors, seven major festivals in the year, and so on."

"What do you think those tables mean, then?" asked Shōin. He was tracing the marks with his finger, as if trying to devise their meaning through touch.

"I'm guessing that this is the way they plan to relocate the *dorako*," answered Bran. "After all, if the Black Wings are to assist the *Taikun*'s army, they need to be spread out over Yamato, in vulnerable places. Even a dragon needs some time to reach, say, Satsuma or Chōfu from Edo. It also needs to be fed and stabled," he added.

"That means infrastructure," said Shōin.

"A castle," Bran added, remembering his daydream of conquering coastal fortresses with Emrys.

"*My* castle," Lord Mori said, clenching the paddle in his fist.

He remained silent for the longest time, eyes down, tapping the end of the paddle against his chin.

He is the exact opposite of Nariakira, thought Bran. The lord of Satsuma would have had three different answers ready the moment Bran stopped talking. Lord Mori was taking everything slowly, with deliberation.

Perhaps he makes better decisions that way… or perhaps he's just not as fast a thinker.

"If they come here…" the *daimyo* said at last, "how can we fight those – Black Wings?"

Bran wasn't sure who was supposed to answer the question, so he waited until Shōin spoke.

"We studied Bran-*sama*'s *dorako* through the night," the boy spoke, "and we are fairly confident we might defeat these creatures, if need be."

I'd like to see you try.

"What do you say to that, Bran-*sama*?"

"I'm afraid even the best of your wizards are no match to a fully grown *dorako*. They are *famously* resistant to magic."

"We already managed to subdue your beast once," Shōin said, looking at Bran defiantly.

"Black Wings are far bigger, stronger and more powerful than Emrys. In fact, they are the largest I've ever seen." He tried not to let his irritation show. "I have faced the power of Ganryū's orb before, if that's what you mean, and I sincerely doubt it would do much against even one of those monsters. Not to mention *seven*."

"Ah-hm." Lord Mori fell into another long period of silence. A large mosquito flew in from somewhere and hovered, irritatingly, in the air beside Bran's ear. The droning noise and the heat were making him drowsy.

"We seem to be in a rather dire situation here," the *daimyo* said. "I can't risk the well-being of my people in such an unfair combat."

"But," Shōin raised up from his knees by an inch, "I don't understand. Why are you so worried about all this, *kakka*? What combat? The *Taikun* has no obvious reason to attack us, does he? We are a law-abiding province, we pay our taxes on time, we obey the decrees. We are not Satsuma."

"You are right, Yoshida-*sama*. We may be safe, for now. But with that kind of power, the *Taikun* might soon start making unreasonable demands. What then? What if, for example, they demand we arrest Bran-*sama* and all his friends and acquaintances, and hand them over?"

"I'm fully aware my presence here is troublesome, *kakka*," Bran said quickly. "At any moment I can do the same as the Black Wings did – 'disappear' into some remote location."

"I don't think Edo would fall for the same trick twice," the *daimyo* said with the gentlest of smiles. "And too many people know you're here by now. No, I'm afraid there is only one thing I can do."

He clapped thrice this time. All the walls around the room slid open, revealing a troop of samurai, armed too the teeth.

Bran leapt up, summoning his *tarian* around him. The Lance flickered in his hand. His head spun and the room swayed.

"I wouldn't do that," said the *daimyo*, still sporting the same gentle smile. "Think of your friends back in the Meirinkan."

"They will fight," said Bran, remembering how Dōraku and Satō forced their way through Ganryū's army. And Torishi would protect Nagomi with his life.

310

The *daimyo* would not frighten him so easily.

"Fight? I don't need to fight them," Lord Mori replied. "But I can make their life so miserable they'll wish they were dead. How do you think your wizardess friend, for example, would react to being disowned from her new family and sent into another exile – because of *you*?"

That hurt, almost physically so. Bran felt weakened by the *daimyo*'s words… or was it the *cha*? *Daimyo* said something that escaped Bran. The walls wobbled around him. He blinked and focused.

"I don't understand…what new family?"

"Oh – you mean you still don't know? But I thought you said you were close with Takashima-*sensei*… or should I say, Yoshida-*sensei*…?"

A slow understanding dawned on Bran. He looked at the boy beside him and remembered Satō's ominous-sounding words.

"I had to stay and live here."

"Mori-*dono*, I must protest…" he heard Shōin say feebly.

"Must you, Yoshida-*sama*? Think again. Do your loyalties lie with me, or with your wife's… *friend*?"

You bastard. You're even worse than Nariakira.

The Yamato wizard lowered his hand in resignation.

"I thought so," scoffed Mori-*dono*. He rose; the gentleness in his face was gone, replaced by mockery, as he addressed Bran. "You foreigners are too soft. You may dress

311

like a samurai, and talk like a samurai, but no samurai would surrender without a fight. You bring shame to your clan."

He's right, Bran thought in a daze. *Father would never have gone down so easily.*

"Take him away," the warlord spat out the order in disgust.

His *tarian* buzzed off. The floor escaped from his feet. As the samurai grabbed Bran and pulled him outside, he heard the *daimyo* speak to a bewildered Shōin.

"Now, Yoshida-*sama*, there is a more important matter for us to discuss..."

The two black palanquins disappeared beyond the gate. The rest of the Mori samurai followed them out, leaving the school unguarded for the first time in two days.

Satō entered freely into the infirmary, and saw Nagomi helping to clear Bran's room up.

"There you are," she said. "Why didn't you come out to say goodbye to Bran?"

The priestess paused on the way to the mattress cupboard.

"Goodbye? Why? He's coming back soon, isn't he?" she replied, not looking at Satō as she spoke.

"Have you actually managed to speak to him yet?"

"I sat by his bed all night."

"But did you *talk* to him? Nagomi." She grabbed the priestess by the hand as the girl passed her. Nagomi dropped the rolled-up blanket she'd been holding. "Why didn't you tell me you were in trouble?"

The priestess smiled sadly. "Aren't we all?"

She bent to pick up the blanket.

"Leave that, for the Gods! You're not a servant. Come with me outside." Satō pulled her towards the door. "You have to tell me what happened on the way from Nagoya."

Satō felt the disconcerting stare of the *dorako* on herself. The beast lay in its usual place in the middle of the courtyard, with its head on its front paws, like an old dog, glancing at the wizardess from time to time from underneath a lazy eyebrow. She did her best to ignore it.

They were sitting under the only large tree on the school grounds; a gnarled, vine-stifled, half-dead camphor, the last remnant of what must have once been a garden sprawling where the Meirinkan now was.

"What are your plans now?" she asked.

"Plans?" said the priestess, shaking her head. "I didn't have time to think of any plans. I just wanted to get here in time for your wedding."

"You must have thought of *something*. I mean, all those visions, prophecies – it's obvious what you're part of is greater than any of us."

"I never asked to be a part of anything," said Nagomi.

A gust of wind picked up a bunch of brown, dry camphor leaves off the ground and scattered them across the sand.

"Sometimes... sometimes I feel like those dry leaves, just blown here and there in the wind."

Satō reached out a hand and caught one of the leaves and crushed it in her hand. A fresh, cool smell spread through the air.

"Well, looks like the wind is carrying you straight to the *Taikun*'s prison, unless you act now."

Nagomi raised her head. "I'm safe here, aren't I?"

"I suppose so, but for how long? Sooner or later the winds will blow again. As long as there's a *Taikun* in power, neither of us is safe. And what about your family? They're in Edo, at the government's mercy."

"You don't have to remind me," said Nagomi. "I worry about them every night. But what can I do? What can we do against the *Taikun*? Many people have tried and failed. Powerful people. Even Kazuko-*hime*."

She swallowed the tears and grit her teeth. She touched the High Priestess' necklace and raised her head and looked into the dazzling sun.

"I want to do my bit to help... Not just to help my family – but to fulfil Kazuko-*hime*'s legacy, to finish the mission she left to me ... If only I knew how."

Satō smiled. "That's all I needed to hear, really. I'm sure we'll find a way. We only need to stick together again."

Nagomi nodded and picked up a handful of the leaves from the ground.

"It smells like Suwa," she said. "Remember? There was this great camphor tree by the carp pond."

"We used to climb it when the priests weren't looking." Satō smiled.

They sat in silence for a while, listening to the rustle of the wind in the branches, and the chirp of starlings in their nest, before Satō spoke again.

"How did it feel?" she asked. "When you stabbed that man?"

"It was awful," replied Nagomi, shivering. "Nauseating. It made me never want to fight again. But…"

"Yes?"

The priestess smiled wryly.

"That whole situation… It felt good to be finally doing something on my own. To be in control, if only for a brief moment."

Satō chuckled.

"Kazuko-*hime* chose well," she said. "You're definitely not just an ordinary leaf."

Another gust blew more sand and debris around them, then another, stronger, forceful.

"That's no wind," said Satō, standing up. "It's Emrys!"

The dragon beat its wings one more time and launched itself into the air. The buffeting air threw dirt in Satō's eyes.

315

Through forced tears, she saw the beast turn towards the castle.

"Something's wrong with Bran!" said Satō and ran off after the dragon. Nagomi followed close behind.

Right as Emrys disappeared over the wall, the school gate opened, and in came Shōin. The boy looked up and traced the green dragon's flight with curiosity, until the beast was no longer visible.

He turned towards the approaching girls. His face was grey, sullen. He was alone. Nagomi shivered.

"Where's Bran?" asked the wizardess. "Did you see that? His dragon just got up and flew away!"

The boy raised his hands defensively.

"He… he won't be coming back." He swallowed. "There will be an announcement of his arrest later today. No, wait – " he silenced her protests, "this is only to appease the rEtainers. In reality, Mori-*dono* asked him to undertake an urgent secret mission."

"That's strange." Satō looked at him suspiciously. "He wouldn't even come for his belongings?"

"It's all part of the bluff. Mori-*dono* will send for them later." He swayed. "I'm sorry, it was a tiring day – I really have to rest now…"

"No," said Nagomi, stepping forward. "This is wrong!"

"What is?" Satō asked, frowning.

Nagomi grabbed Shōin by the collar of his kimono and shook him. "Why are you lying?" she cried. "This isn't how it should be – this is not what I saw!"

The boy laughed nervously.

"What do you mean? I'm – I'm telling the truth."

He avoided her accusing stare, and looked to Satō for help.

"Nagomi!" the wizardess grabbed her hands. "Let him go! What's wrong with you?"

She stepped back, trembling with a mixture of emotions. Anger, fear and confusion surged through her.

None of the visions showed this. None of the visions… what's happening?

"You saw this?" Satō asked. "What did you see?"

Satō's voice trailed off as the visions flashed before Nagomi's eyes again.

Bran standing next to Shōin in Lord Mori's audience room, confused and angry.

Guards taking him away on a boat, beating him mercilessly.

A suicide sword in the sand, stained with blood.

His dead body on a beach, bloated and battered.

Nagomi shook her head and rubbed her eyes to stop the images from coming.

"I'm sorry," she said. "I think I should go and rest."

"I think you better should," said Satō, touching Nagomi's forehead with a worried look. "You're burning. Drink some water."

Once she got back to her room, Nagomi dropped to her knees, and shut her eyes tight, unable to stop the barrage of images.

"Will she be all right?" Shōin asked, leaning heavily on his wife's shoulder.

Satō bit her lips in hesitation, looking towards the dormitory. Shōin followed her gaze and noticed Nagomi's great hairy companion hurrying after the priestess.

"She'll be fine," Satō said, turning away. "It's just the strain of recent events. She's not used to it."

"I am sorry to hear that," Shōin said.

Satō helped him sit down on a shaded bench and beckoned to one of the students to bring them water.

"What did you talk about?" she asked. "What secret mission?"

Shōin grabbed the water gourd and drank from it far longer than he needed to. He used the pause to think of a satisfactory answer. Lord Mori had not given him too much time to invent a story.

"Those papers he brought," he started. That, at least, was a safe topic – and true. He told her of the news the foreigner had related before the *daimyo*, and of the strange markings on the pieces of paper.

"Mori-*dono* thinks those mean the castles where each of the *dorako* is supposed to be relocated," he added, counting out on his fingers. "Chōfu, Kagoshima, Edo, Heian…"

"The *Mikado*'s palace?" Satō gasped. "They wouldn't dare…"

"To protect the court? Isn't that the *Taikun*s' duty?"

"Yes, but – to use foreign armies … to ally with the heretics… it's unthinkable."

"It's still uncertain…" The right-wrong answer finally jumped into Shōin's mind. "That's what the foreigner's mission is about – to find out what's really going on."

"Yes, that makes sense." Satō nodded thoughtfully. "It's just so… sudden. He wouldn't even come back to say goodbye… *again*," she added quietly, and Shōin wondered, not for the first time, what exactly connected the Westerner to his wife.

"Well, he couldn't really be seen travelling up and down the streets of Chōfu," he forced a chuckle. "Mori-*dono* has a reputation to keep."

A shadow fell on his face. He looked up – it was Takasugi, handing him another gourd.

"Thanks, but I've had enough water," Shōin said.

Takasugi laughed. "You think *I'd* bring you water? I brought this all the way from Naniwa – it will put you back on your feet."

"Ah." Shōin reached for the gourd. "It's good that you're here, Takasugi-*sama*. There's something urgent I need to discuss with you."

"You're in bad shape, little priestess."

Nagomi slowly sat up. Torishi slid the door closed discreetly, making sure there was nobody outside.

"I can't take it anymore. I want it to stop."

"Is it really so bad? Seeing the future?"

"I don't want it!" she cried. "I hate Scrying, I hate what it does to me!"

"I don't understand," he said, frowning.

She hid her face in her hand.

"Scryers can't be healers. It's something I've learnt in Atsuta. And it's true. My healing power has diminished. It's now just a fraction of what it once was... At first I thought it was because of what happened on Ganryūjima, but now I know... I hate it," she repeated.

He came up and knelt in front of her, putting his large hands on her arms. "If this is your true calling, don't fight it. There will always be other healers to take your place."

"*True calling?* All my life I wanted nothing else but to heal people."

"You're still young. You'll change your mind."

She wiped her eyes and sniffed. Her golden necklace jangled. She picked it up to the light.

"And who will train me, now that Kazuko-*hime* is dead? How will I even know which visions are true? I was already wrong about Sacchan. And now Bran…"

"What about him?" Torishi asked sharply.

"Shōin said Mori-*dono* has sent him on a secret mission. But that's not what I saw."

Torishi frowned and smoothed his beard deep in thought.

"You must renew your training at once," he said eventually.

"Haven't you been listening? I don't know how. I don't know anything. And there's noone who can help me."

She dropped her head. He reached out his hand and raised her chin gently.

"Do you forget?" he rumbled. "I am the Prince of the Kumaso. I am Chief Shaman. I know the ways of the Spirits."

She raised her eyes. "You would help me?"

He put his fist to his chest in a solemn gesture.

"I will do all that's in my power."

Shōin stood up on the Western-style lectern, and looked at the small crowd of men before him. Some of them were as old as his father, if not more. Most were in their twenties; there was nobody as young as himself.

THE CHRYSANTHEMUM SEAL

He still found it overwhelming to speak to them as a teacher. His authority over them was not his own: it had been bestowed upon him by the *daimyo*. He was not their superior in any of the usual samurai ways: experience, wealth, status, kinship. All he had going for him was his raw magic talent – and even that was not as exceptional as he wanted them to think – and the kind of wizardly intuition which put him ahead of the pack, and into Mori-*dono*'s attention.

And a willingness to betray those who put their trust in me, it seems, he thought bitterly, but then dismissed that notion. It was just some foreigner I met the day before. I had no obligations towards him.

If any of the men in front of him resented his position, they did not show it. They were all commoners or low-ranking nobles, and so, if anything, they looked up to him as an example of the kind of lightning-fast career that was only possible nowadays in an enlightened domain such as Chōfu, or – Shōin was the first to admit – Satsuma. They may have hoped to take his place, but it was a healthy ambition, without malice – and Shōin was ready to step down at any moment, should the need arise.

I'm tired of all this governing and conspiring, anyway. I'd much rather focus on my magical studies. I still haven't even figured out my attunement…

And now they all stood here, waiting patiently for him to speak. Even standing by the lectern he had to look up to see their faces. He cleared his throat.

"This is the message from Mori Takachika-*dono* to the students and staff of the Meirinkan Academy of Western Learning," he started, unravelling a scroll sealed with the Mori crest. He hoped nobody would notice that the scroll

322

was just an empty piece of paper. The *daimyo* had only given him rough guidance as to what he was about to say. *You'll know best how to talk to them*, he'd said.

Shōin wasn't so sure. He had consulted his words with a few others, including Takasugi and the strange samurai who had arrived at their wedding, and who seemed to be another mysterious acquaintance of his wife. They were more familiar with the ways of the world than he was, but each refused to actually speak to the gathering.

"You are our leader," Takasugi, who now stood beside him in case any help was needed, had said, "whether you like it or not. You must start acting like one."

Shōin took a deep breath.

"The attack on our loyal r*Eta*iners in the forest of Hinoyama Mountain was an unforgivable breach of law, etiquette, and trust. The usual punishment for that kind of transgression is beheading of the ringleaders, and an order of suicide for the followers."

He paused to see their reaction. Their faces remained grave, silent, unmoved. Were they really all ready to die for this? Shōin wasn't sure he would have remained so calm himself in similar circumstances.

"However, having considered the loyalty shown *personally* to me by the headmaster of the school," he continued, "and taking into account the progress made by the school in recent weeks and the incalculable benefits that its students bring to the well-being of our domain, we have decided one last time to remain gracious and forgiving in this case."

Not to mention, it will rub Satsuma all the wrong way, Shōin thought with an inward chuckle. The message from Lord Nariakira demanding the rendition of Takashima Satō and those who helped her escape, could not have come at a better moment.

Not even a sigh of relief. The air in the hall remained dense with unease. They knew they wouldn't be let off *that* easily.

"Those responsible *will* be punished, with fines and public shaming, the dEtails of which will be announced at a later date." This sounded harsh, but Shōin knew the punishments would be extremely lenient: fines for the noble-born, who could afford them, shaming for the commoners, who wouldn't care. The *real* retribution was still to come.

"To avoid similar altercations in the future, we have decided to adjust the Meirinkan statute. It is no longer a school of Western learning, and you are no longer just students. With this decree, all those who decide to remain at the school are elevated to rEtainer status of the Mori clan. *Loyalty* will be paramount. Furthermore, the Meirinkan is to become a military academy, with the sole purpose of developing modern methods of warfare. There will be strict discipline. Your orders will be coming directly from the castle."

Now there were gasps. And whispers. Every word of what Shōin said was revolutionary. To elevate so many of the commoners to noblemen, in one sweeping statement, was unheard of; to open a military academy without the *Taikun*'s permission was a crime. Why would a small, distant domain like Chōfu need to develop its own, new style of army? Was Mori-*dono* heading the same way as Satsuma – towards open rebellion?

"So there you have it," Shōin rolled back the scroll. He didn't feel at all well: his stomach rumbled, his brow was covered in sweat. *I need to lie down, he thought.*

"We are now a war school. No more Western literature or history, except the history of warfare. No more medicine, other than dressing wounds and the like. No more studying artefacts, unless they can be somehow used for combat. And so on, and so on. In short, we are to become the Mori clan's personal militia. Our new name is *Kiheitai*, 'the Irregulars'."

One of the students at the front raised a hand.

"Yes, Aoki-*sama*?"

"How long do we have before the changes come into effect?"

"The decree is read out publicly tomorrow at noon. Those of you who so wish can leave the school before then – except for those who took part in the fighting. For them, the only other choice is suicide."

There were nods and murmurs, some of agreement, some of astonishment. It was a fair deal – almost too fair.

One voice broke away from the hubbub. "Isn't it great? Shōin-*sama* saved us from the hangman! May he live ten thousand years!"

Shōin searched the owner of the voice out in the crowd. *I don't remember you having taken part in the battle*, he thought. It was just as Mori-*dono* had warned him: *they will crawl out in time of change, like worms crawl out of wood when there's a fire. Turncoats, sycophants, trying to secure their position in the chaos.*

He raised his hand, and they quietened down.

"You are now all retainers of the Mori clan," he said, finishing his speech. He could barely stand. The strain of the last two days was taking a terrible toll on his frail physique. "At the beck and call of the *daimyo*. It is a harsh duty – but a great privilege. Remember this when…" he gasped and clutched his chest. Takasugi ran up to him and helped him down, then climbed to the lectern.

"That will be all," he said. "You are dismissed."

CHAPTER XV

"Are you sure you don't want me to try pleading with Mori-*dono* one last time?" Satō asked Nagomi.

The wizardess looked stronger and more warlike than ever, wearing the raven black uniform of the new Chōfu army, with the sword and the thunder gun thrust under the belt. Across her chest ran a white sash with a golden hem, marking her as an officer in the *Kiheitai* militia. Shōin and other officers had already boarded the ship that would take the newly-fashioned troop on its first assignment to deal with a minor peasant revolt in the eastern part of the province.

"I'm sure," replied Nagomi. Her voice was shakier than she wanted it to be. "There is something I need to work on with Torishi-*sama*, and I need peace and quiet."

"Well, you'll have plenty of that here," said Satō with a wry smile. "Almost everyone is leaving with us…"

The priestess nodded. She was to be left with just Torishi for her companion. Lord Mori's house arrest remained in place for them both. But she didn't mind. In her current state she was not fit for travel – or combat, if that was what Satō was expecting of her.

THE CHRYSANTHEMUM SEAL

This is nothing but another gust of wind, isn't it?

Everyone else was leaving the Meirinkan for their own particular reasons. Bran had his secret mission from the *daimyo*. The Swordsman had "borrowed" a few of Satō's students on some errand of his own and disappeared the day after Bran's waking. Satō and Shōin, too, had their orders. The priestess was the only one without an assignment, the only one who could go where she pleased, and with whom she wanted – and she was growing weary of it.

I have to follow my own mission. As soon as I learn to control those visions…

Torishi had assured her he already had something prepared. For the first time in weeks, she was again full of hope.

"Takasugi-*sama* will be disappointed," Satō said with a snicker.

"W-what?"

"He keeps talking about how you dealt with those guards and spies – he thinks you're some kind of a *shinobi*."

Nagomi felt her cheeks burn red. She looked away.

"You know I don't like to remember that day. Too many people died."

"Then I suppose it's better that you don't come with us," said Satō, nodding in sympathy. "We are going to a war. People will die."

"Don't take me for a coward, Sacchan."

"I'm not! You've always been the bravest of us all. But you're not a warrior, and I respect that."

Satō waited for her to answer, but Nagomi remained silent, looking at the wizardess, and to the ships and beyond, across the strait. There, past two tiny, nameless islets, the hump-backed mountain she was seeing often in her dreams lately rose up.

Mekari-yama... what secret do you hide from me?

From asking around the school, she had gathered that the shrine had been damaged in a fire the previous year, and hadn't since been fully rebuilt. But that wasn't much to go on – minor shrines like that one burned down all the time.

"Nagomi?" Satō's voice broke her out of her daydream. "I have to go."

"Yes," she said distractedly, and then she wrapped her arms tightly around the wizardess. Satō laughed nervously and looked around to see if anybody noticed this unusual public show of affection.

"We were supposed to stick together," Nagomi whispered.

"Don't worry, I'll be back soon," Satō said, patting the priestess on the back.

"I'll be waiting," said Nagomi, though she knew from her visions it would be a long time before they'd meet again.

From the safety of his hilltop hideout, Shōin watched the village patrol return from its round and disappear beyond the make-shift palisade.

"They seem well organized," he said. "Not at all the sort of mindless rabble my father used to tell me about."

"I didn't know your father was a soldier," said Satō. There were just the two of them in the observation post. Most of the militia - once teachers and students of the Academy, now "officers" and "soldiers" of the *Kiheitai* – were hiding in the thick forest at the foot of the hill, preparing for the battle.

Shōin chuckled quietly. "He was a tailor in the army train. There are no warriors in my family."

The village below was one of two fortified camps guarding the opposite banks of the Nishiki River, and formed part of the rebel rear-guard – the first of several lines of defence they had formed around Iwakuni, the harbour city besieged by the rebels for nearly a month now.

That was all the information Shōin had, and all that he needed. He was only an observer in this campaign. He knew nothing about fighting battles, waging wars; he left that part to Takasugi, a man much better suited to the job thanks to his education and samurai upbringing.

Not that much fighting was necessary until now. The bulk of campaigning was done by the domain's regular troops, and the rebels seemed to melt away before them like sand before the storm.

"I can't believe our first task is to destroy a rebellion of commoners," Shōin said, shaking his head. "This wasn't what I had in mind when I started teaching at the Meirinkan."

"Why are they revolting now?" asked Satō.

"I don't know," replied Shōin. "The peasant revolt my father saw was before I was born, almost thirty years ago. There have been no disturbances since then. And now this," he nodded at the village below.

"Don't they have any demands?"

"Oh, you know." Shōin shrugged. "The usual. Lower taxes, less work, more respect from the upper classes... the grievances of the common folk are always many. And always right," he added, quietly, to himself. "But," he said quickly, before Satō could think on his words, "there is something odd about this one. Nobody knows what caused it in the first place, who the ring-leaders are... They have better weapons and tactics than usual – or so I've been told – and they were joined by some warrior monks and *onmyōji* from the mountains, which is why *we're* here. Look out – " He pointed to the bare hillside, where a man camouflaged in a coat and hat made of green straw climbed quickly towards them. "Takasugi's coming back."

The newly-appointed commander of the *Kiheitai* scrambled into the observation post and took off the straw garments, revealing the black-and-white uniform underneath.

"How did it go?" asked Shōin.

"It went well, I think," replied Takasugi. "But they made no promises. I don't think they believe us yet."

"I don't believe it myself," said Shōin. "It's too radical. Mori-*dono* will never consent to it."

"What's radical?" asked Satō, "what are you two talking about?"

Takasugi reached for the gourd at his waist and drank from it in deep gulps, before answering.

"There's a group of dissenters among the rebels," he said, wiping his mouth. "We made them an offer in exchange for joining our side. It remains to be seen whether they accept it or not."

"Have you learned what the rebels' plans are?" asked Shōin.

Takasugi nodded. "That's what caused the dissent. The leaders are very keen on capturing Iwakuni. The others, not so much. The peasant headmen I talked to simply wanted to present their grievances before the *daimyo*."

"What's so precious about Iwakuni?" asked Satō. Takasugi shrugged.

"A city… a harbour… a residence of a minor branch of the Mori clan… not much worth fighting for, except maybe the provincial treasury and they must know that doesn't amount to much – Iwakuni is a poor land."

"Odd," said Shōin, looking down again at the twin villages. The river between them flowed calmly, the water was bright green in the noon sun.

"When do the samurai attack?" he asked.

Takasugi looked at the sky. A lone black kite flew between the hilltops in search of prey. "Any minute now."

As if in answer, the blast of a war conch resounded over the hills, followed by a salvo of arquebus fire. Before the smoke dispersed in the wind, more than fifty samurai, bearing Mori banners, poured forth from the forest, screaming and waving swords, towards the furthest of the fortified villages.

"That's our cue, *sensei*," said Takasugi. Shōin nodded, put his hands together and shot a beam of red-coloured flame from his fingers high into the sky. At the signal, the soldier-students of the *Kiheitai* emerged from their hiding places. In their simple black-and-white uniforms they looked nowhere near as impressive as the samurai, in their simple black-and-white uniforms; and there was maybe twenty of them altogether. But they moved in a tight formation toward the nearest village, silent, determined, ominous. Takasugi had only a week to transform this random group – hand-picked from among the students of Meirinkan – into some kind of fighting force. At least in their appearance they looked the part.

"Now we'll see if our deal came through," remarked Shōin. "Let's go."

The three of them ran down the slope, to join the rest of the students. Catching glimpses of the battle through the trees, Shōin watched the samurai across the river reach the stockade and clamber up, ignoring the arrows that poured on them from above. The rebels fought bravely, but they were quickly overwhelmed, and the Mori warriors broke inside with little trouble.

Meanwhile, the *Kiheitai* approached the gates of their target village and spread out in a fan-shaped formation, waiting for orders, glancing at each other nervously. Shōin bit his lips.

I don't want any of them to get hurt.

He hoped the gambit paid off, but the wait was unbearable.

There were cries and the sounds of brief fighting inside the stockade, and then silence. The wicket gate opened wide, and out came a small, stocky man in short peasant trousers, an ancient black lacquer breastplate a few sizes too large, and a conical hard hat of blackened tin. He was chewing on a long straw, exuding the unmistakable practical authority of a village headman. He first looked across the river to where Mori's samurai were finishing mopping up the remains of the defenders, and winced. It was a slaughter: in close quarters, the rebels, armed with bamboo spears and farming tools, stood no chance against the trained swordsmen.

"Where is the man who spoke with us?" the headman asked.

"Here I am," said Takasugi, stepping forth.

"The village is yours," the headman said, spitting out straw, "but you'd better keep your part of the bargain."

Shōin nodded at Satō, and together they followed Takasugi and his *Kiheitai* past the palisade fence. The cries of the dying across the river resounded in Shōin's ears, but he grit his teeth and ignored them.

I can't help them, he thought, *but maybe I can help the people here.*

They marched down a corridor of grim, tough faces; bothhopeless and hopeful at the same time. They were farmers, merchants, craftsmen, monks... all classes of the Yamato society, except the samurai. Following the headman, they reached the centre of the village. The line of men before them parted, revealing the remnants from a scene of the fighting they had heard earlier.

Bodies of four of the rebels lay strewn on the dirt, hacked almost to pieces; several more knelt or crouched, supporting themselves on their spears, their many wounds taken care of by a few shrine acolytes. In the middle of this carnage lay a swordsman, a rōnin in an unmarked, monotone grey kimono, his hands still clutching his sword, his body pierced with arrows and broken-off spear blades.

"He wouldn't let us surrender," commented the headman.

Satō gasped and knelt down by the dead swordsman, examining his clothes and weapon.

"You know who that is?" Shōin asked.

"I know *what* he is," she replied. "He's one of Ganryū's men."

Before Shōin managed to ask what she meant, a huge explosion shattered the air and shook the ground beneath his feet. A shower of dirt and splinters rained down from the sky, and a column of black smoke rose across the river.

The small mountain monastery where the Chōfu loyalist forces had made their camp, had been requisitioned as an infirmary. The priests scurried around from one samurai to another, trying to patch up as many light wounds as they could; but many of the injured, still being brought to the camp from the burned village, were beyond their help.

The few who were already dead lay in biers awaiting burial at the local cemetery. Satō whispered a short prayer as she passed them on her way to the temporary *Kiheitai* headquarters.

The small building was bursting with people. It was prepared to accommodate no more than twenty soldiers, but the ranks of the militia had swelled more than twice, and they all wanted uniforms and weapons. Takasugi and Shōin tried their best to bring a semblance of control over this crowd, but in the end they too gave up, left the building, and sat down on the porch: Shōin with his head in his hands, Takasugi puffing ravenously on a long clay pipe. An old battered three-string shamisen lay on Takasugi's lap.

This was where Satō found them.

"*Ah*, Satō-*sama!*" Takasugi welcomed her between puffs of *tabako*.

"Is this yours?" she asked, nodding at the instrument.

"I found it in one of the abandoned houses. Surprisingly good sound. It's been a while since I last played."

"Where have you been?" asked Shōin.

"At the village, or what was left of it," she replied, "investigating the explosion."

"What is there to study?" asked Takasugi. "It looked like a barrel of gunpowder to me."

"I'm not sure." Shōin stretched his legs and moved aside to make way for Satō. "The priests say they haven't seen such injuries before. It's not just shrapnel and burn wounds, it's something that resists their healing power."

"The wounds will not heal," said Satō. "It's blood magic – as I suspected. Our enemies are no mere humans."

Takasugi took the pipe out of his mouth and shook his head.

"What is going on here, Shōin?"

They had moved to friendly terms shortly after the battle. Shōin felt uneasy as Takasugi's superior, especially in a war zone, where it was Takasugi who played the main part, and Shōin could do nothing but stand on the sides, his assistance needed only when magic was involved.

"I thought we were going to fight some peasants."

"I don't know. Ever since that barbarian came to Chōfu, it's been mysteries on top of mysteries."

"The *foreigner* would be our best bet to deal with this threat," said Satō. "We could really use his *dorako* now."

Shōin avoided her stare. The double bluff devised by lord Mori was eating him from the inside. It was a complex web of lies, and Shōin wasn't sure how long he was able to keep it up. He wasn't made for lying. His father had always tried to raise him as an honest, straightforward kind of man.

"Still, it looks like our gamble paid off," he changed the subject, nodding at the crowded headquarters.

"And how!" Takasugi laughed.

"They don't seem very disciplined."

"I know. But they are eager. It's funny how fast their loyalties shift when they are given the chance. Without those commoners, this expedition would already be a failure."

"I hope Mori-*dono* will see it the same way. Commoners fighting alongside samurai... this has not happened since the Civil War."

"And may not happen yet," said Takasugi, sucking thoughtfully on the nearly empty pipe. "I hoped the attack would be easy and without casualties. Now the samurai are resentful and angry." Then he added wistfully, "Too bad priestess-*sama* had to stay behind...."

A lit particle of *tabako* fell into his mouth and he coughed furiously, fanning his mouth with his hands.

"Here, have some water," Shōin handed him a gourd, holding back laughter.

"I don't see what use these peasants are in a war," said Satō, annoyed. "No matter what, they will just be arrow fodder. They don't have the guts to fight."

"You're wrong, Satō-*sensei*," Takasugi countered, having coughed out the fire. "The Chōfu farmers are a tough breed. They formed the bulk of the Mori armies in the Civil War — armies which conquered land from here to Okayama."

Satō was doubtful. "Even so — to train the farmers and merchants in handling swords and halberds will take months."

Takasugi tapped the pipe against his mouth. He pointed to Satō's waist.

"How easy is it to use this thunder pistol?" he asked.

Surprised at the question, the wizardess drew the weapon and stared at it for a few seconds before aiming casually at a nearby tree and squeezing the trigger. The thunder blast echoed throughout the temple, and the dazzling bolt ripped the bark off the tree and scorched a deep hole in the trunk.

Suddenly everyone around was looking at them, and Shōin bowed repeatedly with an apologetic smile until the passing monks moved away nervously.

"This is what we need," Takasugi's eyes lit up. "Easy to handle, easy to aim, devastating. Weapons that commoners could use. Lightning throwers, air guns, cannons, rockets... *Rangaku* weapons."

Satō laughed, but then noticed the look on Takasugi's face.

"You... you're serious?"

"Why not?"

"*Why not?* Let me tell you about *Rangaku* weapons. My father made airguns, it was his life's work – and he only made about a dozen working models. This thunder pistol Tanaka-*sama* gave me is the only one I've seen. And you want enough to arm a – a battalion, or whatever you call it."

Takasugi smiled. "A *platoon*. Fifty men is a *platoon*. Battalion is five hundred."

"Fifty, or five hundred, doesn't matter. We don't even have *five* guns."

"Then the *Kiheitai* as I imagined it is impossible."

Satō shrugged. "I told you, we're wasting our time on these peasants. You tell him, Shōin."

Shōin frowned. "You're being unreasonable, Takasugi. Mori-*dono* only wanted us to provide him with a troop of battle wizards, not an army of gun-toting peasants. We are overreaching our authority as it is with this lot," he waved a hand at the building behind them.

The first of the new recruits emerged from its walls. They had no uniforms yet, but each wore a sash of white hemp across their chest – and a weapon, assigned from the stash they had discovered in the village: a short sword, half a spear, a halberd blade, a hunting knife...

"Look at them," Takasugi said, "so proud. So much prouder than those samurai over there."

"Those samurai would have their heads if they could, you know," replied Satō. "Look, here comes one of them."

Lord Kunishi, the commander of the r*Eta*iner troops, walked towards them at a brisk, if lightly limping, pace. Most of his face was scarred with a myriad of tiny, fresh scratches, which bled constantly.

"What is the meaning of this, Yoshida!" he shouted, shaking his fist. Another farmer passed him, waving an old, chipped *katana*. The samurai reached for it and tore it from the farmer's hands. "A commoner cannot wield weapons, you know that!"

"They are all members of the *Kiheitai*," said Takasugi, calmly. "We are waiting for the letter of confirmation from the *daimyo*."

"Don't be ridiculous!" The samurai's lips trembled with anger. "What use would the *daimyo* have of rice farmers and shoe makers?" He stared at Satō. "I should've known it would end like this. First *women*, now *peasants*."

The wizardess looked as if she had been struck by her own thunder gun. She stood up.

"*Control yourself,*" whispered Shōin.

"Your samurai have suffered great losses in the morning attack," said Satō. "The priests can't heal them in time – I can see even your face is beyond their help."

"Yes." Kunishi eyed Satō suspiciously. The veiled insult escaped him. "This expedition will have to be postponed until we receive reinforcements. What's it to you?"

"Do you think Mori-*dono* will appreciate your retreat from a handful of peasant rebels?"

The samurai grunted in response. This time, Satō hit a nerve.

"We have your reinforcements right here." Satō pointed to the recruits. "You won't have to wait, you won't have to retreat. We can push on with the offensive as planned."

"My offensive plan requires samurai. Trained warriors. Not this… *rabble.*"

"Just give us a few days to prepare these men," Shōin said. "You will not be disappointed."

He stared at the back of the samurai as the man walked off in a huff, then looked back at Satō.

"You look like you have a plan."

"Not sure if it will work. I will need everyone's help."

There was no castle at Iwakuni. No white keep rose over the town like a watchful heron. It had been demolished a long time ago when the Mori clan took control over the surrounding territory and gave the remainder for the governor's residence. But the ramparts remained; layers of curved granite guarding the wide bend of the Nishiki River and the small harbour nestled in its mouth.

All of this paled into insignificance compared to the bridge spanning the river, leading into the former castle grounds. Five massive arches, like five rainbows of wood and stone, floated gently in the air, almost defying gravity. Admiring it made Satō proud to be Yamato; surely, nowhere else in the world could such a graceful and at the same time powerful structure exist.

And now, it was threatened. The rebel siege closed all access to the city, leaving only the bridge as the last intact passage. A fortified bridgehead across the river was still holding on, but barely, as the bulk of the rebel army gathered around it for one last push. Once the bridge fell, the city and the governors' residence would have lain open to the victorious and loot-thirsty soldiers.

"Look how many of them there are," whispered Satō.

"A thousand, at least," replied Takasugi. "This must be the entire rebel army. They know we're coming, and yet they put up barely any defences from this side."

"They must know how small our numbers are."

They were crouching in tall grass on a low, rice bowl-shaped hill, no more than a quarter of a mile from the enemy camp. The wide beach and muddy flood-plain to the south of it were both filled with campfires and tents. The day was coming to an end, and it seemed there would be no more action until the morning, giving Satō and the others plenty of time to survey the future battlefield.

"They're running out of time," said Shōin. "Their leaders know it. You were right; this was never about the peasants' demands. There's something in that governor's residence that they want."

The sound of horns blowing stirred the twilight, echoing throughout the rebel camp. The soldiers came out of their tents and shacks and ran towards muster points marked with rectangular banners of azure cloth.

"Are they going to attack?" asked Shōin. "It's almost dark!"

"You said it yourself, they're running out of time," replied Takasugi, standing up. "And so are we."

"They're not ready yet," opposed Satō. "We haven't finished preparing the weapons."

"We won't get a better chance. The bridge will fall today, I can tell. Come, let's gather the troops."

The ranks of the *Kiheitai* had been swelling ever since the rumour had spread throughout the river and mountain valleys of the region. The promise of being armed and getting paid to fight in the name of the Mori clan was enough to sway dozens of new recruits to join the cause.

Still, the hundred or so mountain farmers standing before Shōin seemed a feeble force compared to the rebel horde, no matter how proudly they wore their white sashes and bamboo spears.

"You all know what you're supposed to do?" asked Takasugi one last time. The recruits grunted. Shōin looked to the other side of the muster field, and caught a sceptical shake of head from the samurai commander. They too were preparing for the battle, but their preparations were of a different quality altogether. Donning the armour, sharpening the swords, strapping on the helmets; it all resembled a complex ritual, a dance even. Seeing their preparations made Shōin lose all confidence in his wizards' efforts. If anyone was going to win the battle for the Mori clan, it was these samurai – armed, armoured and skilled. Satō was right: the peasants were only good for arrow fodder.

But there was no way to tell her any of that now. The wizardess was pacing up and down the first line of the troops; serious and focused, adjusting the stance and bearing of the soldiers as if her own honour depended on their performance.

He glanced again at the samurai; without a word, in grim silence, they marched off towards the bridge. Some were limping – the commander ordered anyone who could still wield the sword to join in this final combat – but that did not diminish their powerful presence in the least.

He turned back to the militia and his heart sank even lower. Despite Takasugi and Satō's best efforts, the soldiers

344

slouched, slumped, chewed *tabako*; most were unable even to stand to attention.

"Takasugi," he said with resignation, "that's enough. Let's go."

By the time they reached the flood plain, the rebels had already overrun the bridgehead. The fighting moved on to the bridge arches, and the shallows below it.

"We're too late," said Shōin.

"No," replied Satō, "this is perfect. They are trapped."

"The samurai are moving in," noted Takasugi. "Right on time."

The Mori rEtainers charged from their positions on the bowl-shaped hill in a neat, disciplined wedge. Their task was simple – to drive a hole into the rear guard of the enemy for the militia recruits to pour through. As soldiers, the *Kiheitai* were far too poor to attempt such a charge on their own.

The wedge of swordsmen struck the rebel army in a clash of blades. There was confusion at first, and signs of panic, but soon the rebels realised how tiny the samurai force was and began to push it back.

"Now!" cried Takasugi. The hillside erupted with a salvo of magic missiles, carefully prepared by the Meirinkan wizards. Before the noise and smoke dissipated, Takasugi and Satō leapt onwards with their swords raised and the hundred mountain men armed with bamboo spears followed them into action. Raising plumes of dust from under their feet they ran, head-over-heels, like a herd of deer. The rebels paid even less attention to the approaching rabble than they had to the samurai. It seemed the charge would simply crash and dissipate against the wall of the enemy rear guard.

Will they remember? doubted Shōin. *Will they be focused enough?*

The first lightning strike shot from the first bamboo spear, then another. A blast of flame followed, and a blade of ice. The *Kiheitai* ran forward and kept shooting for as long as the magic charges remained in their weapons. Not all farmers remembered to fire, not all missiles hit the target, and not all shots were fatal, but it didn't matter. The plan's success depended on surprise, shock, and the resulting chaos – and it seemed to work. The rebel rear guard, dismayed and bewildered at an attack which they could not comprehend, turned and fled even before the first of the militia reached their line.

For the past several days, all the wizards of the *Kiheitai* had been hard at work on the bamboo spears. The process was called *imbuing*; every scholar of *Rangaku* was familiar with the term, but few had as such dEtailed knowledge of it as the Takashima family. Indeed, it was at the heart of the Takashima-ryū style. Satō's sword was always imbued with powerful frost magic, a trick which enabled her to cast combat spells fast and easily.

There was no time to learn all there was about *imbuing*, but the basic process proved simple enough, and easy to teach. Each wizard would transfer some of his elemental power into a make-shift bamboo spear, or any other weapon the militiamen possessed. The weapons could hold just a few spells before disintegrating – and not for long, either; it was a hasty, slapdash job after all, even with the blood rune which Satō had inscribed into every bamboo shaft. The risk of misfiring or exploding in one's hands was grave, but the ability to turn any peasant into a spell-caster, even if for only a few seconds, far exceeded the risks. The rebel intelligence knew by now about the presence of twenty or so wizards in the Chōfu force... but nothing had prepared them for a mass attack of a hundred of them.

The strategy worked. The battle was over as soon as it had begun. Once the smoke and dust cleared, Shōin saw the samurai climb the five-span bridge. They had the bulk of the rebel army exactly where they wanted it; trapped on the narrow passage between two groups of trained and vengeful and bloodthirsty Mori swordsmen.

The militia dispersed. Unarmed – the bamboo spears having expended all the imbued charges – and leaderless – Takasugi, Satō and the other wizards entered the fray on the bridge – they quickly began doing what the victorious rabble had always done at the rear of the battle: chasing after the marauders and looting the camp.

If there are traps, they will all die, he thought. But there was nothing he could do to help. Preparing for the battle took virtually all his strength, and he could only watch it from afar, cursing his weakness.

The pincers on the bridge were closing in on the rebel core. The river below was filled with bodies of the dead, and foaming as the deserters leapt into the water, trying to make for the shore. It was turning into a massacre, and Shōin felt great pity at the loss of so much life.

The sound of explosions and beams of bright red light made him forget all about the dying rebels. The chaos came from the middle span of the bridge, and resembled, not the single powerful blast he remembered from the previous battle, but a barrage of gun fire. It was a regular, if brief, magic battle, and Shōin could not tell who was winning.

"Satō!" he cried, and ran towards the bridge as fast as he could.

Satō was in the middle of a bloody slaughter – and she was loving every moment of it.

She had never imagined herself taking part in an actual battle like the one unfolding around her. Noone of her generation had. There was supposed to be eternal peace in Yamato. No samurai was ever to raise the sword against another samurai in war as long as there was a *Taikun* sitting on the throne in Edo.

She had fought bandits and wolves, and she had fought Ganryū's swordsmen and his assassin, but she was fighting for her life back then and there was never the time to enjoy the pure thrill of combat, the joy of clashing sword against sword. This time was different. This time, she was a part of a charge, a victorious strike – and it was the others who had to fear for their life, others fled before her vengeful, ice-cold blade and others cowed before her magic power.

She ducked a spear thrust, cut through the shaft of an incoming halberd, dodged a flying chain-blade and grabbed it, pulling its owner onto the point of her sword. She cut

348

with right hand, and let loose a volley of ice missiles with the left.

"*Bevries!*"

She blocked a short-sword blade and kicked the man who held it in the stomach. She punched, cut, slashed and blasted her way through the rebel throng. Next to all the other Mori samurai in the fray, she felt a part of a well-oiled war machine. In the midst of the melee it didn't matter whether she was a man or a woman. Those fighting alongside her only cared whether her blade was in the right place in the right time.

In the beginning of the battle, she was trying to stay close to Takasugi and the other wizards; but they were too slow and too defensive, and she moved to the head of the charge, where the real fight was happening.

Her kimono was soaked in blood; some of it was her own. She was no Dōraku, no Gensai – no untouchable master of the sword. But she didn't care. The smell of it was heady, m*Eta*llic, intoxicating. She couldn't get enough of it.

If only Father could see me today…

She didn't notice the first crimson missile fly past her. The next one she parried instinctively, the frost blade soaking in the fiery blast. Then, when the samurai before her was felled by a well-aimed magic strike, she saw him. Standing at the top of a bridge span, surrounded by a guard of several grey-clad swordsmen, was a bald man wearing the blue sash of a *Butsu* monk, his entire body covered in tattoos. *Blood runes*, everywhere, lighting up in sequence as the spell-caster executed barrage after barrage of deadly magic.

THE CHRYSANTHEMUM SEAL

The bridge's timber barriers lit up in flame, trapping within anyone who hadn't fallen or fled. Another line of fire ran down the middle, but Satō blocked it, rising a column of ice in its way. The man narrowed his eyes and smiled at her. It was a clear challenge.

They got separated again by other fighters, and for a while she had to focus back on deflecting spears and slashing down panicked farmers. The air around her exploded with magic as other wizards finally joined the fighting at the front. She felt the electric tingling on her tongue. Ice crystals, electric sparks, flames and smoke filled the air around her. The ground beneath her feet trembled and cracked.

Again, the strange caster rose right in front of her. It was as if he was searching her out among the fray, ignoring everyone else. He shot with both hands, a dozen fire lances at once; she parried and dodged, but a few hit her, sharp, deadly blades piercing her arms and stomach. She doubled over in pain.

The world around her changed colours: everything was coated in rust-red hue. The blood in her veins ran hot and fast. Her wounds, old and new, glowed bright blue, and her body filled with radiant energy.

With a roar she rose and charged at the tattooed wizard. Two grey-clads stood before her, but she just swiped them aside with a gesture.

How am I doing that?

She leapt into the air with the sword high above her head to fall on the tattooed man like thunder. He grinned at her, licking his lips, and reached out his hand. A blinding flash and a great force repulsed her and struck her down against the bridge floorboards.

She rolled aside, dodging a fireball smashing the boards where her head had just been, and jumped up. She charged again, parrying and blocking the attacks as she ran. He made no attempt to block her blade as she drove it straight through his chest. A fountain of blood spurted from the wound. Its smell made her almost faint. He grabbed her neck with a dying grasp.

"*Join us,*" he uttered, spitting blood. "*You'll have all the power you want.*"

She felt her strength sap, and her breath give out.

"Who are you?" she croaked. "You're not a Fanged."

"*I am merely the servant of the Serpent. But you... you could be so much more.*"

She had no force left to resist him. His voice was so smooth, sweet – and convincing... Her sword slipped from her hand and she closed her eyes.

"Satō!"

She winced. A wave of light, four rays in different colours, blasted one by one right through her and into the body of the tattooed man. He blinked in surprise and then blew up into a million tiny pieces of scorched flesh.

She dropped to her knees, close to fainting. Once she was able to see again, she found her sword on the ground and stood up. Around her, the battle continued to rage, but all the grey-clads lay dead, and the rebels were on the run, fighting for mere survival as the battle-raged samurai took no mercy. She tried to raise her sword and join the fight, but she swayed. Hear head was spinning. Somebody caught her from falling.

"Come, *sensei*" someone said, pulling her out of the fray. "We've won. Time to rest."

CHAPTER XVI

Wulf woke up with a groan. It was already bright outside. He lay for a while yet, breathing the faint smell of Yokō's body on the still-warm futon mattress next to him.

The door slid open. The girl smiled at him and beckoned outside.

"*Gohan,*" she said.

It meant it was time for breakfast. He rose and fumbled with the confusing Yamato garments until she came over to help him.

They ate the rice, egg omelette and soup in silence, not knowing enough words of each other's language to strike a conversation. Instead, he simply stared at her. She was no beauty, he was first to admit it, but there was *something* about the girl that made him go crazy with lust. He knew it made her uncomfortable – she blushed and giggled nervously – but that only made her seem more adorable in his eyes.

They finished the meal and he moved to embrace her, but she squeezed out of his arms.

"*No,*" she said. "*Come.*"

From her gestures he understood they were supposed to leave the house. He frowned. He didn't feel comfortable going outside without his Qin companion – and the only interpreter.

"Shouldn't we wait for when Li's back?" he asked. She tilted her head, trying to understand the words. "Li-*sama*," he said.

"*Come*," she repeated, pulling him gently towards the door.

They walked out through the garden of pink and blue flowers towards the castle gate. He stopped.

"The city?" he asked. "I don't think that's a good idea…"

But she had none of it. "*Come*," she said, forcefully this time.

She led him a short distance down a broad street linking the gate with the castle moat. It was lined with a dozen wooden scaffolds, upon which hung bodies of criminals, some still barely alive, others dead, quickly decomposing in the summer sun. Wulf covered his nose and averted his eyes.

The men were Nariakira's guards, punished by the lord for their failure in stopping the Black Lotus from running away. Wulf remembered the day of the execution well. It was a grim spectacle. There was no trace of emotion on the warlord's face as the men were tied to the scaffolds. The convicted too had remained silent, throughout their ordeal.

Like everyone living in the castle, Wulf had to pass the line of bodies several times a day, but he still could not quite get used to the sight – or the smell. He breathed in only once he and Yokō had crossed the deep moat.

Turning right, they went up a low-rising hill until they reached a large, two-storey mansion of thick white-washed walls, covered by a lattice of black wooden slates under a blue-tiled roof. He carefully opened the door and looked inside. The house was empty. Yokō pointed down the corridor.

What's happening?

Expecting the worst, and prepared to defend himself from any danger, he entered the room at the end of the hallway. It was completely empty, lacking even the ubiquitous packed straw mats. On the naked floorboards in the middle of the room Wulf spotted a large bronze stain.

The man standing by the window turned around with a broad smile. It was Shimazu Nariakira.

The warlord's arm swept around the room, and then pointed at Wulf.

"*Jouw!*" he said.

"This room? Mine?" Wulf asked, uncertain.

"*Ruim? Nej. Huis!*"

"The entire house…?"

"*Ja, ja! Uw huis!*"

The warlord then took the sheathed *katana* from his belt and thrust it into the hands of a stunned Wulf. He grunted forcefully, until the boy took the sword.

He slapped Wulf's shoulder with a grin. "*Samurai!*" he said, and then left the room in that purposeful manner of his.

Wulf stared at the sword for a moment, trying to comprehend what had just happened. He walked over to the window in a daze. He unsheathed the sword by a few inches. The blade was razor sharp and patterned in a complex manner; the scabbard was richly decorated with golden dragons and crossed circles of Satsuma.

He heard Yokō slide the door close behind him and shuffle across the floor. He smoothed his clothes bearing the Satsuma crest. New clothes to go with his new life. A new woman. A new weapon. And now, a new house. Things were changing quickly around him; he didn't understand all of the changes or reasons for them, but he didn't mind at all the direction in which they were taking him.

He looked at the dust-shrouded city below, the bright blue sea beyond, and the peak of the volcano in the distance. Not for the first time, he thought of Bran ap Dylan. Was he really still somewhere in this strange land? Had Lord Nariakira offered him the same rewards before presenting them to Wulf? The sword, the house – maybe even… Yōko? His hand tightened on the sword's hilt.

The girl's warm, soft hand slid under his kimono from behind and she nibbled his ear. He forgot all about the jealousy. It didn't matter. Bran wasn't here. He obviously wasn't up to the task – whatever task Lord Nariakira had in mind for him. But Wulfhere would not fail. He was a Warwick – a scion of kings. The *daimyo* must have noticed that in him. He smiled, triumphal.

Now all I need is a new dragon, and this place is as good as mine.

Samuel finished packing his papers into the leather satchel and considered the view from the window; the bright summer sun dazzled the waves, gently lapping against the walled shore of *Dejeema*, spreading like a fan out into the *Keeyo* bay.

He had spent less than two months in this place, but he knew he would miss it – even though at times the island felt like a prison, as it must have done for those who actually had to live in the tiny space between the sea and the single-gated bridge leading onto the mainland.

In a way, it was Samuel's first real holiday in years. With his status half-way between prisoner of war and a guest, there was little for him to do other than amble through the narrow, cobbled streets lined with pastel-coloured houses built in an odd manner that mixed the styles of the Bataavians and the Yamato. Sometimes he stood on the wall with the Porro glasses borrowed from the Admiral, and watched the comings and goings of the *Keeyo* harbour; as busy a port as any he had ever seen. The Yamato men, mostly, seemed to ignore the presence of the foreign outpost in the middle of their city, never even consciously turning their faces towards the island. Only the children and the women acknowledged *Dejeema*'s existence, each in their own way. The children would stand on the edge of the waves, trying to see who could throw a stone far enough to reach the outpost wall; the women, meanwhile… Samuel sighed at the thought. Yes, the fair city of *Keeyo* would be sorely missed.

At first, he had thought they were there merely for entertainment. And, sure enough, some of them were… but he soon discovered there was a lot more to it. The term *Dejeema Wife* that he began to hear a lot around the city was not a euphemism. The men – and there were only men on *Dejeema* according to the local law – really did take local women for wives, even if only by custom.

The *Keeyo* women – apart from those who got paid to fake interest – did not pay much attention to Samuel; the bushy black beards and fierce eyes of the Varyaga sailors drew far more of their notice. But, as he had eventually learned, there was more than a craving for the exotic at play.

"They are regarded as outcasts, yes," explained the Overwizard; the commander and governor of the outpost, who had arrived at *Dejeema* from some distant errand half-way through *Diana's* stay. "The children of the union even more so. Shunned from most of society, especially if they are noble-born."

"And what do they get for all that trouble?"

"Protection. A way out. Escape from an arranged marriage, or from an unwanted life. They may not be officially wedded, but everyone in Keeyo knows not to touch a *Dejeema Wife*. There was enough trouble over women in the past to make it into an unwritten law. Women of Yamato are an unhappy race," the Overwizard said. "My men don't need much – a loving touch, a friendly smile… and they know how to show their gratitude. Compared to what those women would suffer in a loveless marriage, it's paradise."

"And what about you, Overwizard? Do you have a *Dejeema Wife*? Or an actual one, back home?"

The plump man smiled sadly. "I had both and I lost both. I gave up."

"I'm sorry to hear that."

"Don't be. I've learned to deal with death the Yamato way. These people don't dwell on the past, Doctor. It's a useful trait."

Samuel remembered well the sad smile. The Overwizard was a strange man: short, portly, and innocuous in stature, but he exuded energy. He was, of course, a powerful mage, though he rarely used magic in every-day life. But he had, above all, an immense authority over the rough rabble of hardy sailors and cut-throat merchants that made up the *Dejeema* crew, and that kind of power did not come from magic skills. In a quiet, subdued way, the Overwizard was at least as much of a leader of men as Dylan ab Ifor had been.

He tied the satchel up with a piece of string. Borrowed from the Overwizard it had, of course, a magic lock, but Samuel did not trust it. *What if it broke? I would need to find a wizard to get to my notes.*

The notes contained crucial clues to what Samuel believed to be the greatest secret of Yamato. As one of the few Western-trained and experienced doctors in the city, he had been giving his assistance in various medical matters during his stay on the island, both to the Bataavians and their Yamato kindred. It was then that he had begun to notice a curious pattern.

THE CHRYSANTHEMUM SEAL

The Yamato knowledge of diseases and various illnesses was appallingly poor. Certainly, they were making progress under the watchful eye of their Bataavian teachers, but their country still suffered from bouts of smallpox, measles, and other easily preventable diseases, which they tried valiantly to fight with the usual remedies of the primitives: herbs, diet and hygiene.

But their treatment of injuries, no matter how violent, was something else entirely... it went far beyond anything Samuel had ever seen. No Yamato ever requested his help with a broken arm, a sprain, or a cut. Several times he had seen a porter or shipwright suffer from what would normally be a crippling mishap – a busy harbour never lacked in those sorts of incidents – only to see him seemingly unharmed and fully fit just a few days later. Whatever was going on, it was nothing short of miraculous.

The Bataavians never mentioned the phenomenon, at least never near Samuel. They seemed to ignore its existence and avoided the subject, even when asked directly. He had to rely on his observations, and they could only get him so far without actually descending on the mainland and talking to the injured Yamato themselves. There was no way to do it on *Dejeema*.

Admiral Otterson was a generous man: he had offered to leave Samuel on the island, from where he could return home with the next Bataavian ship. A month earlier, Samuel would have jumped at the opportunity; not anymore. The *Diana* was heading for a bigger city than Keeyo, a place where he would perhaps be allowed to land and speak directly with the locals. It was his best chance of discovering the truth behind the mystery. He had to board the Varyaga underwater ship once more… even if it meant travelling with whatever was locked in that deep, cold cargo hold again.

Bran drew the pail full of icy cold water from the well. He dipped his fingers in, and touched the still tender bruises on his eyebrow and a cut on his forehead. He washed his arms, wincing and hissing. Once again, his "custodians" had decided to show him how much they loathed the "barbarians". There was no point in protecting himself from their blows with magic – he knew it would only make them angrier and force them to come up with more subtle, more frustrating ways of harming him – such as withholding food for a few days.

Bran's skin, where bare, had gone beyond tan and into deep, burnt red, peeling in places; his lips were parched, and his eyes glued with dry dust. He scratched his itchy cheek. He needed a shave, badly. He had grown thin over the last few weeks and that only made the problem worse, as the skin on his face seemed to shrink; to wither.

He put on the *yukata* – the only clothes he had were the ones in which he'd been arrested – and poured the rest of the water onto the hot scales of his dragon. The Yamato summer was scorching hot – just like the one in Gwynedd had been… and just like then, Bran's main concern was to stop the parching heat from drying out Emrys's hide.

"Has it really been a year?" he asked the air. "The *Ladon*… the disaster…?" He wiped sticky sweat from his brow.

The beast opened one eye, startling a fly, looked around, then closed it again.

"This is ridiculous," Bran said, irritated, and threw the pail away. "I went through it all just to be stuck here with you, like some hermit?"

He stormed off and sat down inside the dilapidated boat shed – the only structure on the tiny island which was now his "home", or rather, his prison.

The Chōfu coast was a mere mile away, and on most days he could easily see the city's ochre-yellow walls and gold-plated palace roofs glistening in the summer sun, or track the busy boat traffic in the harbour. "His" island – the larger of the two clumps of rock in the middle of the Dan-no-ura Straits – was a little smaller than Ganryūjima, and completely devoid of any features apart from a few clumps of trees, the boat shed, and a deep well dug out in the middle. Bran guessed it must have served as a refuge for fishermen during the fierce winter storms, but in the summer, no ships ventured near it.

The earth beneath his feet rumbled gently. He knew well what it meant.

"Are you hungry *again*?" he asked, irritably. "Well, you'll just have to wait. It's still light."

Having convinced Lord Mori that he'd be unable to control Emrys for too long if the dragon grew hungry, Bran was allowed to let the beast loose at night, hunting in the forested hills of the Ogasawara land – the Mori clan's sworn enemy – on the other side of the strait. His own needs were

362

more or less satisfied by a boat of supplies arriving once every few days at the narrow strip of a beach.

It was a strange prison. There were no guards, no bars, no chains; and yet, Bran could not escape. The deal he'd struck with Lord Mori was enough to keep him on the tiny island indefinitely.

As long as I'm here, Satō is safe from harm.

"How long are you planning to stay here?"

Bran jerked up in surprise, hitting his head on the shed roof.

"You," he said, noticing Dōraku leaning on the edge of the well, smoking his pipe. "How in Annwn did you get here?"

The Swordsman raised a brow.

"Are you still surprised by my ingenuity?"

Bran shrugged. "I suppose not."

He didn't like the idea of being alone with this man. Much like Nagomi, he never managed to completely bring himself to trust the Fanged.

"You're hurt."

Bran didn't answer. He gazed gloomily at Dōraku's sandals, avoiding his inquisitive stare.

"It's time for you to run away," the Swordsman said.

Bran went over to pick up the pail and filled it with water again.

"If I leave now, something may happen to Satō."

"Well, if it's the wizardess you're so concerned about…" said Dōraku, "that should be motivation enough for you to haul your bottom out of here. She sacrificed a lot so that you might live – and you squander that away?"

"I live," Bran said, and shrugged again. "And where would you have me go? There is nowhere in Yamato where my presence would be welcome."

"You do realize she doesn't even know you're here. She thinks you're away on some spy mission for Mori."

Bran pondered the news briefly, but he couldn't find it in him to be surprised by such trifles anymore. He poured the water on the dragon's back.

"It might be better that way," he said. "No need to worry her."

Dōraku tapped the pipe against the rim of the well and put it away into his sash.

"Sooner or later, Mori will have to do something about you."

"I'll cross that bridge when I come to it," said Bran. He was growing tired of the conversation.

"What if he decides to kill you? What if the choice is your life or hers? How far are you willing to go?"

Bran had no answer for him. He didn't feel comfortable at Dōraku's line of questioning. What did the Swordsman want from him? To put his friends' well-being on the line for his own sake once again?

"I thought you, at least, would understand," he said carefully. "There are more important things in life than… well, life."

"You're not a samurai, boy," the Swordsman replied. "You don't have to act like one."

"I will choose the way I behave myself, thank you very much."

Dōraku's lips narrowed, and his nostrils puffed.

"You're wasting everyone's time," Dōraku said, anger creeping into his voice "Stop this sulking, boy!"

Bran stood up. "Leave me alone! Who do you think you are, coming here, telling me what to do? You're not – "

He bit his tongue. He had almost blurted *my father*. But that would have been such a childish thing to say…

He shook his head. "Just go. I'll think about what you've said."

"That you will," said Dōraku with a slight bow and walked off towards the sea.

Bran turned his back on him and punched the sand with his fist.

Emrys snored.

As they approached the cliff, a sudden updraft caught Emrys unawares, bringing with it the heady smell of iron – the inescapable scent of the dry red dust below. Emrys pulled up and then levelled its flight over the scarred plateau, which Bran called the Wounded Highland.

THE CHRYSANTHEMUM SEAL

Other than watching ships in the Chōfu harbour, exploring the Otherworld was his only pastime during the days of exile. He had been plotting its strange, inexplicable topography, trying to figure out a way to map it to the real world. He knew it was possible ever since he had managed to locate Nagomi by tracking her on the red dust plain… but it was not a straightforward task. The Otherworld was an idea, rather than a place. It had a few common points with the physical plane – hot spots of power, like the Takachiho Mountain – which enabled Bran to orientate himself in his journeys, but other than that, the relation seemed to be random. The distances changed, the locations moved around.

This was an empty, lonesome land – but Bran was not alone here. He could sense other minds, in the distance… the Black Wings were a constant, faint presence, for instance, puttering about somewhere in the North, always on the move. But there were others who travelled through the Otherworld, darker, more sinister spirits that he tried to avoid.

Reaching other minds, other red light towers was a nigh-impossible task. Even if Bran spotted one, it seemed to move away almost as fast as he tried to reach it. There was a secret to finding them that only the Gorllewin possessed; Bran suspected it had to be voluntary, agreed upon prior to contact. If that was true, then all his attempts were futile. He hoped there was a way to overrun that limitation.

At times he reached Nagomi's tower. Physically, they were a mere two miles apart, but in the Otherworld the distance varied from a few hours to a day of flying, sometimes over the Wounded Highland and across the

Canyon of Pain, sometimes down the Slopes of Gravel – all names Bran had put on an ever changing map he'd been trying to draw in the sand of his little island. The school of magic was a bright yellow – sometimes blue – beacon which was present on both planes, and that always helped Bran to find his way around.

Nagomi's "tower" was, fittingly, a small shrine, with white-washed walls and blue tiles on the roof. The door was shut and guarded by a sleeping black bear, which Bran assumed had something to do with Torishi. Every time Bran got too near the shrine door, the bear woke up and snarled at him, his fierce, dumb eyes showing no recognition.

At length, he stopped trying to contact the priestess. He sensed a dark, creepy presence. The shadowy beings were getting closer every day, and stronger. It was as if they were looking for him, and he didn't want them to find Nagomi as well.

A few days after he had first detected their presence nearby, Bran resolved to stage an ambush. He landed Emrys in a deep crevice on one of the Slopes of Gravel and waited. As soon as he felt the creature near enough, they leapt into the air. A shapeless shadow crept and crawled over the red surface. It spotted Bran and began to crawl away with surprising speed. Emrys swooped down towards it; Bran summoned his Soul Lance and slashed it through. The shadow disappeared without a sound, leaving only a faint scent of ozone.

The smell of salty air and the burning rays of the sun told him he was back. He opened his eyes and stared into the sea. What were those things, and what did they want? There was no doubt now that they were after him. Was there reason to it, or were they simply drawn to him, an anomaly in the otherwise empty land?

As he pondered the question, a drop of rain fell on his sun-blistered shoulder. He looked up, surprised. It hadn't rained for days, and the sun was relentless in its brilliance, turning the whole sky into a blazing haze of azure, so bright it was almost white. This time, however, half the sky had gone dark blue; a torn curtain of rain approached from the north, and the wind had picked up, raising whirls of sand on the beach.

The supply boat made it just in time before the full rage of the storm opened over the Dan-no-ura Strait. The warden thrust a large, richly decorated bento box in Bran's hands. It was filled with succulent fish, fresh fruit, and even a few moist slices of cured venison from the mountains.

"What is this?" asked Bran, astonished.

"Your last meal," replied the warden brusquely, angry at having to even talk to the barbarian, and irritated by the first drops of rain falling on his bald head.

Bran's heart raced.

"Last meal?"

"His Excellency Mori Takachika-*dono* orders you to commit suicide," the warden said, throwing a piece of paper and an unsheathed short sword, without the scabbard, on the ground before Bran. "He grants you this rare privilege as a mark of his graciousness. *Far* too generous, if you ask me."

368

"Nobody asked you," mumbled Bran, picking up the sword with shaking hands. A sudden, sharp blast of pain flashed in his eyes. The warden whacked him in the face with full force, causing him to drop the box and the sword in the sand. He staggered and spat blood.

"I could kill you right now, barbarian!" the man growled. "But I respect Mori-*dono*'s wish. I will be back to pick up the body…" he added, and looked to the sky. A thick drop of rain hit him right in the eye. He grunted. "…as soon as I can. And make sure that monster of yours is dealt with, too!"

In a hurry, he pushed the boat back into the swelling sea, leaving Bran alone to his thoughts.

An order to commit suicide?

He picked up the paper. It was a clear enough statement – and once again, the *daimyo* mentioned Satō's well-being in what seemed a casual passing, but which was an obvious threat against her. *The girl's life and happiness is in my hands, the letter said, between the lines. And don't you forget it.*

Bran cursed and crushed the letter in his hand. Was that it? Was this the choice Dōraku was taking about? But why now? What had happened in Chōfu to change the *daimyo*'s decision?

He sat down and started picking at the food randomly. *Maybe it's just another bluff*, he clung to a sudden hope. *Or a test.*

A gust of wind threw sand and sea in his face. The storm had finally come, and it looked like it was here to stay for a while.

369

A man, dressed in a cloak of oiled straw and holding on to his bamboo hat, torn and soaked through, burst into Bran's boatshed home, past the sleeping Emrys, whom he failed to notice. Huffing and puffing, he sat down by the campfire burning under the roof and rubbed his hands.

"Oh good," he said, "you've managed to get the fire going."

The storm had been rampaging for three days now, and Bran lay huddled on his bedding, wrapped in cloaks and dirty blankets next to the fire he had built out of damp wood and sustained with regular bursts of dragon flame. He tried to move as little as possible to conserve heat. The man didn't see Bran's face in the shadow and mistook him for just another castaway.

"What weather, eh? And in the middle of the summer!"

Bran grunted in vague agreement and sneezed.

"I didn't see another boat," the man continued, "are you stranded here? I can take you back on shore."

"Don't you know where you are?" Bran asked from under the blankets.

The other man looked around, perplexed. "This is Kanju Island, isn't it? I have been away for a few months, but I think I know my way around Dan-no-ura, even in this storm."

"So you haven't heard about the prisoner on Kanju? This island is off-limits by Mori-*dono*'s orders."

"Oh!" The man covered his mouth. "I'm sorry. I didn't know – I was in Naniwa all this time… As soon as the weather clears, I'll… wait – " He pointed at Bran. "If it's a prison, where are the guards?"

"There are no guards here. Only me."

"*You're* the prisoner?"

"I am. Don't worry, I won't tell anyone you were here." Bran pointed into the corner of the boatshed. "There's some rice in the crate. I don't have much to spare – I haven't had any supplies since the storm started."

"Ah, thank you! I have some fish in the boat, I'll bring it in the morning."

The fisherman reached for the box and grabbed a handful of wet rice.

"You're very kind," he said, with his mouth full of sticky grains, "for a criminal. What did they put you in for?"

Isn't that obvious? thought Bran, before remembering the fisherman couldn't see his face and of course his flawless, if archaic, Yamato wasn't at all helpful.

He sat up and moved closer to the light of the campfire. The fisherman stared at him, dropping bits of rice to the floor, then screamed, scrambled on all fours and ran out of the shed.

"Wait!" Bran shouted, but it was no use. The fisherman was gone, pushing his wobbly boat into the stormy waves, away from the island, into the darkness and inevitable death.

THE CHRYSANTHEMUM SEAL

Looking out of the second floor window onto the smooth surface of the sea, dazzling in the summer sun, and the wide, calm bay bound by rolling green hills, Dylan thought of fate, and chuckled quietly.

This place was supposed to be the closest guarded secret in the East. And yet, if Admiral Reynolds was to be believed – and Dylan had no reason not to believe him – he was only the *third* of his family to visit the fabled island of Dejima.

"What is so funny, Dracalish?"

The question was posed by a man who looked like a bank manager, who was sitting on the other side of a simple walnut table: Overwizard Hendrik Curzius, the master of this island prison in which the Yamato held the Bataavian merchants, the chief of the inmates.

Dylan scratched the walnut surface lightly.

"I was just wondering how you had managed to keep this place a secret for so long."

"Why did you attack my ship, Commodore… ab Ifor, was it? Our nations are not at war. I will be forced to write a stern note of protest to your government."

"I did not come here as a Dracalish officer. And I would appreciate it if you didn't involve the official channels. This is a private mission – I'm looking for my son."

Curzius tapped his fingers on the table.

"Can you describe him to me?"

"Seventeen, black hair, green eyes, about your height…"

"Aren't you forgetting something in this description?" Curzius chuckled. "A certain green dragon? But, I'm afraid you have been misinformed. The boy is no longer in Yamato."

"That's not what Nariakira told me."

There was a pause in the conversation as Curzius pondered his reply. Dylan chipped at the edge of the table with his fingernails. Outside, a black kite screeched a warning.

"I'm not sure where Nariakira-*dono* got that information. According to my sources, your son was seen flying towards Qin a little over a month ago. I'm sorry, Commodore, but it looks like your little endeavour, however costly to us all, was unnecessary."

Dylan frowned. *So that's it? All that effort for nothing?*

The Overwizard leaned forward, pressing his fingers firmly against the table.

"What does Nariakira-*dono* get from you for his assistance?" he asked.

"I don't know what you mean."

"Ha!" Curzius laughed. "That sly fox wouldn't serve you a cup of saké if you hadn't promised him a barrel in exchange."

"Whatever it was, it doesn't matter now." Dylan stood up. The chair screeched from underneath him. "Well done, Overwizard," he said, looking at the scratches he had left on the walnut wood. "You're just as good as I've heard you were."

THE CHRYSANTHEMUM SEAL

He was playing cool, but in reality, he was exhausted. All through the conversation the two men had been using their magic to play a deadly game of power, using tiny charms to imbue the table with energy. It was the kind of Gornestau Dylan preferred to the showy, theatrical magic duels other wizards were fond of, and, just as he had guessed, Curzius did too.

It was a hard-fought stalemate, leaving both of them on the verge of collapse. The Overwizard waved a hand over the table, grim in silence, clearing it from all charges.

"If you'll excuse me," said Dylan, "I must make preparations for my departure."

"Departure?" Curzius raised his greying eyebrows. "How? You have no ship and no mount. I hope you're not planning to hijack Soembing again."

A sizzling, glinting golden spark flew past the window with a loud whoosh and crackle. Dylan smiled.

"I think my ride's just arrived."

CHAPTER XVII

Prince Mutsuhito stood smiling in the door of his father's Bamboo Room. The *Mikado* was not only sober, but beaming with energy and good humour. He was discussing agitatedly with a stocky, balding nobleman wearing a simple black kimono with a single Satsuma crest on the back. The Prince watched his father laugh and then get serious, wave his hands about and then scratch his head in thought; he hadn't seen His Highness behave in this way in a long time.

The *Mikado* and the nobleman finally noticed Mutsuhito leaning against a pillar. The aristocrat bowed and excused himself out of the room. The Prince took his place at his father's side.

"Who was he, Father-*sama*?" he asked, scratching his thigh. The shimmering green scales had by now spread to both his legs, and he had to go to increasingly elaborate ways to hide the disfigurement from prying eyes – not least those of his father.

"That was Maki Izumi, recently arrived from Satsuma. A priest and a philosopher. Great mind. He has some very interesting ideas regarding the future of this country. What brings you here, son?"

"I just passed the courier bearing gifts and messages from the new *Taikun*. I wanted to see what he brought."

"Ah, yes. The old fox finally met his end." The *Mikado* grinned. Ever since he had received news of the *Taikun*'s untimely demise, his mood had been steadily improving. "*And* there's a new Chief Councillor in. Hopefully that will put all that barbarian nonsense to rest. I tell you, son, I expect things to only get better from here."

They moved to the audience chamber just as the palace Chamberlain announced the courier's arrival, and soon the delegation consisting of three men in Tokugawa garb entered the room. One of them stepped forward, handing the Chamberlain a sealed scroll, while two others put black lacquer boxes on the floor before the dais upon which the *Mikado* sat behind the gauze curtain.

Prince Mutsuhito watched the Chamberlain open the two boxes with care before presenting their contents to his father.

"Silk handkerchiefs with seasonal motif," the *Mikado* grunted approvingly. "Reasonable enough. What's in the other one?"

The Chamberlain took out a bottle of thick glass containing some orange liquid. It had a paper label attached, with Western runes written all over. The *Mikado*'s face turned sour.

"And what is *this*…?"

"*Bu-Ran-Ji*," the Chamberlain deciphered a translation scribbled at the bottom of the label.

"It is a Western spirit, *denka*," explained the courier. "The Chief Councillor grew fond of it. You drink it with..."

"Enough."

The *Mikado* waved for the bottle to be put away.

"How dare they suggest I would drink this barbarian swill!"

"I'm sure they meant well, Father-*sama*," Mutsuhito interjected. "It is quite a novelty. The court ladies might enjoy it."

"Hrm." The *Mikado* breathed in and out, calming down. "Well. Let's see what the letter says."

The Chamberlain unrolled the scroll and read: "*His Illustrious Highness, Taikun Tokugawa Iesada, to His Exalted and Divine Majesty, Mikado Kōmei...*"

"Give me that," the *Mikado* tore the letter from the courtier's hand and read it himself.

"Greetings... mmhmm... the new Chief Councillor – some man named Hotta Naosuke – never heard of him... riots in Mito – I don't care about that... *Ah*! A mention of the Shimazu girl. That will cheer Izumi-*sama* up...wait, what's this...?"

Mutsuhito observed his father's face change expression from neutral through vaguely contented, to irritated, to furious. Purple and with veins nearly bursting, he crushed the letter in his fist.

"*Bastards.*"

THE CHRYSANTHEMUM SEAL

The faces of those gathered in the audience paled, hearing the sacred lips utter such profanity.

"Father-*sama*… calm down. Remember what your physician said…"

"They signed the damn treaty!" the *Mikado* shouted to the Prince. "They. Signed. The. Treaty."

He breathed heavily, looking around with maddened eyes, as if for a target. His gaze fell on the box of handkerchiefs. He grabbed a handful and blew his nose noisily, then threw them at the courier.

"This is my answer. Take it to your *Taikun*. Now out! All of you!" he cried, his jowls shaking, spittle spraying on the gauze curtain. The Chamberlain and the messengers bolted out the door.

"What treaty?" asked Mutsuhito. "What's this all about?"

"The Barbarians," his father wheezed, gasping for breath, "the ones who landed near Edo."

"I thought they were driven away?"

"It was just a trick… The Council bowed to all their demands. They gave them the right to land, to trade, to build an embassy."

He slumped on the pillow. "It's over. Yamato is lost."

He searched around again and noticed the bottle of Western alcohol. "I need a drink. This will do." He struggled with the opening and then took a full swig of the orange liquid. He coughed and spluttered, but his eyes lit up.

"No! Not yet. Go, son. Bring me Izumi. I have a letter to write."

"Another missive, Father-*sama*? Don't you think the *Taikun*…"

"Not to him. I will not be writing to *those* traitors any longer."

Satō moved in a numb half-trance down the wide avenue bound by two walls of curved granite, and into the lush garden surrounding the governor's villa. Her wounds were now healed but her body still hadn't recovered from the strain and loss of blood. Shōin shuffled beside her in silence, pale and broody, and also tired from last night's battle.

She stopped and breathed in the scent of flowers and pine needles, soothing and calming; it felt good to be back to the peace of civilization. She even found enough strength to admire the villa's architecture. It was light and neat, built in a style she wasn't familiar with, more modern than she was used to. The impeccable grid of straight black lines and broad swathes of white rice paper made it look more like an ink painting than a building.

No commoner could build something like this, she thought. *Only the samurai know how to appreciate such refinement.*

She'd had enough of the company of farmers, merchants, and craftsmen for a while. They were noisy, uncouth, and they smelled of fermented rice and saké. She cared little for Shōin's lofty ideals. She had only helped him out of spite; but she could certainly see the samurai commander's point of view. Once the imbued spears had lost their charges, the commoner "army" was good for nothing, despite Shōin and Takasugi's boasts. In the end, it was down to the swordsmen and wizards to deal with the enemy – as expected.

And couldn't they see how dangerous it was, giving the peasants such radical ideas? Arming them with *Rangaku* weapons… She scoffed at the thought. Could anyone guarantee their loyalty? What did a peasant know about honour? They would rebel again in no time. With the weapons, they would surely overrun this striking villa, turn the gardens into rice fields and tea houses into manure barns. They would not care for the precise proportion of the dividing walls, nor the arrangement of flowers and scrolls placed in the *tokonoma* alcove.

No, a commoner's place was not in the army. She could make an exception for those with magic talent and a drive to study, but that was all.

With these unhappy thoughts, she entered the glorious building. A servant led them down the equally refined black-and-white corridors to the dining hall; a perfectly simple room, with one wall facing the finest part of the lush green garden, opened wide to let in the scent of summer flowers and the shimmer of a small waterfall.

When she and Shōin entered, they were welcomed by subdued cheers and applause. They were the last to arrive to the feast prepared by the governor to celebrate the victory.

The samurai commanders sat at one low, square table, together with the governor and his retinue; the wizards at another, smaller, on the side, like younglings. None of them seemed to mind the slight. Satō hesitated for a moment. She belonged to the Meirinkan, but in battle she fought alongside the Mori r*Eta*iners… Yet today, the samurai ignored her; today she was a mere woman again. In a badly concealed huff, she sat down next to her husband.

The Iwakuni governor rose with the saké cup in his hand. The conversation at the two tables fell silent.

"I want to toast our brave defenders and rescuers, Commander Kunishi and his samurai! *Kanpai!*"

"*Kanpai!*"

They all drank their saké in one gulp and slammed the cups against the tables.

That's it? thought Satō, as the governor sat down. What about us? She looked around, bewildered. The wizards were pouring themselves more alcohol.

Lord Kunishi was the next to stand. He bowed to the governor and then turned towards the wizards' table.

"And I would like to toast the *onmyōji* of the Meirinkan Academy, who helped us achieve our victory. *Kanpai!*"

"*Kanpai!*"

Satō raised the cup again. "We're not *onmyōji*," she mumbled, but she knew the commander meant well. Finally, it seemed, he was learning to appreciate the value of *Rangaku* on the battlefield. Satisfied with the toasts, she reached for the plate of sliced lotus roots, when, unexpectedly, Shōin stood up with his cup. The diners murmured in surprise; the boy waited until they filled their drinking vessels for the third time.

"Lastly, I would like this toast to thank those without whom we would not be able to celebrate this victory, and who were not invited to dine here with us."

Oh, no. Shōin, what are you doing…

Satō did not join the toast. She wanted no part in this farce. Takasugi and a few others nodded in agreement; the remaining samurai seemed confused, unsure yet whom the boy could mean.

"The brave common men of the *Kiheitai* militia! *Kanpai!*"

Only the wizards raised their cups. The men at the governor's table remained silent, stony-faced. Kunishi's face turned purple; the never-healing pinpricks on his cheek made it look like he was sweating blood.

"I have never…" he blurted; his hand wandered towards the short sword at his waist. It took the governor's gentle, but stern gesture and gaze to calm him down.

Shōin's face was now as red as the silk pillow he sat down upon heavily. The silence in the room was palpable. Takasugi nudged him with an encouraging smile, but Shōin searched for approval in Satō's face. He found none.

"You idiot," she whispered, looking into her rice bowl. She felt her ears burn with embarrassment. "What were you thinking?"

"Those men were ready to die for our cause, just as much as those samurai," Shōin whispered back. "They deserve a mention."

"You might as well have toasted the bamboo spears they carried!"

"That's unfair, and you know it."

"Honestly, sometimes I think Bran understood Yamato better than you do." She shook her head. "Maybe that's why Mori-*dono* sent him on a secret mission, instead of you," she added quietly. Shōin winced, but said nothing.

The feast was coming to an end. A few flasks of saké later, the moods mellowed, and everyone seemed to have forgotten about Shōin's gaffe. At some point, Takasugi asked a servant to bring him the battered shamisen. The room quietened.

"It is a song I heard sung in our camp before the battle," he said, tuning the three strings. He cleared his throat and began to sing in a surprisingly clear and strong voice:

Kiite osoroshi

Mite iyarashii

Soute ureshii

Kiheitai!

To hear them is dreadful

To see them is obscene

To be with them is joyful

Kiheitai!

The song made everyone laugh, even the haughty samurai – it was just the kind of bawdy humour everyone in the army liked. Takasugi sang a few more songs before putting the instrument away. At that cue, a few young girls entered the room and joined the samurai table to entertain them further. There were none for the wizards.

It didn't matter. The conversation at the Meirinkan's table turned to the d*Eta*ils of last night's battle. Who was the tattooed man? Where had he come from? What kind of power was he using? Satō took no part in this exchange. The pain from her fresh wounds was making her cranky and ready to snap for no reason, so she just dabbed at her meal of pressed rice and thinly sliced veg*Eta*bles in silence. Besides, she knew the answer to all those questions, and it wasn't something she wanted to talk about with anyone.

The more she had been learning about blood magic, the less she understood it. It seemed to throw all the rules of magic out of the window; there were no spell words, no set rites… it was as if by using the blood runes, wizards could write whatever magic they wanted. It went so far beyond simply enhancing one's spells, beyond raw power… Healing wounds, throwing people around, building exploding traps – was there no limit to what blood magic could do?

She kept mulling the tattooed man's words in her head over and over.

Join us.

The Serpent knew about her. Were they searching her out, or was it only a coincidence that she found herself on the same battlefield…? If they were actively looking for her… she shivered at the thought.

384

There was more else at stake, too. The short-lived rebellion the monk had led – what was that all about? She raised her head. Oddly enough, the conversation at the table had just come to the same topic.

"What did they *really* want?" the wizards wondered. "Why were they besieging Iwakuni, anyway?"

"Oh, that's right," she said, turning on her pillow to face the governor. He looked up in surprise, trying to focus his eyes on her. Most of the samurai had by now managed to drink themselves into a stupor.

"Would you mind showing us your treasury, governor?" she asked.

"Tre- treasury?" he blurted, his eyes wide open and wandering.

"That's right. We'd like to see what the rebels thought they could find here. They fought hard to get through that bridge, was there anything they could have been looking for?"

"Chests of tax gold," the governor shrugged, "debt documents…nothing out of the ordinary, really."

She elbowed Shōin. *Make yourself useful.*

"We'd still like to see it," her husband added, "if you don't mind."

"Of course." The governor stood up and straightened his kimono. This made him sway; he supported himself on one of the girls. "Follow me."

They climbed into what must have been the castle's foundations, a deep, two-storey cellar. As they reached the

385

end of the corridor on the upper floor, the governor nodded at the guard, who opened a great timber door leading to the treasure room.

Satō's eyes glazed over the chests full of copper and silver coins, and nuggets of precious m*Eta*ls on the shelves. This was not what she was looking for. She wished she had Bran's ability to see magic… She closed her eyes and focused, but couldn't detect anything out of the ordinary.

"What's in the room below us?" asked Shōin.

"Can you sense it?" she whispered.

"I'm not sure," he whispered back.

"Oh, it's just where I keep some of the prisoners," answered the governor. "Before sending them to Chōfu for further interrogation."

"And are there any here now?"

"No… not as such." He grimaced and winced. For a government official he was a terrible liar – or the amount of saké he had drunk had rid him of the ability to keep a straight face.

"Please, show us."

Or we'll think you have something to hide from Lord Mori, was the unspoken threat.

Sour-faced, the governor led them to the lower floor of the cellar. This one was a true dungeon, dark, damp and cold, smelling of dead rats and moulding bamboo. There were several cells along the corridor, all empty except the last one.

"What's this?" cried Shōin. "A child? Give me that torch!"

He beckoned a servant. Satō took the light and peered inside. Cowering in the corner of the dank, tiny room, was a creature the size of a child, dark-skinned and bald, with features hidden by a layer of dirt and grime. It – or he – was naked and trembling; its only accessory was a leather cord tied around its neck, upon which hung a jagged piece of blue-coloured, translucent stone.

"That stone - !" cried Satō. She tried to reach for it, but the creature hissed and scratched at her hand.

"Careful," the governor said, approaching. He slapped the poor creature on the face. It hid its head in its lanky arms. "It's vicious."

"What is this... thing?" asked Shōin.

"My men found it sneaking through the forest about a month ago. It was trying to reach the northern border."

"Can it speak?"

"Yes, but it's difficult to understand. It lost most of its teeth when my men... handled it."

Satō leaned over the creature. She was trying to remember something... she shook her head to get the remnants of saké out of her head.

Little people in the cave... exactly like him. I have seen this.

She knelt down to have her face on the same level as the little dark man.

"Are you... an Ancient?"

His eyes glinted.

"How...?" he croaked through bloodied lips. His voice surprised her; she expected it to be high-pitched and child-like, but it was mature and hoarse.

"I have a – friend, who told me about your people. He is of the Kumaso."

"*Kumaso*..." He nodded sagely. "So there are still Sons of Bear in the south."

The accent was hard; she could tell Yamato was a foreign language for him.

"What are you doing here?"

"Going north. To my land."

She stood up and turned to the governor.

"What were you planning to do with him?" she asked.

The governor shrugged. "He's been trespassing without a permit. I can do with him whatever I want."

"He should have been sent to Chōfu, and you know it."

"I don't even know if it's *human*," the governor scoffed.

"We have to take him back with us," she said to Shōin.

"Now listen here – " the governor straightened himself, his hands and jowls shaking. "I don't know who you think you are, woman, but – "

Satō felt something snap inside. She grabbed the governor by the collar and, even though the man was stout and towering above her by a good foot, she pinned him to the cold stone wall. The world around her was shrouded in the rusty red hue again.

"Mori-*dono* must be informed of anyone caught crossing the border," she seethed. Her voice sounded like a snake's hissing in her ears. "You know the law. Shall I inform him of what happened here? Shall I tell him it was your negligence that caused the rebellion?"

Frost crackled around her fist. A blade of ice grew in her other hand, pointing at the governor's head.

"N-no... I didn't think... rebellion?" He flustered. "What does any of this have to do with the rebellion?"

Shōin grasped her hand.

"That's enough, Satō."

The ice blade dissipated. The normal colours of the world returned. She breathed deep and, reluctantly, she let go.

The governor gasped for air and staggered towards the door, a broken man, shaken to the core. "Well, I never..." he murmured to himself. "I never..."

"What's so important about that man-child?" Shōin asked. "Is he really involved in the revolt?"

"I'm certain of it. That stone... it would take too long to explain here," she said, pointing at the governor with her eyes. *I'll tell you when we're alone.*

Shōin hesitated, before nodding. "Very well, I'll arrange for his transfer to the capital right away."

Satō turned to the little man again.

"What is your name?" she asked.

"The man I was with called me Koro."

"We are going to get you out of here, Koro."

"Chōfu… the wrong way," he croaked.

"It's better than this dungeon."

The little man's eyes dropped in resignation. "I hope."

Satō woke up from a shallow sleep; she had dreamt of the tattooed man. It was dawning outside, and the thin paper walls of the room were tinted a sickly purple-grey. The birds in the garden burst into a cacophony of screeches and whistles.

She rolled from side to side; the grit in the mattress beneath her ground noisily. She reached for the red orb hidden in the bundle of her clothes. As always, it lit up faintly under her touch. She used to think the glow was cold and evil, but now she was beginning to grow accustomed to it, even fond of it.

It must be worth as much as a village, she thought. *A jewel of this size… How old can it be? Seven, eight centuries? That was the last time anyone in Yamato needed a dragon weapon… and here I am, using it as a night lamp.*

The orb vibrated in her hand and hummed softly.

"You can't sleep either?" asked Shōin quietly.

They were sleeping in the same room, to keep up the pretence of a married couple, but on separate beddings, at least a foot apart.

"What's wrong?" she asked. She didn't want to discuss her own problems right now.

Shōin was silent for so long that she thought he'd fallen asleep again.

"I'm scared, *sensei*," he replied, his voice breaking.

He hadn't called her *sensei* since the first few days after their wedding, when he still kept slipping into his old manner.

"Scared? Of what?"

Another long pause, punctuated by a rhythmical screeching made by some irritated bird outside.

"I blew that man apart with just one spell."

"I know, I've been there."

"I don't know how it happened. I should not have such power."

"Well, isn't it great, though? You are growing up to be a mighty wizard."

"But it drains me so… when you were with the priests – healing – I was recovering from that single spell for the whole night. I felt like dying."

"That's only natural."

She heard him shuffle. Judging by the faint silhouette carved by the light of the orb, he supported himself on his elbow.

"Is it? I don't remember you teaching us about things like that. But I do remember learning about something else."

He laid back and sighed.

"I am a *Vriesmatic*, aren't I?"

"A *Prismatic*," she corrected him instinctively, and then added quickly, "but that's impossible."

"Why?"

"The *morfisch veld* of Yamato… the potentials…" She ran through the complex *Rangaku* theory in her head. Her father had always tried to teach her as much of the system as he could and she liked to think she had a fairly good grasp of it.

"It's far too early," she said. "It would take generations to accumulate enough potential for a Prismatic to be born."

"Then how do you explain what I did? You saw that spell… I don't even know what to call it. And I still can't find my affinity, no matter how I try."

"Don't worry, Shōin. You're still young. You'll grow out of it."

The screeching bird outside flew away, and instead of its song, Satō could now hear the ringing of morning bells in a nearby temple. She put the orb back, got up and slid open the wall panel.

From the room's veranda she could see down the hill upon which stood the governor's residence, all the way to the silver flowing river and the five-span bridge.

"Look, there's a ship down in the harbour. With red and white sail."

"That's a Mori ship!" Shōin sprang up. "News from Chōfu!"

By the time Shōin and Satō arrived at the pier, the porters were carrying down the last of the crates. The ship listed on the side, half-buried in the mud as the Nishiki River receded with the tide. It looked like a typical single-sail cargo barge, except for the ornate, gold-plated superstructure in the middle, which made it seem as if the ship carried a huge festival shrine on its deck.

"What's in these?" Shōin asked Takasugi, who was looking through the registry letters.

"Two hundred uniforms and two hundred spear heads," Takasugi announced, beaming. "That's a lot more than we asked for."

"So Mori-*dono* approved of our plan," said Shōin, trying to sound cheerful. He alone knew that the crates were *daimyo*'s promised, belated reward for his help in "capturing" the *dorako* and the rider.

"It seems so. I haven't actually seen any letter from Chōfu yet, it's just been these crates so far."

As he spoke those words, an unexpected whinny came from the deck of the ship, along with the tingled clopping of silver-clad hooves.

"*Eeeh!* Is that...the Imperial Messenger?" gasped Satō.

The courier, riding a resplendent, snow-white horse, approached the gangway and descended down it majestically, straight and proud in the gem-encrusted saddle. Shōin had never seen one like this before. The messenger from Heian, sent by the *Mikado* himself. He would only appear during major festivals to send ritualized holiday message from Yamato's spiritual leader.

What is he doing here?

"Which one of you is a Mori r*Eta*iner by the name of Yoshida?" asked the courier.

"That would be me." Shōin stepped forward.

The courier reached into the folds of his white silk kimono and drew a letter stamped with a sixteen-p*Eta*l chrysanthemum flower embedded in gold foil.

Shōin dropped to his knees in the mud, as did Satō and everyone else. It was the *Mikado*'s personal seal, an object as sacred as the *Mikado* himself. They were receiving a letter from a God – the *Mikado*, descended from the Sun Goddess Amaterasu herself… What business did a God have with one as lowly as Shōin?

He raised the golden seal to his lips and kissed it before carefully breaking it open. The missive was written in elegant, flowing, slightly archaic letters, in silver ink which made it difficult to decipher.

My loyal and devoted subjects, the missive started, like many of you, We have become aware of strange and ominous tidings coming from all around our Sacred Land. The Barbarians are within our borders; the monsters are invading our frontiers; laws are flaunted and ancient customs are abandoned; the morals have become loose.

The Taikun, *in whose care We have entrusted this Sacred Land, and his Council, are doing nothing to prevent any of this from happening. Therefore, there remains nothing else for Us than to call on you, my subjects, to defend the islands of Yamato and Our Holy Person.*

The Barbarian menace must be dealt with swiftly and without mercy. The Sacred Land must be defended at all cost. The Imperial Capital must stand forever in the heart of our nation, united in face of this danger.

Worship the Mikado!

Vanquish the Barbarians!

Jōi!

Blood rushed to Shōin's head. He folded the letter gingerly with shaking hands. What was happening was unthinkable. He didn't know much about politics, but he knew this much – the *Mikado* could never contradict the *Taikun* so openly. What was going on? And more importantly, what did any of this have to do with him?

"Your lord *daimyo* requested that I give you this letter also," the Imperial Courier said, handing Shōin another missive. "Now move aside, I must speak with the governor."

Shōin stepped out of the way of the white horse and, as the messenger rode away, he unfolded the letter. He read through it several times to make sure he understood it completely.

"What is it?" Satō looked over his shoulder.

"It's a new order for the *Kiheitai*," said Shin, folding the letter before she could read it. He stood up.

"Takasugi, gather the men. We are ordered to sail to Heian."

"Heian? The capital? Are you sure?"

Shōin nodded.

"Mori-*dono* has tasked the *Kiheitai* with guarding the *Mikado* from the barbarians... and whoever may be allied with them. We are to go to Heian immediately and join the Chōfu forces already gathered there."

He hid the missive into the folds of his gi jacket. There was another message added on to the letter, in Lord Mori's personal code; a message he chose not to read out loud in front of Satō. He hoped she would realize herself what the *Mikado*'s edict meant for her friend.

Bran ap Dylan had finally been sentenced. By the time the letter had arrived in Iwakuni, he was probably already dead.

CHAPTER XVIII

"You should be there," said Stirling, looking outside. "This was your victory."

Edern stood beside him; beyond the shot-through windows of the fortalice, the flames of the battle were ebbing. The Imperial troops were securing the perimeter around the ruined city, making sure no rebel marauders interrupted the prepared entry of the Qin victory parade.

Edern shrugged. "You're right. But the army staff decided they don't want us to show our presence in the war too much. I think they're plotting again."

"I still think it's unfair."

Edern turned and gave him a tired look. He really didn't need this conversation now.

"Oh, don't give me that look," Stirling scowled. "I know I'm only *human*, but I try my best!"

He popped a pellet of Cursed Weed in his mouth, and chewed slowly.

Stirling had been the *aide-de-camp* of the fallen Admiral, but since Reynolds' death, he had not received a new appointment, remaining as a non-commissioned officer within the corps. Instead, he tried to do the work of a staff

Reeve for Edern – be for him what Gwen was for Dylan back when he had been the Commodore.

But Stirling was right – he was just a human, and Edern was slowly growing bored of him; his mind not quick enough, his stamina not up to what a Faer lover required. It was supposed to be just a random fling back at Huating, but the man remained with him through all the weeks, clinging needlessly; Edern was hoping he would eventually get an assignment somewhere else, but it wasn't forthcoming.

Before he could reply, he heard the unmistakable sizzling and slithering sound of a Qin dragon in flight. The beast landed before the fortalice, and a boy in clothes of a Qin Imperial Messenger leapt from its back. Having asked the guard for the way, he ran up the stairs; a few moments later, Edern heard him knock on the door of his bedroom.

"Out," Edern ordered Stirling. The officer nodded and promptly made himself scarce.

"Come in!"

The messenger entered shyly; he was rather handsome, if a bit too young for Edern's liking. He handed over a tightly wrapped scroll of thick mulberry paper.

"*We* – uh – *have this* – " the boy started, in a stuttered, broken Seaxe.

"It's alright," said Edern, "you can speak Qin. Just keep it slow and simple – I've only been learning for a few weeks."

The boy's face brightened with relief. "This message came to the *Bohan's* headquarters. It has your name on it, but we can't read it."

"My name?"

Edern unrolled the scroll and tensed.

"When did you get it?"

"Last night."

How…?

"Was there anything else?"

The boy shook his head. "Only this."

"Are you able to send a message back?"

"Yes."

"Then go down and wait for my answer."

With the boy gone, Edern reached into the drawer in his desk and took out the Cipher Disk granted every senior officer in the Marine Corps. The message, calligraphed in the broad strokes of a Qin brush, was written in Dracalish, in a complex, polyalphabetic code. Edern pressed the disk to the paper and drew an activation rune on its surface. The disk glowed green then turned and moved about the page, changing the black ink letters into a legible message before Edern's incredulous eyes.

Follow the White Eagle. Bring two green colts in a wagon to 31,127 Airy. Fly due NEbE to 33, 130 Airy, until landfall. Ignore the sky. Will meet there. Stay on course, dancer.

"Follow the White Eagle." The message was from Dylan. Coordinates and directions. Two young, rider-less mounts on a dragon carrier, and then some two hundred miles by air… Edern's nostrils flared with excitement. At last, a chance to leave this wretched place and re-join Dylan and Gwen; things were going to be as they should always have been.

But… he grew instantly suspicious. What did *he* have to do with Dylan's mission? He was no secret agent, no spy. Never before had Dylan involved him so directly in any of his clandestine endeavours. Besides, Edern was a

Commodore now; Dylan was no longer his superior officer. He was now taking orders straight from the High Command – and if they knew anything about Dylan's whereabouts, they weren't telling anyone.

And those coordinates… Edern looked to the wall, where a map of the local seas hung forgotten among battle plans and sketches of enemy fortifications.

It's been so long since I've been to sea, he thought briefly.

The directions were baffling. There was nothing out there, between thirty first and thirty third meridian. Just an empty swathe of ocean, and… and a rough white spot, dashed along the edges, marked "Rough seas, possibly around Yamato".

Yamato? Was this where Dylan wanted him to go? By whose authority? Edern's doubts grew. Was this really a secret mission… or had he gone off on some errand of his own? *Why was he using a Qin messenger?* Had he *deserted?* And was he asking Edern to desert too?

"What's going on?" Edern said out loud.

Stay on course, dancer.

He knew what it meant. Dylan had only ever called Edern "dancer" to remind him of his Tylwyth blood: that of the Faer Folk of Brycheinniog. Edern was not of human race, and not a subject of the Dragon Throne.

In theory, he could leave the Lloegr Navy at any time. *Unlike Dylan,* he thought. Taking a few dragons with him was a different matter, but in the chaos of a war, who would count them…? The only question remaining was…

Do I want to do it?

He crushed the message in his fist and destroyed it with a sizzle of dragon spark.

"Damn you, Dylan," he muttered to himself. "Of course I'll do it."

He called the messenger back.

"Yes?" the boy asked.

"Send back only this," said Edern, and scribbled two symbols on a piece of paper.

"A crescent moon and burning torch...?"

"Yes. And make sure it's delivered today."

Moon and Torch - the symbols of the old Roman Feast of *Diana*. The fifteenth day of the eighth month. This would give Edern enough time to prepare his grand exit.

He would fly to the Gates of Annwn to see the Ardian again... but Yamato was close enough.

Torishi turned away from the lashing rain outside and slid the wall panel shut. The thin paper wall shuddered from the buffeting of the wind.

"I wish this storm would end already," said Nagomi.

"This is no normal tempest," replied Torishi. "Can you not hear the souls wailing in the gale?"

She nodded. The weather was strange, not only because there should have been no storms at this time of year, but because there was something unnatural about the wind. It reminded her of the night they swam to Ganryūjima, but this was different still. The Spirits she sensed in the wind were not angry or malicious, but rather... confused and lost.

And it's been going on for days.

"We should've gone to Mekari when we had the chance," she said.

"You were not ready to face your visions," said Torishi. "You still aren't. Let's begin."

He sat down heavily on the polished wooden floor opposite Nagomi, beside the irori hearth pit. With so many of the students gone, they had the entire dining room of the school to themselves. Torishi removed the pot from the hook over the hearth and put it aside, saying to himself, "we won't need that." He lay his bow to one side, and a bunch of arrows to the other, then opened his shaman's box and stuck the wooden slates into the ash.

"Speak nothing, little priestess," he warned Nagomi. "When I say, drink this and enter the fire. Don't worry, it will not hurt."

He handed her a cup of strongly smelling, murky saké. He put a bowl of the same before the hearth as an offering.

"I understand," she said.

"This is not what you're used to, priestess. This is raw and wild. But as long as you're with me, we may just make it."

She nodded. Torishi started the fire in the hearth and threw some leaves on it. Soon the room filled with thick, wet smoke, and the bear-man began to hobble back and forth, entering the trance.

He started muttering words in his own strange language, at first too quiet to tell apart. The flames in the hearth rose, and formed into the shape of a woman, old and wise. Nagomi bowed inadvertently, sensing she was in the presence of a mighty Spirit. Torishi threw his head back and chanted aloud.

Kamui huchi
Ires huchi
Iairaig'ere!
Tan tonoto
Chise otta tuki
Soita tuki
Ekas nomi kamui
Anomi shiri nena.
Pirika-no nuian!

The fire woman crouched and took a sip from the saké bowl. She smiled broadly and then disappeared, and the flames rose even higher and brighter. Torishi opened his eyes for a moment: they were dark and empty, like bottomless pits.

"Now!" he called.

Nagomi swallowed the warm, sharp liquid, and the world around her swirled. The fire in the hearth turned blue and parted in the middle, forming an entrance. She stood up and, fearless, stepped into the portal.

She felt herself pulled, and torn, and twisted; she was squeezed through some narrow opening, and then thrust into what felt like layers of slime; another force tore her from there and cast her into warm liquid, smelling faintly of iron, and then shoved her against a wooden floor.

Not this again…

She rose and faced the familiar, gold leaf-trimmed door. She slid it open. The putrefied corpse of the girl was still there among the candles.

"You again," it croaked. "You mustn't be here. This is not your place."

"I know you," said Nagomi, "why do I know you? Wait – you look just like... that blind girl from Kirishima!"

The creature howled in anguish and raised a skel*Eta*l hand. A great force pushed Nagomi away, back into darkness. Her body whirled again and she landed face-first into fine, dry dust.

She stood up, spluttering and coughing. The world around her spun one more time and then stopped. She retched, took a few deep breaths and looked around.

There was nothing there but an endless plain of fine red dirt. Behind her rose a vermillion *torii* gate and a small white thatched shrine. Before it stood a large black bear.

"Torishi-*sama*?" she asked, uncertain.

"I'm here," replied Torishi behind her. "You took a long time to get here."

She turned around. He was wearing his finest treebark garments, with many-coloured beads tied into his beard and long hair; he had his bow and arrows over his back and the broad sword at his belt.

"How do you feel?" he asked.

"My stomach hurts."

He winced. "I'm sorry. There was no other way."

"Is this the Otherworld?"

"A part of it, yes. This is where the Living Spirits can get to unguided. But we won't dwell here long."

He looked around and sniffed.

"Something is amiss. There's evil abroad. Maybe we should go back."

"No," Nagomi said firmly. "Let's do it."

Torishi grinned. He leaned over to the bear and whispered. The animal grunted and shook its head.

"Sit on its back, little priestess," he told Nagomi, "it will lead you to the Place on the Mountaintops."

"What about you?"

"I will be waiting there. Hold tight! This is a wild animal, after all!"

He slapped the bear on its behind and the beast charged forth, faster than any horse Nagomi had ever seen, and smooth, like the Ikazuki mounts. She rode for what seemed a long time, and yet when she looked back, she could still see the white shrine clearly behind her.

They reached a range of tall, steep mountains, and the bear started climbing the dusty slope, leaping from shelf to shelf and scratching at the dark red rock until at last it reached the summit, half-hidden in white and orange clouds.

Nagomi looked down — she no longer saw her shrine, but she could now see, through the openings in the clouds, many other buildings scattered around the red dirt plain: towers, pagodas, temples and palaces, each of them alone, each of them radiating red light and each surrounded by a mighty wall.

Torishi appeared beside her and helped her dismount. The animal grunted again.

"When I was a child," said Torishi, watching it disappear in the red haze, "I caught this bear as a cub, in a trap of my own making. I raised it myself, feeding the best meat and fruit, until it grew strong and powerful."

"What happened to it?" asked Nagomi.

"I killed it."

She covered her mouth in shock.

"*Why?*"

"So that it could return here," Torishi explained. "Bears are Spirits from the Otherworld. They only come to our world to find a hunter with whom they bond. Forever. Without it, I would be lost in this land."

"Why did it bring me here?"

"So that you could meet someone."

He turned his back to her, put his hands to his mouth in the shape of a trumpet, and yelled a resounding, wordless cry, which echoed through the mountaintops.

"I found him here not long after our fight with the demon," Torishi explained. "I should've asked him for help earlier. He knows more about these things than I do."

"Who is it?"

The mists and clouds solidified into the shape and form of a tall and burly man. She had seen this man before; she recognized the long, braided hair, the colourful garments much like those Torishi wore, and the jangling bronze bracelets. A mighty eagle was sitting on his outstretched arm.

"*Irankarapte, nipa,*" he said in a deep voice.

"*Irangarapte na,*" said Torishi.

"You!" She gasped. "But... we let you go free!"

"And for that I am grateful," the man replied, raising a fist to his chest. "But somebody else wished me dead, it seems."

"I am sorry," she whispered.

"Leaves in the wind, priestess. Leaves in the wind."

She shivered.

"They may have lost the Way of the Bear in the North," added Torishi, "but they r*Et*ained some of the old lore."

The man looked at Torishi with slight annoyance. "The Bear is still strong in our land. We just do things differently.

406

But let us not argue here. We have precious little time left to train you before I pass beyond the mountains."

"Are you a Scryer?" Nagomi asked.

"I was taught the Way of the Eagle in my youth, but I never had the patience to pursue it... I will teach you what I can, *Shamo* priestess, but from there you are on your own."

"I understand," she replied with a short bow. "I'm sorry – I never learned your name."

"I am Shakushain, Prince of the North," he said, running a hand across his beard. He then smiled, closed his eyes and, with the speed of a lightning strike, he slammed his fist into the rock underneath him.

A crack spawned in the stone floor, spewing white, green and yellow fumes, similar to those Nagomi remembered from the Suwa Shrine.

"The Waters of Scrying!" she whispered in awe. Shakushain grimaced.

"*Hah*! This is the real thing, not your pale, *Shamo* imitations," he said. "These mountains are built of Time itself. Each wisp of this smoke is a moment in the past, present or future."

He waved his hand, and the coloured mist split into separate strands.

"What you see in your Waters is already cleansed and chosen by the Spirits out of all possibilities... But you know already there's more to Scrying than that. Here, you can learn how to do it yourself. That is the skill of *true* Scryers."

He blew at the smoke, and the strands enveloped Nagomi's head. Instinctively, she held her breath.

"No, no!" Shakushain said. "Breathe it in."

She did as she was told, and her head filled with images. There were dragon wings and precious jewels; thick forests, high mountains, and deep caves; bloody battles and fierce duels, flashing guns and slashing swords; children being born and conceived, cities burned and rebuilt anew, iron ships steaming in the high seas and walking machines roaming the land.

"Too much!" she cried. "I can't see..."

"Focus, girl. Only one of those is real."

"Which one?"

"Which one do you *think*?" his voice boomed, but she no longer saw him.

She tried to concentrate on each strand of vision separately, but they all seemed identical. There was no specific feature she could grasp onto. Until...

A strand floated past which was brighter and crisper than all others, a vision of a sea battle between several fleets of monstrous iron ships.

"That one!" she cried and tried to grab it in her hands. The strand disappeared.

"Wrong!" Shakushain rebuked her. "That was the one that's least likely. Try again!"

Least likely? But it seemed so real...

She breathed in again, and another set of visions overwhelmed her. This time, she watched calmly as each strand passed before her eyes. She now noticed a few other wisps were as clear and sharp as the one she had grabbed before, and she dismissed those. She looked beyond them and saw something else: a vision so plain and insignificant, it was almost invisible; a faint, grey light, weak and shimmering, moving quickly and difficult to pinpoint.

She reached for it, but it was like trying to catch a fish in the pond with her hands. Slippery, the wisp slipped away and vanished among the others, and once again, all the strands around her dissipated into the air.

"I couldn't get it…" she said.

"Good." Shakushain smiled. "That means it was the right one. The truth is the hardest to spot and impossible to hold on to. That's the difficult part of Scrying – and one I never mastered myself…"

He stopped abruptly and looked sharply past her, towards the red dirt plain below.

"You must go," he said.

Nagomi followed his gaze and saw something move on the plain; a black, crawling dot, scurrying rapidly towards them, then another behind it, and another. She sensed dread emanating from the dark forms that tightened up her throat and covered her skin with goose bumps.

"What are they?"

"I don't know," replied Shakushain. "But it's best you leave now."

"He's right," said Torishi, and helped Nagomi mount the black bear again.

"Goodbye, priestess," said Shakushain.

"We'll be back soon, won't we?" she asked, looking from him to Torishi. "I have so much to learn from you."

The men looked at each other.

"Go now," said Torishi. "Once you reach your mind shrine, remember to close the door behind you."

The bear leapt down the slope in a great hurry and raced on, even faster than before. The mountains soon disappeared beyond the horizon, and the red dirt beneath her became a blur. But the dark, crawling shadows were fast, too. She sensed them behind, slithering on the ground like black snakes. Soon they were near, reaching her back with their shadowy tentacles. The bear roared and picked up the pace, its sides steaming with sweat. At last, Nagomi saw the white walls of the shrine. With a few great leaps, the bear swallowed the remaining distance and ground to a halt before the *torii* gate.

The black shadows were almost upon her. The bear turned and bared its teeth at them, and they stopped. Nagomi hesitated.

"Will you be all right?" she asked the animal, but it did not respond. The shadows crept closer. The air around Nagomi grew cold, smelling of blood and rot.

One of the dark shapes leapt into the air and struck at her with its arms; she covered her head and heard a sharp whiz of an arrow. The missile pierced the shadow and it vanished. Another arrow destroyed the second one. Torishi showed up behind it, holding the bow aimed at the last of the creatures.

"What did I tell you?" he snarled at her with wild fury. "Get inside and close the door!"

He looked more like a furious bear than a human being. She had never seen him like this before, not even in the midst of battle. She turned back, ran inside the shrine and slammed the door behind her.

On the fourth day of the storm, Bran ran out of food. On the fifth, he felt the first pangs of starvation and began to wonder whether the storm would ever cease. Even Emrys was growing annoyed: the foul weather had caused all its prey to hide in dens, lairs, and thicker forest, where the dragon couldn't reach them.

On the sixth day, Bran had another visitor.

"I thought you could use some supplies," said Dōraku, throwing a bundle at Bran.

"All right," the boy said, unpacking the food in hurry, "now I'm intrigued. How *did* you get here in this weather?"

The Swordsman smirked. "Your dragon did not eat all of the Ikezuki horses."

"What about the Dan-no-ura spirits? Wouldn't a storm like this get them out?"

"This storm is not their doing. Something else is going on, and I'm not yet sure what. I was just on my way to investigate."

He turned back towards the sea. Bran stood up.

"Wait."

"What is it?"

"I was thinking... if I perished in this storm, nobody would suspect anything, would they?"

Dōraku turned around with a grin. "What prompted this change of heart?"

Bran shrugged. "A change of circumstances."

The episode with the fisherman, though brief, had destroyed his confidence. It had been the first time he had shown his real face to an ordinary Yamato man, and that man preferred to succumb to raging waves rather than risk spending any more time in Bran's company.

Bran realized at last that he had been clinging to a fool's hope. The Mori clan's disgust with him was more than just an act.

The death order was no bluff. They really hate me — and fear me.

"Hold on a few hours," said Dōraku. "I'll be back at nightfall to help you out."

"I don't need your help. I can fly away any time." Bran said, preparing to mount the dragon.

"They will suspect something if you don't make it convincing enough."

Bran stopped.

"Convincing – how?"

"Just wait, and you'll see."

"We must go back," said Nagomi firmly.

The freak storm continued to batter the walls and doors unabated, adding its hollow wail to the eerie silence that filled the school buildings. The Meirinkan was shut down, and even the few pupils that had remained behind after the *Kiheitai* departed, had returned to their families. There was nobody left apart from the essential staff, which moved about the corridors silent and invisible like the *shinobi* assassins.

Rice, pickles, and dried seaweed was all Nagomi and Torishi had prepared for their meal. Not that it mattered; Nagomi was too distracted to think of eating.

"Too dangerous," said Torishi, biting into a slice of radish. "You saw what happens. Every time we go there, the shadows get closer and more numerous."

"But there is so much I have yet to learn! And Shakushain-*sama* – "

"He's gone," replied Torishi. "Departed beyond the Mountains, at last."

"So you *did* go there – without me."

He gave her a long look, and chewed the radish over slowly. She pushed the half-empty rice bowl away, despondent, but then she had another idea.

"What if we stayed close to my shrine? That way we could escape at any moment."

"What good would that do? The Mists of Time do not reach that far."

"I can still see things without them, you know. I have visions here all the time."

"Then you can study them here, too. Just like you always have. I'm beginning to regret – "

"I have to get back there!" she blurted out.

He put down the chopsticks, burped into his fist, and stared at her.

"What is it *really* about…?"

She averted his gaze. She didn't want him to know that the real reason why she had insisted on repeating their journey to the Otherworld had nothing to do with Prince Shakushain's training.

She was too overwhelmed with the new and alien surroundings to notice it on her first visit, but she had clearly felt it the second, and subsequent, times.

Bran.

He was there, somewhere. She sensed his presence, and his thoughts, the way she had sensed them a few times before in the real world, only stronger and more persistent. It was almost as if he was trying to contact her again, but could only do so in that strange world of red dust.

"I felt him too, you know," Torishi said. She gaped at him in surprise. "Your instinct was right, after all. There is something strange going on. I didn't believe for a moment that he was sent on any mission."

"All the more reason to go back! You said you would do all that's in your power to help me."

"Out of the question. I can't protect you alone and Dōraku-*sama* is not here to help us. Will you be eating those mushrooms?"

"No, you can have them," Nagomi replied. She stood up from the table grumpily, bowed sharply, and left the room.

The tiny flame flickered in the draught coming through the thin paper walls. The dancing shadows writhed on the floor and the heated floor-boards under the charcoal pot whistled a quiet, wailing song.

Nagomi stuck the thin wooden slats into the ash inside the pot, and put a bowl of warm saké in front of it. She had stolen both from Torishi's box earlier that day. She didn't know the songs he sang to his Gods, but she had her own – and she was a priestess. That had to count for something.

She wished she still had her Spirit Light, but having lost two in such a brief time during her adventures, she couldn't bear risking another one. She hoped the make-shift fire she managed to light up in the bronze pot was good enough.

She started whispering a long, improvised prayer. Last time she had checked, Torishi was fast asleep in his room, but she could never be too careful. She cast some leaves she had picked up in the courtyard onto the flames; the fire belched a mushroom-shaped cloud of dark smoke, and Nagomi erupted in a fit of coughing.

When she cleared her eyes from tears and soot, she saw that the flames had formed into the woman she knew from Torishi's rituals. She gazed at the priestess inquisitively, and then looked around, as if searching for the bear-man.

"He is not here. Please…" Nagomi offered the bowl. The woman reached for the saké and took a sip. Her stare remained suspicious, but she raised her hands to the ceiling and then vanished. A portal of blue flame appeared in her place. It was small and dark, but large enough for Nagomi to pass through.

The black bear growled at Nagomi, forcing her to step back into the shadow of the *torii* gate. It would not let her pass any further.

It didn't matter. She was in the Otherworld again, and again she could sense Bran's beckoning call. Not knowing how else to respond, she put her hands to her mouth and cried into the air:

"Bran! I'm here! Come quickly!"

Nothing happened. She waited a while and then called him again. Again, the only response was the howling of the wind in the distance.

And then the air grew cooler and something moved in the dirt. The shadows. They appeared out of nowhere, sliding from all directions, surrounding the white shrine. The bear snarled and growled at them, but they would not stop.

Nagomi stepped back. She turned around only to see one of the shadows had bypassed the shrine's wall and had now wrapped itself across the door. She was trapped outside, and there was no place to run. She ignored the heavy feeling in her stomach and rising panic and prayed to Spirits of this place to bring forward the light that had helped her in the past.

One shadow shot a dark tentacle at her. She cowed, but the missile bounced off the thick hide of the black bear that leapt to her defence. Another shadow crept up from the right, launching a second attack. The bear snapped its maw at it, but its teeth caught only air. The shadows moved too fast. A thin black feeler reached Nagomi's shoulder; she felt icy cold pain and screamed. She jumped back and tripped.

415

The tentacle wrapped around her leg; a slimy, crushing limb, pulling her beyond the shrine wall. There was nothing for her to grab onto; her fingers scratched at the red dirt in vain.

A familiar whoosh rang out in her ears. A plume of bright fire poured from the sky and scorched the shadowy attacker into dust. Nagomi looked up to see the jade-green dragon circling above the shrine.

"Bran!" she cried. Her heart jumped with joy.

The dragon swooped down, spitting flame, destroying the shadows all around the shrine. Bran leapt off its back in mid-flight, rolled under a shooting tentacle and, rising, cut through the enemy with a lance of bright golden light. With each strike, one shadow perished in a noiseless explosion.

Finally, all the dark creatures were vanquished. Emrys landed on the ground beside the black bear, who growled at it in fear and anger.

She ran up to Bran and for a brief, too brief moment, she held him in her arms, feeling his warmth.

"It was you! I knew it!"

I waited so long for this...

"Yes," he replied, his voice tired and weak. "I was trying to contact you for days. I almost gave up."

"Are you hurt? What's happened to you?"

She let him go and lead him to the shrine wall, where he sat down, breathing heavily. She knelt beside him.

"I am imprisoned by Mori-*dono* on a small island not far off the Chōfu shore. No, wait," he raised his hand to stop her from interrupting. "I *agreed* to that. It doesn't matter. Today I'm running away – and I suggest you and Satō do the same. If the *daimyo* learns I'm gone – "

"Sacchan is no longer here," she said, "she was sent to the north with the others, to fight some rebels."

"The north?" He frowned.

"Iwakuni, I think. It's just me and Torishi left."

"Then take him and hide somewhere. Or better yet, flee, as soon as this storm ends - somewhere far from that *daimyo*. Maybe try to reach Satō. I might do the same. I haven't decided yet."

He stood up and studied the horizon. "The shadows are coming again. They never really die, just disappear here and reappear somewhere else."

She stood by his side.

"What are they?"

"I don't know. I've only started seeing them after... after my accident."

Is it because of what Sacchan did to save him?

"I must go," he said.

"But..." She caught hold of his hand. "I haven't seen you in a month... There's so much I want to – "

Taking her by surprise, he drew her in, held her tight and planted a kiss on her cheek

"A week from today," he said, "I will come here again. Stay safe."

"I'll be waiting."

Just as Bran had enough of waiting and prepared again to mount Emrys, the grey bulky shape of a tired horse emerged from the crashing waves onto the beach.

Dōraku dismounted and unbound a large bundle from the saddle.

"What's wrong?" he asked, seeing Bran's face. "You look worn."

"Never mind that, what have you got there?"

"Yourself."

He threw the bundle at Bran's feet and unravelled it from a blanket. It was the body of a boy, roughly Bran's size, naked and severely bruised. His face was battered out of all recognition.

"The sea threw out plenty of bodies these last few days," explained Dōraku, "It took me a while to find the right one."

"That's your plan?"

"It's good enough. The *daimyo* will not be too concerned with d*Eta*ils. Now put your clothes on it."

Bran choked on vomit as he wrapped his *yukata* around the boy's slimy torso. As he leaned down to do so, he thought he smelled a faint stench of smoke and leather.

"Is he an *Eta*?" he asked, turning his head away.

"Probably." Dōraku shrugged. "That way nobody will miss him."

"What about his family?"

"An *Eta* family," the Swordsman scoffed. "Give me that sword."

He grabbed the short blade and thrust it into the boy's belly, then wrapped his cold, stiff hands around the hilt.

"Now hurry up. Something tells me this is the last night of this storm."

Bran washed his hands in the sea and mounted his dragon. He looked into the sky. The clouds were as dark and dense, and the rain lashed just as sharp against his face as before.

"Where will you go?" asked Dōraku.

"Find Satō, make sure she is safe and apologise for everything."

"What, and risk being captured again? Why not fly straight back to Chōfu!"

418

"I'll be discreet."

"How will you even know where she is?"

"I know she was sent to a place called Iwakuni."

That caught the Swordsman by surprise. He raised an eyebrow.

Yes, thought Bran with satisfaction, *I don't need to rely on you to tell me everything.*

"And do you think that will not be the first place they will be looking for you?"

Bran rolled his eyes. "Fine, let's hear *your* plan."

"There's only one place in Yamato where a foreigner can be safe for now, without involving himself in too much trouble."

"Dejima," Bran guessed.

"And you already know your way."

He frowned. He knew Dōraku was playing him again; there was something going on in Kiyō, or in its vicinity, and the Swordsman needed Bran to be there for some mysterious reason. But he was making a convincing point, and if Bran ever decided to fly to Qin, Kiyō was a better starting place than most.

"Very well. I'll try to make it to Dejima in one piece. I suppose I'll be hearing from you sooner or later."

"It's likely," Dōraku replied with a smile. "I'm guessing sooner rather than later. Things have begun to move fast in Yamato."

"What makes you think I want to take part in any of it?"

"You're here, aren't you?"

To this Bran found no answer. He sent out a command and Emrys leapt up, struggling against the howling wind and pouring rain.

THE CHRYSANTHEMUM SEAL

CHAPTER XIX

Gwen emerged from the wooden tub, water pouring down her naked body in glistening waterfalls. She walked across the grass, past a group of bathing, giggling Yamato women, and welcomed the towel that Dylan handed to her.

"You look... *resplendent*," he said, dazzled by the view.

She laughed. "I don't think that's the word you wanted to use."

"Maybe," he agreed, "but it's hard to think in these...conditions."

"It's nice, isn't it," she said, "all this..." She waved her arm at the surroundings.

She leaned back into his arms and looked at Kiyō. The women's bath on Dejima was set up outside in a small garden next to the kitchens, and it commanded a grand view of the city's white walls and blue roofs across the bay. She studied it in silence; Dylan noticed her nose wrinkle, as it would every time she was in deep thought.

"What are you thinking about?" he asked.

"How easy it would be to capture this city with our dragons," she said. "You could control the entire air-space from that hill to the right, and then strike the ships at the harbour…"

He burst out laughing.

"Don't tell me you haven't been thinking the same," she said.

"I have," he admitted. "This place would make a fine new jewel in the Dragon Queen's crown. If we brought it to her, she might even forgive us the desertion."

"You know, I'm glad we came here. Even if it was all for nothing… even if it cost us our dragons."

They kissed.

"Do you think he'll come?" she asked when they stopped to catch a breath.

Dylan stroked her arm. "I hope so. Otherwise I'll have to steal Li's dragon, and that would really complicate matters."

"How are *they* reacting to all this, I wonder?" she pointed to the haze-covered Kiyō. "They're so cryptic, these Yamato. I can't tell anything from their faces."

"I hear the governor of the city tried to kill himself when Li arrived."

"Kill himself?" she turned to him in surprise. "Why?"

"It's his duty to protect this bay from foreigners. And he knows he can't do it anymore. Not against dragons, not against those... underwater ships that the Khaganate had brought."

And that we missed by just a few days, he remembered. *I'd so love to see them. I've heard rumours, but the real thing must be amazing...*

"So, why didn't he?" Gwen interrupted his thoughts.

"I don't know. Something's changed. The old rules are being scrapped. The Overwizard says they're going to let them move freely around the city any day now."

"Oh! I'd love that. The city looks so nice from here."

"I thought you were only admiring its lack of defences," he said with a smile.

She sneezed in response; the Yamato women giggled even more. She pushed Dylan gently away and bowed to pick up her clothes, letting the towel slide gracefully to the ground.

They walked back down the narrow lanes of Dejima to their lodgings on the top floor of a pastel-blue house overlooking the vegetable garden. The colony reminded him of the Fragrant Harbour in its beginnings – only even more claustrophobic, if that was even possible.

Two hundred and fifty years of this? He boggled. The Bataavians were a tougher bunch than he had been giving them credit for. Or at least more stubborn.

He heard cries of awe and fear around him, and looked to the sky. The golden Qin dragon was weaving its coils in the air above the bay, glinting in the sun like the water trickling down Gwen's back.

"Look, he's flying again," he said.

Li's arrival had caused an enormous stir on the island, and, Dylan imagined, even greater on the mainland. As far as he knew, there had never been a dragon in Kiyō before, other than an odd fossil gifted to the local rulers by the Bataavians. Just like in Kagoshima before, hundreds of the city's inhabitants had fled to the hills at the first sight of the monster – and they were only now slowly returning to their homes as the week moved on and not a tile was blown off the roof by the "vengeful" beast.

The golden dragon turned and swooped northwards, as if chasing something, and disappeared from sight.

"Show-off."

"Lucky bastard."

They said these two sentences in unison and laughed, but then Gwen's face turned wistful.

"Oh, Dylan, I want to fly again."

"Soon, I promise."

"Why did you only ask for two extra mounts?"

"Even Edern wouldn't manage to get more through the Sea Maze on his own. And I couldn't risk getting anyone else involved."

She pouted.

"We'll take shifts," he promised.

424

"What about Warwick?"

"Who do you think will fly Nariakira's dragon?"

The other of the two dragons Edern was bringing had been promised to Shimazu Nariakira in Kagoshima – and Dylan decided he was still going to keep his part of the bargain after all. If his instincts were right – and they rarely weren't – Shimazu's friendship had the potential to be worth a lot more than one small mount.

"You knew!"

"I wasn't buying that 'hunting trip' excuse for a minute. And just as I expected, the boy stayed in Kagoshima after all. I guess he got a taste for those little oranges of theirs."

"Do you think it's wise to give these people a dragon…?"

"It's only one mount, how much harm can it do? And I want to keep Nariakira close. He may be a rascal, but it would be great if he was our rascal. When Dracaland finally decides to turn its attention towards Yamato… what is it?"

"Your diplomat self is back," Gwen smiled. "I haven't seen him for ages."

"Yes," Dylan scratched the scar on his face distractedly, "it feels rather good, I must say. I missed that."

They reached the pastel-blue house. A Corrie-like servant – a *kabout*, as the Bataavians called the diminutive race – showed his small, wrinkly face in the corridor.

"*Diner word geserveert,*" he screeched.

"That means food is ready," said Dylan.

"I got that." She walked towards the dining room. "Aren't you coming?"

He looked to the second floor. He had an odd feeling about the house ever since they came in...

"In a minute, love. I need to get something from upstairs."

He slowly climbed the rickety, squeaky stair. The door to the small room he had been using as his office was ajar.

Odd, he thought. *I'm sure I locked it.*

Carefully he creaked the door open, peering inside through True Sight.

Sitting in Dylan's chair, by Dylan's desk, was a Western boy, dressed in nothing but a Yamato loincloth, morbidly thin, deeply tanned, scarred, and dripping wet. His face, peering from under a layer of muck and seaweed, with deep green eyes and a sharp, straight nose, was strangely familiar. His name was at the tip of Dylan's tongue...

"Welcome, Father," the boy said. "Long time no see."

APPENDICES

GLOSSARY OF TERMS

(Bat.) — Bataavian

(Yam.) — Yamato

(Pryd.) — Prydain

(Seax.) — Seaxe

aardse nor *(Bat.)* spell word, "Earth Tomb"

amazake *(Yam.)* a traditional sweet drink from fermented rice

ardian *(Seax.)* the Commander of a Regiment in the Royal Marines

banneret *(Seax.)* the Commander of a Banner in the Royal Marines

bento *(Yam.)* a boxed lunch, usually made of rice, fish and pickled vegetables

bevries *(Bat.)* spell word, "Freeze"

biwa *(Yam.)* fruit of loquat tree

blodeuyn *(Pryd.)* spell word, "Flowers"

bugyo *(Yam.)* chief magistrate of an au*tono*mous city

bwcler *(Pryd.)* magical shield covering a fighter's arm, a buckler

cha *(Yam.)* green tea

chwalu *(Pryd.)* spell word, "Unravel"

Corianiaid *(Pryd.)* a race of red-haired dwarves from Rheged

cwrw *(Pryd.)* beer

dab *(Pryd.)* creature, thing or a person

daimyo *(Yam.)* feudal lord of a province

daisen *(Yam.)* chief wizard

dap *(Pryd.)* the same size and shape as something

dengaku *(Yam.)* a meal of grilled tofu or vegetables topped with sauce

denka, —*denka* *(Yam.)* honorific, referring to the member of the royal family

derwydd *(Pryd.)* druid

dōjō *(Yam.)* school of martial arts or fencing

dono, —**dono** *(Yam.)* honorific, referring to a noble man of a higher level

doraco *(Yam.)* Western dragon

doshin *(Yam.)* chief of Police

dōtanuki *(Yam.)* a type of *katana*, longer and heavier than usual

draca hiw *(Seax.)* spell word, "Dragon Form"

draigg *(Pryd.)* a dragon

duw *(Pryd.)* a swearword

dwt *(Pryd.)* a young child

egungun (Yoruba) a holy spirit, also a shaman dancer representing Egungun

enenra *(Yam.)* a spirit born of smoke

faeder *(Seax.)* father

fudai *(Yam.)* an "inner circle" clan; one of the vassals of the Tokugawa *Taikun* before the battle of Sekigahara

futon *(Yam.)* a roll-out mattress filled with rice husks

gaikokujin *(Yam.)* a foreigner, non-Yamato person

genoeg *(Bat.)* spell word, "Enough" (to mark the end of a continuous spell)

gornestau *(Pryd.)* magical duel

graddio *(Pryd.)* school graduation ceremony

gwrthyrru *(Pryd.)* spell word, "Repel"

hakama *(Yam.)* split trousers

hamon *(Yam.)* visual effect created on the blade through hardening process

haori *(Yam.)* a type of outer jacket

hatamoto *(Yam.)* the *Taikun*'s retainer, samurai in direct service to the *Taikun*

hime, —**hime** *(Yam.)* honorific, referring to women of high position

igo *(Yam.)* a board game for two players, using identical black and white tokens

ijslaag *(Bat.)* spell word, "Ice Layer"

inro *(Yam.)* a wooden container for holding small objects, hanging from a sash

inugami *(Yam.)* a dog spirit

jawch *(Pryd.)* a swearword

jutte *(Yam.)* police truncheon

kabuki *(Yam.)* a form of classical dance theater

kagura *(Yam.)* a type of theatrical dance with religious themes

kakka *(Yam.)* honorific, referring to lords of the province or heads of the clans

kambe *(Yam.)* a shrine servant taken from an adjacent village

kami *(Yam.)* God or Spirit in Yamato mythology

kanpai *(Yam.)* Cheers!

kappa *(Yam.)* a water sprite, reptilian humanoid

katana *(Yam.)* the main Yamato sword, over 60cm in length

kaya *(Yam.)* a bright yellow wood used for making igo boards

kekkai *(Yam.)* a magical shield, similar to *tarian*

THE CHRYSANTHEMUM SEAL

kimono *(Yam.)* official layered robe of the noble class

kirin *(Yam.)* a chimerical creature of Qin, body of a deer and the head of a dragon with a large single horn

kodachi *(Yam.)* a short Yamato sword, less than 60cm in length

koenig *(Seax.)* the monarch of the Varyaga Khaganate

kosode *(Yam.)* basic, loose fitting robe for both men and women

kun, —kun *(Yam.)* honorific, referring to young persons of the same social status

kunoichi *(Yam.)* a female *shinobi* assassin

kuso *(Yam.)* a swearword

lloegr *(Pryd.)* Dracaland east of the Dyke

llwch *(Pryd.)* spell word, "Dust"

long (Qin) Qin dragon

mam *(Pryd.)* mother

mamgu *(Pryd.)* grandmother

Matsubara *(Yam.)* the family of *katana* swordsmiths

metsuke *(Yam.)* inspector representative of the *Taikun*

Mikado *(Yam.)* the divine Emperor of Yamato

mikan *(Yam.)* fruit of tangerine tree

mithraeum (Latin) temple of Mithras

mitorashita *(Yam.)* worshippers of Mithras

mochi *(Yam.)* a sweet made of rice gluten

mogelijkheid *(Bat.)* magical potential

monpe *(Yam.)* workman's trousers

naginata *(Yam.)* a polearm formed of a *katana* blade set in a bamboo shaft

nodachi *(Yam.)* a large, two-handed sword, over 120cm in length

noren *(Yam.)* a curtain hanging over the shop entrance, with the logo of the establishment

oba (Yoruba) chieftain

obi *(Yam.)* a silk sash wrapped around the waist

obidame *(Yam.)* a buckle for tying the obi sash

oden *(Yam.)* a type of stew

omikuji *(Yam.)* fortunes written on a strip of paper

onmyōji *(Yam.)* a practitioner of traditional Yamato magic

onmyōdō *(Yam.)* traditional Yamato magic

oppertovenaar *(Bat.)* overwizard of Dejima

pilipala *(Pryd.)* spell word, "butterfly"

proost *(Bat.)* Cheers!

Rangaku *(Yam.)* "Western Sciences", study of Western magic and technology

*Rangaku*sha *(Yam.)* a practitioner of Western magic

reeve *(Seax.)* the Staff Sergeant in the Royal Marines

rhew *(Pryd.)* spell word, "frost"

ri *(Yam.)* measure of distance, approx. 4 km

rōnin *(Yam.)* a masterless samurai

ryū *(Yam.)* a Yamato dragon

Saesneg *(Pryd.)* (slur) Seaxe

sakaki *(Yam.)* a flowering evergreen tree, used to produce **sacred** paraphernalia

sama, —sama *(Yam.)* honorific, referring to peers of the same social status

sencha *(Yam.)* popular kind of tea

sensei, **—*sensei*** *(Yam.)* honorific, referring to teachers and doctors

shamisen *(Yam.)* a three-stringed musical instrument

shinobi (Yam.) assassin

shōchū *(Yam.)* strong liquor (25-35% proof)

shōgi *(Yam.)* strategic board game similar to chess

shukubo *(Yam.)* accommodation for temple pilgrims

soku*kamiButsu* *(Yam.)* a self-mummified monk

stadtholder *(Bat.)* the ruler of Bataavia

swyfen *(Seax.)* a swearword

tabako (Yam.) tobacco

tadcu *(Pryd.)* grandfather

tafarn *(Pryd.)* tavern, inn

tafl *(Pryd.)* strategic board game, played on a checkered board

taid *(Pryd.)* grandfather

Taikun *(Yam.)* military ruler of Yamato

taipan (Qin) leader of a trading company

Taishō *(Yam.)* field marshal, commander-in-chief of all the forces in the field

tarian *(Pryd.)* magical shield surrounding entire body

tengu *(Yam.)* a forest goblin

tenpura *(Yam.)* small fish and vegetables fried in batter

teppo *(Yam.)* a "thunder gun" — hand-held lightning thrower

terauke *(Yam.)* a passport produced by an affiliate temple

tono, —**dono** *(Yam.)* honorific, referring to a noble man of a higher level

torii *(Yam.)* wooden or stone gate to the shrine

tozama *(Yam.)* an "outer circle" clan that was forced to become the vassal of the Tokugawa *Taikun* after the battle of Sekigahara

tsuba *(Yam.)* a handguard of the *katana*

twinkelbal *(Bat.)* sparkleball; a stone used for thaumaturgy practice

twp *(Pryd.)* insult, "stupid, simple"

tylwyth teg *(Pryd.)* Faer Folk, a race of tall, silver- or golden-haired humanoids

waelisc *(Seax.)* (slur) Prydain

wakashu *(Yam.)* an "unbroken" youth, a virgin

THE CHRYSANTHEMUM SEAL

wakizashi *(Yam.)* a short sword used as a side arm, 30-60cm in length

xiexie *(Qin)* "thank you"

y ddraig goch *(Pryd.)* Red Dragon

yamabushi *(Yam.)* an ascetic mountain hermit

yōkai *(Yam.)* evil spirit, demon

yukata (Yam.) casual summer clothing, simple light robe

GLOSSARY OF CHARACTERS

GWYNEDD

CANTRE'R GWAELOD

IFOR AP MEURIG o Cantre'r Gwaelod
b. 2541 a.u.c. Midshipman on *Phaeton* under Captain
Broughton Reynolds. Married to Branwen ferch Rhodri.

DYLAN AB IFOR o Cantre'r Gwaelod
b. 2566 a.u.c. Formerly Ardian of the Second Dragoons
Regiment of the Royal Marines. Married to Rhian ferch
Rhys.

Former Mount: Highland Silver, Afreolus (*Unruly*)

BRAN AP DYLAN o Cantre'r Gwaelod
b. 2590 a.u.c. A graduate of Dracology at the Llambed
Academy of Mystic Arts.

Mount: Rhos Jade, Emrys (*Ambrosius*)

RHIAN FERCH RHYS
b. 2569 a.u.c. Cunning-woman from southern Gwynedd.
Married to Dylan ab Ifor. Bran's mother.

ROYAL MARINES

EDERN mab Gwyn
b. 2526 a.u.c. Commodore of the Ever Victorious Army,
formerly Banneret of the Second Dragoons Regiment of the
Royal Marines. A Tylwyth Teg.

Mount: Highland Silver, Nodwydd (*Needle*)

GWENLLIAN ferch Harri
b. 2577 a.u.c. Reeve of the Second Dragoons Regiment of the
Royal Marines.

Former Mount: Highland Silver, Tywyll (*Dark*)

SAMUEL ben Hagin
b. 2546 a.u.c. The ship's doctor.

ALEXANDER SETON
b. 2567 a.u.c. Ardian of the Twelfth Regiment of Light
Dragoons

WULFHERE of WARWICK
b. 2589 a.u.c. Soldier of the Twelfth Regiment of Light
Dragoons. Descendant of Richard Warwick the Kingmaker.

Former Mount: Highland Azure, Eolhsand (*Amber*)

EOGAN STIRLING
b. 2576 a.u.c. Aide-de-camp of late Admiral Broughton
Reynolds.

YAMATO

HEIAN

MUTSUHITO
b. 2595 a.u.c. Crown Prince of Yamato

KŌMEI
b. 2576 a.u.c. 121st Divine *Mikado* (Emperor) of Yamato

MATSUDAIRA KATAMORĪ
b. 2579 a.u.c. Chief Commissioner in Heian

SASAKI TADASABURO
b. 2586 a.u.c. Chief of City Guards in Heian

KOYATA JŪMONJI
b. 2570 a.u.c. Deputy Chief of City Guards in Heian

HAJIME SAITŌ
b. 2587 a.u.c. Student of the Ganryu Dojo, now a ronin in employment of Matsudaira Katamori.

ISHIDA TAKUYA
b. 2566 a.u.c. Lieutenant of Koyata

THE CHRYSANTHEMUM SEAL

HIRATA MITSUYU

b. 2574 a.u.c. Lieutenant of Koyata

NAMIKOSHI TOKOJIRO

b. 2581 a.u.c. An interpreter of Seaxe language, lieutenant of
Koyata.

ITŌ

ITŌ KEISUKE

b. 2556 a.u.c. A Western-style physician, formerly owner of the
Sōfukuji Infirmary.

ITŌ TAKI, neé Kusumoto

b. 2556 a.u.c. Wife of Itō Keisuke, also a physician.

ITŌ INE

b. 2580 a.u.c. A nurse and physician, formerly at the Sōfukuji
Infirmary. Daughter of Von Siebold.

ITŌ NAGOMI

b. 2591 a.u.c. A priestess, formerly of the Suwa shrine. Friend
of Satō. Daughter of Von Siebold.

KUMASO

KAYA TORISHI

b. 2569 a.u.c. Chieftain and shaman of the last village of the
Kumaso People.Officialy servant of Itō family.

440

TANAKA

TANAKA HISASHIGE
b. 2552 a.u.c. A scholar of Rangaku magic, mechanician and thaumaturgist.

KIYŌ

HOSOKI KAZUKO
b. 2567 a.u.c., d. 2608 a.u.c. High Priestess of Suwa Shrine.

IKŌ
A servant girl at the Suwa Shrine.

TAKASHIMA

TAKASHIMA SHŪHAN
b. 2544 a.u.c., d. 2608 a.u.c. A *Rangaku* scholar, head of the Takashima School of Wizardry.

TAKASHIMA SATŌ
b. 2589 a.u.c. An ice-wizard and former heir and teacher of Takashima School of Wizardry. Friend of Nagomi.

THE CHRYSANTHEMUM SEAL

SATSUMA

SHIMAZU NARIAKIRA
b.2562 a.u.c. Daimyō of the province of Satsuma, lord of
Kagoshima Castle.

SHIMAZU HISAMITSU
b. 2570 a.u.c. Younger brother of Shimazu Nariakira

SHIMAZU ATSU
b. 2589 a.u.c. Adopted daughter of Shimazu Nariakira, princess
of Satsuma.

TORII HEISHICHI
b. 2557 a.u.c. *Daisen,* Arch-wizard of Satsuma

YUKIHIGE "SNOW BEARD"
b. 2567 a.u.c. An ice-wizard and teacher at Satsuma School of
Wizardry.

KURODA RYŌSUKE
b. 2583 a.u.c. A retainer of Shimazu, stationed in Edo.

SAIGŌ TAKAMORI
b. 2581 a.u.c. A retainer of Shimazu, Captain of Castle Guards
in Kagoshima.

ŌKUBO SHOSUKE
b. 2583 a.u.c. A retainer of Shimazu..

ŌKUBO MINEKO
b. 2591 a.u.c. A court servant girl in the court of Satsuma.

YOKŌ
Lord Nariakira's truth-sayer. Formerly, a servant girl at the
Kirishima Shrine.

442

KUMAMOTO

KATŌ KIYOMASA (II)
b. 2570, d. 2608 a.u.c. Captain of the Guards Regiment at
Kumamoto Castle.

KAWAKAMI GENSAI
b. 2577 A retainer of the Kumamoto Domain. Master
Swordsman.

MIYABE TEIZŌ
b. 2572 A retainer of the Kumamoto Domain.

HŌJŌ

YOKOI SHŌNAN
b. 2562 a.u.c. A scholar and reformer at the Hosokawa's
court in Kumamoto.

ARIMA

MAKI IZUMI
b. 2566 a.u.c. High Priest of the Suiten-gu Shrine, formerly
retainer of Arima clan, scholar and revolutionary.

MORI
(CHŌFU)

MORI TAKACHIKA

b.2572 a.u.c. Fourteenth *daimyo* of the Chōfu domain.

YOSHIDA SHŌIN

b. 2594 a.u.c. Headmaster of Meirinkan School of Wizardry, formerly a student at the Takashima School of Wizardry. Adopted to Mori clan.

TAKASUGI HIROBUMI

b. 2592 a.u.c. A Student of Meirinkan School of Wizardry, Commander of the *Kiheitai*, friend of Shōin.

KUNISHI SHINANO

b. 2575 a.u.c. Retainer of Mori clan, a student of Meirinkan School of Wizardry.

YOSHIKAWA KEIMIKI

b. 2572 a.u.c. Governor of Iwakuni.

KORO

b. 2558 a.u.c. A man of the ancient native race of Ezo, friend of Shakushain.

TOKUGAWA

TOKUGAWA IEYOSHI
b. 2546 a.u.c., d. 2608 a.u.c. Twelfth *Taikun* of Yamato

TOKUGAWA IESADA
b. 2577 a.u.c. Thirteenth *Taikun* of Yamato

MORIYAMA EINOSUKE
b. 2573 a.u.c. Interpreter of Dracalish at Edo court, school friend of Tokojiro Namikoshi

HOTTA NAOSUKE
b. 2568 a.u.c. Chief Senior Councillor in the *Taikun*'s government.

DATE MUNENARI
b. 2561 a.u.c. Former Senior Councillor in the *Taikun*'s government.

SAGA

NABESHIMA NAOMASA
b. 2568 a.u.c. *Daimyo* of the Saga Domain.

EIGHT-HEADED SERPENT

GANRYŪ OF THE CRIMSON ROBE
Formerly Sasaki Kojirō. A Fanged, one of the Eight. Master Swordsman.

CHIYO OF THE EMERALD ROBE
A Fanged, one of the Eight

DŌRAKU OF THE PURPLE ROBE
Also known as Shinmen Takezō. A renegade Fanged. Master Swordsman, Ganryū's rival.

OZUN
b. 2581 a.u.c., d. 2608 A renegade *Yamabushi* priest

AZUMI
b. 2585 a.u.c. The last of the line of *shinobi* assassins of Koga

SHAKUSHAIN
b. 2569 a.u.c., d. 2608 A native warrior from the northernmost island of Ezo

DEJIMA

HENDRIK CURZIUS
b. 2566 a.u.c. *Oppertovenaar* (Overwizard) of the Bataavian outpost of Dejima.

GERHARDUS FABIUS
b. 2559 a.u.c. Captain of the *Soembing*

PHILIP VON SIEBOLD
b. 2549 a.u.c. Chief physician on Dejima from 2576 to 2582. Father of the Itō sisters.

QIN

LI HUNG-CHANG
b. 2576 a.u.c. A scholar, officer and translator. Personal aide to Tseng Kuo-Fan.

THE CHRYSANTHEMUM SEAL

TYR GORLLEWIN

MATHIUN PERAI
b. 2547 a.u.c. Komtur of the Western Navy of Tyr Gorllewin.

HARRI AULICK
b. 2540 a.u.c. Vice-Komtur of the Western Navy of Tyr Gorllewin.

LEIF EIRIKSSON
b. 2577 a.u.c. Chaplain of the *Star of the Sea*.

THORFINN KARLSEFNI
b. 2588 a.u.c. Dragon rider on the *Star of the Sea*.

FRIGGA RHYDD
b. 2587 a.u.c. Dragon rider on the *Star of the Sea*.

VARYAGA KHAGANATE

FRIDRIK OTTERSON
b. 2568 a.u.c. Varyagan admiral, Captain of the *Diana*.

MAGNUS INGVARSSON
b. 2549 a.u.c. The ship's doctor on *Diana*.

HJALMAR NOBELIUS
b. 2554 a.u.c. Varyagan inventor and thaumaturgist, creator of the *Diana*.

Thank you for reading *The Chrysanthemum Seal*
If you enjoyed it, why not leave a comment on Amazon or
Goodreads?

The Year of the Dragon cycle contains the following volumes:

The Shadow of Black Wings

The Warrior's Soul

The Islands in the Mist

The Rising Tide

The Chrysanthemum Seal

The Year of the Dragon: Books 1-4 Delux Edition